**Praise for *New York Times* bestselling author
Joseph Finder and his novels**

THE ZERO HOUR

"Thrilling."   —*The New Yorker*

"Breathlessly exciting."

—*Kirkus Reviews* (starred review)

"A labyrinth of suspense . . . brilliant . . . a master story-
teller."   —*Pittsburgh Post-Gazette*

"A thinking person's thriller with bite."
—*Publishers Weekly* (starred review)

HIGH CRIMES

"Fast and furious."

—*The New York Times Book Review*

"Exciting . . . deliciously absorbing . . . full of hairpin
turns."   —*The Washington Post*

"A powerhouse tale."   —*Chicago Tribune*

"Provocative and chilling."
—*Publishers Weekly* (starred review)

"Rattling good entertainment."
—*Kirkus Reviews* (starred review)

VANISHED

"If Jack Reacher met Nick Heller in a dark alley, my money's on Reacher. But it would be ugly. Or would it? Actually, I think they'd go for a beer together and set the world to rights—because Joseph Finder has given me a terrific new hero to root for. This is an action-packed, full-throttle, buy-it-today-read-it-tonight series that you definitely shouldn't miss."
—Lee Child

"A humdinger. . . . a thriller to enjoy for its Washington locales, convincing familiarity with cutting-edge spy gadgetry, and taut action scenes." —*The Washington Post*

"Cliffhangers galore, the fascinating tradecraft of corporate espionage, and an engrossing story will propel readers through this outstanding thriller. Highly recommended as a great summer read."
—*Library Journal* (starred review)

"Written in staccato chapters that are emotionally supercharged and action-packed, this thriller will more than satisfy adrenaline junkies and have them guessing until the very end." —*Publishers Weekly*

"If you read only one book this summer, make it *Vanished.*" —*Crimespree* magazine

"Moves at the pace of an injected neurotoxin...You'll curse Finder for keeping you up into the early hours."
—*Shots* magazine

"Even though I'd been warned that everyone who'd read it did so in one sitting, I cracked the cover at 10 p.m., figuring yeah, yeah, one sitting, right. When I passed out at 4 a.m., I was thinking, boy, if I could just keep my eyes open long enough to finish this!"

—Myles Knapp, *Contra Costa Times*

POWER PLAY

"A white-knuckle tale of suspense."

—*Chicago Sun-Times*

"A fast-paced fun ride . . . a delicious, perfectly prepared mixture."

—*Boston Globe*

"A bloody, rollicking thrill ride . . . the plot moves at light speed."

—*Richmond Times-Dispatch*

"The action is swift . . . keeps the plot bubbling and the pages turning."

—*The Wall Street Journal*

"Thrilling . . . Start *Power Play* this afternoon and you'll have the nightstand lamp burning at bedtime."

—*Pittsburgh Post-Gazette*

KILLER INSTINCT

"Unstoppable."

—*USA Today*

"Masterful."

—*Houston Chronicle*

THE ZERO HOUR

HOUR

Joseph Finder

St. Martin's Paperbacks

This is a work of fiction. All of the characters, organizations, and events portrayed in this novel are either products of the author's imagination or are used fictitiously.

THE ZERO HOUR

Copyright © 1996 by Joseph Finder.

For information address St. Martin's Press, 175 Fifth Avenue, New York, NY 10010.

ISBN: 978-0-312-93492-7

Printed in the United States of America

William Morrow and Company Inc. hardcover edition / May 1996
St. Martin's Paperbacks edition / June 2011

St. Martin's Paperbacks are published by St. Martin's Press, 175 Fifth Avenue, New York, NY 10010.

10 9 8 7 6 5 4 3 2 1

For Emma,
our "excellent creature"

The terrorist and the policeman both come from the same basket. Revolution, legality—countermoves in the same game; forms of idleness at bottom identical.

—Joseph Conrad, *The Secret Agent*

The prince of darkness is a gentleman.

—William Shakespeare, *King Lear*

Part 1

TRICKS

The supreme art of war
is to subdue the enemy
without fighting.

—Sun-tzu, *The Art of War*

CHAPTER ONE

Prisoner number 322/88—he was known to the prison authorities as Baumann, though that was not his name at birth—had been planning this day with meticulous precision for quite some time.

He rose from bed very early and, as he did every morning, peered through the narrow barred window at the verdant mountainside that glittered emerald in the strong South African sunlight. Turning his gaze, he located the tiny, shimmering patch of ocean, just barely visible. He took in the distant caw of the seagulls. He could hear the jingling of chains worn by the most dangerous convicts as they tossed and turned in their sleep, and the barking of the Alsatians in the kennels next to the prison building.

Dropping to the cold concrete floor, he began his morning ritual: a series of limbering stretches, one hundred push-ups, one hundred sit-ups. Then, his blood pumping vigorously, he showered.

By the standards of the outside world, Baumann's solitary cell was cramped and narrow. But it had its own shower and toilet, a bed, a table, and a chair.

He was in his early forties, but might have been taken for a decade younger. And he was strikingly handsome.

His hair was full, black, and wavy, only slightly sprinkled with gray. His closely trimmed beard accentuated a jaw that was strong and sharp; his nose was prominent but aquiline, beneath a heavy brow; his complexion was the olive so prevalent in Mediterranean countries.

Baumann might have been mistaken for a southern Italian or a Greek were it not for his eyes, which were a brilliant, clear, and penetrating blue, fringed by long eyelashes. When he smiled, which was rarely and only when he wanted to charm, his grin was radiant, his teeth perfect and brilliantly white.

In his six years in Pollsmoor Prison he'd been able to achieve a level of physical training he could never have otherwise. He had always been remarkably fit, but now his physique was powerful, even magnificent. For when he wasn't reading there was little else to do but calisthenics and *hwa rang do*, the little-known Korean martial art he had spent years perfecting.

He changed into his blue prison uniform, which, like everything he wore, was stenciled with the number 4, indicating that it was property of his section of Pollsmoor Prison. Then, making his bed as usual, he began what he knew would be a long day.

Pollsmoor Prison is located just outside Cape Town, South Africa, on land that was once a racetrack and several farms. Surrounded by high stone walls topped with electrified razor-wire fences, it is a rolling landscape of palm and blue gum trees. The warders and their families live within the prison walls in comfortable apartments, with access to recreation centers, swimming pools and gardens. The four thousand prisoners normally incarcerated here are kept in conditions of legendary squalor and severity.

Pollsmoor, one of only eleven maximum-security prisons in South Africa, never had the fearsome reputation of the now-defunct Robben Island, South Africa's Alcatraz, the rocky island off the Cape Peninsula coast isolated by icy, ferocious waves. But it succeeded Robben Island as the repository for those South Africa considered its most dangerous criminals, a group that included first-degree murderers and rapists—and, once, political dissidents who battled apartheid. It was here that Nelson Mandela completed the last few years of his quarter-century prison sentence, after Robben Island was closed and converted into a museum.

Baumann had been moved here in a van, in leg irons with twenty others, from Pretoria Central Prison, immediately following his secret trial. To most of the *boers*, or warders, and all of his fellow inmates, prisoner number 322/88 was a mystery. He almost always kept to himself and rarely spoke. At supper he sat alone, quietly eating his rotten vegetables, the maize and cowpeas glistening with chunks of fat. During exercise periods in the yard, he invariably did calisthenics and *hwa rang do*. After lockup, rather than watching a movie or television like everyone else, he read books—an enormous and peculiar range of books, ranging from histories of the atomic bomb or of the international oil business to biographies of Churchill or Nietzsche, an exposé of a recent Wall Street scandal, Max Weber's *The Protestant Ethic and the Spirit of Capitalism*, and a treatise on sixteenth-century Italian Renaissance architecture.

The other prisoners (called *bandiete* or *skollies*) smoked contraband *zolls*, long homemade cigarettes wrapped in brown paper, while Baumann smoked Rothmans. No one knew how he had got them. He never took part in the smuggling schemes of the others, nor joined in their escape attempts, which were usually amateurish and always failed, ending in capture or, most often, death.

Nor was he a member of any of the numerous gangs,

which, with the encouragement of the prison officials, controlled the inmate population. These were rigid, highly stratified organizations, controlled by governing councils called *krings*. They engaged in ritual killings, beheadings, dismemberment, even cannibalism. They were hostile to nonmembers, whom they called *mupatas*, or sheep.

Once, a few days after Baumann had arrived at Pollsmoor, one of the gangs dispatched their most vicious *lanie*—a leader serving a long sentence, whom everyone knew to avoid—to threaten him in the exercise yard. The *lanie* was found brutally murdered—so horribly mangled, in fact, that the men who discovered him, all hardened men, were sickened. Several inmates were unlucky enough to witness the act, which was done quickly and efficiently. The most terrible thing about it was that even in the thick of the struggle, there was no visible change in Baumann's glacial demeanor. Afterward, no one would ever admit having seen the killing. Baumann was treated with respect and left alone.

About Baumann, it was known only that he was serving a life sentence and that he had recently been reassigned from kitchen duty to the auto shop, where repair work was done on the prison officials' cars. It was rumored that he had once been employed by the South African government, that he used to work for the state intelligence and secret service once called the Bureau for State Security, or BOSS, and now called the National Intelligence Service.

It was whispered that he had committed a long string of famous terrorist acts in South Africa and abroad—some for BOSS, some not. It was believed that he had been imprisoned for assassinating a member of the Mossad's fearsome *kidon* unit, which was true, although that had merely been a pretext, for he had been ordered to do so. In truth, he was so good at what he did that he frightened his own employers, who much preferred to see him locked away forever.

A *boer* had once heard that within BOSS Baumann was known as the Prince of Darkness. Why, the warder could not say. Some speculated it was because of his serious mien; some believed it was because of his facility at killing, which had been so vividly demonstrated. There were plenty of theories, but no one knew for certain.

In the six years he had been imprisoned here, Baumann had come to know the place extremely well. He had become so accustomed to the smell of Germothol disinfectant that it had become a pleasant part of the ambience, like the salty sea air. He was no longer startled by the whoop of the "cat," the siren that went off without warning, at odd moments, to summon guards to an incident—a fight, an escape attempt.

At half past nine in the morning, Baumann entered the auto shop and was greeted by the warder, Pieter Keevy. Baumann rather liked Keevy. He was basically a good sort, if a bit slow on the uptake.

The relationship between *boer* and *bandiet* was a strange one. Warders were famously cruel, to the point of sadism—yet at the same time, touchingly, they desperately wanted to be liked by the prisoners.

Baumann was aware of this vulnerability and took advantage of it whenever possible. He knew that Keevy was fascinated by Baumann, wanted to know about his life, where he came from. Baumann duly provided the guard with morsels from time to time—morsels that piqued Keevy's curiosity without ever satisfying it. He liked Keevy because it was so easy to manipulate him.

"We've got a new one in for you boys today," Keevy announced heartily, clapping Baumann on the shoulder. "Food-service lorry."

"Oh?" Baumann replied equably. "What's wrong with it, *baas*?"

"Don't know. They're saying it smokes whenever they shift gears."

"White smoke?"

Keevy shrugged. "Thing sort of shifts with a bang."

"I see. Probably drinking up transmission fluid, too. Not a big deal. Probably a bad vacuum modulator."

Keevy cocked an eyebrow and nodded sagely as if he understood. "Bloody pain in the arse."

"Not really, Piet. And we're almost done with the chaplain's car." Baumann indicated the small black Ford sedan he'd been working on for the last few days.

"Let Popeye do it," Keevy said. "Popeye" was the prison nickname for Jan Koopman, the other *skolly* who worked in the auto-repair shop. "Like I said, it's a food-service lorry. We wouldn't want to miss any meals, now would we?"

Baumann chuckled at the warder's pathetic attempt at humor and replied dryly: "I'd hate to miss out on another ear." This was a reference to a time when Baumann, tucking into his maize and cowpeas at supper a few weeks ago, discovered a large, hairy, filthy pig ear.

"Oh!" Keevy gasped as he exploded with laughter. "Oh—the hairy ear!"

"So why don't I ask Popeye to take a look at the lorry, while I get the chaplain's car out of here." Keevy was still laughing, silently and helplessly, his large round shoulders heaving.

Popeye, whose shoulder boasted a large, crude tattoo, which signified he'd knifed a warder, arrived a few minutes later and sullenly obeyed Baumann's directions. He was actually larger than Baumann and weighed a good deal more, but he knew enough to be afraid of his co-worker and did what he was told.

As Baumann opened the trunk of the chaplain's car, he furtively glanced over at Keevy, who was by now taking a drag on a cigarette. Sure enough, as he did every morning after he lit his cigarette, Keevy lumbered to the door and went off to get a mug of coffee and take a ten- or fifteen-minute break with the warder at the next station.

Standing at the trunk of the car, Baumann called over to Popeye, "Could you check out this fucking tailpipe? Think it's got to be replaced?"

Popeye came over and knelt down to inspect the tailpipe. "Shit, what the hell are you talking about?" he said belligerently, seeing nothing wrong with it.

"I'll show you," Baumann said quietly as he reached down with both hands, grasped Popeye's chin from behind and above, and, with a sudden, violent shake from side to side, pulled the chin upward to a forty-five-degree angle. It was all over in a few seconds, and there was not even time for Popeye to cry out before he slumped, dead, to the concrete floor.

Baumann quickly dragged the inert body across the floor to the glossy cinnamon-red tool cabinet. He opened it, removed the shelves of drill bits, wedged the body inside, and turned the lock. He glanced back at the door. Old reliable Keevy still hadn't returned from his break. At least five minutes remained before Keevy would be relieved by the next guard. Always there was a routine: human beings thrive on routine.

Baumann reached deep into the trunk of the chaplain's car and lifted a section of the tan carpeting that lined it. Behind the flap of carpeting were the latches he had installed during the last few days of work on the car. He opened the latches and pulled back the false wall, which he had installed and camouflaged by gluing the carpet liner over it.

Behind the panel was a concealed compartment between the trunk and the car's backseat, just big enough for him to crawl into. All of this he had accomplished while doing the requested bodywork on the car. Keevy, who paid no attention to Baumann's work, suspected nothing.

He climbed into the trunk and positioned himself in the compartment. As he was about to pull the panel closed behind him, he heard the approach of a heavy set of footsteps. He struggled out of the space, but too late. Standing a few feet away, his mouth gaping, was Keevy.

Keevy was not supposed to be here, and it saddened Baumann. "What the fucking—" Keevy said in a funny, strangled little voice, trying to comprehend what Baumann was doing. In one hand he held a clipboard, which Baumann now realized the guard had absentmindedly left behind before taking his break.

Baumann chuckled to himself and gave Keevy a radiant, endearing smile. "Trunk's coming apart," he explained to the guard as he casually crawled out, swung his feet around, and stood up. "With what they pay that poor old man of the cloth, it's not surprising."

But Keevy, suspicious, shook his head slowly. "Coming apart?" he said stupidly.

Baumann put an arm around the warder's shoulders, feeling the soft flesh yield like a bowl of quivering aspic. He gave him a comradely squeeze. "Look," he whispered confidingly. "Why don't we keep this between you and me?"

Keevy's eyes narrowed with greed. His mouth was slack. "What's in it for me?" he said at once.

"Oh, quite a lot, *baas*," Baumann said, his arm still around Keevy's shoulders. "A pig's ear, for one thing."

He smiled again, and Keevy began to chortle. Baumann laughed, and Keevy laughed, and Baumann made his right hand into a fist, and in one simple motion swung it back and then slammed it into the hollow of Keevy's armpit with enormous force, crushing the brachial nerve, which is wide at that point and close to the surface.

Keevy collapsed immediately.

Baumann caught him as he sagged and crushed Keevy's trachea, killing him at once. With some difficulty, he pushed the body underneath a workbench. In a few minutes, he had installed himself within the hidden compartment in the chaplain's car and tightened the latches. It was dark and close in there, but there wasn't long to wait. Soon he could hear the footsteps of another prison official entering the shop.

With a loud metallic clatter, the blue-painted steel doors, which led to the vehicle trap and the courtyard outside, began to lift. The car's ignition was switched on; the engine was revved exactly three times—signifying that all was according to plan—and the car began to move forward.

There, a minute or two went by, during which time the guards in the vehicle trap carefully inspected the car to make sure no prisoner was hiding in it. Baumann was thoroughly familiar with how they inspected vehicles, and he knew he would not be caught. The trunk was opened. Baumann could see a tiny sliver of light appear suddenly at a gap where the panel met the trunk's floor.

He inhaled slowly, noiselessly. His heart hammered; his body tensed. Then the trunk was slammed and the car moved forward.

Out of the vehicle trap. Into the courtyard.

Baumann could taste the exhaust fumes and hoped he would not have to remain here much longer. A moment later, the car again came to a halt. He knew they had arrived at the prison gates, where another cursory inspection would be done. Then the car moved on again, soon accelerating as it merged with the main road to Cape Town.

Clever though he was, Baumann knew he could not have orchestrated his escape without the help of the powerful man in Switzerland who for some reason had taken a keen interest in his liberty.

The car's driver, a young man named van Loon, was an accountant in the office of the prison commandant as well as a friend of the chaplain's. The young accountant had volunteered to pick up the chaplain, who was arriving on a Trek Airways flight from Johannesburg to D. F. Malan Airport in Cape Town, in the chaplain's own newly repaired car.

By prior arrangement with Baumann, however, van Loon would find it necessary to make a brief stop at a petrol station along the way for refueling and a cup of coffee. There, in a secluded rest stop out of sight of passersby, Baumann would get out.

The plan had worked perfectly.

He was free, but his elation was dampened somewhat by the unpleasantness with the warder in the auto shop. It was unfortunate he had had to kill the simple fellow.

He had rather liked Keevy.

CHAPTER TWO

Several hours earlier, at eight o'clock on a rainy evening in Boston, a young blond woman strode brusquely across the lobby of the Four Seasons Hotel and toward the bank of elevators.

The set of her pretty face was all business, her eyebrows arched, her lips slightly pursed. She wore the uniform of an affluent businesswoman: a navy-blue double-breasted Adrienne Vittadini suit with padded shoulders, an Hermès scarf, an off-white silk blouse, a simple strand of pearls and matching mabe pearl earrings, black Ferragamo pumps, and, under one arm, a slim cordovan Gucci portfolio. In the other hand—somewhat incongruously—she grasped a large black leather bag.

To the casual observer, the woman might have been a high-powered attorney or an executive returning from a dinner with clients. But a more thorough inspection would have revealed tiny details that punctured the illusion. Perhaps it was her too obviously dyed, shoulder-length ash-blond hair. Perhaps her restless blue eyes, which betrayed a discomfort with the hotel's modern glass-and-marble opulence.

Whatever it was that didn't fit, the concierge glanced

up at her, back down to the petty-cash-disbursement sheet before him, then back again to the beautiful blond woman for the briefest instant. Then he inclined his head slightly to one side and caught the eye of one of the hotel's security people, a woman who sat in a large comfortable armchair feigning to read *The Boston Globe*.

Security arched her eyebrows a fraction to signal that she, too, was suspicious—or at least amused—then smiled and gave the tiniest shrug, invisible to anyone but the concierge, which said, Let her go, we can't be entirely sure.

The Four Seasons did all it could to discourage call girls, but in uncertain cases such as this, it was far better to err on the permissive side rather than risk offending a legitimate hotel guest.

The blond woman entered a waiting elevator and got out on the seventh floor. When she reached room 722, she let herself in with a key.

About twenty minutes later, a well-dressed man in his mid-fifties unlocked the same door. Although he was not an especially handsome man—he had a high, speckled forehead, beaky nose, large pouches under his eyes, fleshy jowls—there was about him the patina of prosperity.

His face and hands were deeply tanned, as if he often sailed the waters off St. Bart's, which he did. His hair was silver and neatly combed. His navy blazer was well tailored and expensive, his tie from Ermenegildo Zegna, his tasseled loafers polished to a high sheen.

Entering the room tentatively, he glanced around, but the only evidence of the woman was the clothes hanging neatly in the closet. The bathroom door was closed. He tingled with enormous anticipation.

In the exact center of the king-size bed an envelope had been placed. He reached across the bed and retrieved it. On its front was his name in large, loopy script. The note inside contained a simple set of instructions, which he read and immediately began to follow.

With trembling, clumsy fingers, he placed his briefcase on a desk and started undressing, dropping his jacket and then his pants in crumpled heaps on the gray carpet beside the bed. Fumblingly, he unbuttoned his shirt and then slipped off his monogrammed silk boxer shorts. He stumbled twice trying to remove his socks. Momentarily alarmed, he looked up to make sure the drapes were drawn. They were. She had, of course, taken care of every detail.

As he knelt in the corner of the room, naked, he felt his half-swollen member throb fully, almost painfully, to life, arching away from his body, proud and distended and flushed.

He heard the bathroom door open.

When the woman emerged, he did not turn to look: he had been ordered not to do so. In her black patent-leather boots with heels, the blond woman was just under six feet tall. Her body was covered entirely in a skin-tight black cat suit of four-way-stretch PVC, a wet-looking material made of a plastic substance bonded to Lycra. Her black gloves went to her elbows; the mask over her eyes was of thin black leather.

Silently, with fluid movements, she approached him from behind and placed a blindfold on him, the soft sheepskin against his eyes, the supple leather on the outside, its closure made of elastic. It looked like an oversize pair of goggles.

As she fastened the blindfold, she touched him gently, caressed him, wordlessly reassured. She placed a gloved hand under each arm, lifted him to his feet, and guided him over to the bed, where he knelt again, his engorged phallus compressed tightly between his abdomen and the side of the bed.

Next, she placed handcuffs on his wrists and clicked them shut. For the first time, she spoke. "It's time for your hood," she said in a husky contralto.

He inhaled deeply and quaveringly. His shoulders hunched with anticipation. He could sense her towering over him, could smell her leather gloves and boots.

She removed his blindfold, and now he was able to look at her. "Yes, mistress," he said in a soft, childlike whisper.

The hood was made of leather, too, form-fitting and lined with rubber. It had no holes for eyes or mouth, only nose holes for breathing. His eyes widened in fear as he took in the severity of this piece of apparatus. She slipped it over his head, heavy and cold and stifling, and he trembled with mixed terror and excitement.

She pulled the hood's collar tight, adjusted it, pulled the zipper down at the back, and fastened the zipper's tag end to the collar with a loud click.

The man was now overwhelmed with delicious fear. An icy, sickening terror lodged itself in the pit of his stomach. He wanted to vomit, but was afraid to do so, for it would suffocate him.

He felt his breath catch somewhere deep in his throat, just above the lungs. He gulped, gasped for air, forgetting for an instant that in this hood the only way he could breathe was through his nose, and he panicked.

He whimpered, trying to scream, but unable to.

"You've been bad," he heard her admonish him. "I like looking at you, but you've been a bad boy."

Control your breathing! he told himself. *Regular, rhythmic! Through the nose—breathe!* But the panic was too powerful; it overwhelmed his feeble efforts to take control of his body. He gulped for air, but his mouth tasted only the rubber, now warm and damp. Rivulets of perspiration ran down his face in the darkness, and trickled, hot and salty, into his gasping mouth. Even when he somehow managed to compel himself to breathe through his nose, snorting in stingy, leathersmelling nosefuls of air, he knew he remained on the very precipice of losing control entirely.

Yet at the same time—such a peculiar, wonderful blend of the deepest terror and the most extraordinary tingling arousal!—he could feel his penis throb with excitement, as if it were about to explode.

And then—and then!—he felt the sting of her leather riding crop on the backs of his thighs, teasing and painful. And—my God!—even a sting on the head of his very penis!

"I'm going to keep you on my leash," he heard from very far away. "You certainly haven't behaved properly, not at all."

He whimpered again, then moaned, and he realized he was gyrating his pelvis to some imagined rhythm, waving his butt at her, a coy offering.

"I'm going to flog the skin from your back," she said, and he knew she meant what she was saying, and he could barely contain himself.

The woman could see that he was on the verge of climax. And she hadn't even yet applied the device that was sold in medical supply houses as the Wartenberg Neurological Stimulator. From her black bag she withdrew a medical instrument that resembled a pinwheel at the end of a scalpel handle. Radiating out from the small-diameter pinwheel were dozens of sharp pins. She ran the instrument lightly across his legs and up to his chest.

His moans now came in waves, plaintively; he sounded to her very much like a woman nearing orgasm.

With her left hand she lightly grasped his testicles

and caressed them; with the other hand, she ran the pin-wheel over the backs of his legs, the backs of his knees. She moved her left hand up to the shaft of his penis and began slowly to pump, knowing it would not take much time at all. He was already throbbing, rocking back and forth, moaning. Now she ran the pinwheel up the crack of his ass, up the center of his spine, all the while masturbating him vigorously, and even before the pin-wheel reached the sensitive skin at the back of the neck, he started to come, spasming and bucking, moan-ing, moaning.

"Now," she said, as he collapsed onto the bed, "I'm going to your wallet to take what I deserve." So blissed out was he that he didn't even hear what she said, but it made no difference; he had utterly ceded control.

The blond woman got to her feet and briskly walked over to the desk where he had left his briefcase. She popped it open—he hadn't locked it, rarely did—removed the glinting gold disk, and dropped it into her black leather toy bag, where it disappeared among the whips and crops and restraints.

She looked over at the bed and saw that he had not moved: he was still slumped over the side of the bed, still breathing hard and deep, the sweat pouring off his chest and his back in glistening streams, darkening the pale-green bedspread beneath him. The dark, damp bor-der around him reminded the woman of the snow an-gels she and her sisters used to make years ago by lying prone in the new-fallen New Hampshire snow and wav-ing their hands and feet. Then another, very different association: the even, wet border around the man also looked a little like the crude white paint tracings you sometimes see around dead bodies at crime scenes.

Quickly, she bent over and retrieved his wallet from the seat pocket of his pants, withdrew four fifty-dollar bills, and slipped them into her portfolio.

She returned to her spent client and caressed him. A submissive must always be brought back to earth slowly and gently. "Turn around and kneel in front of me," she ordered with quiet authority. He did so, and she unlocked his handcuffs. Then she unzipped the leather hood, tugging at it with great effort until it began to slide off.

His silver hair stood up in crazed, sweaty clumps, and his face was deep crimson. He blinked slowly, his pupils adjusting to the light, his eyes coming slowly into focus.

She patted his hair flat. "What a good boy you've been," she said. "Have you had a good time?"

His only reply was a faint, weak smile.

"Now I've got to run. Call me next time you're in town." She ran her fingers lovingly across his cheek, over his lips. "What a good boy you've been."

Down the block from the Four Seasons, a gleaming black van was parked. The blond woman tapped on the mirrored, opaque passenger's side window, which was then lowered a few inches.

She removed the golden disk from her leather bag and placed it in the outstretched palm.

She hadn't even seen anyone's face.

CHAPTER THREE

The flashing turret lights atop the cruisers pulsed blue and white along most of the block of Marlborough Street. Five patrol cars were double-parked on the narrow street, roiling the rush-hour traffic all the way to Massachusetts Avenue and infuriating the already short-tempered Boston drivers.

A dozen or so residents of this normally staid Back Bay neighborhood (although "neighborhood" wasn't an accurate description of these connected rows of nineteenth-century town houses whose inhabitants did everything they could to avoid one another) leaned out of their bay windows and gawked like children at a schoolyard fistfight. Very un–Back Bay.

But the presence of all these police cruisers, unusual in this proper stretch of Marlborough Street, promised that something fairly exciting might actually be going on here. Sarah Cahill double-parked her aged Honda Civic and walked toward the building, in front of which stood a beefy young uniformed patrolman holding a clipboard. She was wearing jeans, running shoes, and a Wesleyan sweatshirt—hardly professional attire, but after all, she had been in the middle of making dinner for herself and her eight-year-old son, Jared. Spaghetti sauce: her hands reeked of garlic, which was too bad, because she'd be shaking a lot of hands. Well, she thought, screw 'em if they don't like garlic.

The responding officer, the guy with the clipboard, couldn't have been out of his twenties. He was crew-cut and pudgy and awkward and was joking with another cop, who was laughing uproariously and had traces of doughnut sugar on his face.

Sobering momentarily, the crew-cut officer said, "You live here, ma'am?"

"I'm Sarah Cahill," she replied impatiently. "Special Agent Cahill, FBI." She flashed her badge.

The patrolman hesitated. "Sorry, ma'am. You're not on my admit list here."

"Check with Officer Cronin," she said.

"Oh, *you're*—" He gave a crooked smile, and his eyes seemed to light up. He looked her up and down with unconcealed interest. "Right. He did mention you'd be here."

She signed her name and returned the clipboard to him. She smiled back and pushed ahead through the front door, her smile disappearing at once. From behind she could hear a whispered comment, then loud laughter. The crew-cut cop remarked loudly in his foghorn voice: "I always thought Cronin was an asshole." More laughter.

Sarah got into the elevator and punched the button for the third floor, overcome by irritation. What the hell was that supposed to mean—a jibe at Peter Cronin for having had the bad taste to marry an FBI agent? Or for having had the bad taste to *divorce* her? Which hind-brain instincts were these two chuckleheads responding to, raunchy sexuality or hatred of the feds?

She shook her head. The elevator, a musty, old-fashioned Otis with an accordion gate inside that shut automatically, provoked a moment of claustrophobia.

The grimy mirror inside reflected her image duskily. She quickly took out her new M.A.C. coral lipstick (a shade called Inca) and reapplied it, then, with her fingers, combed her glossy auburn hair.

She was thirty-six, with a sharp nose, wavy shoulder-length hair, and large, luminescent, cocoa-brown eyes, her best feature. She was not, however, looking her best at this moment. She looked a wreck, in fact; she wished she'd taken the time to change into a suit, or any outfit, for that matter, that would garner some respect from the hostile audience she was about to face. The Bureau, finicky about the way its agents dressed, would not look kindly on her attire. Well, screw the Bureau too.

The elevator door opened, and she took a deep breath.

The door to 3C was open. In front of it stood a uniformed officer she didn't know. She identified herself and was admitted to the apartment, which was crawling with homicide detectives, photographers, patrolmen, medical examiners, an assistant district attorney, and all the other usual guests at a murder scene. Crime scenes are supposed to be orderly and methodical, but, for all the police department's lists and rules and procedures, they're inevitably chaotic and frenzied.

Sarah elbowed her way through the jostling crowd (someone was smoking, though that was strictly verboten) and was halted by someone she didn't recognize, a homicide detective from the look of him. He stood before her, blocking her entry, an immense monolith. Fifties, a hard drinker, balding; tall, muscular, spiteful.

"Hey!" he boomed. "Who the hell are you?" Before she could reply, the detective went on: "Anyone who's not on the list I'm going to issue a fucking summons, you understand? Plus, I'm going to start asking you all for reports."

She sighed, contained her exasperation. She produced

her leather-encased FBI badge, and was about to speak when she felt a hand on her shoulder.

"Sarah."

Peter Cronin, her ex-husband, told the other detective: "Sarah Cahill, from the FBI's Boston office. Sarah, this is my new boss, Captain Francis Herlihy. Frank, you okayed this, remember?"

"Right," Herlihy conceded sullenly. He looked at her for a moment as if she'd said something rude, then pivoted toward a gaggle of non-uniformed men. "Corrigan! Welch! I need some evidence bags. I want that Hennessey's bottle and the drinking glasses in the sink."

"Hello," Sarah said.

"Hello," Peter said. They exchanged polite, frosty smiles.

"Look, we can't seem to turn up any of the deceased's friends or relatives, so I'm going to have to ask you to identify the body."

"I was wondering why you invited me here." Peter never did her a favor, either personal or professional, unless there was something in it for him.

"I also figured we could help each other out on this."

Captain Herlihy turned back toward Sarah as if he'd forgotten something. His brow was furrowed. "I thought the feds didn't do murder, except on Indian reservations or whatever the hell." A little, sardonic smile, then: "Thought you guys just went after cops."

"Valerie was my informant," Sarah said curtly.

"She screwed cops?"

"OC," she said, meaning Organized Crime, and didn't elaborate.

As Herlihy walked off he said, "Don't let her touch anything or fuck anything up, got it?"

"Do my best," Peter told his boss. As he led her

toward the body, he remarked *sotto voce*, "Captain Francis X. Herlihy. Grade Double-A asshole."

"A gentleman and a scholar."

"Yeah, well, it's a favor to me he's letting you in here. Says a friend of his on the job shook down a gay bar in the South End last year and you guys jammed him up or something."

Sarah shrugged. "I wouldn't know anything about it. I don't do police corruption."

"Lot of the guys aren't so happy you're here."

She shrugged again. "Why so crowded?"

"I don't know, bad timing or something. First time in five years I've seen everyone respond at once. Everyone's here but the *Globe*. Place is a fucking three-ring circus."

Peter Cronin was in his mid-thirties, blond, with a cleft chin. He was good-looking, almost pretty, and was not unaware of his effect on women. Even during their short-lived, tumultuous marriage, he'd had several "extracurricular activities," as he blithely put it. No doubt there was a woman right now sharing his apartment who was wondering whether some bimbo—no, some *other* bimbo—would be attaching herself to Peter like a limpet this evening.

As he pushed through the crowd with one hand, murmuring his hail-fellow-well-met greetings to his fellow cops, he asked: "How's my little buddy?"

"Jared's probably watching *Beavis and Butt-head* even as we speak," she replied. "Either that or *Masterpiece Theatre*, I'm not sure which. You're not the primary on this, are you?"

"Teddy is. I'm assisting."

"How was she killed?"

"Gunshot. This is not a pretty sight, I should warn you."

Sarah shrugged, as though she'd visited thousands

of murders, though in fact, as Peter knew, she'd seen no more than a dozen, and they always sent a wave of revulsion washing over her.

She had never been to Valerie's apartment before—they'd always met at bars and restaurants. This studio apartment, with its improvised kitchenette off to one side, had once been an upstairs parlor in some nineteenth-century industrial magnate's town house. Once this room had been done up in opulent high-Brahmin style. Now the walls and ceilings were covered with mirrors, a high-tech bordello. The furnishings were cheap, black-painted. A worn mustard-yellow bean-bag chair, a relic of the seventies. An old tape deck and a towering set of speakers whose cloth was fraying. Valerie's home looked the way it was supposed to look, like the lair of a hooker.

"Here you go," Peter announced. "The body snatchers have come and gone. The ME on call is Rena Goldman. She looks like a resident, but she's a real doc."

"Where is she?"

"Over there, talking to your pal Herlihy."

Valerie Santoro lay on her back, sprawled on her enormous bed. The black coverlet was encrusted with her dried blood. One hand was splayed back coyly as if beckoning one and all into her bed. Her hair was shoulder-length and dyed ash-blond; her lips bore traces of lipstick. Sarah felt her stomach lurch, looked quickly away. "Yeah," she said, "that's her. Okay?"

CHAPTER FOUR

In the small parking lot adjacent to a petrol station, the Prince of Darkness located the rented four-wheel-drive vehicle, a Toyota Double Cab with four seats, a canvas cover over the back, and a long-distance fuel tank. A tent was strapped on to the roof rack, and in the back were a gas stove and lamp, a change of clothes, and a pair of sunglasses. A sticker on the back identified the car's owner as Imperial Car Rental of Cape Town. If anyone happened to stop him for any reason, he'd just be another poor fool on a camping tour of the desert.

He felt the hood. It was warm, which told him the car had not been here long. This was good.

Looking quickly around the lot, he assured himself that no one could see what he was doing. Then he knelt to the ground beside the Toyota's door and felt underneath the frame until he came upon a smooth, newly soldered patch. Baumann pushed at it until the ignition key slid out from beneath the soldering.

A few blocks away he parked the car next to an international telephone box and removed a handful of one-rand coins from the glove box. He dialed a long series of numbers, fed the coins into the slot, and in twenty seconds had an international connection.

A man's voice answered: "Greenstone Limited."

"Customer service, please," Baumann said.

"One moment, please."

There was a pause, a few clicks, then a male voice said: "Customer service."

"Do you ship by air?" Baumann asked.

"Yes, sir, depending on destination."

"London."

"Yes, sir, we do."

"All right, thank you," Baumann said. "I'll call back with an order."

He hung up the phone and returned to the Toyota.

It was almost dusk when he passed through Port Nolloth, on the Atlantic Coast. From there, he headed northwest. Asphalt-paved highways became gravel roads and then dirt paths, which ventured feebly across the parched savannah. A few kilometers down the road, a forlorn cluster of huts sprang up. Beside them nattered a scraggly herd of goats.

When he passed the last hut, he checked his odometer. After traveling exactly four and a half kilometers farther, he pulled to a stop and got out.

The sun was setting, immense and orange, but the air remained stiflingly, staggeringly hot. This was the Kalahari, the great sand veld thousands of kilometers broad. He had just crossed the South African border into Namibia.

The border between Namibia and South Africa is for the most part unmarked, unguarded, and unfenced. It bisects villages where tribes have lived for centuries, oblivious to the outside world. Crossing back and forth between South Africa and its neighbors— Namibia, Botswana, Zimbabwe, and Mozambique—is simple. Thousands of Africans cross in either direction every day.

Wearing his dark sunglasses, Baumann stood beside

the vehicle, drinking greedily from his flask of cold water and enjoying the eerie, otherworldly landscape: the cracked, dry riverbeds, the high ocher and russet sand dunes, the gray-green shrubs and the scrubby acacia bushes. The heat rippled up from the striated expanse of sand.

For ten minutes or so he enjoyed the silence, broken only by the high whistle of the wind. Mere hours ago he had been looking through a narrow, barred window at a miserly patch of sky, and now he was standing in the middle of an expanse so vast that, as far as he looked in any direction, he could see no signs of civilization. He had never doubted he would taste freedom again, but now that it was here, it was intoxicating.

The noise came first, almost imperceptibly, and then he could make out the tiny black dot in the sky. Slowly, slowly, the dot grew larger, and the noise crescendoed, until, with a deafening clatter, the helicopter hovered directly overhead.

It banked to one side, righted itself, then swooped down for a landing. The sand swirled around him in clouds, raining against the lenses of his sunglasses, stinging his eyes, bringing tears. He squinted, ran toward the unmarked chopper, and ducked down beneath the whirring blades as he approached the fuselage.

The pilot, in a drab-green flight jacket, gave him a brusque nod as he hopped in. Without a word, the pilot reached down to his left side and pulled up on the collective pitch control lever, which resembled the arm of an emergency brake. The helicopter rose straight up into the air.

Baumann put on the headphones to block out the sound and leaned back to enjoy the flight to Windhoek, the capital of Namibia and the site of the country's only international airport.

Baumann had not gotten much sleep the night before, yet he was still alert. This was fortunate. For the next few hours he would need to remain vigilant.

CHAPTER FIVE

Valerie Santoro, call girl and entrepreneur, had been a beautiful woman. Even in death her body was voluptuous. She'd worked hard to maintain it for her clients. Her breasts were pert, too perfect: she'd obviously had silicone implants. Only the face was Sarah unable to look at: part of the forehead was missing. Dark blood was caked around the irregular-shaped chunk removed by the bullet at the point of exit. Inconsistent, Sarah knew, with suicide.

The pale-blue eyes looked challengingly at Sarah, regarding her with contemptuous disbelief. The lips, pale and devoid of lipstick, were slightly parted.

"Not a bad-looking babe," Peter said. "Check out the bush."

Her pubic hair had been shaved into the shape of a Mercedes-Benz emblem, a perfect, painstaking replica. Who had done this for her?

"Classy chick, huh? The snitch's snatch."

Sarah did not answer.

"What's the matter, lost your sense of humor?"

The photographer from the ID unit was hard at work with his Pentax 645, snapping still photos of the crime scene and the body "in cadence," as they call it—in sequence, in a grid, providing a photographic record designed to anticipate all of a jury's questions. Every few seconds some part of her—her right cheek; her left hand, loosely curled into a fist; a perfectly oval breast—was illuminated by the camera's lightning.

"What was the name of that call-girl service she worked for again?"

"Stardust Escort Service," Sarah replied distantly. "The poshest call-girl business in Boston."

"She used to brag she was doing the mayor, or the governor, or was it Senator—"

"She had an impressive clientele," Sarah agreed. "Let's leave it at that."

"Ah, yes." Peter laughed mordantly. "Eat like an elephant, shit like a bird." It was the old police refrain: the FBI always asks questions, sucks up information, never gives it out.

In truth, Sarah owed her ex-husband a debt of gratitude for putting her in touch with Valerie Santoro, who'd turned out to be a valuable FBI informant. About a year and a half ago, Peter had mentioned a call girl he knew named Valerie Santoro, who'd been hauled in on a drug bust and "jammed up" by the locals, and wanted to deal.

Prostitutes, because of their unique access, make good FBI informants. But you always have to be careful with them; you can never direct them to commit prostitution, or the case is blown. Everything must be done subtly, many things left unsaid.

Sarah had invited her to lunch at the Polynesian Room, a horrifying pink shrine to bad taste on Boylston Street. Val's choice. The restaurant's interior was blindingly pink and scarlet red, decorated with golden dragons and fake-oriental gargoyles. Some of the booths were upholstered in early 1960s red leatherette. Val preferred to sit at one of the straw booths fashioned in the shape of a sampan. Here and there were potted, dried palms spray-painted green.

She was five foot eight, had honey-blond hair, long legs. She ordered a White Russian and the Pu Pu Platter. "I may be good for nothing," she said, "but I'm never bad for nothing." She had a client who owned a lounge in Chelsea that was used for drug-trafficking and money-laundering. She figured Sarah might be interested. Another client of hers, one of the highest elected officials in Massachusetts state politics, had mob ties.

So a deal was struck. Following standard procedure, Sarah drafted a memo to get Valerie Santoro into the Bureau's informant bank, requested an informant number and a separate file number. This was a system devised to keep the informant's identity confidential and yet ensure she got paid.

Valerie heard enough gossip—enough boasting from the men she serviced, who needed to impress her—to allow Sarah to wrap up several major organized-crime cases. She'd been worth all the White Russians the government had ever bought her.

Running an informant, Sarah had been told by a potbellied good-old-boy supervisor in her first office, in Jackson, Mississippi, is like having a mistress on the side: she's always giving you trouble, always wanting something. Never put them on retainer, or they'll spin, invent information, keep you on a string. They bring in a nugget, it's evaluated, and then they get their chunky nut.

At Quantico they gave lectures on running informants, on what motivates them (money, greed, a desire for revenge, even once in a blue moon a flash of conscience), on how to develop your relationship with them. Unlike local law-enforcement agencies, which are perennially strapped for cash, the FBI has plenty of money to dispense for informants. You'd get as much as five thousand dollars to "open" an informant, more if you were courting a major player. You were encouraged not to be stingy. The more generous you were with the cash, the more dependent upon you the informant became.

You were warned about how tangled the relationship inevitably became. You became a proxy authority figure, a parent or a sibling, an adviser. By the end of the relationship, it was like a love affair gone sour. You wanted to throw them away, never see them again. Yet you had to wean them, or they'd keep calling.

Most of all you had to protect your informants. They placed their lives in your hands; the game you were inducing them to play was often dangerous.

Sarah snapped on a pair of latex gloves. "Was there forced entry?"

"No sign of it."

"But you printed the door anyway."

"Sure."

The photographer, snapping away, called out to Peter: "You check out the hood ornament?"

"Classy broad, huh?" Peter replied.

"Place doesn't look ransacked," Sarah said. "Probably not a burglary. Any neighbor report the gunshot?"

"No. A friend of hers called 911, reported her missing, didn't give a name. District office determined she lived alone, got the key from the apartment building supervisor. Who, by the way, wasn't exactly grief-stricken about this. Wanted her out of the building."

"Well, now he's got what he wants," Sarah said with a grim half-smile. "Where's the ME—what's her name, Rena something?"

"Rena Goldman." Peter beckoned to a woman in her early forties, with long gray hair, horn-rimmed glasses, a long, pale face, no makeup. She wore a white lab coat. She and Sarah, both wearing surgical gloves, shook hands.

"Do we know anything about time of death?" Sarah asked the medical examiner.

"Lividity is fixed, so it's at least eight hours, and she hasn't been moved," Rena Goldman said. She consulted a small, dog-eared spiral notebook. "No evidence of decomposition, but there wouldn't be any in this cool weather. She's out of rigor, so it's got to be at least, say, twenty-four hours."

"Semen?"

"I don't see any, not at first glance anyway. I can tell you for certain in a couple of hours."

"No, there probably won't be any," Sarah said.

"Why not?" Peter said.

"Apart from the fact that Val always, but always, made her clients use condoms—"

He interrupted: "But if it was a rape—"

"No signs of that," the medical examiner said.

"No," Sarah echoed. "And it sure wasn't a client."

"Oh, come on," Peter objected. "How the hell can you say that?"

With a slightly chewed Blackwing pencil, Sarah pointed to a folded pair of glasses on the bedside end table. The frames were heavy and black and geeky.

"She told me she never saw clients at her apartment. And she wasn't wearing these when she was killed. They're too ugly to wear regularly—I certainly never saw her in them. She wore contacts, but you can see she didn't have them in, either."

"That's right, now that you mention it," Rena Goldman said.

"Of course, it *may* have been a disgruntled client who tracked her down at home," Sarah said. "But she wasn't on a business call. She fought, didn't she?"

"Oh, yeah. Defense wounds on the body. Contusions

on the arm, probably from warding off blows." Goldman leaned toward the body and pointed a thin index
finger at Valerie's head. "Wound across the face. A
curved laceration about half an inch wide, with diffuse
abrasion and contusion approximately one inch around,
extending from the temple to the zygoma."

"All right," Sarah said. "What about the gunshot?"

"Typical contact gunshot wound," Peter said.

Rena Goldman nodded and tucked a wisp of gray
hair behind one ear.

"The hair's singed," Peter said. "Probably a big gun,
wasn't it?"

"I'd guess a .357," the medical examiner said, "but
that's just a guess. Also, there's stippling." She was referring to fragments of gunpowder embedded around
the point of entry, indicating that the gun was fired at
close range.

Sarah suddenly felt nauseated and was relieved that
she had no more questions to ask. "Thanks," she said.

Rena Goldman nodded awkwardly, turned, and
drifted away.

In the "efficiency" kitchen area a few feet away, a
handsome young black man, attired in a double-breasted
Italian blue blazer and foulard tie, gingerly placed an
empty beer can into a paper evidence bag. Peter's partner, Sergeant Theodore Williams, was the best-dressed
cop on the force. A few years younger than Peter but
unquestionably the better homicide investigator.

Next to him at the Formica kitchenette counter stood
a tech from Latent Prints, a round-shouldered, older
black man, delicately applying with a feather brush the
fingerprint powder the techs liked to call "pixie dust"
to a bottle of Baileys Irish Cream. Sarah watched him
lift a print from the bottle with a clear plastic Sirchie
hinged lifter.

"So who kills a call girl?" Peter asked. "A john?"

"I doubt it," Sarah said. "She told me she only did outcalls, mostly hotel rooms."

"Yeah, but these mirrors . . ." he began.

She sighed. "Who knows? She did have a personal life. But a *sex life*, outside of work? I don't know. A lot of these girls hate sex. What about her little black book?"

"Nothing. A date book, that's all. Purse, wallet, cigarettes. A fucking *arsenal* of makeup in the bathroom. Some Valium and a couple of tabs of speed. A Port-a-Print. But no little black book."

"A what?"

"Port-a-Print. One of those things they use in department stores or whatever to imprint your credit card, you know? I guess she took Visa, MasterCard, and Discover."

"Most call girls do these days. Though they still prefer cash."

"Bad form to have the wife doing the bills and discover a Discover Card charge for a blow job."

"Which is why you used to pay cash, right?"

"Touché," Peter replied, unperturbed.

CHAPTER SIX

A Latent Prints technician sat on the floor of the dark bathroom wearing foolish-looking orange plastic goggles. An eerie orange light emanated from the Polilight, a heavy, compact gray-and-blue box attached to a flexible metal tube that, using liquid optical technology, emits light in various hues: white, red, yellow, orange. Shone obliquely, it is used to check for fingerprints on walls and other hard-to-inspect areas.

"Anything?" Sarah asked.

Startled, the tech said: "Oh. Uh . . . no, nothing." He got to his feet and switched on the light.

More mirrors here, Sarah noted: the medicine cabinet above the sink, and another one, strangely placed, low and directly across from the toilet. Newly, and maladroitly, installed. Both mirrors were dusted with splotches of the gray pulverized charcoal and volcanic ash used to lift prints. In a few places, the gray was overlaid with smudges of Red Wop powder to bring out more ridge detail.

She watched him dust an area of one of the mirrors. "You know," she said, "a little Windex'll get those real clean."

The tech turned around, confused, not getting her

joke, but at that moment a voice boomed from just outside the bathroom threshold: Frank Herlihy.

"Is that the famous twenty-thousand-dollar paper-
weight I keep hearing about?"

"This is it, sir," the tech said gamely, patting the
Polilight as if it were a buddy.

"Oh, Ms. Cahill again. Can we help you with anything?" His tone professed sincerity, but his beefy red
face betrayed no desire to help.

"I'm fine," Sarah said.

"Hey, Carlos, what's up?" Herlihy said bluffly. "Fum-
ing tank explode on you again?"

The tech laughed and shook his head. "No, sir, but I
was up all night charting prints, and then at six this
morning the prick pled."

Herlihy laughed gutturally, malevolently. "You know,
Carlos, I'd be careful with that Polilight, there. Semen
fluoresces, doesn't it? Wouldn't want the little lady here
to see how much you jerk off."

Carlos snorted, and Sarah excused herself, her attention suddenly distracted. She stood outside the bathroom
and looked in. Her eyes narrowed. "The mirror," she
said, returning slowly to the bathroom.

"Huh?" asked Carlos.

"It's that mirror," she said. More to herself than to
Herlihy or Carlos, she murmured: "It's in a weird place,
isn't it? I mean, if you're sitting on the toilet, you can
see yourself in it. That's odd. Why would you . . ."

"Thanks *so* much, Ms. Cahill," the homicide captain
said with a nasty inflection. "Any other observations I
can pass on to the deceased's interior decorator?"

She flashed the captain a contemptuous look and
went on, aloud but to herself: "Most women wouldn't
want to look at themselves sitting on the toilet. *Two*
medicine cabinets . . ." Sarah approached the mirror.
Carefully grasping the mirror's edges with her gloved

fingers, she pulled at it. It popped off, as she expected it would. Behind it was a crude plywood compartment, in which sat a small, grimy Rolodex.

Sarah cast a glance at Captain Herlihy. "Well, now," she announced. "The little black book. Could I get some help here, please?"

Astonished, Carlos from Latent Prints helped Sarah tug at the plywood compartment until it too came off, revealing a plaster-and-sheetrock grotto in which sat several neatly wrapped stacks of fifty-dollar bills, unremarkable except that each bill had been cut precisely in half.

"Anyway," Sarah said to Peter, "she operated in a cash economy." They emerged from the elevator into the lobby of the apartment building, lit with a garish, stuttering fluorescent light.

"That was almost five thousand dollars," he said. "With the missing half-bills, I mean. Tells me drugs."

"Or organized crime."

"Maybe. Nice work on the mirror thing."

"Damn, I'm good."

"I wouldn't go that far."

"Actually, it wasn't rocket science," she said. "We busted a drug dealer in Providence last year who hid his telephone answering machine in a secret compartment built into the floor."

"Take credit when it's thrown your way, Cahill. Your friend sure did have an impressive clientele. You have any idea?"

"Yes," Sarah admitted.

"What was it, five or six CEOs in Boston and New York. *Two* United States senators. One circuit court judge. How much you bet it had something to do with one of them?"

Someone entered the building, not a face either one

recognized. They fell silent. Outside he added, "You liked her, didn't you?" He nodded to the officer with the clipboard, clapped him on the shoulder.

They stepped into the dark street. "Kind of. Not my kind of person, really. But a good sort."

"Whore with a heart of gold."

Sarah looked around for her car, but couldn't locate it, forgot where she'd parked it. "Bronze, maybe. She really took a liking to me. Practically lived for our meetings. Lonely girl—sometimes she'd call five times a day. It got so I had to duck her calls."

"She tell you anything that might indicate, you know . . . a client she was afraid of, someone who knew she was ratting for the FBI, something like that?"

"No."

"But you have theories."

"Maybe," Sarah said.

"Care to share?"

"Not yet. But I will, okay? I need a copy of the Rolodex."

"Well, we own all that, you know."

"Yeah, and without FBI cooperation you don't have dog shit."

Peter gave a strange half-smile. His face reddened. When he was angry, his face flushed like litmus paper. "If it wasn't for me you wouldn't have met her."

"Probably not," she conceded. "But that still doesn't change—"

"I mean, I took a chance introducing you two, you know. Given your record with informants—"

"Fuck off, Peter," she snapped.

He beamed as he turned away. "Give the little guy a hug for me, huh?"

She spotted her Honda Civic a moment later, being dragged by a tow truck. And she'd taken the standard precautions against towing: placed her FBI calling card on the dashboard, next to the blue bubble light.

"Shit," she said, realizing there was no point in running; it was too far down the block already. But she was able to make out a small violet sticker on the tow truck's bumper:

PRACTICE RANDOM KINDNESS & SENSELESS ACTS OF BEAUTY

CHAPTER SEVEN

Just after midnight, Sarah Cahill unlocked the front door to her Cambridge house. The only light came from the parlor at the front of the house, where the babysitter, Ann Boyle, snoozed in the La-Z-Boy recliner, the *Boston Herald* tented over her wide bosom.

Ann Boyle, broad and sturdy, with blue-rinsed curls and small, tired eyes, was at sixty-seven a great-grandmother and a widow. She lived in Somerville, the working-class town that bordered Cambridge, and had taken care of Jared since he was small. Now that Jared was eight, she came over much less frequently, but Sarah's hours were so unpredictable that it was important to have Ann on call.

She woke Ann, paid her, and said good night. A few minutes later she could hear the cough of Ann's ancient Chevrolet Caprice Classic starting up. Then she went upstairs to Jared's bedroom. She navigated the cluttered floor by the dim yellow glow of the night-light and narrowly averted demolishing her son's latest project, a desktop basketball hoop he was constructing with a Styrofoam cup for a hoop and a square of foam core as the backboard.

On the shelf above his bed a platoon of stuffed animals kept watch, including a pig he'd named Eeyore and a bear, Coco, who wore a pair of Carrera sunglasses. Another bear, Huckleberry, kept him company in the bed.

Jared was sleeping in a tie-dyed T-shirt he'd picked out at the flea market in Wellfleet and Jurassic Park dinosaur pajama bottoms. His brown hair was tousled. His breathing was soft and peaceful. His eyelashes were agonizingly long. On his wrist was a soiled yellow rubber band imprinted "Cowabunga!"

She sat there on the edge of the bed, staring at him— she could stare at him for hours while he slept—until he suddenly murmured something in his sleep and turned over to one side. She kissed him on the forehead and went back downstairs.

In the kitchen, Sarah took a highball glass from the cabinet. She needed something to lull her to sleep. Whenever she was called out of the house for work she came back wired. But Scotch had its costs, and she was growing less tolerant of awaking with even a mini-hangover. She set the glass down and decided to microwave a mug of milk instead.

While the microwave oven whirred, she straightened up the kitchen. All the supper dishes were still on the kitchen table; the spaghetti sauce still sat parched in a pot atop the stove. She'd asked Jared to clean up, and of course he hadn't. Ann should have done it, but probably hadn't been able to tear herself away from the TV. She felt a wave of annoyance, which merely compounded her foul mood.

Just seeing Peter could depress her, whatever the circumstances. Certainly there were times when she missed having a lover and partner around, and a live-in father for Jared.

But not Peter. Anyone but Peter, whom she'd come to loathe. What had seemed roguishness in the early days of their relationship had revealed itself as simple malice. He was a coarse, self-centered person, and she had only discovered that too late.

Not only did Jared sense her contempt for her ex-husband, but he seemed to feel the same way. There was an odd distance in the boy's attitude toward his father, who behaved with his eight-year-old son like a Marine drill sergeant. Peter probably imagined this was the only manly way to bring up his son, whom he saw just once a week. The court-ordered custody terms allowed Peter to take Jared one weekend day a week, which usually turned out to be Saturday. Jared dreaded the visits. When Peter did come by, sometimes accompanied by his bimbo *de jour*, he would take Jared to breakfast at a diner and then to watch the pro boxing at Foxboro, above the track, or to his gym in the South End to learn how to fight. Saturdays with Daddy were always sports-related. It was the only way Peter could reach out to his son.

Jared was a creative, lively kid, sometimes moody, and intensely intelligent. Recently he was obsessed with baseball—collecting baseball cards, reeling off baseball statistics. Sarah was afraid this was some misguided attempt to snag his father's approval. Bright and intuitive though Jared was, he still hadn't figured out that whatever he did, it would never be enough. He wanted a father, but in Peter he'd never really get one, and the faster he learned that, the better for him.

A month ago, Sarah found herself recalling, Jared had arrived home late one Saturday afternoon after a day with his father, in tears and visibly bruised. One of his eyes was swollen shut. Sarah gasped and ran out to the street to flag Peter down before he drove off in his clattering AMC Pacer.

"What the hell did you do to him?" she shouted.

"Oh, calm down," he'd replied. "I threw him a left

THE ZERO HOUR   45

hook and he forgot to duck, is all. I was trying to show him you gotta use your elbows to absorb the blow."

"Forgot to duck? Peter, he's a *child*!"

"Jerry's got to learn how to take his lumps. It's good for him." To Peter, Jared was always "Jerry" or "little buddy."

"Don't you ever do that to him again!" she said.

"Don't tell me what I can't do with my son," Peter said. "You got him taking piano lessons and writing *poems*, for Christ's sake. You trying to raise a faggot?" And he gunned the engine and took off down the street.

The microwave beeped, then insistently beeped once more. The milk had boiled over, spilling inside the oven. She mopped up the mess with paper towel, removed the milk skin from the mug with a spoon, and stirred in a little maple syrup.

Then she put on some soft chamber music (the Beethoven piano trios, which, with the Schubert piano trios, she played more than anything else—something else Peter liked to mock her for) and sat in the La-Z-Boy.

She thought of Valerie Santoro, not posed on her bed in the indignity of death, but alive, beautiful, and re-membered the last time they'd met. She had talked about quitting "the business," something she talked about quite a lot recently and getting a "high-powered" job on Wall Street. She'd begun to ask for more and more money so she could quit working—realizing that she was near the end of her career as a call girl and the money wasn't coming in the way it used to.

Valerie Santoro, rest in peace, was a user who thought she'd finally found her sugar daddy, her ticket out. She affected to disdain the money Uncle Sam gave her, while at the same time angling desperately to get more of it.

Sarah, for her part, had found her own ticket out, or at least up. A good informant boosted your stock immeasurably, but an informant like Val, with access to some of the high and mighty, the high rollers and the mafiosi, was truly a prized commodity.

Now her prized racehorse was dead, and something about the murder didn't make sense. Prostitutes were more prone to be victims of violence, even of murder, than the run of society. But the circumstances didn't indicate she'd been killed in the line of her particular kind of duty. It was unlikely that rough trade had been involved.

The cash Valerie had hidden behind the dummy medicine cabinet—the almost five thousand dollars in fifty-dollar bills, cut in half—was persuasive evidence that Val had done a job for someone.

But for whom? If it was Mafia-related, why had the money been left there? Wouldn't whoever killed her have known about the cash and taken it back? If she'd been killed by elements of organized crime because they'd discovered she was informing for the FBI, where had the money come from? Had she been killed because she'd been an informant?

The FBI normally doesn't concern itself with homicide, but a case that involved the murder of an FBI informant was a clear-cut exception.

Peter Cronin hadn't called his ex-wife to the crime scene just to identify a body, and certainly not out of generosity. Well, informants weren't the only ones who did horse-trading. If Peter wanted access to the FBI's databases, he'd have to pony up some pieces of evidence himself, like the Rolodex and the address book. He'd deal; he had little choice.

At two in the morning, Sarah climbed the stairs to her third-floor bedroom, got into the extra-long T-shirt she liked to sleep in, and got into bed. Visions of the crime scene flashed in her mind like a gruesome slide show, with snatches of remembered conversation as a disjointed sound track, and not before a good hour of tossing and turning was she able to fall into a fitful, troubled sleep.

CHAPTER EIGHT

Seven kilometers outside of Geneva, Switzerland, at a few minutes before noon, a late-model, cobalt-blue Rolls-Royce limousine pulled off a small, tree-shaded road not far from Lac Léman and came to a halt at a high wrought-iron gate. Embedded in a stone pillar before the gate was a keypad and speaker. The driver punched in several numbers, and when a voice came over the intercom he identified himself. The iron gate swung slowly inward, and the limousine maneuvered along a macadam-paved access road, through a narrow *allée* of apple trees that went on as far as the eye could see. At once, the magnificent grounds of an enormous, secluded estate came into view.

The vehicle's sole passenger was Baumann, dressed impeccably, yet casually, in a tweedy sport coat of black-and-white Prince of Wales plaid over a navy-blue crewneck sweater and white shirt. He had shaved off his beard, and his dark wavy hair was combed straight back, which gave him the appearance of a prosperous young Genevois banker on holiday. He seemed quite relaxed.

Late the previous evening he had been flown into a

small, unmarked airstrip outside Geneva. He had journeyed from Cape Town without having legally crossed a single national border—and, therefore, without a trace in any computer records anywhere.

In Geneva he stayed at the Ambassador Hotel, on the Quai des Bergues on the Rive Droite, overlooking the crystal-clear waters of the Rhône and the Pont de la Machine. A suite had already been reserved for him, in the name of a British merchant banker, whose passport he was also given. As soon as he had entered the room, he had jerry-rigged the door to ensure that no one could enter uninvited without enormous commotion. Then he took a long hot shower, and passed out. Late in the morning he was awakened by a call from the concierge, who told him his car was waiting.

Now, languidly staring out the window of the Rolls, he took in the manicured grounds. Hundreds of perfectly trimmed golden yew hedges stretched before him. The grounds, which seemed to go on forever, occupied some fifty acres of prime Lac Léman real estate.

From this distance, he could just make out the thirteenth-century castle that belonged to his host. The castle (restored and renovated most recently in the late 1980s) was said to have once been the home of Napoleon III.

The present owner and occupant of this enormous estate, another sort of Napoleon entirely, was a man named Malcolm Dyson, an American expatriate financier, a billionaire, about whom the world knew very little.

In the last few months, however, Baumann had steadily put together a sketchy portrait of the legendary, reclusive Malcolm Dyson. The confines of Pollsmoor Prison had given him unlimited time for his research, and the prison library had yielded a small amount of public-record information. But the best network of resources by far had been the prison's inmates, the petty crooks, the smugglers, the shady dealers.

The American newspapers had christened Malcolm Dyson the "fugitive financier," a phrase now fastened to his name like a Homeric epithet. He had made a fortune on Wall Street, in bonds and commodities and by playing the stock market brilliantly. In the mid-1980s, Malcolm Dyson was one of Wall Street's most glittering tycoons.

Then, in 1987, he had been arrested for insider trading, and his vast corporate empire had come tumbling down. All of his U.S. assets had been confiscated.

After his trial, and before he was slated to be sent off to prison, he fled to Switzerland, which has no extradition treaty with the United States. He and his late wife had lived in Switzerland ever since, rebuilding his empire from the ground up. Now, at seventy-two, Dyson was one of the richest men in the world, controlling assets estimated at several hundred billion dollars. Yet he could never return to the United States, nor travel to any country from which he might be extradited, or he would promptly be thrown in prison for the rest of his life. So he remained a prisoner of sorts, but in the most lavishly gilded of cages.

He lived in a Swiss Xanadu, a restored thirteenth-century castle he called Arcadia. More significantly, however, Malcolm Dyson had become a major trader in commodities and the world currency markets. He was widely rumored to have come close to cornering the world's supply of gold and platinum and to have major holdings in gem diamonds and strategic minerals such as titanium, platinum, and zirconium, which were vital in the defense and space industries. Dyson's corporate empire, which was sometimes called "the Octopus," had in the last few years outgrown the other leading diamond and precious-metals firms that made up the cartel whose offices were located in Charterhouse Street in London, just off High Holborn and Farringdon Road. His holdings were by now larger than those of the other precious-metals behemoths, including De Beers Consolidated Mines Ltd., the Anglo American Corporation, Charter Consolidated, the Mineral and Resources Corporation, and Consolidated Gold Fields Ltd. He was enormously wealthy, but beyond that he was an enigma.

The limousine came to a stop at a tall hedge, into which was carved a topiary gate. Standing in front of the gate was a tall man in his late thirties, with a high forehead and receding hairline, wearing rimless spectacles. He wore a dark-gray sack suit. He was clearly an American.

He approached the limousine and opened the door. "Welcome," the man said. "I'm Martin Lomax." He shook hands and ushered Baumann into the dim labyrinth of an English hedge maze. The path wended maddeningly through acute angles and around cul-de-sacs. Baumann permitted himself a smile at Dyson's affectation. He wondered what other sort of eccentricities Malcolm Dyson would entertain.

Then the tall hedges gave way to an open area of immaculate jade-green lawn, bordered by brightly colored flowers—lavender, nepeta, agapanthus, daylilies, roses, honeysuckle, euphorbia—in wild and lush profusion.

Lomax led Baumann through this meticulously tended garden and through another opening in the winding hedge, then stopped. There were faint sounds of gurgling, plashing water. Baumann's curiosity was piqued. He took a few steps forward and entered the verdant, shaded stillness of another garden. At the exact center of this garden was a swimming pool, an irregular oval of smooth rocks that looked almost natural.

In a wheelchair nearby, next to an ancient, crumbling sundial, sat Malcolm Dyson, speaking on a cellular telephone. He was a small, rumpled man, almost rotund. His head was round and almost completely bald. There were dark liver spots at his temples and on the backs of his gnarled hands. He was wearing a loose, open-necked white muslin shirt that resembled a tunic. His legs were covered by a plaid wool blanket; his shoes were comfortable Italian leather loafers.

Whoever Dyson was speaking with was obviously making him angry. He concluded the conversation abruptly by flipping the phone closed. Then he looked straight across the garden at Baumann and gave a warm, engaging smile.

"So at last I meet the famous Prince of Darkness," Dyson said. His voice was high, throaty, adenoidal. Only his eyes, steely gray, did not smile.

There was a high mechanical whine as Dyson urged his electric wheelchair closer to Baumann, but it was only a symbolic gesture; he stopped after a few feet.

Baumann approached, and Dyson extended a round, speckled hand. "Mr. Baumann," he announced with a chuckle and a dip of his head. "I assume you know who I am."

Baumann shook his hand and nodded. "Certainly, Mr. Dyson," he said. "I do know a bit about you."

"Glad to hear it."

"I've recently had some spare time to do a little research."

Dyson chortled, as if to share Baumann's joke, but Baumann was not smiling. "Do you know why you're here?" Dyson asked.

"No," Baumann admitted. "I know that I'm not sitting in Cell Block Nineteen in Pollsmoor Prison. And I know that you made the arrangements for my jailbreak. But to be entirely honest, I have no idea why."

"Ah," Dyson said, arching his brows as if the matter hadn't before occurred to him. "Right. Well, I hoped we might have a little talk, you and I. I have sort of a business proposition for you."

"Yes," Baumann said mildly, and then gave one of his brilliant smiles. "I didn't think it would take you long to get around to that."

CHAPTER NINE

Early the next morning, Sarah arrived at the FBI Boston field office and took the photocopies of Valerie Santoro's handwritten Rolodex cards to the counter where the computer searches were done. A young Latino clerk-trainee named Hector took the sheets and squinted at Sarah amiably. "You want these run through NCIC?"

The FBI's computerized National Crime Information Center database is used by police whenever they stop a motorist, to check for stolen vehicles, cash, and guns, as well as fugitives, missing children, and missing adults. It would also tell her which of Val's clients had criminal records or warrants outstanding.

"Right," she replied. "And Intelligence and Criminal. And of course FOIMS. See if we get a hit." FOIMS, the Field Office Information Management System, was the FBI's main database.

The Boston office of the FBI occupies four floors of an enormous curved modern building called One Center Plaza. Sarah's cubicle was located on the building's fifth floor, where the Organized Crime and drug squads shared space. The vast expanse of floor was covered in tan wall-to-wall carpeting. Long blue partitions separated small office areas known as pods, two or three desks equipped with telephones, walkie-talkie radios, and, on some desks but not all, computer terminals. The younger agents tended to be computer-literate, unlike their older colleagues, who left the computer-search headaches to the folks in Indices, at the other end of the floor. Next to her desk was a paper shredder.

Apart from the usual equipment, Sarah's desk held her Sig-Sauer pistol in its holster in a small green canvas bag (a pistol was standard issue in both drugs and OC), her pager, and a few personalizing touches: a framed photograph of her parents sitting on the couch at home in Bellingham, Washington, and a framed snapshot of Jared in his hockey uniform, holding a stick, smiling broadly, displaying his two large front teeth.

The atmosphere was quiet, yet bustling. It could have been any private corporation in the country. The FBI had moved here a few years ago from the John F. Kennedy Federal Office Building across the street, where the whole Boston office had been crowded onto one big open floor, noisy and boisterous and gregarious, and you could hear what everyone else was doing at every moment.

She returned to her desk, gazed for a moment out at the Suffolk County Courthouse, leafed through the photocopies of Val's appointment book that Peter had had made.

The entries were brief and unrevealing. Val did not record the names of her clients, just times and places. On the night she was murdered, she'd had two appointments, one at eight o'clock at the Four Seasons, the other at eleven o'clock at the Ritz. It wasn't out of the question that one of these two "clients" had followed her home after an assignation and murdered her. The possibility couldn't be ruled out.

Had Valerie Santoro been murdered because someone had discovered she was an FBI informant? If so, was it one of her clients? Valerie's information had helped Sarah make two major OC cases; quite likely she'd been the victim of an organized-crime hit.

Sarah was one of a handful of women in the Boston office, and for some reason she hadn't become friends with any of the others. Her closest work friend was her partner and podmate, an immense grizzly bear of a man named Kenneth Alton, who was speaking on the telephone. He waved at her as he sat down. A computer junkie who'd gone to MIT, Ken had long hair, hippie wire-rimmed glasses, and a great protuberant belly. He probably weighed over three hundred pounds and was always on a diet, always sipping Ultra Slimfast milk shakes. He wasn't exactly what the public expected to see in an FBI agent, and he'd never make management. But he was valued for his extraordinary computer skills, and so his idiosyncrasies were tolerated. J. Edgar was probably spinning in his grave.

Sarah had been with the FBI for almost ten years. Her father had been a cop who hated being a cop and had urged his only child to avoid law enforcement if it were the last job on earth. Naturally, she went into law enforcement and married a cop, in that order.

Though for the last several years she'd been working Organized Crime in Boston, her main interest was in counterterrorism, where she'd developed something of a reputation within the Bureau while working the Lockerbie case.

A Pan Am jumbo had exploded in the skies over Lockerbie, Scotland, on December 21, 1988, at 7:03 p.m., resulting in the death of 270 people. The FBI launched SCOTBOMB, the largest international terrorist investigation ever, conducting fourteen thousand interviews in fifty countries.

Sarah was a single mother—Peter had moved out by then—living in Heidelberg, Germany, with a sick infant. Jared, then four months old, had developed a bad case of bronchiolitis. Neither baby nor mother got any sleep. The first several weeks in Heidelberg Sarah spent in a state of complete sleep deprivation. It was a trying, exhausting time, but it was where she had made her bones within the Bureau.

She'd been assigned to interview the friends and families of U.S. soldiers who'd been stationed at the base at Heidelberg to see whether any might have been targets. The days were long; they usually weren't done until nine at night. The Army provided a command post and a secretary for dictating reports.

Each investigator was assigned one victim. You had to follow up all connections to that victim, all friends, even casual contacts. In the process, you couldn't help digging up dirt. One victim had been cheating on his wife, another was in financial trouble, another was using drugs. Were any of these problems connected to the bombing?

Sarah became a sponge, soaking up information, rumors, overhears. It soon became apparent that the answer was not in Heidelberg.

The important forensic work was going on else-where. Sarah began to hear details through Bureau channels. The bomb had consisted of a plastic explo-sive and a timing device concealed in a Toshiba radio cassette recorder, which had been placed in a Sam-sonite suitcase. The suitcase was traced to Air Malta flight KM-180, from Malta to Frankfurt, then trans-ferred as unaccompanied luggage to Pan Am 103A from Frankfurt to Heathrow. There it was transferred to container AVE-4041 on Pan Am 103.

Then she learned that a fragment of a green circuit board, part of the timing device, had been identified.

Sarah asked and received permission to do some digging into the matter of timing devices—who used what, what had been used where. This was pure scut work, and it wasn't her "ticket," as they say in the Bureau, but she had gotten reluctant approval to search.

All the intelligence on timing devices was on-line at the Bureau. There was a match. The circuit board was similar to one used in an attempted coup in Togo in 1986. It was also similar to one seized at the Senegal airport in 1988.

That was her contribution, and although it turned out to be crucial, at the time she had no idea where it would lead.

But the timer was eventually traced to a Swiss company, Meister et Bollier Limited, Telecommunications. In 1985, it turned out, twenty of these timers were sold to Libyan intelligence.

And the case was cracked. Her file reflected a "contribution above and beyond."

But when her Heidelberg tour was done, she found that there were very few Counterterrorism slots in the United States open and none in Boston, which she still considered home—and where, by the terms of her custody agreement with Peter, she had to live. So she'd requested a transfer to Organized Crime, and there she'd been ever since.

She called a few informants, worked a few leads. For almost two hours she filled out forms, wrote up a few 302s, or interview reports, did the paperwork that takes up most of an FBI agent's work, got caught up. She called the airport and talked to a member of an FBI surveillance team on a case that was all but wrapped up.

Then a thought occurred to her, and she picked up the phone. Fortunately, Ted answered the phone; Peter was out of the squad room.

"Can you pull Val's phone records, or should I?" she asked.

"Already did."

"You're kidding me. You got a subpoena that fast?"

"I've got a friend at New England Telephone Security."

Sarah shook her head, half in disgust and half in admiration. "I see."

"Oh, don't tell me you feebees always play by the rules," Ted replied. "Phone company's impossible to deal with through channels anymore, you know that."

"So what'd you find?"

"According to her local phone records, at three forty-four in the afternoon of the day she was killed, she received a three-minute call."

"So?"

"So she wasn't at home at the time. Between three and quarter after four, she was at a salon on Newbury Street called Diva. Take a look at her appointment book. Both her hair stylist, a guy named Gordon Lascalza, and her manicurist, Deborah something, placed her there then."

"You've never heard of answering machines?" Sarah said.

"Oh, there's messages on her answering machine, all right," Ted replied. "Three messages. One from the owner of the Stardust Escort Service, a Nanci Wynter. Her madam. And two from creditors—Citibank Visa and Saks. Apparently she didn't like paying her bills, or she was short of funds, or both."

"And?"

"None of them remotely approached two minutes. Also, they were received between five o'clock and six-thirty. They also match up with her phone records."

"So you're saying that Val came home after her haircut and manicure," Sarah said, "played her answering machine, and rewound, right?"

"Exactly," Ted said.

"And whoever called her at three forty-four that afternoon and left a long message—we don't have that message, because it was recorded over by later messages."

"Right."

"But you know who placed the call, right? From the phone records?"

Teddy hesitated. He was not a good liar. "According to the phone records, that three-minute phone call Valerie Santoro got on the day she was killed came from a cellular phone, a car phone. Registered to a limousine-rental agency. The limo company has twenty-some cellular phones in its name, probably all installed in the cars it rents out."

She nodded, sensed he was holding back. "Did you already talk to the limo company, or should I?"

An even longer pause. "Uh, I did already."

"And?"

"All right, the phone call came from a limo rented for two days by a guy named Warren Elkind, from New York City."

She hesitated. "Know anything about the guy?"

"Nothing."

"Do me a favor. Forget to mention to Peter you told me about this guy, huh?" There was a long silence. "Hello?"

"Yeah, I'm here. All right. Understood," Teddy said reluctantly.

"Thanks, Teddy. I owe you. Oh, and one more thing."

"Now what?"

"Can I have the tape?"

"The what?"

"The tape from Valerie's answering machine."

"You asking me to get it transcribed? Or copied?

"I want the original."

"Shit, Sarah, why are you doing this? It's in the evidence locker already—"

"Because we have jurisdiction. She's one of our informants."

"It's not going to do you any good, Sarah—I already told you what's on it."

"Can I borrow it for a little while anyway?"

He sighed. "I'm hanging up before you ask me for anything else."

"Ms. Cahill? Excuse me." Hector, the database trainee, approached her awkwardly. He was holding a long sheet of computer paper and smiling bashfully. His face looked like that of a child who'd accomplished something for which he knew he'd be praised.

"We got six hits," the trainee said.

Sarah perused the computer printout. The six names had little in common. One was a United States senator whose name had come up in a bribery investigation. Another was a professor at Harvard Law School who specialized in defending celebrities; he was probably being watched for no other reason than that someone high in the Bureau disliked him. A third was a well-known construction executive tied to the Mob; then there were two lowlifes who'd done time for drug trafficking.

And there was Warren Elkind: a prominent New York banker, the chairman of the Manhattan Bank, the second-largest bank in the country. The accompanying biographical information indicated that he was a leading fund-raiser for Israel and had been the target of numerous threats from Palestinian and Arab groups.

Sarah called the Ritz and asked for the security director.

"Is there a problem?" he asked in a pleasant baritone.

"Absolutely nothing involving the hotel," she reassured him. "We're looking for someone we believe stayed there four days ago. I'd like to get a list of all hotel guests from Monday night."

"I wish we could do that, but we're very protective of our guests' privacy."

Sarah's tone cooled slightly. "I'm sure you're aware of the law—"

"Oh," he said with a tiny snort, "I'm quite familiar with the law. Chapter one hundred forty, section twenty-seven, of the Massachusetts General Law. But there *is* a legal procedure that has to be followed. You'll have to get a subpoena from Suffolk District Court and present it to our keeper of records. Only then can we release documentation."

"How long would that take?" she asked dully.

"After you get the subpoena, you mean? It takes several days for us to go into our records. A two-week register check will take at least three days. And then you've got to make sure the scope of the subpoena is specific enough. I doubt any judge will issue a subpoena for the names of *all* hotel guests that stayed here on any given night."

Frustrated, Sarah lowered her voice and asked confidentially: "Is there any way we can speed things up a bit? I can assure you the hotel will not be involved in any way—"

"Whenever the FBI comes here asking for the names of our guests, we're involved, by definition. My job is to protect the security of our guests. I'm sorry. Bring me a subpoena."

The second call she placed was to the Four Seasons, and this time she decided to take a different tack. When she was put through to the accounting department, she said: "I'm calling on behalf of my boss, Warren Elkind, who was a guest at your hotel recently." She spoke with

the glib, slightly bored assuredness of a longtime secretary. "There's a problem with one of the charges on
his bill, and I need to go over it with you."

"What's the name again?"

Sarah gave Elkind's name and was put on hold. Then
the voice came back on. "Mr. Elkind checked out on the
eighteenth. I have his statement here, ma'am. What
seems to be the problem?"

CHAPTER TEN

"I see you collect pictures," Baumann said.

"You know something about art, I take it?" Malcolm Dyson asked, pleased. The word "pictures," as opposed to "paintings," seemed to indicate that Baumann was not entirely ignorant about the art world.

The conversation had been relocated to the main house, whose walls were crowded with paintings, mostly old masters but a few contemporaries, from the marble-tiled entrance hall to the immense Regency dining room—even, Baumann observed, in the washroom off the conservatory. A Rothko nestled between a Canaletto and a Gauguin; canvases by Frank Stella and Ellsworth Kelly, Twombly, and Miró jostled against a Correggio and a Bronzino, a Vermeer, a Braque and a Toulouse-Lautrec. An astonishing collection, Baumann saw, but grotesquely jumbled together. A collector with a lot of money and no taste.

Hanging above a Louis XIV gilt console table in a hallway—poorly lighted, Baumann thought, and ineptly displayed—was a *Nativity* by Caravaggio. In one corner of the sitting room, oddly juxtaposed, were Antonella da Messina's *Ecce Homo* and a Modigliani. Only after they had moved into the library did a switch go on in Baumann's head, and he suddenly realized what many of these paintings had in common. The Caravaggio had disappeared thirty or so years ago from the oratory of a church in Palermo, Sicily; *Ecce Homo* had been looted by the Nazis from the Kunsthistoriches Museum in Vienna. Much of the art in Dyson's collection had been obtained on the black market. The stuff had been stolen.

They sat in the library, an enormous, high-ceilinged, dimly lit chamber lined with antiquarian books and paneled in mahogany. It smelled strongly, and not unpleasantly, of fireplace smoke. Dyson had boasted that he had purchased the library in its magisterial entirety—from the books to the vaulted ceiling—from a baronial estate outside London.

The floors were covered in antique Persian carpets, over which Dyson had navigated his wheelchair with some difficulty. He sat behind a small writing table; Lomax, taking notes on a yellow pad with a silver ballpoint pen, sat beside him. Both of them faced Baumann, who was sunk into a large, plump armchair upholstered in green-and-white-striped taffeta.

"Just a passing familiarity," Baumann said. "Enough to know that the Brueghel used to live in a gallery in London. And the Rubens—*Baccanale*, is it?—vanished from a private collection in Rome sometime in the seventies."

"*Baccanale* it is," Dyson said. "Very good. The Brueghel's called *Christ and the Woman Taken in Adultery*—very special, I've always thought." He sighed. "Most of the Renoirs are from Buenos Aires; the El Greco came from Saarbrücken, as I recall. The Vermeer, I'm told, came from the Gardner in Boston, but what do I know? The Dalís were picked up in Barcelona, and the Cézanne . . . Marty, where the hell'd the Cézanne come from?"

"A private collection outside Detroit," Lomax answered without looking up from his notes. "Grosse Pointe Farms, I believe."

Dyson extended his hands, spread them out, palms up. "Don't get me wrong, Baumann. I don't put on my cat-burglar togs and rip off the stuff myself. I don't even commission the heists. They just come to me. Black-market dealers around the world must just figure me for an easy mark—man without a country and all that."

"But not without a checkbook," Baumann said.

"Right," Dyson said. A housekeeper appeared with a tray of coffee and smoked salmon sandwiches, served them, and noiselessly vanished. "I mean, let's face it," Dyson went on, "I'm not exactly going to just show up at Sotheby's Important Old Masters sale, am I? Not if I want to stay out of Leavenworth or wherever the hell it is the U.S. government wants to stash me. Anyway, stolen art's a bargain—stuff goes for maybe seven or ten percent of the crazy prices they hold you up for at Wildenstein or Thaw or Christie's—"

"I assume you didn't break me out of Pollsmoor to talk about art, Mr. Dyson," Baumann interrupted. "You had a 'business proposition.' "

Dyson regarded Baumann for a long moment over his reading glasses, his eyes steely. Then his face relaxed into a smile. "I like a fellow who's all business," he said to his assistant.

Dyson's cellular phone trilled on the table in front of him. He picked it up, flipped it open, and barked: "Yes? . . . Good God, what time is it there? . . . Does Mr. Lin ever sleep? . . . All right." He pushed a button to sever the connection. Looking directly at Baumann, he went on: "The Chinese are going to take over Asia, believe you me." He shook his head. "So they say you're the best in the world."

Baumann nodded curtly. "So I've been told. But if I

were really so good, I wouldn't have spent the last six years in jail, would I?"

"Too modest," Dyson said. "My sources tell me BOSS screwed up. Not you."

Baumann shrugged but did not reply.

"You were instructed to take out a member of the Mossad's assassination unit, the *kidon*. Someone who was getting under Pretoria's skin. Only it turned out the guy you whacked was some big-deal case officer—what's the term, a *katsa?* Do I have this right?"

"More or less."

"And then there's lots of diplomatic fallout between Tel Aviv and Pretoria. Which sort of threatened to screw up Pretoria's A-bomb program, which relied on Israel's cooperation. So you get locked away. Life sentence. Spare them any embarrassment. Right?"

"Roughly." Dyson had the basic idea right, and Baumann was uninterested in correcting the details. The salient fact was that this enigmatic billionaire had gone to great trouble to extract Baumann from prison, and men like this did not do such things out of humanitarian impulses.

About two months earlier, Baumann had been visited in his cell one afternoon by a priest, who, after a few moments of aimless chatter about Baumann's religious faith, had leaned close and whispered to the prisoner that a "friend" from the outside wanted to aid his escape. The patron, a man of great resources, would be in touch soon through confederates. Baumann would be reassigned to the auto-repair shop at once.

Baumann had listened without comment.

A few days later, he had been transferred to auto repairs. A young fellow from the prison commandant's office came by a month or so after that, ostensibly to discuss a problem with his car's ignition system, but really to let him know that things were now in place.

"Now then," Dyson said, opening a folder that Martin Lomax had slid before him. "I have a few questions for you."

Baumann merely raised his eyebrows.

"Call it a job interview," Dyson said. "What's your real name, Mr. Baumann?"

Baumann looked at Dyson blankly. "Whatever you'd like it to be. It's been so long I really don't remember."

Lomax whispered something to Dyson, who nodded and went on: "Let's see. Born in the western Transvaal. Only son of tobacco farmers. Boers. Members of the Nationalist Party."

"My parents were poorly educated and hardly political," Baumann interrupted.

"You left the University of Pretoria. Recruited there to BOSS—what's it called now, the Department of National Security or something, the DNS?"

"It's been renamed again," Lomax said. "Now it's the National Intelligence Service."

"Who the hell can keep track of this shit?" Dyson muttered. He went on, almost to himself: "Trained at the Farm as an assassin and a munitions expert. Top marks at the academy and in the field. Service loaned you out to various friendly spook services." He glanced at the sheaf of notes. "Says here you're single-handedly responsible for some fifteen documented terrorist incidents and probably a good many more undocumented ones around the world. Your cryptonym within the service was Zero, meaning you were top dog or something."

Baumann said nothing. There was a tentative knock on the library door, to which Dyson abruptly shouted: "Come!" A tall, thin man in his late forties entered, bearing a sheet of paper. His face was sallow and concave. He handed the paper to Lomax and scurried from the room. Lomax scanned the paper, then handed it over to Dyson, murmuring: "St. Petersburg." Dyson glanced at it and scrunched it into a ball, which he tossed toward a burgundy leather trash can, missing it by a few feet.

"In 1986, you were hired, on a freelance basis, by Muammar Qaddafi to bomb a discotheque in West Berlin. Bomb went off on April 5. Killed three American soldiers."

"I'm sure whoever did it," Baumann said, "had been assured by the Libyans that no American military would be present that night. Always better to do one's own intelligence work."

"If I wanted to hire an assassin, a mercenary, a soldier of fortune, they'd be lining up out the door all the way to Paris, you know," Dyson said. "Guns for hire are cheap and plentiful. You fellows, on the other hand— rare as hen's teeth. You must have been quite in demand."

"I was, yes."

"Says your native language is Afrikaans. But you usually speak with a British accent."

"A reasonable facsimile," Baumann replied.

"But persuasive. How the hell old were you when you did Carrero Blanco?"

"Hmm?"

"Luis Carrero Blanco."

"I'm afraid I don't recognize the name."

"The hell you talking about? Luis Carrero Blanco, the president of Spain under Franco. Blown up in 1972. The Basques claimed credit, but they'd really hired some mysterious outsider. A professional assassin who got a quarter of a million dollars American for pulling it off. That wasn't you?"

Baumann shrugged. "I wish it had been."

The old man furrowed his brow and shifted in his wheelchair. He looked puzzlingly at Lomax, then back at Baumann. "If you're trying to conceal something from me, I'd advise you to—"

"Now I've got a few questions for you," Baumann interrupted, raising his voice ever so slightly.

Annoyance flashed in Dyson's gray eyes. He scowled.

"How many people were involved in the operation to extract me from Pollsmoor?"

"That's my business," Dyson replied curtly.

"I'm afraid not. It directly concerns me and my welfare from now on."

Dyson paused for a moment and then relented. He turned to Lomax, who said: "Two."

"In all? Including the phony priest and the chap in the prison commandant's office?"

"Just those two," Lomax repeated with irritation. He inclined his head toward his boss for an instant, saw Dyson nod, and said quietly: "They're both dead."

"Excellent," Baumann said. "All loose ends tied?"

"Professionally," Lomax said.

"Let's just hope," Baumann said, "that whoever did the wet work was more professional than whoever's in charge of security here at whatever this is called . . . Arcadia."

Lomax compressed his lips into a thin line. His eyes flashed with anger, his face reddened.

"Look, goddammit," Dyson said, his voice choked with fury. "You should be eternally grateful—you should damn well kiss the ground I wheel on for what I did to break you out of that hellhole."

At this, Baumann rose slowly to his feet. He smiled wanly and turned to leave. "I do appreciate your assistance, Mr. Dyson," he said, "but I didn't ask for it. If I'm not satisfied that you have taken the necessary basic precautions to ensure that I am not traced, then I must refuse to have anything more to do with you."

"Don't even think about it," Dyson called out.

"Mr. Dyson, you've presumably brought me here because of my proficiency at the type of work you want me to do on your behalf. I suggest that we respect each other's areas of expertise. Now, please tell me how the arrangements were made."

Dyson told him about how his people contacted certain officials in South Africa and paid them off. Baumann nodded. "All right. I'll listen to what you propose. But I should warn you that I may well not accept. It all depends on the nature of the job you want done, and the amount of payment you're prepared to offer."

Dyson backed up his chair by pushing at the writing table, rattling the inkwell and the Meissen urn. "Do you seriously think you have much choice?" he said. "You're a goddam international fugitive now. And I know your whereabouts!"

"Yes, you do," Baumann agreed equably, looking around the room. "And the same could be said of you."

Dyson stared furiously at Baumann. Lomax visibly stiffened and slowly lowered a hand toward the concealed pistol Baumann had observed in the garden.

Baumann went on as if he hadn't seen this: "And I'm certainly familiar enough now with the security here, the weakness and the permeability. Anytime I wish, I can pay you a return visit. Or come to call at your corporate offices in Geneva or Zug. You obviously know some of the particulars of my background, so I'm sure you don't for a moment doubt my ability to hunt you down."

Dyson put a restraining arm on Lomax. "All right," he said at length. Lomax glowered. "I'm sure we'll be able to come to some happy agreement." His expression eased somewhat. "We Americans call it 'getting to yes.' "

Baumann returned to the armchair and settled into it. He crossed his legs. "I hope so," he said. "Six years in prison can make one long for something productive to do."

"You understand that what I want you to do must be done in absolute secrecy," Dyson said. "I can't stress that enough."

"I have never advertised my accomplishments. You don't know even one small part of the work I've done."

Dyson fixed him with a stare. "That's the way I like it. I must not be connected to this in any way, and I intend to take measures to ensure that."

Baumann shrugged. "Naturally. What is it you want done?"

Martin Lomax, who knew every last detail of the plan his employer had been brooding about for months, returned to the library about half an hour later. He understood that Dyson wished to close the deal in private, as Dyson always did.

When he entered, discreet as always, the two men appeared to be finishing their conversation.

He heard Baumann speak just one word: "Impressive."

Dyson gave one of his odd, cold smiles. "Then you're interested."

"No," Baumann said.

"What, is it the money?" Lomax found himself asking, a tad too anxiously.

"The fee would certainly be a consideration. Given the risks to my life it would entail, I'd certainly be better off back at Pollsmoor. But we will discuss finances later."

"What the hell are you—" Dyson began.

"You have spelled out your conditions," Baumann said quietly. "Now, I have mine."

CHAPTER ELEVEN

"Crime Lab, Kowalski," said a man's voice.

"Michael Kowalski? This is Special Agent Sarah Cahill in the Boston office."

"Yup." He made no attempt to hide his impatience.

"You're an acoustic engineer, is that right?"

Kowalski sighed. "What's up?"

She leaned forward in her chair. "Listen, do you guys know how to . . . unerase tapes?"

The phone line was silent for a long time. She gestured hello with her chin at Ken Alton, who was getting up from his desk and heading toward the break room.

Finally, Kowalski spoke. "Audio, video, what?"

"Audio."

"No."

Sarah could hear his hand covering the phone. There were muffled voices on the other end of the line.

"Hello?" she said.

"Yeah, I'm back. Sorry, I'm raked. All right, you got an audio tape you accidentally erased over or something? Not likely we're going to be able to bring it back for you. No way. That tape's gone. Sorry."

"Thanks." Sarah glumly put down the phone and said, "Shit."

She found Ken sitting at a table in the break room, drinking a Diet Pepsi and eating a Snickers bar. He was reading one of the William Gibson novels he constantly toted around. She sat down beside him.

"I liked the old one better," she said.

He closed his novel, using the Snickers wrapper as a bookmark. "The old what?"

"Break room. Across the street. The rats always snarfed your brown-bag lunch if you left it out. I miss the rats."

"Was that Technical Services you were talking to?"

"Right."

"Warren Elkind blew you off, eh?"

"He wouldn't even take my call—not after he heard it was about Valerie Santoro's murder. I guess I'm really reaching now."

"Hey, don't take it so hard," Ken said. "Life sucks, and then you die." He bit his lower lip. "Technical Services is pretty good. If they can't do something, it usually can't be done."

"Great," she said bitterly.

"But not necessarily. Are you really serious about this?"

"What's that supposed to mean?" she asked, turning to look at him. Her phone rang, and she ignored it.

"Well, there's a guy I went to MIT with. A real genius. He's on the faculty there now, an assistant professor or something. Electronics engineer. I could give him a call if you want."

"Yeah, I'd like that. Hey, have you ever done a full-scale search of the computerized central files?"

"Sure. Why?" The Pepsi machine hummed, then rattled.

"Warren Elkind. I want to see if his name comes up anywhere. How do I do it?"

"You make the request through Philly Willie. He

sends it on to Washington, to the professional searchers at headquarters. The correlation clerks are excellent."

"I want to find all references to Elkind. Can they do it?"

"They use software called Sybase, which is pretty good. Only question is whether they'll let you do it. Costs a lot. What makes you think Phelan's going to authorize it?"

"Warren Elkind is one of the most powerful bankers in America. He's also been a target of terrorist threats. If I leave things the way they are, we have one dead prostitute and one rich banker. No connection. A big, fat goose egg. But if we can do a fully cross-referenced search, it's possible we'll turn up something someplace we wouldn't have thought to look. Some investigation somewhere, some *lead* somewhere—"

"Yeah, but Phelan's just going to tell you about how the Bureau's file clerks cross-reference better than any file clerks in the world. If it's not in Elkind's file now, what makes you think a computer search is going to yield anything more?"

"You're the computer nerd. You figure it out. I want an all-out, interagency search. CIA, DIA, NSA, INS, State, the whole shebang. Stuff that *our* people don't necessarily cross-reference."

"Go talk to Willie."

"He's just going to say, 'Sarah, this isn't Lockerbie.' "

"Well, it isn't." He took a huge mouthful of Snickers and, chewing, smiled wickedly. "But ask anyway. You think Elkind killed your informant?"

She sighed. "No. I mean, anything's possible, I wouldn't rule it out. But there's something . . . I don't know, sort of *off* about her death. A five-thousand-dollar payoff . . . and murdered hours after servicing one of the most powerful men on Wall Street. Something's not quite right."

CHAPTER TWELVE

Malcolm Dyson, Baumann thought, was faux-casual yet tightly wound; shamblingly relaxed yet ferociously observant. And he had made a point of keeping Baumann waiting a good half hour while he changed for dinner; where he was having dinner, whether in or out, the old billionaire hadn't volunteered. He guarded his personal life like a state secret.

Dyson's only revealing comment had been an aside, uttered as a liveried butler escorted him into a cherry-wood elevator and up to his personal quarters. "I've learned," he'd said apropos of nothing, "that I don't even miss the States. I miss New York. I had a nice spread in Katonah, thirty-four acres. Town house on East Seventy-first Street that Alexandra put endless time into redoing. Loved it. Life goes on." And, with a dismissive wave: "New York may be the financial capital, but you can goddam well pay the rent out of a shack in Zambezi if you want."

Dyson reappeared in the smoke-redolent library, wearing black tie and a shawl-collar dinner jacket. "Now, then. Your 'conditions,' as you call them. I don't have all day, and I'd prefer to wrap this up before dinner."

Baumann stood before Dyson. For a few moments he was silent. At last he spoke. "You have outlined to me a plan that will wreak terrible destruction on the United States and then the world. You want me to detonate a rather sophisticated explosive device in Manhattan, on a specific date, and disable a major computer system as well. I am now privy to your intent. And you, like me, are an internationally sought fugitive from justice. What makes you think I can't simply go to the international authorities with a promise to divulge what I know of your plan, and strike a bargain for my freedom?"

Dyson smiled. "Self-interest, pure and simple," he replied phlegmatically. "For all intents and purposes, I am beyond reach here. I'm effectively protected by the Swiss government, which receives enormous financial benefit from my corporate undertakings."

"No one is beyond reach," Baumann pointed out.

"You are a convicted murderer and terrorist," Dyson said, "who broke out of a South African jail and went on the lam. Why do you think they will believe you? It's far more likely you'll simply be rounded up and returned to Pollsmoor. Locked up in solitary. The South Africans don't want you talking, as you know, and the other governments of the world sure as hell don't want you at large."

Baumann nodded. "But you're describing a criminal act of such magnitude that the Americans, the FBI and the CIA in particular, will not rest until they locate the perpetrators. In the aftermath of such a bombing, the public pressure for arrests will be enormous."

"I've selected you because you're supposed to be brilliant and, most important, extremely secretive. Your job description is not to get caught."

"But I will require the services of others—this is hardly a job I can do alone—and once others are involved, the chance of secrecy dwindles to nothing."

"Need I remind you," Dyson said hotly, "that you've got talents you can use to make sure no one talks? Anyway, the FBI and the CIA, and for that matter MI6 and Interpol and the fucking International Red *Cross*, will all be looking for parties with a *motive*. Parties who claim responsibility for such an act, who have some agenda. But I want no credit, and as far as the world knows, I have no agenda. Whatever my legal troubles in the United States, I have all the money anyone could ever want and much more. Much, much more. Beyond, as they say, the dreams of avarice. After a certain point, money becomes merely abstract. I have, you see, no financial motive."

"I can see that," Baumann agreed, "but there are flaws in your plan I can see already—"

"You're the expert," Dyson exploded. "You're the goddam Prince of Darkness. Iron out the wrinkles, straighten out the kinks. Anyway, what sort of flaws are you referring to?"

"For one thing, you say you're unwilling to give up operational control."

"If I want to call it off, I need to be able to reach you—"

"No. Too risky. From time to time I may contact you, using a clandestine method I deem safe. Or I may not contact you at all."

"I'm not willing—"

"The point is nonnegotiable. As one professional to another, I'm telling you I will not compromise the security of the operation."

Dyson stared intently. "If you—*when* you contact me, how do you plan to do it?"

"Telephone."

"Telephone? You've got to be kidding me. Of all the sophisticated ways—"

"Not landlines. I don't trust them. Satellite telephone—a SATCOM. Surely you have one."

"Indeed," Dyson replied. "But if you plan on calling me through satellite transmissions, you'll need a portable—what are they called—"

"A suitcase SATCOM. It's the size of a small suitcase or large briefcase. Correct."

"I have one I use when I'm out of telephone range, or on my boat, or whatever. You can take that."

"No, thank you. I'll get my own. After all, how do I know the one you'd give me isn't bugged?"

"Don't be ridiculous," Dyson said. "Why the hell would I want to do that?"

"You want to keep track of my whereabouts—you've made that clear. How do I know there isn't a GPS built into the receiver?" A Global Positioning System, Baumann did not bother to explain, is a hand-held device that can be modified to transmit an inaudible signal as a sub-carrier of the audio signal transmitted over satellite link. It would enable the receiving party to determine within a few meters the precise location of the party using the portable SATCOM.

"In any case," Baumann went on, "I don't know where you acquired your portable unit. It's simple technology these days for a government intelligence agency, using a sensitive spectrum analyzer, to identify the characteristic emissions from a particular transmitter and map its location. Just as the CIA, a few decades ago, followed certain automobiles of interest in Vietnam from space by picking up their unique sparkplug emission patterns."

"That's the most far-fetched—"

"Perhaps I'm being overly cautious. But I'd much rather procure my own, if you don't mind. It's an expenditure of approximately thirty thousand dollars. I assume you can afford it."

Baumann's tone made it eminently clear that he would do as he pleased, whether Dyson minded or not.

Dyson shrugged with feigned carelessness. "What else?"

"You are offering me two million dollars. Unless you are prepared to multiply that figure, there's no sense in our talking any further."

Dyson laughed. His even false teeth were stained yellow. "You know what the first rule of negotiation is? Always bargain from strength. You're standing on quicksand. I sprung you; I can burn you in a second."

"That may be true," Baumann conceded, "but if you had another alternative, you wouldn't have gone to all the trouble to pull me out of Pollsmoor. I wouldn't be standing here before you. There are indeed other professionals who could do the job you describe—but you will get only one shot at it. If it fails, you will never have another chance, I can assure you of that. So you want the best in the world. And you've already made that decision. Let's not play games."

"What do you want? Three million?"

"Ten. Money for you is, as you say, abstract. Theoretical. To you, another five million is a telephone call before your morning coffee."

Dyson laughed loudly. "Why not fifty million? Why not a billion, for Christ's sake?"

"Because I don't need it. In a dozen lifetimes, I could never need that kind of money. Ten million is enough to buy me protection and anonymity. This will be the last job I do, and I'd like to live the rest of my life without the constant fear of being caught out. More important, though, any more than that is a risk to me. The basic rule in my circles is never to give anyone more than he can explain. I can explain, by various means, a fortune of ten million dollars. A billion, I cannot. Oh, and expenses on top of that."

Dyson stared, his steely-gray eyes penetrating. "Upon completion."

"No. One-third up front, one-third a week before the strike date, and the final third immediately upon completion. And before I do anything, the money must begin to move."

"I don't have ten million dollars in cash sitting around, stashed in my mattress or something. You make a withdrawal of that magnitude, you're inviting all kinds of scrutiny," Dyson objected.

"The last thing I want is wads of cash," Baumann said. "Much too easily traceable. And I don't want you to be able to grab my money."

"If you set up an account in Geneva or Zurich—"

"The Swiss are not reliable. I don't want my funds impounded. I know for sure that at some point in the future, some small part of this will come out. I need plausible deniability."

"Caymans?"

"I don't trust bankers," Baumann said with a grim smile. "I have dealt with far too many of them."

"Then what do you suggest?"

"The payment must be put in the hands of someone we both trust to serve as a go-between."

"Such as?"

"There is a gentleman we both have met in the Panamanian intelligence service G-2." Baumann spoke his name. "As you may or may not know, during the American invasion of Panama, Operation JUST CAUSE, his family was inadvertently killed."

Dyson nodded.

"He was always anti-American," Baumann went on, "but since then, you'd be hard pressed to find someone with a greater hatred for America. He has a motive to cooperate with both of us."

"All right."

"He will act as our executive agent, our go-between. You will issue him a letter of credit. He'll be unable to touch the money himself but he'll be authorized to release it according to a schedule we work out. He approves the transfer of funds, and the Panamanian bank disburses them. That way, he can't abscond with the money, and neither can I. And you'll be unable to withhold it from me."

For a long while, Malcolm Dyson examined his manicured fingernails. Then he looked up. "Agreed," he said. "A very intelligent plan. Your knowledge of the financial world is impressive."

Baumann nodded modestly and said, "Thank you."

Dyson extended his hand. "So when can you begin?"

"I'll begin my preparations as soon as I have received my first installment of the funds, my three point three million dollars," Baumann said. He took Dyson's hand and shook it firmly. "I'm glad we were able to come to an agreement. Enjoy your dinner party."

Part 2

CIPHERS

All warfare is based on deception.

—Sun-tzu, *The Art of War*

CHAPTER THIRTEEN

The largest intelligence organization in the world also happens to be the most secretive. It is the U.S. National Security Agency, or NSA—which is sometimes archly said to stand for either "No Such Agency" or "Never Say Anything."

The NSA, which occupies a sprawling, thousand-acre compound at Fort Meade, Maryland, is in charge of America's SIGINT, or signals intelligence. This includes communications intelligence (COMINT), radar, telemetry, laser, and nonimagery infrared intelligence. It has been described as an immense vacuum cleaner, sucking up electronic intelligence the world over and, if necessary, decrypting it.

Crudely put, the NSA has the ability, among quite a few other abilities, to eavesdrop electronically on most telephone conversations throughout the world.

Under the provisions of two laws—Executive Order 12333, Section 2.5, and the Foreign Intelligence Surveillance Act, Section 101/F-1—the NSA cannot *target* the telephone conversations of any U.S. citizen without a warrant from the attorney general of the United States, based on probable cause that the individual is an agent of a foreign power.

The operative word here is *target*. The law doesn't apply to communications that the NSA's satellites *happen* to pick up as they rummage through the international telecommunications network.

Not only is the law full of loopholes and clever wording, but all of the NSA's targeting requests are approved by a top-secret rubber-stamp court. And in any case, if the NSA's satellites intercept a phone call between London and Moscow, there's simply no way to tell whether the caller is a United States citizen.

So, in effect, the NSA has the ability to intercept *any* telephone call coming into or out of the United States as well as any telex, cable, or fax anywhere in the world, by means of microwave interception. The agency is believed to sift through millions of telephone calls daily.

In order to make such a vast undertaking remotely manageable, the NSA programs its supercomputers' scan guides with highly classified watch lists of certain "trigger words," including word groups, names, and telephone numbers. Thus, any telephone conversation or fax, for instance, that contains a reference to "nuclear weapons" or "terrorism" or "plutonium" or "Muammar Qaddafi," or to names of terrorist training camps or code names of certain secret weapons, may be flagged for further analysis.

Telephone calls that are encrypted or scrambled also tend to pique the NSA's suspicion.

The same evening that Baumann agreed to work for Malcolm Dyson, a random fragment of a telephone conversation between two points in Switzerland was captured by a geosynchronous Rhyolite spy satellite, moving 22,300 miles above the earth's surface at the exact speed of the earth's rotation—in effect, hovering. The conversation was sent over landlines using microwave linkage, via two microwave towers located in Switzerland, in line of sight to each other.

In many areas of the world, topographical concerns—mountains, bodies of water, and the like—make it impossible for telephone conversations to travel exclusively by landlines. So an enormous volume of telephone traffic is beamed between microwave towers. Because each microwave tower sends out its transmission in the shape of a cone, some of the waves continue to travel into the ether, where they can be picked up by satellite.

The captured signal, which contained a fragment of the telephone conversation, was scooped up by a hovering NSA Rhyolite satellite and relayed to another satellite over Australia, thence to a relay site, and then to Fort Meade, where some twenty-seven acres of computers are located deep below the National Security Agency's Headquarters/Operations Building. It is said to be the most formidable concentration of computational power in the world.

Within minutes, the signal was classified and reconstructed. Only then were a couple of interesting things learned about the captured telephone conversation.

First, the NSA analysts discovered that the signal was digital: it had been converted into a series of zeroes and ones. Digital signals have a great advantage over analog signals in that they are received with maximum clarity.

Digital signals have another advantage over analog. Once scrambled, they are secure, impenetrable, impossible to be understood by anyone outside a handful of government agencies in the most developed countries.

Then the NSA analysts discovered a second interesting thing. The captured conversation had been rendered even more secure from eavesdropping by means of a state-of-the-art digital encryption system. It is not uncommon these days for private citizens—particularly in the world of high finance—to make their most sensitive calls on sophisticated, secure telephones that digitally encrypt their voices so that they can't be bugged, tapped, or otherwise eavesdropped on.

But the vast majority of suppliers of these secure phones (one of the biggest is Crypto A.G. of Zurich) cooperate with law enforcement by selling their encryption schemes to both the National Security Agency and the British GCHQ (the Government Communications Headquarters, in Cheltenham, England, which is the British counterpart of the NSA). So even most encrypted phone conversations can be listened to by the NSA and GCHQ. International businessmen discussing illegal schemes and drug cartels discussing transactions all tend to speak carelessly over "secure" phones, not realizing that most of them really aren't secure at all.

But this particular digitally encrypted format was unknown to either NSA or GCHQ. And that was the third peculiar discovery.

The scrambled signal was sent immediately to the Cryptanalytic Division at NSA's Headquarters/Operations Building. There it was run through a Cray supercomputer, which tested the signal against all known encryption schemes. But the Cray came up blank. The signal wouldn't break. Instead of voices speaking, there was only a bewildering sequence of ones and zeroes that the computer couldn't comprehend.

This in itself was extraordinary. The NSA's computers are programmed with the keys to virtually every known cipher ever invented, every mechanism to encipher that has ever been used. This includes any system ever used by anyone at any time in history, anything ever written about in a technical paper, in a book, even in a novel, any cipher that's ever been even floated as a hypothesis.

As long as the computers are fed a large enough sample of the cipher, and the encryption scheme is known to the NSA, they will crack the code. Most digital signals are broken immediately. But after minutes, then hours of churning, the computers were stumped.

The NSA abhors the existence of any encryption scheme it doesn't know. To a cryptanalyst, an "unbreakable" encryption is like an impenetrable safe to a master safecracker, an unpickable lock to a master lockpick. It is a challenge, a taunt, a red flag.

Two cryptanalysts—cryppies, as they're called within the Fort Meade complex—hunched before a screen and watched with mingled fascination and frustration.

"Jeez, what's wrong with this one?" George Frechette said to his officemate, Edwin Chu. "Everything's processing except this one string. Now what?"

Edwin Chu adjusted his round horn-rimmed glasses and peered through them for several moments at the flashing numbers on the screen. "We got us a new one."

"What do you say we have a look at it?" George suggested. "Play with it a little?"

"Sure," Edwin said. "Hey, I'm there."

CHAPTER FOURTEEN

Professor Bruce Gelman, a small, slender, balding man with a wispy beard, was an assistant professor of computer science at MIT with a national reputation in the field of electronic engineering. According to Ken Alton, he was also a legendary hacker skilled in the intricacies of telephony and one of the founders of the Thinking Machines Corporation.

He could have been in his thirties or forties; it was impossible to tell. Dressed in a woolen lumberjack shirt over a plaid flannel shirt, he did not look like a typical university professor, but then, computer types rarely did. His office was located in the Artificial Intelligence Laboratory in a tall, anonymous office building in Kendall Square, Cambridge.

"I thought you guys were up to speed on this stuff," he said, sipping coffee from a giant plastic cup. "You're telling me the FBI labs threw in the towel?"

"Basically, yes," Sarah said.

Gelman rolled his eyes, scratched at his beard, and chuckled. "*I* see," he said with exaggerated politeness, leaving no doubt what he thought of the FBI. "Of course, this technician you talked to is right: it's not exactly *easy* to restore a tape that's been erased. That's true."

She removed from her briefcase a black cassette sealed in a plastic evidence bag and marked with a number, took it out of the bag, and handed it to him.

He gulped some more coffee, set down the cup, and knitted his brow. "We could get lucky," he said. "Might be an old answering machine. Or just a poorly constructed one."

"Why would that help?"

"Maybe the tape wobbles up and down in the machine, relative to the heads. Possible the tape guides are loose, and the tape wandered up and down some."

"That would make it easier?"

He shot his left hand out for the enormous cup of coffee, and accidentally tipped it over. "Oh, God. Yuck." Pulling some sheets of pale-blue Kleenex from a plastic dispenser, he mopped up the muddy spill, which coursed over a stack of papers. "Yuck."

He retrieved the enormous cup, managing to salvage half the coffee. "You see, that would leave us a stripe of recorded information above or below what's been recorded over it."

"And if the answering machine isn't old, or the tape guides aren't loose?"

"Well," Gelman said, "tape is three-dimensional, right?" He slurped loudly from the coffee cup, then gingerly set it down. "It has a thickness to it. The front and the back surfaces of the tape are affected differently by the recording process."

Sarah didn't entirely understand what he was driving at, but nodded anyway.

"So you compare the front and back surfaces of the tape," he went on, "to see if there are any traces of magnetic information on the *back* of the tape. Sometimes that works."

"And if not?"

"Well, then there's an effect called 'print-through,'

where you find traces on *one* section of the tape of what's been recorded on a section right *next* to it. So there are various places to look for data. I'm surprised your labs didn't think of this." He shook his head disapprovingly. "So we can scan the tape and reconstruct it two-dimensionally, using VCR technology."

"Can you explain that?"

He frowned and looked down at the coffee-stained papers arrayed on the desk before him. "So, it's like this," Gelman said. "This is a technique I developed for a— another government agency, under contract. Oh, hell, it's obviously the NSA. Anyways, normally an audio tape is magnetized, negative or positive, on a stripe, okay?"

Sarah nodded.

"But on a *videotape*, the information is laid down differently. It's recorded on stripes put down at a transverse angle to the tape, in order to fit more information on the same length of tape."

"Uh huh."

"So when it comes time to play back, a VCR uses a helical-scan playback head to read that information. Meaning the tape head moves at sort of an angle across the tape, okay?"

"Okay."

"So if you want to play back a really narrow stripe of leftover information that's sort of on the *edges* of a broader band—the vertical information as well as the horizontal—you can use this VCR technology, a similar helical-scan playback device."

He paused a moment, and Sarah nodded to encourage him to proceed.

"So the helical scan goes across the tape, transversely, moving up through the *newly* recorded stuff and then over the narrow band of leftover information—the stuff we're interested in, right? So, at regular intervals, we have these little blips of the stuff we want. The rest is garbage." Gelman spoke more and more rapidly, with growing enthusiasm. "So, then the question is, how do you sort the wheat from the chaff, you know what I mean? How do you separate out the sound you want from the sound you don't? Well, what you do is, you write a program to differentiate it out, right?"

"Right."

"Now, I know the distance and the time between the bits of the stripe we're interested in—the sequence of magnetic impulses, let's call it. I can calculate it on the basis of the rate at which the playback head is revolving. I know the *periodicity*. So, I tell the computer what I'm looking for and to pull out any signals of interest. Then we put sort of a digital 'picture' of the magnetic information onto a computer, using a specially constructed piece of equipment, a helical-scan tape playback mechanism that converts the analog signal to a digital signal. It's the same technology as a compact-disc player or a digital audio tape, right? Really, it's a modified digital compact cassette playback unit that can play back the recovered audio tape as if it were high-density digital tape."

"Look," Sarah broke in at last. "Computer stuff is obviously not my area of expertise, which is why I'm talking to you. You're saying you may be able to un-erase this tape, right?"

"That's right."

"How long would it take you?"

"The process might take a few hours, maybe. But to do it right, a week, probably—"

"Okay. I'd like to hire your services on a contract basis. Could you have something for me in two or three days?"

"Three days?" Gelman gasped. "I mean, theoretically, yes, but—"

"That would be great," Sarah said. "Thanks."

CHAPTER FIFTEEN

Baumann awoke with a pounding headache, covered in a cold sweat. The linen bedsheet around him was soaked, as if he'd been doused with gallons of cold water. He drew back the heavy drapes to let in the strong morning sunlight. Looking down at the Avenue des Portugais, then up at the sky, he estimated that it was eight or nine o'clock. He had badly needed the sleep, but there was much to be done today.

For a few moments he sat on the edge of the bed and massaged his temples to ease the headache. His head spun with the residue of nightmares. He had dreamed he was back in the hole, that black chamber of horrors.

He had abided the floggings, the "cuts" with a cane while you were strapped, spread-eagled, to the three-legged mare, a prison physician standing dourly by. But the hole, or the "bomb," as some called it, was the worst place in Pollsmoor, a dank horrific place it had taken all of his strength to endure without cracking. The hole was where they put you to punish you for fighting in the exercise yard, for striking a *boer*, for no reason at all other than that the chief warder didn't like your face. Actually, he had spent no more than a month there in all his years at Pollsmoor. It meant solitary confinement, a bare concrete cell, a "punishment regime" of maize porridge and watery broth and more porridge.

No cigarettes, no newspapers, no letters, no visitors. No radio, no television. No contact with the outside world; no leaving the tiny, fetid, unlighted cell, whose walls began to close in on you. You lived like an animal in a cage rank with your own urine and excrement from the shallow hole in the ground into which you had to relieve yourself.

Why was he having this dream again? What did it mean? That his subconscious didn't believe he was out of prison? That his mind understood things on a higher plane: he was still not out of prison?

He took a long, almost unbearably hot shower. Then he got into one of the hotel's thick white cotton robes ("Hôtel Raphaël Paris" stitched in gold on the breast), settled into one of the suite's chaises longues, and began to make telephone calls. As he spoke—his French, slightly British-accented, was impeccable—he idly combed his damp hair straight back.

He'd flown into Orly from Geneva's Cointrin Airport, on a false passport provided by Dyson's staff. Travel within the European Economic Community had become remarkably casual since he'd been locked away. No one gave his Swiss passport so much as a passing glance. But however Dyson's people had procured the passport, he didn't trust it. If it was forged, was the forgery top-notch? Was the forger an informer for the Swiss authorities? If it was a legitimate passport, what if it had been flagged as missing? If someone in the Swiss government had been paid off, how secure was that transaction?

Dyson had offered to supply a full set of the documents he'd need—passports, driver's licenses, credit cards—but he'd politely turned down the offer.

Dyson-supplied paper was a sheep's bell: if he chose, Dyson could keep close tabs on his whereabouts.

Until he made contact with a professional forger, he needed to create a plausible identity from scratch. Things had gotten more complicated in the last five or six years. Passports were more difficult to forge; you could no longer rent a car with cash. The emergence of worldwide terrorism had spurred the airlines to impose random security checks of checked and carry-on baggage on transatlantic flights. It was a much more suspicious world. Also, he didn't dare acquire all of his documentation in one place, from one source. He would have to travel to a number of countries in the next few days.

He had reserved suite 510 at the Raphaël, on Avenue Kléber in the 16th Arrondissement, a luxurious and discreet place. He had never stayed here before (he would never be so careless) but had heard of it from acquaintances. The suite was immense by Parisian standards, with a large sitting room, and cost a fortune, but he was spending Dyson's money, after all, not his own. And it was important to cultivate the right sort of appearances.

He had money enough to last for a while, U.S. dollars, Swiss and French francs. The first payment from Dyson had already been transferred from a bank in Panama.

He needed clothes. All he had were the suit and shoes he'd bought off the rack at Lanvin, on Geneva's Rue du Rhône. He would have to pick up a selection of shirts from Sulka, a few pairs of shoes from John Lobb, and a couple of conservative businessman's suits at Cifonelli or Marcel Lassance.

All of this would have to be done in a matter of hours, for there was even more important business to conduct.

An hour later he was sitting in the spare, inelegant showroom of a microwave-communications firm on the sixth floor of a building on Boulevard de Strasbourg, in the 10th Arrondissement. The company did business with corporations, news organizations, and anyone who required the use of a satellite-linked telephone.

The company's director, M. Gilbert Trémaud, treated Baumann with the utmost deference: the British gentleman traveled widely in the Third World and needed an Inmarsat-M- and Comsat-compatible phone.

"The most compact model I have," Mr. Trémaud explained in fluent English, "is an MLink-5000, about one-fifth the size of most other portable satellite telephones. With battery, it weighs thirteen kilos. Eighteen inches long, fourteen inches wide, and five inches thick. It's extremely portable, highly reliable, and glitch-free." He brought it out of a locked display case. It looked like an aluminum briefcase.

Baumann popped the clasp. It opened like a book. "The antenna—?"

"A flat-plate array antenna," Trémaud said. "The days of the parabolic antenna are over, thankfully. Beamwidth is much broader, which means aiming accuracy is much less crucial."

"I don't see it," Baumann said.

Trémaud touched the lid. "This *is* the antenna," he said, and watched his visitor smile.

"Very convenient," Baumann said.

"Yes, it is," Trémaud agreed. "You can use it in an apartment or hotel room quite easily. Just sit it on the windowsill, flip the top open, and it's deployed. The signal-strength meter helps you adjust the angle. The unit will compute the azimuth for you. Do you know where you'll be using it?"

Baumann thought for a moment. "Why do you ask?"

"There are four satellites in use now. Depending upon where you are, you will transmit via any of the four. If you're in Moscow, for example, make sure your hotel room faces west. But if you're, say, in—"

"How quickly can I get it?"

"You can buy it today, if you wish. I have three in stock. But you cannot take it with you yet."

"Why not?"

"These units are very strictly controlled. First, you must apply for an identification number, which will serve as your telephone number. The application takes three days at least to go through—"

"That's impossible," Baumann said. "I'm leaving tonight."

"*Tonight?*" Trémaud exclaimed. "But there's simply no way!"

"I'll buy it without an identification number."

Trémaud shrugged, spread his palms, and widened his eyes. "If I could do that, sir, I would do so gladly. But I must enter an identification number in the computer next to the serial number of each unit I sell. Otherwise the computer will not release it from inventory."

"I'll tell you what," Baumann said quietly. He took an envelope from his breast pocket and began counting out thousand-franc notes. "I am in a difficult position, because I need to have this immediately. I am prepared to pay you"—he continued to count out the bills—"lavishly . . . for your attention to this matter. There are ways to circumvent foolish restrictions such as this, are there not?"

Trémaud watched as Baumann counted out the rest of the cash. Then he pulled the pile toward himself and counted them again. Finally he looked up at Baumann and swallowed hard. His throat was dry.

"Yes, sir," he said with a slight nod of his head. "There are ways."

CHAPTER SIXTEEN

Alexander Pappas had been retired from the FBI almost a year, but he was one of the least retired retired people Sarah knew. He had been her boss when she first moved to the Boston office, before Lockerbie, and had become a good friend, then mentor. There was sort of a father-daughter thing between them, yes, but Alex Pappas felt strongly about women getting ahead in the Bureau. He seemed to have made up his mind that of all the women in the Boston office, Sarah Cahill was the one who most deserved his support. The two had become close when Sarah's marriage was breaking up and she needed someone to talk to; Pappas became an adviser, father confessor, sounding board. Sarah sometimes felt he'd saved her sanity.

There was another kind of bond as well: both had worked major terrorism cases. In March 1977, when Pappas was assigned to the Counterterrorism Section in the Washington metropolitan field office, a religious sect calling themselves the Hanafi Muslims seized three buildings in Washington. They took 139 hostages and threatened to kill them if their demands weren't met, chiefly vengeance against a rival sect. The FBI and the local police surrounded the buildings but had little success until Pappas managed to convince the Hanafis to surrender without violence. Which was fortunate, because as Pappas later explained it to Sarah, the Justice Department had made it clear to the FBI that force was not to be used under any circumstances.

And then, at the end of his career, he was called to New York to help investigate the terrorist bombing of the World Trade Center on February 26, 1993, when an explosion in the parking garage beneath one of the twin towers killed six and injured a thousand. Although he repeatedly downplayed his role in the effort whenever discussing the Trade Center matter, and rarely talked about it, Sarah knew that Pappas was far more central than he let on.

He was content to let others grab the credit. "Look," he once explained to Sarah, "for the younger guys this was a CTM—a Career-Threatening Moment. Make or break. What the hell did I need the credit for? I was an old man about to get out of there." Then he added, with a wicked cackle: "Now, if this had been twenty years earlier, you'd have read my goddam name all over *Newsday* and the *Times*, believe me."

Pappas was a widower who lived in a small, comfortable house in Brookline, near Boston. Once a month or so, he'd invite Sarah and Jared over for a home-cooked dinner. He was an excellent cook. Jared loved dinners at Pappas's house and was fond of the old man.

Pappas greeted them at the door by reaching down to give Jared a hug and—his usual joke—pretending to try to lift Jared into the air. "I can't do it!" he wheezed. "You're too heavy!"

"You're not strong enough!" Jared replied delightedly. "You're too old!"

"Right you are, young man," he said, giving Sarah a kiss on the cheek.

He was a large man, large-boned and thick around the middle. He was sixty-seven and looked at least that, with a round, jowly face, rheumy brown eyes, a full head of silver hair, and oversized ears.

The entire house smelled wonderfully of garlic and tomatoes. "Lasagna," he announced. He asked Jared: "You ever have *Greek* lasagna?"

"No," Jared said dubiously.

He tousled Jared's hair. "Greek lasagna is called spanakopita. I made that for you guys once, didn't I?"

Jared shook his head.

"I didn't? What's wrong with me? Next time. My wife, Anastasia, made the best spanakopita you ever had."

"*I* never had it," Jared said.

"Don't be a wiseacre. Now, come here. I've got something to show you."

"I want to play with the Victrola in the basement," Jared said, running ahead toward the basement steps.

"Later. This is more interesting, I promise you," Pappas said. "All right? All right?" He produced a small, flat package wrapped in silver paper and handed it to Jared.

"A baseball card!" he squealed.

"No, it's not," Pappas said solemnly.

"Yes it is," Jared replied, just as solemnly, carefully tearing the package open. "All *right! Awesome!*" He held the baseball card up for Sarah to see and explained, "It's a Reggie Jackson rookie. This is worth, like, thirty or forty *dollars.*"

"Oh, God, Alex," Sarah scolded. "You shouldn't do that."

Pappas beamed. "Now, if we're going to eat anytime within the next ten hours, Jared's going to have to help me make the salad. Come on."

Jared stuck out his tongue but followed Pappas into the kitchen eagerly. They talked baseball. "The greatest player who ever was," Pappas rumbled, "was the Babe."

Jared, who was not actually helping make the salad but was instead watching Pappas slice cucumbers, replied with exasperation: "He was a big, slow white guy."

"Excuse me?" Pappas said incredulously and put down the paring knife. "Excuse me? Babe Ruth stole seventeen bases twice in his career. And they didn't even run much back in the twenties. In those days, there were hardly any stolen bases."

"Who had more home runs?" Jared said.

"Sure, Aaron did, but over a much longer period of time. Babe Ruth's career was shorter than Aaron's, for one thing. The Babe wasn't even a full-time hitter—for the first six years of his career, he split his time between pitching and playing outfield, Jared."

Jared hesitated, fixed Pappas with a long stare. "The best was Willie Mays."

"Oh, so you're dumping Hank Aaron now."

"Mays was one of the greatest fielders ever. And Ruth had an advantage—the ballparks in the nineteen-twenties were smaller."

"Oh, for God's sake—" Pappas began.

"Boys," Sarah interrupted. "If we don't eat, I'm going to pass out and Jared's going to have to hitchhike home."

Jared finished his supper quickly and disappeared downstairs to the basement to play with Pappas's ancient Victrola. Sarah and Pappas, sitting at the table and poking at the remains of the cannolis, could hear the distant ghost strains of the Paul Whiteman Orchestra.

They talked for a while about the darkroom Pappas was building in the basement, about the adult-education course he was taking in black-and-white photography. Sarah ran the details of the Valerie Santoro murder by him, mentioning the database search and the still-unclear involvement of a banker named Warren Elkind.

"I seriously doubt," she said, "that the head of the Manhattan Bank killed Valerie."

"Why? Rich people don't murder?"

"Come on. There's something more to this."

"There always is, kid. Always is. When someone decides to become an FBI informant, he or she's taking a chance."

"Sure, but . . ."

"You know the pay's the same whether you develop an asset or not."

"My job is to protect the source—"

"Sarah, if you *really* want to protect a source, you'll never use her information, and what good is that? Look, always go with your gut instinct. You're suspicious about your informant's murder, don't leave it to the locals. See if the answering-machine tape turns up anything. Whether it's the Mob or your banker, you'll know soon enough. Speaking of the Mob, you still seeing that Italian guy?"

Sarah gave him a blank stare and said in mock indignation: "Is that supposed to be funny? Do all Italians belong to the Mafia?"

"Yeah, and all Greeks have souvlaki stands," Pappas replied. "What's his name again—Angelo?"

"Andrew," Sarah said, "and he's history."

"He was a nice-looking guy."

"Not my type."

"Not potential father material?"

"Alex, he'd pretend Jared wasn't even *there*. He couldn't deal with the fact that I had a son."

"You probably won't believe me when I tell you you'll find the right kind of guy—for you as well as for Jared. You're the one who's got to fall in love with him. Jared—Jared'll come around."

"You're right. I don't believe you."

Pappas nodded. "It'll happen. Plus, whoever you get serious about is going to have to pass Jared's scrutiny, and he's an excellent judge of character. Gotta be—he likes *me*, doesn't he? So don't worry so much. It'll happen."

CHAPTER SEVENTEEN

Within hours after Edwin Chu and George Frechette, the NSA cryptanalysts, received the encrypted fragment of telephone conversation captured by a Rhyolite spy satellite above Switzerland, Edwin Chu broke the code.

Actually, the NSA's Cray supercomputers, using all available analytical skills, including several cryptanalytic techniques unknown outside the agency, broke it. But Edwin Chu had hovered over the computer and had done what he could to help—sort of a binary backseat driver.

The National Security Agency is always interested in new encryption schemes, so the work Chu did with the Cray late that night and into the early morning wasn't purely to satisfy his own curiosity.

But that was a large part of it.

It wasn't easy. In fact, had Chu been more senior and had more clout, cracking the code would have taken less than an hour, rather than eight hours. He'd wanted to use the latest generation of Cray supercomputers, but had to settle instead for an older Cray.

"I was sort of hoping this would be RC-4," he explained to Frechette, referring to a commercially available encryption package. The only cryptographic software that NSA permitted to be exported out of the United States used algorithms of a certain length, specifically 40-bit. The best-known of these software packages were RC-2 and RC-4, tunable ciphers that were reasonably secure—except from the NSA, which has special-purpose chips designed to crack them in just a few minutes.

"Piece of cake," he modestly announced to George Frechette, handing him a set of headphones. "There's supposed to be this new crypto firm in Zurich that's been making new secure voice-encryption phones and told the Agency to go fuck off."

"Good for them," Frechette murmured. Unknown encryption schemes paid their mortgages.

"I think this is from those guys. Company was founded by some Russian émigré, an encryption specialist, used to be in the KGB's Eighth Directorate." The Eighth Chief Directorate of the former KGB was responsible for the security of all Soviet cipher communications. "Guy was one of their most advanced encryption people. A real big swinging dick. Got fed up with the pathetic level of Soviet technology, and then, when the Soviet Union collapsed, the money dried up. Couldn't produce his most advanced designs. So he went capitalist."

"Huh."

Chu explained that the Russian had developed his own encryption algorithm some years back, while still working for the KGB. The KGB, of course, hadn't let him publish it in a mathematical journal. When he went private, the Russian kept it closely held.

This was his error.

One of the great paradoxes of the crypto world is that the more secret you keep a piece of cryptographic software, the less secure it will be. Unless you make an algorithm widely available to hackers around the world, you'll never become aware of the hidden flaws it may contain.

In this instance, Chu explained, the algorithm depended upon the intractability of a complicated inverse polynomial operation—which the NSA had solved two years ago. The creator likely didn't know this, nor that the NSA had a lot of partial solutions precomputed and stored in fast memory, enabling Chu to take the complicated polynomials and reduce them to a set of simpler polynomials.

In short, it hadn't been easy to crack, but between the NSA's high-powered research and its vast array of the latest computers, it had been crackable.

"Luckily we got a decent hunk of the signal, enough to work on," Edwin Chu said. "Have a listen."

George Frechette looked up, blinking owlishly at Chu. "These guys Americans?"

"Voice One sounds American. Voice Two is foreign, like Swiss or German or Dutch or something, I can't be sure."

"So what do you want to do with this?"

"Get it transcribed and inputted and out of our hands, buddy. Let someone else worry about it. As for me"—he glanced at his watch—"it's Big Mac time."

CHAPTER EIGHTEEN

At a hardware store near the Etoile, Baumann purchased an assortment of tools, and at the Brentano's on Avenue de l'Opéra, he picked up two identical redvinyl-jacketed Webster's pocket dictionaries to use for sending encoded messages. On a brief shopping trip in the 8th Arrondissement, he bought several very good suits and shirts, off the rack but well made, along with an assortment of ties, several pairs of English shoes, an expensive leather attaché case, and a few other accessories.

Then he returned to the Raphaël. Although it was not even noon, the dark, English-style oak-paneled bar was already doing a good business. At a small table, he lingered over a *café express*, going through a stack of American business magazines and newspapers—*Forbes, Fortune, Barron's*, and others. From time to time he looked up and watched the clientele come and go.

It was not long before he noticed a man in his late thirties, an American businessman, from the look of him. Baumann overheard him having a conversation with a man at an adjoining table who appeared to be a junior associate. The first businessman, whose neatly combed dark hair was salted with gray, was complaining to the other that the hotel had failed to deliver his *Wall Street Journal* to his room with breakfast this morning, though he had made a specific request.

The stroke of good fortune came when the businessman was called by his last name by a waiter, who brought a telephone to his table and plugged it into a wall jack. Once he'd finished his apparently urgent telephone call, the two Americans hastened into the lobby. There the junior associate took a seat while his friend got into the elevator.

Just before the elevator door closed, Baumann slipped into the cabin. The businessman pressed the button for the seventh floor; Baumann pressed the same button again, unnecessarily, and then smiled awkwardly at his own clumsiness. The businessman, evidently in a rush, did not return the smile.

Baumann followed the American down the corridor. The man stopped at room 712, and Baumann continued on, disappearing around a turn. From that vantage point, unseen, he watched the businessman enter the room and emerge a few seconds later, wearing a tan gabardine raincoat and carrying a collapsible umbrella, and stride quickly toward the elevator.

Baumann couldn't be sure, of course, but given the time—a few minutes before one in the afternoon—the odds were good that the two Americans were going to a lunch meeting. This was, he knew, a Parisian tradition; such lunches could go on for two hours or more.

Baumann hung the DO NOT DISTURB sign on the American's hotel-room door and, wearing latex gloves, set to work at once. Although room 712 was considerably smaller than his own suite, the basic amenities, including the safe in an armoire near the king-size bed, were, as he expected, the same.

The room safe, as in all hotel rooms Baumann had

ever stayed in, was an amateurish affair, fit mainly for discouraging a larcenous maid from stealing a camera or a wallet full of cash. It was of the type commonly found in the better hotel rooms: a small, heavy, concrete-lined steel box, extremely difficult (though not impossible) to lift.

You punched in a series of numbers of your own choosing into a keypad on the front of the box; the numbers would appear in a liquid-crystal readout; and then when you hit the * key or some such, the locking mechanism would be electronically activated.

He inserted a small hex wrench into the hole in the safe's face, then slid the plate back. That was all it took to reveal the ordinary keyed lock, which required two keys. After a minute or so of grappling with his improvised lock picks, the set of ordinary household tools he'd purchased at the hardware store a few hours earlier, the lock yielded, and the safe popped open.

As was usual with such electronic devices, the safe drew its power from batteries—in this case, two AA batteries—which powered the readout and the locking mechanism. The batteries often went dead and had to be replaced. Or the hotel guest would forget the combination he had himself set. Thus, the manual override mechanism that enabled Baumann to open the safe so easily.

It was there, of course. Whereas Europeans usually carry their vital documents on their person while traveling, Americans tend not to. Mr. Robinson—Mr. Sumner Charles Robinson, in full—had left his passport, along with a good supply of American Express traveler's checks and a small pile of American currency.

Baumann pocketed the passport, then quickly counted the cash (two hundred and twenty dollars) and the traveler's checks (fifteen hundred dollars). For a moment he considered taking the cash and checks, then decided against it. When Mr. Sumner C. Robinson returned late this afternoon or this evening, he might (or might not) open the safe and might (or might not) discover his passport missing. If he did, he'd realize with great relief that his cash and traveler's checks were still there, and he'd probably think that he'd simply misplaced the passport somewhere.

It was preposterous to imagine that a thief would steal his passport and not his cash. Even after searching the room, the pockets of his clothing, and his luggage, and not finding his passport, he might not even do so much as inform the hotel management of the loss. Let alone the municipal police. Taking the cash was simply not worth it.

Martin Lomax, Malcolm Dyson's aide-de-camp, picked up the phone and called the company's Zug, Switzerland, office on a secure telephone to check that all the financial arrangements had been done, and that Baumann's payment had been transferred to the bank in Panama. Lomax had called the Zug office three days in a row, because he was a thorough man, and his boss did not like the slightest detail to be overlooked.

Moreover, Dyson was highly suspicious of the intelligence capabilities of the U.S. government and had instructed Lomax never to speak of the upcoming event on anything but a secure telephone. And not just any secure telephone, because Dyson had not been born yesterday and he knew that virtually all firms that sold encrypted phones—including the famous Crypto, A.G., of Zurich—sold their encryption schemes to the NSA and GCHQ. So there was really no such thing as a truly secure phone anymore, unless you were canny about it.

But Dyson had not purchased his phones from any of these companies. A Russian émigré in Geneva had let it be known that he was in need of financing for his new, start-up venture, a secure-communications company. The Russian, an encryption specialist, had worked for the KGB in the bad old days. Dyson had provided the seed money, and the Russian's company was launched. Its first prototype secure phone went to Dyson. And no encryption schemes were sold or given to the NSA or GCHQ. These phones were truly secure, truly unbreakable. Only on these phones would Dyson and his associates talk openly.

Baumann returned to his own room and, for the remainder of the afternoon, made notes.

Malcolm Dyson's undertaking was indeed brilliant, but the more he thought it through, the more holes emerged. Dyson had made quite a few assumptions that might be false. Also, the billionaire lacked a fundamental working knowledge of the particulars of the site, the security precautions and vulnerabilities, and this was crucial. Dyson underestimated the risk that Baumann would be either caught or killed. But the devil, as they say, is in the details, and Baumann did not intend to overlook a detail.

By the time the bellboy knocked on his door to deliver the suits on hangers, the boxes of shoes, and the rest of the clothing he had purchased that morning, Baumann had sketched out a diagram of action—very rough, but a workable plan, he felt sure. Then he got dressed and went out for a walk.

Stopping into a *tabac*, he bought a *carte de téléphone*, the plastic card with a magnetized strip issued by France Telecom, which would allow him to place several international calls from any public phone booth. He found one in the basement of a café and, after debating this next step for a few moments, placed a call to New Haven, Connecticut. Using the address he'd copied down from the slip accompanying Sumner Robinson's traveler's checks, he obtained Robinson's home number from directory assistance.

A woman's voice answered. It was late in the evening there, and at first she seemed startled, as if awakened by the call.

"Is that Mrs. Robinson?" Baumann inquired in a plummy, grand-public-school, Sloane Ranger British accent. "Name's Nigel Clarke, calling from Paris." He spoke, as someone once said, as if he had the Elgin Marbles in his mouth.

The woman confirmed she was Sumner Robinson's wife and asked immediately whether everything was all right with her husband.

"Oh, my Lord, not to worry," Baumann went on. "The thing of it is, I found your husband's passport, in a *cab*, of all places—"

He listened to her for a moment and went on, "Got your number from directory assistance. But tell your husband he shouldn't worry—I have it here, safe and sound. Tell me what to do, how to get it to him—" He listened again.

"Quite right," he said, "at Charles de Gaulle airport." Baumann's voice was jolly, though his eyes were steely-cold. He heard someone clamber down the stairs. A young woman, exhaling a cumulus cloud of cigarette smoke, saw he was using the telephone and flashed him a look of irritation. He gave her a level, gray, warning stare; she flushed, threw her cigarette to the floor, and went back up the stairs.

"Oh, not leaving Paris till the end of the week, is he? Brilliant. . . . Right, well, the problem is that I'm getting on a plane back to London in just a few *seconds*, you see, and—oh, damn it all, that's the final boarding call, I'm afraid I *will* have to run—but if you'll give me an address I'll send it off by DHL or some other overnight service the very *instant* I get to my house." He pronounced it "hice." He chuckled pleasantly while the woman burbled her gratitude for his generosity. "Heavens, no, I wouldn't *hear* of it. Shouldn't cost more than a few pounds anyway." He pronounced it "pineds."

He had done the right thing, he knew. True, the American businessman might not have reported his passport lost or stolen and applied to the American embassy for a replacement. Now, however, his wife would call him at the hotel, tell him that his passport had been recovered by a nice Englishman at Charles de Gaulle Airport, but not to worry, Mr. Cooke or Clarke or whatever his name was going to send the passport by express mail right away.

Sumner Robinson would wonder how his passport ended up in a cab. Perhaps he'd wonder whether he'd put it into his safe after all. In any case, he would not report the passport lost or stolen today or even tomorrow— since it would be on its way back to him in a matter of hours. The friendly Brit would certainly get around to sending it the next day: why the hell else would he have called New Haven, after all?

The passport would be valid at least three full days. Perhaps even more, though Baumann would never take the chance.

He hung up the receiver and mounted the stairs to the street level. "The phone's all yours," he told the young woman who had been waiting to use the phone, giving her a cordial smile and the tiniest wink.

Baumann had dinner alone at the hotel. By the time dinner was over, a large carton had been delivered to his room containing the MLink-5000. He unpacked it, read through the operating instructions, ran it through its paces. Turning the thumbscrews on the back panel, he pulled out the handset, then flipped open the unit's top, adjusted the angle of elevation, and placed two calls.

The first was to a bank in Panama City, which confirmed that the first payment had been made by Dyson.

The second was to Dyson's private telephone line. "The job has begun," he told his employer curtly, and hung up.

In the last decade it has become considerably more difficult to forge an American passport. Not impossible, of course: to a skilled forger, nothing is impossible. But Baumann, familiar though he was with the rudiments, was hardly a professional forger. That he left to others.

In a day or so he'd contact a forger he knew and trusted. But in the meantime, he'd have to do his best, in the six hours until he had to arrive at Charles de Gaulle for his early-morning commuter flight to Amsterdam.

He examined Sumner Robinson's passport closely. The days when one could just scissor out the original owner's photograph and paste in one's own were long gone. Now, the key page of the U.S. passport, which contained photo and identifying information, was laminated with a clear plastic oversheet, a "counterfoil," designed as a security feature. Another security feature was the emblem of an American bald eagle, taken from the Great Seal of the United States, which grasped in its talons the arrows of war and the olive branch of peace. The eagle, which also appeared in gold ink on the front of the passport, was printed on the counterfoil in green ink, slightly overlapping the passport holder's photograph.

Lost in concentration, Baumann sucked at his front teeth. He knew the U.S. State Department had spent a fortune on special, forge-proof passport paper manufactured by a company called Portal's. Yet the security of the passport actually hinged on a single, cheap piece of clear plastic tape.

He called down to the hotel's front desk, told the

clerk he urgently needed an electric typewriter to prepare a contract. Would the clerk send one up to his room? Certainly, he was told, although it would take a few minutes to open the office containing the typewriters; it was closed for the evening.

A few blocks from the hotel he located a photocopy-and-printing shop that was open all night, blazing with fluorescent light. He instructed the clerk to photocopy and reduce the eagle image on the front of the passport, explaining offhandedly that he needed to put an American eagle on the front of a three-ring binder for a presentation to a major French client early in the morning. No laws against *that*. Then, on a Canon 500 color laser copier, the eagle was reproduced onto a sheet of clear crack-and-peel label stock in green ink. Baumann had several copies made: it was easy to make mistakes. After a brief stop at a coin-operated automated photo booth, he returned to the Raphaël.

There he meticulously removed the old counterfoil laminate from the passport, careful not to rip too much of the paper underneath. With an X-Acto knife, he removed Robinson's photograph and replaced it with his own. Inserting the sheet of clear plastic label stock into the electric typewriter provided by the hotel, he pecked out the exact same biographical data that had appeared on Robinson's passport and had been lifted off with the old laminate.

By three o'clock in the morning, he was satisfied with the result. Only the closest inspection would reveal that the passport had been dummied up. And departing from Paris's busy Charles de Gaulle Airport as he was, on a crowded commuter flight, he knew the French inspectors would scarcely have time for even the most cursory of glimpses at this American businessman's passport.

He ran a steaming-hot bath and soaked in it for a long time while he meditated. Then he dozed for about two hours, arose, dressed, and finished packing his Louis Vuitton suitcase.

CHAPTER NINETEEN

The Prince of Darkness had begun.

Dyson put down the telephone and felt a shiver of anticipation. He had hired the best (he hired only the best), and this savant of the terrorist netherworld would do his thing, and in precisely two weeks the deed would be done.

He pressed a button on his desk phone to summon his aide-de-camp, Martin Lomax.

Dyson & Company A.G.'s corporate headquarters building on the Rue du Rhône in Geneva was a glass cube that, during the day, reflected the buildings around it. It was a stealth office building: depending on the time of day and the angle from which you looked, the glass-walled box disappeared. At night it lit up a fierce yellow-white as Dyson's traders worked, barking out orders halfway around the world.

Dyson's office was on the top floor, southwest corner. It was entirely white: white leather sofas, white wall-to-wall carpet, white fabric covering the interior walls. Even his massive, irregularly shaped desktop had been hewn from an immense vein of white Carrara marble.

Only the artwork, here tastefully sparse, provided splashes of color. There was Rubens's picture of three women, *Virtue*, seized from a rich man during the Second World War. A Van Dyck *(Holy Family with St. Anne and an Angel)* had disappeared some time ago in Italy, only to reemerge at Dyson & Company A.G. Holbein's *St. Catherine* had made its way from a stash in East Germany soon after the Wall fell.

To Dyson, the acquisition of old masters on the black market was one of his greatest post-exile pleasures. It was liberation from legal convention, a way of thumbing his nose at the rest of the world, a wonderfully illicit satisfaction. Let the others buy their second-tier stuff through buying agents with *catalogues raisonnés*, over seafood at Wilton's in Bury Street, London, where the dealers gathered like flies. His pictures, many of them the world's greatest, had been plied off their stretchers and hidden in a table leg or smuggled in via diplomatic pouch.

The art market reminded Dyson of Wall Street, where the rules applied only when you weren't a member of the club. The philanthropist Norton Simon had once admitted he owned a bronze of the god Shiva smuggled from India. In fact, most of the Asian art he bought was smuggled. Even Boston's august Museum of Fine Arts had once been caught red-handed with a stolen Raphael that the museum director claimed he had bought in Genoa.

Embittered was not how Dyson thought of himself. He was liberated. The requirements of vengeance clarified everything.

Malcolm Dyson had been labeled quite a few things before he escaped the clutches of U.S. law enforcement after the great insider-trading scandal, but the most popular seemed to be "the largest tax evader in the nation's history." This was not true. He personally knew of several famous, even legendary, titans of business, household names, who had evaded far more taxes than he'd ever tried to do.

In any case, he had been indicted on no fewer than fifty-one counts of tax evasion, tax fraud, and conspiracy to commit securities fraud. All his U.S. assets were frozen. There were extensive negotiations with the SEC and the Justice Department. He was looking at several years in prison even in the best of circumstances, and that was unacceptable. Had his former friend Warren Elkind not cooperated with the Justice Department to entrap him, none of this would have happened. They'd never have had the proof necessary to indict.

While the negotiations dragged on, Dyson made a business trip to Switzerland with his wife, Alexandra. They decided not to return. The Swiss government refused all American requests to extradite him. Their logic was unimpeachable: under Swiss law, Dyson had been charged with "fiscal violations," which were not extraditable offenses. Was it a coincidence that Dyson also happened to be the largest corporate taxpayer in Switzerland?

Shortly afterward, he went to the bureau of vital statistics in Madrid, took an oath to the Spanish king, and renounced his U.S. citizenship. Now a citizen of Spain resident in Geneva, he never traveled by commercial airliner, because he feared bounty hunters. A very rich man in his position was easy prey. They would kidnap you and then demand a billion dollars or else they'd turn you over to the U.S. government. The U.S. Marshals Service was always trying to ensnare him. He traveled only by private jet.

Now, however, he didn't particularly care whether the bounty hunters came after him. The light had gone out of his life. They had murdered his wife and daughter, and they had put him in a wheelchair, and they would pay dearly.

Dyson sat at his immense desk in his electric wheelchair, a small bald man with liver-spotted head and liver-spotted hands and eyes of gray steel, smoking a Macanudo. The door opened, and Martin Lomax entered. Tall, thin, balding, Lomax was colorless and faithful.

Lomax sat in his customary white-upholstered chair beside the desk and drew his ballpoint pen and pad of paper like a gun from a holster.

"I want to make sure," Dyson said methodically to his assistant, "that we are entirely out of the stock market."

Lomax looked up, puzzled, realizing that this was a question, not an instruction. He glanced at his wristwatch to check the date. "Yes," he said, "we are. As of three days ago, actually."

"And the U.S. Federal Reserve Bank? No change in its policy?"

"Correct. The Fed will no longer bail out banks. Our intelligence is good on this. Washington calls it 'banking reform'—let the large depositors go down when a bank fails. Banks are getting too fast and loose anyway. Teach 'em a lesson."

"All right." Dyson whirred his wheelchair to one side and peered sadly out the floor-to-ceiling window at the rain. "Because our Prince of Darkness has gone to work."

CHAPTER TWENTY

Paul O. Morrison, deputy director of the CIA's Counterterrorism Center, hurtled down a narrow corridor toward a conference room where some twenty-five people had been hastily assembled. In one hand was a manila folder containing a small stack of computer printouts, in the other a half-full mug of cold black coffee that sloshed onto the gray wall-to-wall carpeting as he ran.

He entered the conference room and could immediately sense the tension. Muttering an apology for his tardiness, he set down his mug on the large, gleaming mahogany table and looked around with a worried expression.

Morrison was small and thin, with heavy black-framed glasses and a sallow complexion. Forgoing any opening statement—they knew why they were here—he launched right in: "Um, I've got the complete transcript here."

He handed the pile of printouts to the director of the Counterterrorism Center, a whippet-thin, athletic-looking, squash-playing man in his mid-fifties, Hoyt Phillips (Yale '61), who took one and passed it on.

Morrison waited as the transcripts made their way around the table.

The reaction was swift yet subdued: murmurings of amazement, the occasional whisper, and then a grave silence. He waited, his stomach queasy with acid, until everyone had finished reading.

The Counterterrorism Center—the existence of which was until recently one of the CIA's closely held secrets—was founded in 1986 to deal with the government's embarrassing inability to handle the steadily worsening plague of international terrorism.

The idea behind the center was simple: to give the dozen or so agencies in the U.S. government concerned with terrorism—from the FBI to the State Department, from the Pentagon to the Secret Service—one centralized location into which intelligence from around the world could be funneled, and where all terrorism-fighting efforts could be coordinated.

For years the CIA had resisted the notion. It ran against the very culture of the Agency, whose gentlemen spies much preferred fighting the Soviet menace to soiling their hands with terrorists.

Also, the CIA's leadership never much liked the idea of sharing "product" with its siblings in the intelligence community. And in order for such a center to work, it would have to allow collectors—the people in the field who gather the information—to mingle with the analysts. That simply had never been done. The CIA almost always keeps a Chinese Wall between its analysts and its operators, so as not to taint the product. The folks in the trench coats, it was always believed, should do their spying without any sense of the larger picture, or at least without any agenda or bias. Leave the political bias to the desk jockeys.

But Director of Central Intelligence William Casey

did not share this concern. He ordered the establishment of an interagency "fusion center" where specially chosen representatives of the intelligence community—eighteen or nineteen intelligence officers from the NSA, the FBI, INR (the State Department's intelligence arm), the DIA, and other agencies—are detailed full-time. Although they work at CIA headquarters, their salaries are paid on a nonreimbursable basis by their home departments.

Until the spring of 1994, the twenty-five or so staff members of the center worked in an overcrowded warren of desks and partitions on the sixth floor of the CIA headquarters' original building. Thereafter, they were located in a more spacious, much more modern area in the new building next door. But it was hardly sleek or impressive; no one who has ever been inside CIA headquarters would call the place sleek.

Anything that happens in the world that is in any way related to terrorism will flash across the computer terminals in the center. Armed with secure communications and other secure links to the NSA and other intelligence agencies, the Counterterrorism Center's staff are charged with ensuring cooperation among the various agencies, putting out intelligence products (while protecting sources and methods), and quelling the disputes over credit that are so rife in government bureaucracies.

Since the center is a part of the CIA's Directorate of Operations, the director of the center is always an Ops officer; the deputy director is always an analyst from the Intelligence Directorate. For all his athletic prowess, Hoyt Phillips, the director, was a classic Agency burnout case, bored with a career stymied by his own mediocrity, whiling away his time here until retirement.

Deputy Director Paul Morrison effectively ran the center, deftly managing its six sections. Rare though it is for a CIA office, the center's organizational chart is fairly fluid. There is the Intel staff, who do what is called "target analysis" (evaluating the information collected by CIA and other agencies' sources), a Reports staff, a Technical Attack group, an Assessment and Information group, an Ops group, and so on.

And there are all sorts of meetings, ranging from the monthly Warning and Forecast meeting, to the bimonthly Interagency Intelligence Committee, to the three-times-a-week 8:45 A.M. staff meeting. This meeting, however, had been called for seven-thirty in the morning, which was the earliest all the staff could be gathered.

It was not yet an emergency, but something close to it.

Paul Morrison had been awakened at four-thirty this morning by a watch officer at the center, who had in turn been given a heads-up by the NSA's deputy director of the Office of Telecommunications and Computer Services, concerning a SIGINT intercept deserving immediate attention. By the time Morrison arrived at his office in the center, the complete transcripts of the intercepted telephone conversation had been placed on his desk, having been secure-faxed over from NSA.

NATIONAL SECURITY AGENCY
UNITED STATES OF AMERICA

TOP SECRET UMBRA

FILE: TCS-1747-322
D/OTCS, DD/OTCS, D/DIRNSA
COMINT intercept decryption. Transcription text complete.
VOICE I: . . . Mr. Heinrich Fürst/ [First?] has accepted the sales assignment.
VOICE II: He has? Excellent. When [blank] the field office in New York? [blank segment]

VOICE II: [blank segment] target being?

VOICE I: Warren Elkind [word segment blank] . . . attan Bank including [blank segment]

VOICE II: Oh. Right. Uh, so he's, he's serious about this.

VOICE I: He hired a professional.

VOICE II: I don't doubt that. I've seen the guy's dossier. Probably the smartest [*three-second silence*] . . . uh, one alive—

VOICE I:—the stupid ones don't live—

VOICE II:—know that. But I'm concerned—what if he turns out to be a loose cannon? I mean, he's hardly, he's not fully controllable.

VOICE I:—get the job done.

VOICE II: But not traceable?

VOICE I: He'll be taken care of.

VOICE II: Right. No doubt. But we, couldn't we still be linked? Bringing down Wall Street—well, you saw what happened with the World Trade Center thing and with Oklahoma City. They didn't rest until they found the guys. If we're connected in any way—

VOICE I:—not going to happen. The boss knows what he's doing.

TOP SECRET UMBRA

"All right," said Hoyt Phillips, clearing his throat summarily. "There may or may not be something here."

"Are you and I reading from the same document?" a woman seated across the table from him asked in astonishment. This was Margaret O'Connor, a small, fiery, thirty-four-year-old woman with short brown hair, a face full of freckles, and a surprisingly deep voice. She was the liaison from the State Department's Bureau of Intelligence and Research.

Phillips's thick white eyebrows shot up. "Don't let's

overreact, now, folks," he cautioned. "What we've got here is a couple of guys talking in a roundabout way—"

"Hoyt—" He was interrupted by a handsome black man in his early forties, wearing a blue suit and horn-rimmed glasses. Noah Willkie, the center's liaison with the FBI, had been detailed to Langley for the last seven months. "There's no denying they're referring to a terrorist—'probably the smartest one alive'—who's been hired by someone, presumably their 'boss.' And they're afraid this guy might not be 'controllable,' meaning he's acting as an agent on their behalf, which is why he was hired."

"Noah," Phillips explained patiently, "if you're at all familiar with NSA product, you know you're always getting static, fragments of phone calls that inevitably sound scarier than they are. For heaven's sake, some MIT student doing his junior year abroad in Vienna places a call to a buddy of his in London and uses the phrase 'nuke,' as in 'I got nuked last night'—he got tanked on lager—and suddenly that trips an alarm somewhere and we're all yanked out of bed in the middle of the night."

Deputy Director Morrison watched his boss in silent frustration, wondering whether Phillips was genuinely unconcerned about the intercept or was simply under-mining his deputy for reasons of his own. The director had approved Morrison's suggestion that the meeting be an hour and a quarter earlier than usual, but then maybe Phillips was just covering his ass. Did he honestly believe this intercept was meaningless? Or was he posturing?

"Uh, Hoyt," Morrison said gently, "I think this may bear some scrutiny. The transcript discusses a 'target,' obviously the Manhattan Bank. They're talking about getting a 'job' done in a nontraceable way. They're concerned about being linked. They're talking about 'bringing down Wall Street'—"

"Meaning what, exactly?" asked the DIA liaison, Wayne Carter.

"I don't know if that's a figure of speech or what, frankly," Morrison admitted. "But they're comparing it to the Trade Center bomb and Oklahoma City."

"Do we know who these two are?" Margaret O'Connor asked the NSA liaison, Bob Halpern.

"No, we don't," Halpern replied. "The signal caught the attention of some of our cryppies because of its encryption scheme—they'd never seen one like it before."

"Well, at least we have a name here," said a CIA Operations officer, Richard Jarvis. "The name of the terrorist, right? Heinrich Fürst? That's a hell of a lot."

"It's a code name," Morrison replied. "And it doesn't correspond to any alias or code name in any of our databases."

"Christ," someone snapped in disgust.

"German," Noah Willkie suggested. "Maybe we could check the Stasi archives." The files of the defunct East German secret intelligence service, Stasi, had been captured after the Berlin Wall had fallen and were now in the possession of the Western services, mostly the German intelligence agency, the Bundesnachrichtendienst, or BND. The documents included information on terrorists who had been supported by the East Germans.

Margaret O'Connor, from State, put a question to the group in general: "So who's the smartest terrorist alive?"

"Carlos the Jackal," one of the CIA analysts snickered.

"No, he's only the *sloppiest* terrorist alive," someone else replied with a snort of derision. Carlos, the terrorist of legend—real name Ilich Ramírez Sánchez—had been involved in some of the most horrific acts of terrorism in the 1970s, but despite his fearsome reputation, he was actually a lackadaisical operator overly fond of alcohol and women. He had become enormously overweight, living like a cornered animal in frightened retirement in a drab flat in Damascus. Then in August 1994 the French security service finally snatched him from the Sudan and put him in an underground cell at Le Santé prison in Paris.

"The real question," said Jarvis, the CIA Operations officer, "is who are the most skilled terrorists we know of whose whereabouts we don't have a fix on."

"That's the problem," Morrison said quietly. " 'The most skilled terrorists we *know of*.' The really good ones—the really elusive, masterful ones—we may not even have dossiers on. And in any case, how do you define 'terrorist'? Who's a terrorist? An IRA bombmaker? Qaddafi? One of the Abus—Abu Nidal, Abu Abbas, Abu Ibrahim? Or a country, like Syria?"

"It's obviously an individual, a male," O'Connor said. "Someone who's known to be available for hire. Maybe one of the Agency computer geniuses can have DESIST come up with a list of known terrorists, profile them and all that." DESIST was the CIA's cumbersome computer database system that recorded summaries of all terrorist incidents.

"You're all jumping the gun once again," Hoyt Phillips said. "You're all ready to commit some very expensive resources to chasing down a—a will-o'-the-wisp. We still don't know this is for real."

There was a long silence, at last broken by Noah Willkie from the FBI: "But do we want to take a chance on being wrong?"

"I'm afraid I have to agree with Noah," Morrison said to his boss. "We have to proceed as if this is solid."

Phillips gave a long, exasperated sigh. "If—*if*—we do, I want this thing contained right here in this room. I don't want the White House up in arms about this. I don't want the NSC breathing down my neck." He shook his head. "Soon as the White House is in on this, the shit hits the fan. Then it's amateur hour."

"Well," Paul Morrison said. "We in this room are the only ones outside the NSA who know about it."

"Good," Phillips said. "Let's keep it that way. The contents of this intercept—and the fact of its very *existence*—are to stay right here in this room. Nothing, and I mean nothing, gets put on CACTIS."

CACTIS, which stands for Community Automated Counterterrorism Intelligence System, was a secure communications network: a sophisticated e-mail document system linking the NSA, the CIA, State, the DIA, and the rest of the counterterrorism community. CACTIS had gone on-line in April 1994, replacing the old system, known as FLASHBOARD. Naturally, there is a complete "air gap" between CACTIS and the CIA's internal database, so that the CIA's most sensitive intelligence archives cannot be penetrated from outside the building.

Phillips went on: "I'm still not persuaded we've got anything solid to worry about. When I am, I'll be more than happy to set up a working group or something. Until then, I'm not prepared to dump a lot of resources into this." He clasped his hands together. "No further action," he announced.

"Since when did you take over the terrorism account?" the NSA liaison, Bob Halpern, inquired acidly.

"You know exactly what I'm saying, Bob," Phillips said. "I don't want to be getting a call every five minutes from some chucklehead at NSC who doesn't know an AK-47 from a popsicle stick. That means no working groups, no reports to your home agencies. Nothing. Put nothing in writing. Nothing, is that clear?" He rose. "Let's not make a mountain out of the proverbial mole-hill, okay?"

CHAPTER TWENTY-ONE

An hour or so after the conclusion of the morning staff meeting at which the NSA telephone intercepts were discussed, Special Agent Noah Willkie, the FBI man assigned to the Counterterrorism Center, was standing in the enclosed courtyard between the new and old CIA buildings, smoking a Camel Light. He heard someone call his name, and was surprised to see Paul Morrison, the center's deputy director, approaching him. Morrison did not smoke; what was he doing out here?

"Noah," the deputy director said, "I liked your idea about the Stasi archives."

"The Stasi—oh, right, thanks," Willkie said fuzzily, through a mouthful of smoke.

"You seemed to read the transcript the same way I did."

Noah Willkie furrowed his brow, as if to say, Which way is that?

"In the sense that we could be dealing with a potentially serious act of terrorism here," Morrison hastily explained. "I also sensed you weren't in agreement with the director about ignoring the whole thing."

Willkie took a deep, contemplative drag, then expelled a cloud. "You know what they say: the boss may not always be right, but he's always the boss."

Morrison nodded and was silent for a moment. "How's Duke Taylor doing these days? I haven't seen him in a hell of a long time."

Perry "Duke" Taylor was Willkie's immediate boss at the FBI, a deputy assistant director in the Intelligence Division who was the chief of the Bureau's Counterterrorism Section.

"Oh, Duke's fine," Willkie said. "Same old same old."

"His son ever get into a college?"

"He's doing a year at a prep school. Deerfield, I think. Then he'll try again."

"Hmm," Morrison said. "If he's got any of his father's genes, he'll do fine."

"Hmm," Willkie agreed. He took another drag and peered curiously at Morrison out of the corner of an eye.

"I bet Duke would share your take on the NSA thing," Morrison said.

Ah, so that was it, Willkie thought. "He probably would," Willkie said dryly, "if I showed it to him. But I heard Hoyt."

"Then again," Morrison said, "your primary loyalty is to the Bureau."

"It's complicated. I've also got to abide by Agency procedures."

"Who said Hoyt represents the Agency?" Morrison said with a chuckle. "There are many different points of view here."

Willkie furrowed his brow again, as Morrison turned to leave. "Meaning—"

"I'm just saying," Morrison said with a cryptic half-smile, "that, well, let's say this lead is legit, and some huge bomb really does go off. Who's going to get lynched? CIA? I doubt it. If it's domestic, it's you guys, right?

FBI fucks up. First it's Waco, then the World Trade Center, then Oklahoma City, and now this. And let's say the director of the Bureau learns that one of his agents *actually knew about it* in advance but didn't say anything. . . ." He shook his head as if unable to comprehend the enormity of the consequences. "Anyway, you've got to rely on your best judgment, I guess is what I'm saying."

During the seven months that Special Agent Noah Willkie had been assigned to the Counterterrorism Center at CIA headquarters in Langley, he rarely went to his old stomping grounds, the J. Edgar Hoover Building on Pennsylvania Avenue between Ninth and Tenth streets in Washington. Most of his liaison work could be done by telephone and secure fax. The only reason to visit the Hoover building anymore was to use the gym in the basement, which he never did. He didn't much miss FBI headquarters, and besides, for the time being, working at CIA—the Pickle Factory, as CIA insiders call the place—was a novel experience.

Unfortunately, little had actually happened during his seven months at the center. The work was dull, routine stuff, bureaucratic procedures and the like. But this morning's meeting had been different. The NSA intercept intrigued him. Despite the way the center's director, Hoyt Phillips, was downplaying it, Willkie knew something big was in the works. And that strange encounter with Paul Morrison outside the new headquarters building . . . what was that all about, anyway? Morrison was obviously urging him to brief Duke Taylor, but why? Was Morrison playing out some power struggle with his boss? Was he hinting that no matter what Hoyt Phillips said, CIA was secretly working the lead, in an attempt to grab credit from FBI and everybody else? Or was Morrison simply trying to use the Bureau to do the risky work, launch an investigation CIA wouldn't?

Instead of spending his lunch hour jogging around the CIA campus, he made a phone call and then took a quick drive into Washington to meet with his boss, Duke Taylor.

Perry Taylor was around fifty, close to retirement, but you couldn't tell it from his demeanor. He was a genuine workaholic, driven and exacting. Yet at the same time he was one of the most affable and easygoing people Willkie had ever met.

Handsome in a sort of generic, clean-cut way, Taylor was a man of medium height with short gray hair, small brown eyes, and large wire-rimmed glasses. He'd been married to his high school sweetheart for some thirty years, and the marriage was universally believed to be as close to harmonious as a marriage could be.

But what appeared to be a Norman Rockwell painting on the outside had turned into Hopper. Taylor's closer friends and colleagues knew that he and his wife, unable to bear children, had adopted a beautiful baby girl who had died of measles at the age of five. Then they adopted a four-year-old boy who grew up to be the heartbreak of their lives, constantly in trouble with the law, hostile far beyond the normal adolescent rebelliousness, addicted to drugs, a bafflement to his amiable suburban parents. Though Taylor talked about his home life from time to time, he never brought his problems to work. Noah Willkie respected that.

Taylor was eating his typically Spartan lunch when Willkie arrived: a salad, a roll, a can of Fresca. He greeted Willkie warmly, offered him a cup of coffee, and made small talk for a while.

Willkie remembered hearing that Hoover, who was none too fond of the idea of black FBI agents, disapproved even more roundly of his people drinking coffee on the job. Once Hoover had been so enraged to see an agent drinking coffee in his office that he transferred the offending agent clear across the country.

While Willkie reported on the morning's meeting, and then on Paul Morrison's odd remarks outside headquarters, Taylor nodded thoughtfully. After Willkie had finished, Taylor did not speak for a long while. Willkie noticed for the first time very quiet classical music emanating from a boom-box radio on the windowsill. He looked around at the award plaques on the wall, at the dictionary stand, the FBI ceramic stein with Taylor's name on it, a coffee mug emblazoned "Are We Having Fun Yet?"

"Well, I guess the first thing is to run the name Heinrich Fürst through the Terrorist Information Database," Taylor mused. "Through General, too."

"Right," Willkie agreed, "but Paul Morrison at the CTC says he's already done it, and you know how much better their stuff is than ours."

"They *say* it's better," Taylor said, smiling. "But if we put one of our best searchers on it—Kendall or Wendy, say—maybe we'll turn up something. Don't forget, this is just the NSA's *guess* at how the name is spelled, based on a transcription of a spoken conversation. There are probably hundreds of different ways of spelling, or transliterating, the same name."

"I wouldn't be optimistic."

"Fair enough. No reason to be. Next, we take the profiles of every known terrorist in the world and find some way of narrowing them down, winnowing out the wrong ones."

"I think you can eliminate the pure ideologues," Willkie suggested. "Abu Nidal's people. Hezbollah. PFLP. Sendero Luminoso."

Taylor shook his head. "I don't think it's so easy, Noah. Shining Path, Sendero Luminoso, whatever you want to call them—they may be Maoist, but they contract out to Colombian narcotics traffickers, right?"

Willkie nodded.

"These days, anyone's for sale. Ideology sometimes doesn't seem to matter at all. The only terrorists we can eliminate are those who are dead or locked up. And that still leaves the board wide open—what about terrorists we've never heard of, going out for the first time?"

"This reference to 'the smartest one alive' or whatever," Willkie objected. "You don't call a neophyte the smartest one alive. Anyway, who'd hire a neophyte, right? My guess is, it's someone with a track record. We may not have anything on him—or her—but whoever it is has got to be experienced."

"Good point," Taylor conceded. He shrugged. "But that doesn't help us any. So let's go about this from the other direction: the target. The Manhattan Bank."

"If that's really *the* target. It may be *a* target. Or not a target at all."

"Also true. But what if we run a complete search on the bank and on Elkind? See if there've been any threats. Check out any international operations the bank's involved in. See if Elkind has any enemies. He may have enemies he doesn't even know about. Call up everything we've got."

"Hey, you're talking like you expect me to help you out. I already got a full-time job. Remember? You picked me for it."

"Oh, I don't mean you, Willkie. We've got plenty of people to do stuff like that. But you can keep us plugged in, give us a heads-up if anything comes along of interest. The CIA may not consider this worthy of study, but then, they're full of shit." He gave a big, ebullient smile. "Thanks for coming to me with this. I have to admit I won't exactly be crushed if we catch the asshole before CIA does."

CHAPTER TWENTY-TWO

Jared had invited a friend of his, Colin Tolman, for dinner. The two eight-year-olds sat on the living room rug, an assortment of baseball and superhero trading cards spread out around them. The radio was blasting techno-rap. Both of them wore Red Sox caps, backward. The brim of Jared's hat had been bent into a tube shape. Jared was wearing Diesel jeans and a Phillie Blunts T-shirt. They had their Mighty Morphin Power Rangers back-packs beside them. Both had seen the movie twice and loved it. But eight-year-olds are nothing if not fickle. In a month Mighty Morphins would more than likely be gonzo, dead meat, history, as Jared liked to say.

"Awesome!" Jared shouted as she entered. "Look, Mom, I got a Frank Thomas rookie. That's worth three-fifty *at least*!"

"Will you turn that off, or at least down?" she said. "Hi, Colin."

"Hi, Sarah," said Colin, a pudgy blond kid. "Sorry. Mrs. Cronin."

"She wants to be called *Ms. Cahill*," Jared said, lowering the volume. "Even *I'm* not supposed to call her Sarah. Mom, Colin has a whole binder full of Spider-Man and X-Men."

"Wonderful," Sarah said. "I don't even know what you're talking about. Colin, you collect baseball cards too?"

"Nah." Colin smirked. "No one collects baseball cards anymore, except Jared. Everyone else mostly just collects basketball cards or superheroes."

"I see. How was the last day of school?"

"Jared got thrown out of class," Colin reported.

"You did? For what?"

"For laughing," Colin went on, delighted.

"What?" Sarah said.

"Oh, yeah," Jared said. "You made me, you jerk."

"I didn't make you," Colin said, laughing. "I didn't make you do anything, *dickwad*."

"Hey, watch the language," Sarah said.

"Get out of here! Tell her what *you* were doing, dickwad," Jared said.

"Jared's always bossing people around," Colin explained, "like telling them to do their chores and everything. And Mrs. Irwin was asking us about what we thought about what it's like to be old, and I said I'd love to see Jared a hundred years old in a wheelchair, drooling and everything, and still bossing people around, poking everybody with a cane."

Sarah sighed, shook her head, didn't know how to reply. Secretly it pleased her to think of Jared sent to the principal's office for laughing, of all things, but she also knew that sort of thing shouldn't be encouraged.

"Can we watch Nickelodeon?" Jared asked.

She looked at her watch. "For fifteen minutes while I get supper ready."

"Cool," Jared said.

"Cool, *dude*," Colin amended. "What's on? *Salute Your Shorts? Doug? Rug Rats?*"

"If it's *Ren and Stimpy*, forget it," Jared said. "I hate *Ren and Stimpy*."

Colin gulped air and emitted a loud burp, and then Jared did the same, and both of them cracked up laughing again.

After dinner, Sarah went upstairs to kiss Jared good night. He was lying in bed, holding Huckleberry, the teddy bear, reading the biography of Satchel Paige. He rarely cuddled with his teddy bear anymore; he considered that kid's stuff.

"Is that a kid's version?" Sarah asked.

"Grown-up version." He returned to reading. After a moment, he looked up and asked peevishly, "Yes?"

"I hope I'm not disturbing you, Your Excellency," Sarah said in mock-dudgeon. "I just came up to say good night."

"Oh. Good night." He turned his head to one side to receive a kiss.

Sarah complied. "Didn't you read this already?"

Jared stared at her blankly for a long time, and then said: "Yes, so?"

"Everything okay with you?"

"Yes," he said, and turned back to the book.

"Because you'd tell me if everything weren't okay, wouldn't you?"

"Yes." Not looking up.

"It's this weekend, isn't it?" Sarah asked, suddenly realizing. Saturday was two days away, which meant he spent the day with his father.

Jared kept reading as if he hadn't heard her.

"You're worried about Saturday," she persisted.

He looked up. "No," he said, his mouth curling in sarcasm. "I'm not 'worried' about Saturday."

"But you're not looking forward to it."

He hesitated. "No," he said in a small voice.

"You want to talk about it?"

"Not really," he said, still more softly.

"Do you not want Daddy to come this weekend?

You don't have to do anything you don't want to do, you know."

"I know. I don't know. It's okay. It's just that . . ." His voice trailed off. "Why does he act the way he does?"

"Because that's the way he is." That meant nothing, it was unhelpful, and they both knew it. "We all have our blind spots, and Daddy—"

"Yeah, I know. That's the way he is." He returned to the book and added: "But I hate it."

CHAPTER TWENTY-THREE

Perhaps the greatest difficulty in the business of counterterrorism is deciding what to ignore and what to pursue. You are faced with a vast quantity of intelligence, but most of it is simply noise, static: pillow talk, intercepted telegrams, rumors. Ninety-nine percent of it is useless.

Yet the cost of ignoring the wrong scrap of information may be incalculable. Any intelligence professional who disregards a lead that results in an act of terrorism may be held culpable professionally, not to speak of morally, for the death of a human being—or the death of a hundred thousand.

Duke Taylor's career had been built upon a number of talents, from his ability to get along with just about anybody, to his sharp (though often hidden) intellect, to his golf skills. Not least among his talents, however, was an instinct, the thing that separated an intelligence bureaucrat from a professional.

And his instinct told him that Noah Willkie was right, and the CIA was wrong: there was a major act of terrorism in the planning.

Shortly after his meeting with Willkie, he summoned two of his brightest lieutenants, Russell Ullman and Christine Vigiani, both of them counterterrorism analysts, and briefed them in on the NSA intercept. Ullman, a broad-shouldered, strapping Aryan from Minnesota in his early thirties, was an operational analyst. Vigiani, some years older, and an intelligence research specialist, was tiny, compact, dark-haired, introverted. Both took copious notes.

"For reasons I can't get into, this doesn't go beyond this room. That's why I'm taking the unusual step of having just you guys here without the section and unit chiefs. Now, I want to make sure the boys at Fort Meade add some names to their watch list—Heinrich Fürst, this fellow Elkind. Russell, can you draft a list of all possible trip words?"

"Right," Ullman said, "but how can we ask NSA about this if we're not supposed to know anything about it?"

"Leave it to me, Russ. That's what I'm here for, the diplomacy part. You people do the heavy lifting. Chris, run down whatever you can on Fürst. Have Kendall or Wendy do a complete computer search. Wendy might be better. She's good on Germanic languages, variant spellings, what-have-you. Have our legal attachés in Germany and Austria make discreet contact, see what they can learn."

She nodded and scrawled a note. "I'll try," she said dubiously, "but I'm sure it's not his real name."

"Well, see what you can get. Don't forget about our own people. Maybe somebody knows something. Round up anybody who knows something about Elkind or Manhattan Bank. Field agent, transcriptionist, even the guy who washes the office cars in the Albuquerque field office."

"How am I supposed to do that?" Vigiani asked, genuinely curious.

"Wendy, the computer whiz, can help you. There's a hidden search parameter she can call up, with my authorization." Taylor saw the woman's puzzlement, and added: "She'll explain it. Basically, anytime anyone accesses the Bureau's databases, there's a notation made of it here in the central files, what they were asking about, et cetera.

"Now, and this is the biggest task: I want a pile of files on my desk by tomorrow morning—all possible terrorist suspects."

"You've got to be kidding," Ullman said.

"Put as many people as you need on this, okay? I want all the usual suspects, plus anyone else on the radar screen. Any terrorist with a track record. We've got to start broad."

"Whoa," Ullman said. "You're basically saying, any terrorist alive."

"Every one that fits this MO," Duke Taylor said. "On my desk. By tomorrow morning."

CHAPTER TWENTY-FOUR

Sarah's marriage to Peter Cronin was a mystery that only deepened with time. The reason she'd done it was simple. He'd gotten her pregnant. But that begged several questions: why she decided to keep the baby; why she felt she had to marry him just because he'd knocked her up; and, the biggest question of all, why she had been attracted to him in the first place.

True, he was movie-star handsome, a brawny, virile blond with a dazzling smile. That should have captured her attention for no more than five minutes. Once you got to know Peter at all, it was obvious he was crude, domineering, a creep. Yet at the same time he could be immensely charming when he wanted to.

When he first asked her out, after they'd met on some minor FBI-police task force, she accepted quickly. He's different from me, she told herself, but that's all to the good. She was the overly refined one, perhaps effete, in need of an infusion of street savvy. Their sex life was incredibly exciting. She'd never felt so carried away. They'd fight, his blistering anger would surface, they'd get back together. The roller coaster went on like that for five months until her period was a few days late and a pregnancy test she bought at a drugstore confirmed her suspicion.

There was never even a discussion of abortion; she didn't believe in it. It hadn't happened before. She'd never had the chance to test her moral code.

But Peter wanted to get married, and although the voice of reason in her kept shrilling against it, they went to Boston City Hall and did it several days later. They moved in together, and it was as if nothing had happened. Their relationship remained tumultuous, they still fought constantly, he still knew how to reduce her to tears.

And within a few months, he began to have affairs. First it was a sister of one of his cop friends, then a secretary he'd met at a bar called Richard's, then a whole succession of them.

At first, Sarah faulted herself. She hadn't been much of a wife. She was career-obsessed. Sure, Peter worked long hours, but hers were worse. It hadn't yet occurred to her that if a man works hard, he's ambitious, but if a woman works hard, she's negligent. After one traumatic fight, Peter promised to end the extracurricular activities. Sarah accepted his teary apologies. They would try to rebuild their marriage, for the sake of their unborn child.

At five o'clock one morning, seven months pregnant with Jared, she came home unexpectedly early, rumpled and exhausted. She'd spent the night working a wire on a case involving a precious-metals shop in Cranston, Rhode Island, that was laundering money for the Medellín cartel. She entered the apartment quietly so as not to wake Peter, who happened to be sharing their bed with a woman.

A few weeks after he'd moved out, she saw Peter arm in arm with yet another woman, coming out of a tapas place in Porter Square.

A few months after Jared's birth, Sarah accepted an assignment to go to Germany to help investigate the 1988 terrorist bombing of Pan Am Flight 103 over Lockerbie, Scotland. Separated from Peter for several months already, she leaped at the chance to get out of Boston with her child. The Bureau needed female interviewers who spoke German; counterterrorism she would learn. One block of training at New Agents school had been an overview of counterterrorism, so she knew the fundamentals. Before being sent to Germany she was put through a few weeks of intensive training in terrorism at Quantico. It wasn't easy taking a three-month-old baby to a foreign country, but it was easier than staying in the same city with Peter.

The divorce became final while Sarah and Jared were still in Germany. By the terms of the custody agreement, however, Sarah had to live in the same city as Peter. So she and three-year-old Jared returned to Boston in 1991.

Peter was suddenly interested in his little boy. She and Peter were civil with each other, and occasionally did favors for each other, while at the same time disliking each other as only divorced spouses can.

Though he didn't seem to mind being divorced from Sarah, he was pathologically jealous. Whenever she began seeing a man, he would find out about it, do whatever he could to break it up, always in the guise of protecting Jared.

She'd had a few relatively serious relationships, and each time Peter or his friends on the job would track the man down and harass or threaten him. He'd be questioned at home, stopped repeatedly for minor traffic violations, keep having traffic and parking problems. It didn't do much to sustain the relationships.

But most of her dates never grew into anything long-term. Men didn't want to go out with a woman who had a child, that was one thing. Also, she threw herself into her career, working ridiculous hours, so that even when she did meet someone who didn't mind her having a child, she wasn't available. If she started going out with the guy, she'd keep having to cancel dates because of work. More than once a guy she'd started to get close to had planned something special only to have her cancel at the last minute. And then there was Sarah's attitude, which had hardened since the divorce. She had become self-contained, unwilling to fake vulnerability, even brassy. She had become a woman who didn't need a man in her life, because she'd married one, and look what had happened. Who needed that again?

CHAPTER TWENTY-FIVE

Shortly after the KLM flight from Paris lifted off, Baumann noticed someone seated three rows in front staring pointedly at him, with a penetrating look of recognition.

Baumann knew the face.

The man was big, a hulking figure with round shoulders. Short hair cut into bangs, deep-set eyes. A beefy, jowly face Baumann thought he had seen before . . . but *where*? A long time ago, in connection with something unpleasant. The business in Madrid?

No.

No; he had *not* seen this man before. Now he was certain. The man was no longer staring at him; he was staring instead at the row behind, obviously searching for someone else.

Baumann exhaled silently, relaxed his muscles, sank into his seat. The cabin was stuffy and overheated. A bead of sweat ran down one temple.

A close call. He would have to be ever vigilant. The hulking man had called to mind another man, in another place; the resemblance was uncanny. He closed his eyes for a few seconds and was momentarily in an ice-cold hotel room in Madrid on a preposterously bright, impossibly hot afternoon.

The windows of the suite at the Ritz, Madrid, had been bulletproof, he remembered. Fresh fruit and flowers were brought in every day. The sitting room was oval; everything was painted, or wallpapered, or upholstered in shades of clotted cream.

The four young Basques came into the suite uncomfortably dressed in suits and ties: merely to enter the hotel in those days you had to wear a tie. Their leader was an enormous, bulky, awkward man with short-cropped hair. They seemed awed by Baumann, although they knew him by another name. Baumann, of course, wore a disguise and did not speak. They would never see his face. The only personal habit he allowed himself was a bit of disinformation: though he was not a smoker—that habit he developed only later, in prison—he made a point of smoking Ducados, the most popular Spanish cigarette. They would not be able to determine his nationality.

They knew nothing about him, but he had come highly recommended by a middleman, which was why they were offering a quarter of a million dollars for his services. For 1973, that was a good deal of money. They had gathered their pesetas for a long time, scrimped and saved, robbed banks.

In the privacy of the hotel suite, they told their story. They were Basque separatists—freedom fighters or militants or terrorists, depending upon your politics—and they belonged to an organization called ETA. In Basque, this stood for Euskadi Ta Askatasuna, Basque Nation and Freedom.

They came from Iruña and Segovia, Palencia and Cartagena. They despised the regime of Generalissimo Francisco Franco, which oppressed their people, forbade them to speak their own languages, had even executed Basque *priests* during the Spanish Civil War.

They wanted amnesty for the fifteen ETA members, students and workers, who had been jailed as political prisoners after the December 1970 Burgos trials. Franco was dying—he had been dying forever—and the only way to bring down his detested government was to assassinate his sole confidant, his number two, Admiral Luis Carrero Blanco. That was the only way to shatter the leadership's aura of invincibility.

Carrero Blanco, they explained, was the prime minister and was believed to be Franco's designated successor, the future of the regime. He embodied pure Francismo; he represented the post-Franco era. He was anti-Communist, anti-Semitic, ultrarightist. Because of his fiercely bushy eyebrows he was known by the nickname Ogro, the ogre.

ETA had made several bumbling attempts to eliminate both Franco and Carrero Blanco. These four young Basques had recently seen the film *The Day of the Jackal*, about a fictional plot to assassinate Charles de Gaulle, and were inspired to hire a professional, an outsider about whom nothing was known. In fact, they realized they had no choice if the job was to be done.

Hence, Operation Ogro.

Baumann never spoke with them—not once. He communicated with them by means of a child's magic slate. Not once did they hear his voice. Not once were they successful in tailing him, though they tried.

Ten ETA volunteers were provided for his assistance, but all the logistical details were left to him. Baumann prepared carefully for the hit, researched thoroughly as he always did. He learned that every morning at nine o'clock, Carrero Blanco attended mass at a Jesuit church in the Barrio de Salamanca. He studied the route that

Carrero Blanco's chauffeur took, noted the license plate of his black Dodge Dart.

Baumann rented a basement apartment at 104 Calle Claudio Coello in the Barrio de Salamanca, along the route that Carrero Blanco took to church, located directly across the street from the church. The ETA volunteers dug a two-foot-high tunnel through the apartment wall to the middle of the street, twenty-one feet long, T-shaped. Dirt was carried out in plastic garbage bags; there was an enormous amount to dispose of. Digging the tunnel was brutally arduous labor. There was little oxygen to breathe, and the soil emitted a foul-smelling gas that gave them violent headaches. And there was always the fear that the stench of the gas would seep into the apartment building and alert the neighbors.

The digging took eight days. Meanwhile, an ETA contact procured, from the Hernani Powder Magazine, two hundred kilos of Goma Two explosives, in tubular lengths like Pamplona sausages. Five packages of explosives were placed in large, square milk cans a few meters apart along the transverse of the tunnel. For a long time, Baumann wrestled with the conundrum of how to ensure that the explosion would throw up a vertical, upward, force; he eventually solved the problem by sealing the tunnel up with several feet of tightly packed dirt.

The night before the assassination, Baumann dined alone on fresh baby eels and black sausage, washed down with Oruja. The next day—December 20, 1973—Carrero Blanco's black Dodge Dart turned the corner of Diego de León on Calle Claudio Coello. There, Baumann stood on a ladder, dressed as a house painter. When the vehicle was directly over the tunnel, Baumann threw an electrical switch concealed in a paint can.

There was a muffled explosion, and the burning

wreck of the car was catapulted high up into the air and over the roof of the five-story Jesuit mission and church to the second-floor terrace on the other side. At the Ogro's funeral, Madrileños and right-wing partisans loudly sang the Falange anthem "Cara al Sol."

When the frantic investigation was launched, Baumann fingered, through an intermediary, each of the ETA volunteers who had dug the tunnel. The ten died during the vigorous police "interrogation." Baumann had done the job he was hired to do, and no one alive who was involved in the conspiracy had ever seen his face.

Now visitors to Madrid can find 104 Calle Claudio Coello, the building in which Baumann had rented the basement apartment, still standing and looking rather shabby. Across the street from it, at the exact site of the assassination, a stone plaque is engraved:

AQUI RINDIO SU ULTIMO SERVICIO
A LA PATRIA CON EL SACRIFICIO DE SU VIDA
VICTIMA DE UN VIL ATENTADO EL ALMIRANTE
LUIS CARRERO BLANCO
20-XII-1974

A few years after the bombing, a book was published internationally in which the four Basque leaders claimed total credit for the assassination, neglecting to mention that they had hired a professional. This fraudulent account had been suggested by Baumann. Not only did it redound to the greater glory of the Basque movement, but it deftly covered his tracks. The world didn't have to know that the Basque ETA were bumblers. There were rumors—which persist to this day—that the CIA provided the Basques with intelligence support, to help defeat Franco. (The truth is, sophisticated intelligence was hardly needed.)

By the time Baumann had returned to Wachthuis, the headquarters of the South African security police in Pretoria, word had gotten around of his accomplishment. A story was told and retold of how H. J. van den Bergh, the six-foot-five head of the security police, reacted upon learning what one of his agents, Henrik Baumann—cryptonym Zero—had just done in Madrid. "Jesus Christ," van den Bergh is said to have exploded. "Who the hell is this Baumann? An intelligence agent, my arse. He sounds like the bloody Prince of Darkness!"

CHAPTER TWENTY-SIX

At eight-thirty sharp the next morning, Duke Taylor arrived at his office at FBI headquarters in Washington and was startled to see both Russell Ullman and Christine Vigiani sitting cross-legged on the carpet in front of his closed office door. To either side of them, rising in three towering piles, were folders, striped with various colors. The two looked weary, disheveled. The normally fresh-faced Ullman had heavy purple circles under his eyes. Vigiani's eyes, which usually bulged with ferocious concentration, looked sewn shut.

"Jesus," Taylor said. "You two look as if you slept in your clothes."

"Yeah . . ." Vigiani began with malice.

"Your office door was locked," Ullman interrupted, his voice hoarse. "I hope it's okay we heaped the dossiers here."

Taylor glanced admiringly at the three piles again and said. "Gosh, I didn't think you'd take me *literally*." He shook his head as he unlocked his office door. "Who wants coffee?"

When they were all seated, Ullman said: "Let's start with the most obvious ones. Eliminating all those dead or in custody, that leaves mostly Arabs. Also, most of the better-known terrorists are fairly old by now."

Taylor nodded encouragement.

"Ahmed Jabril, the leader of the Popular Front for the Liberation of Palestine/General Command. Former captain in the Syrian army. Ba'athist. Hard-line Palestinian. He and his group are responsible—"

"Jabril's a creature of Syrian intelligence," Taylor interrupted. "Go ahead." He was leaning back in his office chair, eyes closed. Vigiani and Ullman sat in chairs sandwiched among pillars of dossiers. As Ullman made his presentation, Vigiani pored through a stack in her lap and made notes on her clipboard.

"All right, well, Abu Nidal, of course," Ullman went on. "Nom de guerre of Sabri al-Banna, broke with Yasir Arafat in 1974 to found the Fatah Revolutionary Council. Brutal, brilliant, the shrewdest operator there is. Estimated to have killed a thousand people, two-thirds of them Palestinians. Responsible for terrorism in more than twenty nations, including the Istanbul synagogue massacre in '86 and attacks at the Rome and Vienna airports in '85. Never captured. Lived for a while in Libya. He and his organization are now based in the Bekaa Valley. Do you know, there's no picture of him available?"

Taylor shook his head. "One of that rare breed of terrorist, a true ideologue. Never hire out. Go on."

Christine Vigiani looked up from her dossiers. "Actually, he takes money."

"Only for someone he wants to kill anyway," said Ullman, flashing her a look of profound irritation. "Anyway, this doesn't smell like an Abu Nidal op. But I was intrigued by Abu Ibrahim, a.k.a Mohammed Al-Umari. Leader of the May 15 Group. Expert in the use of barometric detonators and plastic explosives. Perhaps the most technically proficient bomb maker around. Also, there's Imad Mughniya, who masterminded the hijacking of that Kuwaiti airliner back in 1988, who's tied to Hezbollah."

"Problem is," Taylor said, heaving a sigh, "none of them can plausibly pass as Germans. I'm not going to rule them out, but I wouldn't be quick to count them in either. Chris, who are your prime suspects?"

She sat up straight, took a large swallow of coffee, widened her eyes. "Okay if I smoke?"

"I'd rather—" Ullman started.

"All right," Taylor said. "You probably need it."

She pulled out a pack of Marlboros and lighted one, inhaling gratefully. Russell Ullman glanced at her with snakelike distrust and shifted his chair a few symbolic inches away.

"If we're talking Arabs," she said, "I can't believe he didn't mention either Islamic Jihad or Hamas. Particularly Hamas, which has really been acting up lately. If Warren Elkind is such a big Israel supporter, this sounds like a Hamas kind of thing, given how much they hate Israel, and how they set off that car bomb outside the Israeli embassy in London in July 1994. And that bombing in Argentina that killed—"

"Because we're not talking Arabs, we're talking mercenary terrorists for hire, and none of those organizations has anyone that hires out," Ullman said darkly. "Unless you know better."

There was a poisonous silence, and then Vigiani continued: "There's an ETA Basque terrorist who worked as muscle for the Medellín cartel, but that was some time ago. He's believed dead, but reports vary. I'll keep on that one."

"That guy's dead," Ullman said impatiently.

Vigiani ignored him. "And at first I would have thought that among the Provos—the Provisional Wing of the Irish Republican Army—we'd find some good possibilities, but none of them fit the profile. None are known to hire out. Though I suppose any of them *could*. Also, according to the most recent intelligence, some of the Protestant groups in Northern Ireland—the Ulster Defence Association and the Ulster Volunteer Force—have started using mercenaries, paid assassins, for the real serious, clinical operations. I didn't bother with those assholes who did OKBOMB," she said, using the Bureau's code name for Oklahoma City. "Way too primitive. And, let's see, there's a South African guy, but he's locked up for life in Pretoria or Johannesburg or something. And this may seem sort of left-field, but there's Frank Terpil, the former CIA guy Qaddafi hired to train his special forces."

Taylor nodded, eyes still closed.

"Well, his buddy Ed Wilson's serving a long sentence in a federal penitentiary, but Terpil's still at large. File says he's been involved in assassinations in Africa and a coup attempt in Chad in 1978. He's alive and hiding somewhere, and for all I know he may still be active."

Taylor opened his eyes and frowned at the acoustic dropped ceiling of his office. "Maybe."

Vigiani jotted something down on her clipboard. "And all those old East German training camps—they may be history, but some of the folks who trained there are probably still on the market. Problem is, our data on those guys is pretty skimpy."

"You contact the Germans?" Taylor asked.

"I'm working on it," Ullman said.

"All right," Taylor said. "I'm inclined to take a second look at this Terpil fellow and any of the East German-trained personnel we can turn up. Tell your staff to keep digging. Chris, what did you turn up in the computer search on Warren Elkind?"

Vigiani snubbed out her cigarette in the large glass ashtray she'd taken from Taylor's desk. A plume of acrid smoke curled. She presented a quick biographical profile of Elkind, emphasizing his charitable work on behalf of Israel. "Apart from that, there's not much, unfortunately. We've got an agent in Boston who just did a complete computer search on Warren Elkind."

"Really?" Taylor said with interest. "What's he assigned to?"

"OC, I believe. And it's a she."

"What's her name?"

"Cahill, I think. Sarah Cahill."

"I know the name. Big in Lockerbie. Counterterrorism expert. Wonder why she's looking into Elkind. Hmm. I want to talk to her. Get her in here. Meantime, why don't you two go home and get some sleep?"

CHAPTER TWENTY-SEVEN

Early the next morning, after Peter had arrived to take Jared for the day, Sarah drove in to work. Saturdays at the office had become ritual since Peter's weekend visits had begun. Anyway, she had a lot of work to catch up on, and she wanted to search for anything she could find on Valerie's killer.

It turned out not to be necessary.

When she arrived at work, there was a voice-mail message from Teddy Williams. She listened, and immediately took a drive over to the Homicide Squad.

"What have you got?" Sarah asked him.

"Blowback," Teddy said. This was the sometimes invisible spray of a victim's blood found on the shooter's clothing.

"On what?"

"A sport coat we found in the giant closet belonging to a guy named Sweet Bobby Higgins."

Sarah leaned against the wall, eyes closed. She felt queasy. "Sweet—?"

"Sweet Bobby Higgins lives in a big house in Maiden with no less than four wives. They refer to each other as wives-in-law. I think three of them are sisters. Each of them has his made-up crest tattooed below her navel."

"Sort of like you'd brand cattle. Who is he?"

"Sort of an on-again, off-again boyfriend of your friend Valerie's madam. An enforcer."

"I doubt it."

"Valerie was cheating on her, and the madam knew it."

"Maybe she knew it, but I doubt she'd have some pimp whack Val. You got a tip?"

"We were there on a routine search warrant, based on the madam's phone records. Your ex-husband saw it first. A white-and-gold jacket, looked like the sleeves were soiled. Peter looked closer, saw tiny drops, like elongated tears or commas, maybe a sixteenth of an inch long. Sweet Bobby didn't see any blood. When we found it, he looked like he was getting ready to flex."

"You did a PGM test?" She was referring to a phosphoglucomutase enzyme test.

"Precise match with Val's blood. And if you're thinking it's a plant, he doesn't have an alibi. Hinky as hell."

"Does he deny the jacket is his?"

Ted laughed raucously. "Not with a straight face. That's the ugliest jacket I've ever seen."

"Ballistics?"

"Sweet Bobby's got a Glock. Matches the 9mm rounds used on Valerie Santoro."

"You think that clinches it? What did Ballistics tell you?"

Defensively: "They got a match."

She shook her head. "Glocks aren't bored. So it's a lot more difficult to make a definitive ballistic match. But you want to say Sweet Bobby did it, go ahead. That's your business. I really don't give a shit, and as far as I'm concerned, the more pimps you lock up the better."

"Degrading to women, is that it?"

"They're just scumbags. You'd better hope he doesn't have a lawyer slick enough to pick up on the Glock thing, or else the case'll be dismissed without prejudice. You still don't have a witness, do you?"

"This is a guy with priors."

"And if you guys don't get your clearance rate up, you'll both be transferred to Auto Theft. No need to get defensive on me, Ted. I really don't care. Congratulations, okay?"

Late in the afternoon, driving home through the streets of Cambridge, Sarah passed a large grassy field and saw Peter and Jared. Wearing muddy jeans and T-shirts, they were throwing a football. It had just started raining. Peter was making large, sweeping gestures; Jared looked small and awkward. He gave his mother an enthusiastic wave when he saw her get out of the car.

Peter turned, gave a perfunctory thumbs-up.

"You're early," he shouted.

"Mind if I watch for a couple minutes?"

"It's okay, Mom," Jared called out. "Dad's just showing me how to run pass patterns."

Peter now pointed, making jabbing motions. "A square-out," he called to Jared. "Go straight five yards, and then cut right five yards. All right?"

"Straight and then right?" Jared asked. His voice was high, reedy.

"*Go!*" Peter shouted suddenly, and Jared began running. Peter hesitated, then threw the football, and Jared caught it. Sarah smiled.

"No!" Peter yelled. "I said a square-out, didn't I? You're supposed to cut on a dime. You're running a square-out like a fly pattern!"

"I don't even remember what a fly pattern is," Jared said.

"You run straight out, fast as you can, and I throw it over your head. A square-out, you cut right. Get it?"

Jared ran back toward his father. As he ran, he shouted defiantly: "Yeah, but I caught it!"

"Jerry, buddy, you're not catching the ball right either. You're just using your hands. Don't just use your hands. Bring it into your chest. Get your body in front of it."

"I don't want to get hit."

"Don't be a pussy," Peter said. "You can't be afraid of the ball. Don't be a pussy. Try it again, let's go!"

Jared began running, then pivoted to the right, slipping a little in the mud.

"Now when you get it, tuck the ball into your chest," Peter shouted, tossing the football. It soared in a perfect arc. He shouted: "*Tuck* the ball into your chest. *Tuck*—"

Jared stepped aside, and the football slipped through his hands and thunked hollowly into the grass. Vaulting after it, Jared lost his balance and slammed to the ground.

"Jesus," Peter said with disgust. "The ball's not going to hurt you. Get your body in *front* of the ball! Don't be afraid of it!"

"I did—"

"Get *both* hands around the ball!"

Frustrated, Jared got to his feet and ran back toward Peter.

"Look, Jerry," Peter said in a softer voice. "You gotta bring it *into* your body. All right, we're going to do a button hook."

"A button hook?" Jared repeated wearily.

"A button hook. You get out there, run ten yards, and turn around. The ball will be there. You get it?"

"I get it," Jared said. His voice was sullen; he hung his head. Sarah wondered whether her presence was embarrassing him, decided it was, and that she should leave.

"All right, let's go!" Peter shouted as Jared scrambled ahead. As he ran, his pace accelerated. Peter threw the ball hard and fast, a bullet. Just as Jared stopped and turned, the football hit him in the stomach. Sarah heard a *whoof* of expelled air. Jared buckled over, sank clumsily to the ground.

"Jared!" Sarah shouted.

Peter laughed raucously. "Man," he said. "Buddy boy. You really screwed the pooch there, didn't you." He turned toward Sarah. "Wind knocked out of him. He'll be fine."

Jared struggled to his feet, his face red. There were tears running down his face. "Jesus, Dad," he cried. "What'd you go and do that for?"

"You think *I* did something?" Peter said, and laughed again. "I told you, you gotta tuck it into your chest, kid. You looked like a clown out there. You want to learn this or not?"

"*No!*" Jared screamed. "Jesus, Dad! I hate this!" He limped away toward Sarah.

"Peter!" Sarah said. She began to run toward Jared, but the heel of her left shoe caught in a tangle of weeds. She tripped and landed with her knees in the mud.

When she got up, Jared was there, throwing his arms around her. "I hate him," he sobbed against her blouse, muffled. "He's such an asshole, Mom. I hate him."

She hugged him. "You did so well out there, honey."

"I hate him." His voice grew louder. "I *hate* him. I don't want him to come around anymore." Peter approached, his face set in a grim expression, his jaw tight.

"Look, Jerry," he said. "I don't want you to be afraid of the ball. You do it right, the ball's not going to hurt you."

"You get the hell out of here!" Sarah exploded, her

heart racing. She grabbed Jared so tightly he yelped in pain.

"Oh, Jesus Christ," Peter said. "Look what you're doing to him."

"Get the hell out," Sarah said.

"You're a goddam asshole!" Jared shouted at his father. "I don't want to play football with you again. You're an asshole!"

"Jerry," Peter coaxed.

"Screw you, Dad!" Jared said in a quavering voice. He whirled around and stomped away.

"Jared," Sarah called out.

"I'm going home, Mom," he said, and she hung back.

A few minutes later, Sarah and Peter stood on the edge of the field in the drizzle. His blond hair was tousled, his gray Champion sweatshirt smudged with mud. In his faded jeans, he looked as slender and trim as ever. He had never looked as attractive, and she had never hated him more.

"I talked to Teddy," she said.

"Yeah?"

"I heard about Sweet Bobby whatever-his-name-is."

"What, you surprised we made the whore's killer so fast?"

"No. I just don't think you got the right one."

"Jesus, Sarah, we got blood on the guy's clothes, what more do you—"

"You've got evidence enough to lock him up. I just don't think he's the killer."

Peter shook his head and smiled. "Whatever. Mind if I use your shower? Get changed? Jared and I are going out to dinner. Hilltop Steak House."

"I don't think Jared is up to going out."

"I got him till tonight, remember."

"It's Jared's choice, Peter," she said. "And I don't

think he wants to go out to the Hilltop with you tonight. I'm sorry."

"The kid's got to learn to stand on his own," he said gently.

"For God's sake, Peter, he's eight years old. He's a child!"

"He's a boy, Sarah. Kid's got a lot of potential. He just needs a little discipline, is all." He seemed almost to be pleading. "You know, Joey Gamache was a lightweight, but he became a world champ. You want to knock down Floyd Patterson or Marvin Hagler or Mike Tyson, you got to learn to take your lumps. You're raising him to be soft. Jerry needs a father."

"You aren't a father, you're a sparring partner," Sarah said, her voice quiet and malevolent. "Rocket shots to the rib. Jab to the jaw. You're goddam abusive, is what you are, and I'm not going to permit it. I'm not going to let you treat my son this way anymore."

" 'My son,' " Peter echoed with dark irony, chuckling.

They were both silent for a moment. The argument hung heavy in the air between them.

"Look, just make it easier on all of us," Sarah said. "Go home. Jared doesn't want to go out to dinner with you tonight."

"Kid needs a father," Peter said quietly.

"Yeah," Sarah agreed. "It's just not clear you're the one."

CHAPTER TWENTY-EIGHT

At a few minutes after four o'clock in the afternoon, the office mail courier, a chubby middle-aged black man, dropped a small yellow bubble-pack envelope, about four inches wide by five inches long, into Sarah's in-basket. "Just came in," he said. "Rush."

"Thanks, Sammy," she said. The label bore the return address of the MIT Artificial Intelligence Laboratory.

She tore open the envelope, removed the tape, and put it in a tape player.

The voices were indistinct, forlorn, distant conversations in a wind tunnel. Even played on the most high-fidelity tape deck Sarah could wangle from Audio Services, the acoustic quality of the tape recording was woefully bad. But once you got used to it, you could make out the words.

Will Phelan—brow furrowed, intently concentrating, stroking his mustache absently with his pinkie—sat at the conference table beside Ken, who leaned way back in his chair, arms folded across his ample belly, eyes closed.

Sarah provided the narration. "This one," she said, "is just a routine dunning call." A man's voice identified himself as being "from Card Services" and left an

800 number. Then a beep, then the synthesized female voice of the answering machine's day/time stamp announced: "Monday, four-twelve P.M."

"All right," Sarah said. "Listen."

Another man's voice. If the first voice sounded lost in an electronic maelstrom, this one was even more distant, bobbing on crashing waves of static.

"Mistress? It's Warren." A surge of crackly static, then: ". . . the Four Seasons at eight o'clock tonight. Room 722. I've been hard for days thinking about you. Had to jerk off in the lavatory on the plane. Probably against some FAA law. I'm going to have to be punished."

Phelan arched his eyebrows and turned to look at Ken, who seemed on the verge of exploding with laughter.

A beep. The day/time voice stamp announced: "Monday, five-twenty P.M."

Phelan cleared his throat and rumbled: "All right, you got—"

"Wait," Sarah interrupted. "One more."

A rush of static, hollow and metallic. The next voice was male, high-pitched, British-accented. The connection was distant; every few seconds it broke up.

"Valerie, it's Simon. Good evening." Slow, deliberate, phlegmatic. "Your friend is staying in Room 722 at the Four Seasons Hotel. You are looking for a small, round, flat object that looks like a compact disk you might play on your stereo . . ."

A break, then: ". . . gold-colored. It may or may not be in a square sleeve. It will almost certainly be in his briefcase." A long rush of static. "A van will be parked down the street from the hotel this evening. You will take the disk to the van, hand it over, and wait for it to be copied. Then you will return the disk to the hotel's front desk. You will tell them you found it. When you return home, you will be visited by a friend around midnight, who will give you the rest of what we've agreed upon. Goodbye."

A beep, then the mechanical voice: "Monday, six oh five P.M."

Sarah clicked the tape off, looked at the two men.

A long beat of silence.

Phelan said: "Is this admissible?"

"Easily," said Ken. "Bruce Gelman's got credentials up the wazoo."

"This some kind of CD-ROM they're talking about?" Phelan asked.

Sarah said, "Probably. The situation we have here— the five-thousand-dollar payoff in bills cut in half, the theft of a computer disk—this isn't a run-of-the-mill pimp-killing-a-prostitute thing. This is a fairly elaborate setup, I'd guess."

Phelan nodded contemplatively. "By whom and for what?"

"My theory is that Warren Elkind was set up to be robbed by Valerie. That Elkind had *something*, or has access to something—something computer-related— that's worth a lot to some people with a lot of resources." Sarah ejected the cassette tape from the machine and idly turned it over several times.

Phelan sighed long and soulfully. "There's *something* there," he admitted. "But not enough to go on. What'd you turn up from the computer search?"

She explained that the interagency computer search for any mention of Elkind's name had yielded exactly 123 references. The information had come over the teletype, instead of by letter, because Phelan, fortunately, had marked the search "immediate" rather than routine. Most of the references were garbage—"overhears," as they're called in the intelligence community. Some CIA flunky in Jakarta heard Warren Elkind's name mentioned in connection with a major banking arrangement with the Indonesian government. Someone in U.S. military intelligence in Tel Aviv had heard a rumor (false, it turned out) that Elkind had once accepted a bribe from an Israeli minister. Someone else had heard that Elkind had bribed a member of the Israeli government. A lot of junk.

The telephone on a table against the wall rang. Ken got up to answer it.

"I'm inclined to leave Elkind out of this," Phelan said.

"For you, Sarah," Ken said.

Sarah took the phone. "Yes?"

"Agent Cahill, this is Duke Taylor, at headquarters."

"Yes?" she said, her heart hammering. It had to be something serious.

"How fast can you get your bags packed and get on a plane to Washington?" Taylor asked. "I need to see you immediately."

Part 3

KEYS

*Be extremely subtle, even to the point
of formlessness. Be extremely mysterious,
even to the point of soundlessness.
Thereby you can be the director
of the opponent's fate.*

—Sun-tzu, *The Art of War*

CHAPTER TWENTY-NINE

"Goedenavond, Mijnheer," the portly little man in the corner booth said as he half rose to greet Baumann at the Hoppe, a well-known *bruine krogen*, or "brown café." This was a type of pub peculiar to Amsterdam, so named for its tobacco-smoke-stained walls and ceilings. A loud and crowded place, poorly lit, it was located on Spui, in the middle of Amsterdam's university section.

"Good evening," Baumann replied, assessing the man, whose name was Jan Willem Van den Vondel, but—presumably because of his girth—was universally known by the nickname Bones.

Bones was a "mere," an ex-mercenary who had worked in the Middle East and Africa under a bewildering variety of aliases. He had once been one of the dreaded *affreux*, the "frightful ones," the white freelance soldiers who helped keep dictators in power throughout Africa and Asia. In the sixties and seventies, he had worked in the Belgian Congo (now Zaire), in Angola in the days when it was owned by the Portuguese, in white-ruled Rhodesia (now Zimbabwe), in Yemen under the old monarchy, and in Iran under the Shah. In 1977 he had helped lead an unsuccessful effort to oust the Marxist government of Benin, a small country in West Africa. A year later he had been instrumental in aiding Ahmed Abdallah to seize the presidency of the Comoros Islands, an archipelago off the southeastern coast of Africa. A decade later, several of his employees, working as guards for President Abdallah, had assassinated the very man they had put into office.

Van den Vondel was loathsome in appearance, lacking in personal hygiene and malodorous. He had cauliflower ears as well as bad teeth, presumably stained by chewing tobacco, a wad of which bulged in his cheek.

Yet Bones had become one of the best forgers in the business. He had agreed to meet Baumann, a man he did not know, only because Baumann had been vouched for by a mutual friend, an ex-mercenary now residing in Marseilles whom Baumann had hired to do a nasty job in Ostend some ten years earlier. This Frenchman, who'd worked under Bones in the Belgian Congo, knew Baumann only as a wealthy American named Sidney Lerner—a cover Baumann had gone to a great deal of trouble to establish.

"Sidney Lerner" was one of the Mossad's many thousands of *sayanim*, volunteers who help out the Israeli intelligence service out of a sense of loyalty to Israel. A *sayan* (Hebrew for "assistant") must be 100 percent Jewish, but not an Israeli citizen; in fact, *sayanim* are always diaspora Jews, though they may have relatives in Israel. In the United States alone there are some fifty thousand *sayanim*. A doctor *sayan*, for instance, will treat a Mossad agent's bullet wound without reporting it to the authorities. A *sayan* can refuse an assignment—they often do—but can be relied upon not to turn a Mossad agent in.

As Baumann had expected, the forger had asked this mutual friend why on earth Sidney Lerner couldn't get his false papers from his *katsa*, his Mossad case officer. There were reasons, the mercenary said darkly. Are you interested or not? Bones was interested.

Baumann got right to the point. "I need three complete sets of documents."

The forger's eyes narrowed. "Belgian?"

"American and British."

"Passports, driver's licenses, et cetera?"

Baumann nodded, and took a sip of beer.

"But Mr. Lerner," Van den Vondel said, "it's much cheaper to get them in New York or London."

"Speed is of greater importance to me than expense," Baumann explained.

The forger flashed a big, feral gray smile. This was music to his cauliflower ears. "Tell me, please, Mr. Lerner, exactly what sort of schedule are you on?"

"I need them by tomorrow evening."

Van den Vondel burst out laughing, as if this were the most riotously amusing joke he'd ever heard. "Oh, my," he exclaimed helplessly between guffaws. "Oh, my. And I need to be the king of England."

Baumann got to his feet. "I'm sorry we're unable to do business," he said.

The forger's laughing fit immediately ceased. "Mr Lerner, what you ask is absolutely unrealistic," he said quickly. "Impossible. You will find this no matter who you talk to. Unless you have the misfortune of hooking up with some small-time fraud who does the shoddiest work that will have the American or the British authorities on your ass in seconds. I am a craftsman, Mr. Lerner. The work I do is absolutely top-notch, of the highest quality." With another feral smile, he added: "Better, I may say, than the real thing."

Baumann sat down again. "Then how much time do you require?"

"It depends upon what you want exactly. The British documents are no problem whatsoever. The American ones, on the other hand—well, this can be a major challenge."

"So I understand."

"In April of 1993," Bones explained, "the U.S. government began issuing new passports marked with what is called a kinegram, which looks like a hologram, if you know what that is."

Baumann nodded impatiently, closing his eyes.

"It's part of the laminate on the identity page. When you hold it up to the light, it changes between two different images. We still have not devised a satisfactory method to copy that, although in a short time I have no doubt we will. Fortunately, the older-style American passports are still valid and in use. Those are much easier to reproduce. Though still quite difficult. To forge a new passport requires access to the paper, or better still, to the actual passport books that the government uses. It also requires the proper equipment, which is strictly controlled, difficult to obtain, and extremely expensive—"

"And time-consuming, I imagine."

"Very much so. Because of your time constraints, forgery is out. The only possibility is to acquire a valid passport and alter it."

"I'm familiar with how it's done," Baumann said, smiling thinly. He produced Sumner Robinson's passport, opened it to the identity page, and showed it to the forger, covering the name with his thumb.

"You hired an amateur," the forger said disapprovingly.

Baumann nodded.

"This was crudely done." He shook his head. "If you used this and were not caught—well, you were lucky. You must not use this again."

Baumann took the insult to his craftsmanship in stride. "That's why I'm here," he said. "I have no doubt you will do a superior job. But how can you ensure that a stolen passport will not be reported as missing or stolen, and placed on the look-out list on the computers at all American ports of entry? The only way I can think of is to take a passport that belongs to someone who never uses it, and therefore wouldn't notice its absence."

"Exactly, Mr. Lerner. The network at my disposal has the names and addresses of Americans living abroad, in Belgium, the Netherlands, Luxembourg, and other places. Americans who have passports but rarely if ever travel."

"Good," Baumann said.

The two men negotiated a price—a stiff one, as it turned out, because of the number of personnel, including a small ring of petty break-and-enter specialists, who'd require a cut.

As he was about to leave, Baumann added, as if in afterthought: "Oh, and while your people are at it, have them get me an assortment of credit cards. Visa, MasterCard, American Express, and whatnot."

"Credit cards?" Van den Vondel replied dubiously. "Passports that are seldom used are one thing. But credit cards—they're almost always noticed missing. They'd be canceled immediately."

"Quite right," Baumann said. "But that makes no difference to me." He extended his hand; the forger gave a moist, oily squeeze. "Until tomorrow night, then."

CHAPTER THIRTY

Once Baumann concluded his business with the forger, he took a taxi to Schiphol Airport, rented a Mercedes at an all-night car-rental agency, and set out toward the Belgian border. He was bone-tired and in need of a good night's sleep, but there was, to be fair, a certain logic to his middle-of-the-night journey. The distance between Amsterdam and Liège, Belgium, is 120 miles, a drive of only a few hours. In the hours after midnight, the roads were empty and the drive went quickly. Motoring was far less time-consuming than flying to Brussels, then driving to Liège. And Baumann wanted to arrive in the early morning.

There was a black-market armaments dealer who for years had lived and conducted his trade in a village just south of Liège, Baumann had ascertained after a few calls to underground armaments shippers at the Port of Antwerp. Baumann's sources indicated that this dealer, a man named Charreyron, could do the job Baumann needed done.

Historically, Belgium has always been Europe's most notorious, most active arms manufacturer and dealer. It exports 90 percent of the weapons it produces. And the capital of the Belgian arms industry since the Middle

Ages has been Liège, at the junction of the Meuse and the Ourthe rivers: the heart of the Belgian steel industry and Europe's third-largest inland port.

In 1889, the Belgian government decided its army needed a reliable single source for the Mauser Model 1888 military rifle, and founded at Liège the Fabrique Nationale d'Armes de Guerre. Ten years later, Fabrique Nationale, or FN, began making Browning pistols, which it makes to this day, along with machine guns and rifles. (It was FN rifles that Fidel Castro first used upon seizing power in Cuba.) As a result of this industry, a number of small-arms dealers have grown up around Liège in the last half-century, some of them dealing quite profitably outside the law.

By four o'clock in the morning Baumann had reached Liège. The sky was pitch-black; dawn was still a few hours away. He was exhausted, badly in need of a few hours' rest, and he considered what to do next.

He could drive into the Place Saint-Lambert and fortify himself with a cup of strong black coffee, perhaps read a few newspapers. Or park somewhere quiet and doze until he was awakened by first light.

But he decided not to trouble with driving into the city, and instead continued on southwest. As he drove through the darkness, he found himself growing increasingly contemplative. The gloomy landscape reminded him of the western Transvaal of his childhood.

The small town in which Baumann had been born was settled in the early nineteenth century by Voortrekkers. Very quickly it became a *plak-kie-dorp*, a shantytown. When Baumann was a child, the town was made up of Dutch farmhouses and rondavels with thatched roofs. His parents' farmhouse was situated hard by the Magaliesberg Mountains, forty kilometers outside Pretoria, surrounded by broodboom and bread trees.

He taught himself to hunt in the bushveld nearby,

which teemed with wildebeest and springbok, the perfect game. For all of his childhood, and even into his adolescence, he kept to himself, preferring solitude to the company of other children, who bored him. When he wasn't hunting or hiking or collecting rock and plant specimens in the bushveld, he was reading. He had no brothers or sisters: in the years after his birth, his Boer parents tried repeatedly to conceive, but miscarriage followed miscarriage until it became clear his mother was unable to bear another child.

His father, a tobacco farmer who'd sold his farm to the Magaliesberg Tobacco Corporation, the cooperative that owned most of the tobacco farms in the region, was a gloomy, silent man who died of a heart attack when Baumann was six. Baumann's memories of his father were few. His mother supported the two of them by taking in sewing.

She worried constantly about her only son, whom she didn't understand. He was unlike the other children in town, unlike the sons of her neighbors and few friends. She was concerned he had been damaged by the untimely death of his father, had turned inward from the lack of brothers or sisters, had been rendered permanently sullen by his solitary existence. And she despaired of a solution.

The more she urged him to do things the other children did—play games, even get into trouble—the more he kept to himself. Yet he caused her no grief. He excelled in school, made his bed, tidied up his room, read, and hunted. After a while she gave up trying to push her son in a direction he clearly didn't want to go.

Mother and son rarely spoke. During the long, furiously hot December afternoons and evenings—the South African summer—the two of them sat silently in the kitchen. She sewed; he read. They lived in separate universes.

One afternoon in his twelfth year, unknown to his mother, Baumann went hunting for springbok in the bushveld and came upon a drunken Tswana, a local black tribesman. (Baumann had learned to distinguish among the tribes who lived nearby, the Tswanas or Ndebeles or Zulus.) The drunk, a young man perhaps ten years older than Baumann, began taunting the white boy, and Baumann without a moment's hesitation aimed his hunting rifle and squeezed off a single shot.

The Tswana died instantly.

The victim's blood, even his brain matter, splattered Baumann's face and hands and muslin shirt. Baumann burned the bloodied shirt, bathed himself in a stream, and went home shirtless, leaving the crumpled body where it had fallen.

When he returned home, his mother could see he hadn't caught any game and didn't even ask what had happened to his shirt. She'd given up asking questions only to receive monosyllabic replies. He read quietly, and she sewed.

But that evening he was unable to concentrate on his reading, for the killing had thrilled him more deeply than anything had ever thrilled him before. It had scared him, yes, but it had also given him a warm and satisfying sense of control, of mastery, of power over the insolent black man. To Baumann, this was not a racial issue, because he thought little about Coloureds and Blacks. It was the ability to end a human life that intoxicated him—all the more when, after a few weeks, he realized he had gotten away with it, with no consequences whatsoever.

Nothing happened. There was no investigation, no mention in the local newspaper, nothing.

He had gotten away with it. It was like hunting a wildebeest, only a hundred times more exciting, more *real*.

And it had been so simple. Baumann solemnly swore to himself that he wouldn't kill another human being again, because he was afraid that if he continued, he wouldn't be able to stop.

It was then that a complete and stunning transformation overcame the young Baumann. His personality changed almost overnight. He turned outward, became lively and outgoing. He was witty, winning, suddenly popular. He began to play sports, to go out. He made lots of friends. Within a few years he took a great interest in girls.

His mother was baffled, but delighted. She attributed this miraculous change in her son to some mysterious effect of the hormonal surges of puberty. Whatever had clicked inside her son, she was grateful for it.

Only rarely did she pause to observe that her son's newfound demeanor seemed hollow at its center. There was something dead in his eyes, something false in his joviality, something fundamentally false. With her, his closest (and only) living relative, he was polite, proper, even a touch formal. Between them there was, she sometimes felt, a dead space, a coldness.

She died when he was in his late twenties, already an accomplished operative for BOSS, the South African secret police. He made the funeral arrangements with an appropriate measure of grief, which he also displayed at her funeral. The small handful of friends and neighbors from their hometown who attended the service took note of how deeply distraught the young Baumann was, the poor thing, who'd lost his father so early and now his mother, and such a good and polite young man, too.

CHAPTER THIRTY-ONE

Deputy Assistant Director Duke Taylor escorted Sarah Cahill into his office and introduced her to Russell Ullman and Christine Vigiani, who got to their feet and welcomed her with grudging hospitality. They'd have been happier to meet a boa constrictor.

The air-conditioning was particularly strong here on the seventh floor of the Hoover Building. Why, Sarah wondered, did the directors of both CIA and FBI have seventh-floor offices? Did old J. Edgar himself say, "If that's the way the Pickle Factory does it, me too?"

Sarah assessed them quickly. Ullman was big and towheaded, a corn-fed version of Peter. Vigiani looked smart as a whip and was probably trouble. Taylor she liked instantly, liked his serenity, his self-deprecating humor.

Settling into his high-backed leather desk chair, with a huge FBI seal behind him, Taylor said, "So, you were in Germany on the Lockerbie thing."

"That's right."

"You got a lot of raves. Apparently you helped break the case."

With a glint in her eye, she said: "You think if I cracked Lockerbie I'd be sitting here?"

"Where would you be?"

She shrugged. "Who knows?"

"But you know well enough that it took us twenty-one months to find the timing device, and that was what cracked the case. If it hadn't been for you, we'd probably have cracked it—but it would have taken even longer. The Bureau owes you a major debt."

"I'll happily take a pay raise."

"File says you showed strong leadership. You ran a squad in Heidelberg. Obviously you also like to speak your mind."

"When I think it's important. My superiors in Heidelberg got a little annoyed when I insisted there might be more to the case than a couple of Libyans."

"Like what?"

"Like maybe Syria working with Iran. It's just a theory. A few months before Pan Am 103 went down, a couple of guys from the Popular Front for the Liberation of Palestine General Command were arrested in Germany with barometric detonators. Who sponsors them? Syria. But because the Bush administration saw Syria as crucial to the Middle East peace process, they wanted to leave Syria alone. Then we needed Syria to take our side in the Gulf War, so they were definitely off the hook."

"Interesting," Taylor said. "No comment."

"That sounds familiar."

He smiled. "I'm surprised you've lasted this long in the Bureau."

"I have a reputation for getting stuff done. I get cut a lot of slack."

"Do you have a theory on the World Trade Center bombing too? Some people don't think we've completely solved that one either."

"You don't really want to know."

"Try me."

"Well, we never really pursued the international angle adequately. It's like Lockerbie—we just don't want to know, because what do you do if you find out? Everyone seems to be happy pinning the blame on some incompetent followers of some blind sheik. But if you look at the evidence closely, you'll see that one of members of the gang was an Iraqi sleeper agent. I think he was the control. I think Saddam Hussein was behind the Trade Center thing."

"Did they call you in on OKBOMB?"

"No. By then I was in Boston. I wish they had."

"If I'd been in charge then, I would have. Do you miss being in Counterterrorism?"

Sarah paused. "So that's where this is leading. Yeah, I miss it a lot. But I have personal reasons to be where I am."

"I've read your file; I know about your custody situation. I understand about the sacrifices you sometimes have to make for family."

"Is this a job interview?"

"Sort of. You think we're tough enough on terrorists?"

" 'We' being the FBI or the United States?"

"The United States."

"You can't be serious. Of course not. We talk tough, but that's about it. Remember how, during the Gulf War, the Pentagon wanted to target the terrorist training camps in the Iraqi countryside, strike them, but the White House said no? Didn't want to piss off the Syrians, 'cause we needed them in the coalition against Saddam Hussein. That's really tough, huh? And remember when the president of Pakistan, Zia, was killed along with the American ambassador in a plane crash and State wouldn't allow any of our agents into Pakistan to investigate? Pretty damned tough, huh? We've got more than two dozen executive agencies and departments that monitor and respond to terrorism, and we couldn't stop the Gang That Couldn't Bomb Straight at the World Trade Center."

"Why not?"

"Because we're sloppy. The blind sheik behind the World Trade Center incident was on our watch list of suspected terrorists, but he twice got visas to enter the country because his name was spelled wrong on the application, right?"

"You think if we were tougher, things like Oklahoma City wouldn't happen?"

She paused. "I don't know. You can't stop maniacs."

Taylor leaned back in his chair, folded his arms. "All right. We noticed that you've been doing some deep background investigation into a New York banker named Warren Elkind. That seems a little outside your jurisdiction, unless there's an OC connection I don't know about."

Sarah looked at him penetratingly. So that *was* it. "A prostitute who happened to be one of my key informants—helped me wrap up a couple of important cases—was killed. A call girl, actually, not a prostitute—in her line of work they make certain distinctions. Anyway, the Boston police have cleared the case, but I'm skeptical, to be honest. It appears that the call girl was hired to steal something—a CD-ROM disk, I believe—from this Elkind guy."

"What's the connection between Elkind and this prostitute?" Russell Ullman asked.

"A preexisting relationship. She did bondage-and-discipline sessions with him whenever he was in Boston. She was his 'top,' or dominatrix. His mistress. Someone who knew she worked for Elkind must have hired her."

"What was on the CD-ROM?" asked Vigiani.

"I don't know. Bank records, I'd guess. Obviously something pretty valuable."

"But how do you *know* the call girl was hired to do this?" Vigiani persisted. "You haven't talked to Elkind, have you?"

"No," Sarah said. "Not yet. He wouldn't take my call, actually. The reason I know is that I have it on tape."

"Really?" Taylor said, hunching forward. "Phone cover on the prostitute?"

"Her answering-machine tape." She explained how the tape was unerased.

"FBI Crime Labs," Taylor said with a proud smile. "Best in the world."

Sarah cleared her throat. "Actually, I had to go outside the Bureau. MIT. We don't have the technology."

"You have a transcript?" Taylor asked.

"Better than that," Sarah said. "I have the tape right here. I had a hunch you'd want to hear it."

After Sarah played the tape twice, on an old Panasonic that Ullman had rounded up from a nearby desk, Taylor said: "Now we've got a transcript we'd like you to take a look at." He handed Sarah a transcript of the NSA intercept; the three were silent as she scanned it.

Sarah read with puzzlement. When she got to Warren Elkind's name she looked up, then resumed reading. Once she finished, she asked, "Who's speaking here?"

"We don't know," said Taylor.

"Where was the conversation picked up?"

"Switzerland."

She exhaled slowly, looked around at the others. "The 'target,' as they put it, is either Warren Elkind or Manhattan Bank, or both. Elkind is not just one of the most powerful bankers in the world, but he's also a major fund-raiser for Israel. A lot of Palestinians would probably love to see him roast in hell."

Vigiani shrugged, as if to say, *This is news to you?*

Sarah continued, "And this Heinrich Fürst, however it's spelled, who's 'accepted the sales assignment'— what have you turned up on him?"

"Nothing," Taylor said.

"Big fat goose egg," said Ullman. "Under every variant spelling, every homophone, anything remotely close. Nothing."

"Fürst . . ." Sarah said aloud. "You know, I do have an idea."

"Let's hear it," Taylor said dubiously. "We'll take anything."

"Well, I spent a lot of time, when I was in Germany working SCOTBOMB, looking into timing devices for bombs. I talked to one colonel at DIA—an old guy, who died a couple of years ago—about an attempted coup in Togo in 1986. This DIA guy mentioned, really in passing, the name of someone thought to be involved in the Togo affair. He was a mercenary terrorist who went by the alias Fürst. One of many aliases this mere used."

Taylor, who'd been massaging his eyes, suddenly looked at her.

Vigiani said sharply: "*Heinrich* Fürst?"

"Just 'Fürst' or 'Herr Fürst.' "

"German?" Ullman said.

"No," Sarah said. "I mean, the alias was, obviously, but not the mere."

"Did you get a true name on the mere?" Taylor asked.

"No. Just that, and a nickname, sort of a nom de guerre."

"Which was?"

"Well, the guy was good, really good, and apparently as amoral as they come. Brilliant, ruthless, every adjective you can come up with—top-notch in his field. A white South African—rumored to have once worked for BOSS, the old South African secret intelligence service. And some of his admirers called him 'Prince of Darkness.' "

"Loves kids, dogs, Mozart, and walks on the beach," said Vigiani dryly.

Sarah went on: "Well, my German's pretty rusty by now, but doesn't *Fürst* mean—"

Ullman interrupted: "*Fürst*—Prince—oh, Jesus. *Fürst der Finsternis*. Translates as 'Prince of Darkness.' "

"Right," Sarah said. "Just a possibility."

Taylor gave a lopsided grin. "Nice. I think I'm beginning to understand why all the raves in your file. You've got a mind for this stuff."

"Thanks. I did, once."

"You still do. Now, if it's true that our good Prince is really a South African, we should reach out to Pretoria. See what they have on anyone with this alias."

"I'd—I'd be careful about that," Sarah said.

"Oh, come on." Vigiani scowled. "The new South African government is as cooperative as can be. If you think the guy used to work for BOSS, that's where the answer will be. Pretoria."

"Wait a second," Taylor said. "What's your thinking, Sarah? That it might get back to him?"

"I think we've got to consider the possibility—however remote—that certain *white* South Africans might be the ones hiring Herr Fürst."

"White South Africans are out of power," Vigiani said irritably.

Sarah gave Agent Vigiani a blank look. "I don't think it's quite that simple," she said calmly. "Who do you think mainly staffs the South African intelligence service? White South Africans. Anglos and Afrikaners. And they're not happy about how the rug was pulled out from under them."

Vigiani continued to scowl. Sarah noticed that Duke

Taylor's brow was furrowed, so she elaborated: "Say we contact the South African service and ask about a terrorist who calls himself Heinrich Fürst. And some group within that service is in fact running this agent for some nefarious purpose of its own. Suddenly you've set off all kinds of alarms."

Taylor grunted. "So if we're not going the official route to Pretoria, that rules out both State Department channels and our new legat." The FBI had sixteen legal attachés, or legats, in American embassies around the world, which exchange information with foreign police and intelligence agencies. For years the FBI did not have a legat in Pretoria, because of the sanctions applied by the U.S. government. Only recently, since the election of Nelson Mandela as president, had the FBI opened an office there. "We need to reach out and touch some people. Some trusted, private source."

"Do we have a paid asset over there?" Sarah asked.

"Not that I know of. I'll ask around, but I don't think so. At least, not a paid asset high enough in the government."

"Someone with whom the Bureau or the Agency or the government has a relationship, someone reliable?"

"We'll have to shake the bushes. But the first step is to set up an elite, completely secret task force, Sarah, and I'd like you to be on it."

"Where? In New York?"

"Right here," Taylor said.

"I've got a little boy, remember?" Sarah said.

"He's portable. Anyway, it's summer. He's not in school now, is he?"

"No," Sarah said. "But I'd really rather not."

Taylor regarded her for a moment in puzzled silence. In the old days—during the Hoover era—it was unheard of for an agent to refuse an assignment. In the old days, you'd be told, "You want your paycheck, it'll be in Washington in thirty days." They'd have said, "We didn't issue you a son. You want him, bring him."

"Agent Cahill," Taylor said icily, "if our intelligence is accurate, we're looking at a major act of terrorism that's going to take place in New York City in a matter of weeks. You want to tell me what the heck you're working on that's more important, more urgent, than *that*?"

Surprised by his sudden intensity, Sarah sat up straight. She leaned forward and said, returning intensity for intensity: "You're asking me to disrupt my life, pack up my boy, and move out of Boston for what could be weeks or months. Okay, fair enough. But to work here? In Washington? Why don't we set up shop in Altoona?"

"Excuse me?" Taylor said incredulously.

Agents Ullman and Vigiani watched the exchange with fascination, spectators at a bullfight.

"If the terrorism is to occur in New York, we've got to be in New York. You want to do a search, that takes massive shoeleather. That means working closely with the NYPD. It's crazy to be in D.C."

"Sarah, all the resources are here, the computers, the secure links—"

"For God's sake, I had secure links with the Bureau when I was in Jackson, Mississippi, just out of New Agents school. You mean to tell me you can't do that in New York City? I don't believe it."

"Then you're talking about running a secret Ops center out of 26 Federal Plaza," Taylor said. 26 Federal Plaza was the headquarters of the New York office of the FBI.

"Why not take out a full-page ad in *The New York Times*?" Sarah said.

"*Excuse* me?"

"If you want to keep it secret, forget about 26 Federal Plaza. We've got to find another location in the city."

"I take it from your use of 'we' that you accept."

"With a couple of conditions."

Vigiani shook her head in disgust. Ullman studied his notes.

"Such as?"

"We're off-site, for one."

"That's incredibly expensive."

"Look, we're going to need a lot of phone lines, some secure phones. NYO isn't going to have the facilities anyway."

"All right. I'm sure the New York office has something available. What else?"

"I'd like to bring a couple of people with me. A friend of mine on the OC squad, Ken Alton. He's a computer whiz, and we may need his skills."

"Done," Taylor said. "And?"

"Alexander Pappas."

"Alex Pappas?" Taylor said. "I thought he retired a couple of years ago."

"Last year, actually."

"What would he think about going back on the job?"

"I could twist his arm," Sarah said, "but I think he'd secretly jump at the chance. They called him in on TRADEBOM." This was the Bureau designation for the World Trade Center bombing.

"Well, it's highly unusual, but I suppose it can be arranged. All right. So you're on?"

"Yeah," Sarah said. "I'm on."

"Good. Now, how about leading it?"

CHAPTER THIRTY-TWO

The components of a sophisticated bomb are not difficult to obtain. Quite the opposite: the fuse components, wires, and fittings can easily be purchased at any electronics supply shop. Explosives and blasting caps are available at most construction sites.

But the fusing mechanism—the device that fires the bomb at a specified time or under specified conditions—is a far trickier thing. Often it is constructed uniquely for each bomb. It must function under set circumstances with a high degree of reliability. In fact, it takes a good deal of skill to construct a reliable fusing mechanism. For this reason, most terrorists or operatives would no sooner think of assembling their own fusing mechanisms than building their own automobiles. You can't be expert at everything.

Baumann arrived in the small industrial city of Huy, in a manufacturing belt southwest of Liège, by sunrise as he'd planned. The proprietor of a stationery store directed him to the modern brick multistoried building that housed Carabine Automatique of Liège (CAL), a small manufacturer of assault rifles and related components that had long since relocated to Huy, but had kept its name. Although he had no interest in assault rifles, he had made an appointment to see the marketing director, Etienne Charreyron.

It had been easy to arrange the meeting. Posing over the telephone as a British subject named Anthony Rhys-Davies, Baumann had explained that he was a munitions salesman for Royal Ordnance, the vast British arms manufacturer that makes virtually all the small arms for the British military. He was, he explained, a military-history buff on holiday, making a tour of famous Belgian battlefields. But he was mixing business with pleasure and thought he'd stop by to meet Mr. Charreyron and discuss the possibilities of doing business with Royal Ordnance. It would not look at all strange for a businessman on vacation to be dressed in casual attire.

Mr. Charreyron, of course, was happy to arrange a meeting at any time convenient for the British salesman. The possibilities were irresistible. Charreyron's secretary was expecting Mr. Rhys-Davies and greeted him cordially, taking his overcoat and offering him coffee or tea before showing him into Charreyron's cramped office.

Baumann went to shake Charreyron's hand and momentarily started. It was bound to happen, in the small and insular world in which he operated. He and Etienne Cherreyron had known each other years before, though under different names. This was potentially a disaster. Baumann's head spun.

Etienne Charreyron reacted as if he'd seen a ghastly apparition. "What—you—I thought you were dead!" he gasped.

Baumann, who had quickly gained an outward semblance of composure, smiled. "Sometimes I feel that way, but I'm very much alive."

"But you—Luanda—Christ Almighty—!"

For the next ten seconds or so, Charreyron did little

more than babble and stare in horror and incomprehension. His secretary stood in the doorway, uncertain what to do, until he dismissed her with a wave of his pudgy hand.

Ten years earlier, Charreyron and Baumann had served together in Angola. A former Portuguese colony, Angola had since 1976 been racked by civil war, with the Cuban-supported, Marxist MPLA battling the pro-Western UNITA forces, aided by South Africa.

Baumann's employers had sent him there to help orchestrate a covert campaign of terrorism. There he had met a bomb-disposal specialist who went by the nom de guerre Hercule, a mere who had once worked for the Belgian police.

Back in the 1960s, Baumann later learned, this Hercule had built bombs for the legendary mercenary leader Mike O'Hore, the South African leader of the Fifth Commando, nicknamed the Wild Geese. Baumann had always considered O'Hore, whose exploits were world-famous, something of a slacker, a slob whose greatest skill was getting himself good press. But his bomb makers were always the best.

When it became necessary for Baumann to disappear from Angola, he had arranged an "accident" outside the capital city, Luanda, in which it appeared that he had been ambushed and killed. All the other mercs, including, no doubt, Hercule—who knew Baumann only under another name—had always believed that he was dead, one of the many casualties of war.

Bomb-disposal experts are a strange breed. They do their harrowing work in odd corners of the world, traveling to where the work is, often on contract for various governments. Many of them were brought in to clear land mines in Cambodia in the 1970s; in Angola, most of the land mines were cleared by Germans, although a few Belgians were brought in as well. After the Gulf

War, the Kuwaiti government contracted with Royal Ordnance for an enormous number of bomb-disposal specialists to clear the leftover munitions. Their work is so stressful that many of them—those who escape unharmed—retire as soon as they can find good work elsewhere. Baumann now learned that this Hercule/Charreyron had left this hazardous line of work in the early eighties, when he was hired by the small Belgian firm Carabine Automatique of Liège.

"My God, it's great to see you," Charreyron at last exclaimed. "This is—this is just amazing! Please, sit."

"And you too," Baumann said, sinking into a chair.

"Yes," Charreyron said, as he sat behind his desk. "How marvelous it is to see you again!" He was brave, genial, and clearly terrified. "But I don't understand. You—well, the report of your death was some sort of disinformation, is that right?"

Baumann nodded, seemingly pleased to be sharing this secret with his old comrade in arms.

"I take it Rhys-Davies is a cover name, then?"

"Exactly," Baumann said. He confided to the Belgian a fabricated, though plausible, story of his defection from South Africa to Australia and eventually to England, his hush-hush security work on behalf of a London-based sheik. "Now, this client of mine has asked me to undertake a highly sensitive project," he went on, and explained the fusing mechanism that he needed to have built.

"But really, I haven't done that sort of work for a few years now," Charreyron protested mildly.

"I suspect it's like riding a bicycle," Baumann said. "You never forget. And the technology has changed little if at all in the last few years."

"Yes, but . . ." His voice trailed off as he listened to Baumann, taking notes all the while.

"The relay," Baumann said, "must be attached to a

pocket pager. When the pager receives a signal, it will cause the relay to close, which will close the circuit between battery and detonator."

"Won't you need some means of disabling it?"

"Yes, but I want to set the electronic timer to go off automatically if it's not disabled."

Charreyron, his composure returned, simply shrugged nonchalantly.

"One more thing," Baumann said. "There must also be a microwave sensor built into the mechanism that will set off the bomb if anyone approaches."

Charreyron nodded again, arching his brows in mild surprise.

"I will need three of them," Baumann said. "One for testing purposes, and the other two to be sent, separately."

"Yes, of course."

"Now, as to price."

"Yes," the Belgian said. He did some rapid calculations and then announced a large sum in Belgian francs.

Baumann arched his eyebrows in surprise. Fusing mechanisms of such complexity generally went for about ten thousand dollars apiece, and he did not like to be cheated.

"You see," Charreyron explained, "the difficulty lies in acquiring the pagers. You will need three of them, and they must be purchased in the United States. You know how complicated that is—with every pager comes a telephone number and a detailed registration. They must be bought clandestinely. And since I certainly don't want the serial number plate on the pager to be traced through the paging company back to me, I'll have to purchase several and do some alterations."

"But for an old friend . . . ?" Baumann said jovially. Haggling over prices was common in this line of work; the Belgian would expect it.

"I can go as low as fifteen thousand each. But less than that, and it's simply not worth the risk. I will have to go to New York myself to get them, so I have to figure in the cost of travel. And you are asking me to do all this in such a short period of time—"

"All right then," Baumann said. "Forty-five thousand U.S. it is. No, let's make it an even fifty thousand U.S."

The two men shook hands. For the first time, Charreyron appeared relaxed. Baumann counted out twenty-five thousand dollars and placed them on the desk. "The other half when I return in a week. Is there a vacant warehouse on the outskirts of town where we can do a test?"

"Certainly," Charreyron said. "But I think we have a little more business to transact."

"Oh?"

"For an additional fifty thousand U.S., I can assure you that nothing of our past acquaintance will become known."

"Fifty thousand?" Baumann asked, as if seriously considering it.

"And then"—Charreyron clapped his hands together—"the past is gone, just like that."

"I see," Baumann said. "Please understand something. I have many police contacts who stand to benefit handsomely by giving me any information of possible interest to me. Rumors, reports of my presence here, that sort of thing. I am paying you well, with a generous bonus to come. But I don't want to learn that the slightest detail of our talk, or of my past history, has left this office. Not a single detail. You can imagine the consequences for you and your family."

The color drained from Charreyron's face. "I'm a professional," he said, retreating hastily. "I would never betray a confidence."

"Excellent. Because you know me, and you know that I would stop at nothing."

Charreyron shook his head violently. "I would never say a word," he said desperately. "Please. Forget what I said about the fifty thousand. It was a foolish mistake."

"Don't worry," Baumann said pleasantly. "It's forgotten. We all make mistakes. But please don't make the mistake of underestimating me."

"Please," Charreyron whispered. In his days as a bomb-disposal expert, he had constantly faced the possibility of losing a limb, even his life. But nothing terrified him so much as this phlegmatic, ruthless South African, who had suddenly appeared in his office after ten years—a man who, Charreyron had no doubt whatsoever, would indeed stop at nothing.

CHAPTER THIRTY-THREE

A few days after Baumann's first visit to Charreyron, in southwest Belgium, he returned to inspect the fusing mechanisms.

In the intervening time, he had combined a little business with a great deal of relaxation. On his first night back in Amsterdam, he met again with "Bones" Van den Vondel, who provided him with the three sets of stolen documentation he had requested—two American, one British—and a small bundle of credit cards. Bones made it abundantly clear he was happy to do business with Mr. Sidney Lerner, and happier still to have the opportunity to do an ongoing business with the Mossad, should it require any other assistance from an outsider.

Several mornings he slept late. He saw movies, enjoyed expensive restaurants. Several afternoons he spent studying maps of New York City. He took in a few topless bars around Rembrandtsplein and, in the red-light district, bought himself an hour of pleasure with a young prostitute. One night he went to a popular nightclub called Odeon, where he picked up a comely young woman and took her back to his hotel. She was about as randy as he was; they spent most of the night having sex, until each collapsed in happy exhaustion. In the morning, she wanted to stay, or at least to see him again that evening. He was tempted—during his years in Pollsmoor he had almost forgotten how pleasurable sex could be—but knew it was a bad idea to become too familiar to anyone here. He told her he had, regrettably, to catch a return flight that afternoon.

Amsterdam, like New York and San Francisco, is world-renowned as a gathering place for computer enthusiasts, or "hackers." Although Baumann had been in prison too long to be conversant in the latest technology, he knew where to find someone who was. He contacted a member of the Amsterdam-based Dutch organization Hacktic, which publishes a magazine for computer hackers, and arranged a meeting. He described the sort of person he was looking for: a hacker based in New York, without a criminal past.

"No," he was told, "you are looking for a *cracker*—not a hacker. A hacker makes it his mission to understand, shall we say, undocumented technology, so that the government doesn't enslave us, and to make the world a better place. A cracker has the same skills but uses them, so to speak, to break into your house, often for mercenary purposes."

"All right, then, a cracker," Baumann said.

"I have a name for you," his contact said. "But he will only take on your project, whatever it is, if he finds it of interest—and enormously lucrative."

"Oh, that he will," said Baumann. "He will find it both."

On his second-to-last morning in Amsterdam, he purchased a small device at a large electronics supply house for one thousand guilders, which was then equivalent to six hundred dollars. It was an "ATM Junior," used by banks to encode magnetic strips on bank and credit cards. With this device he recoded the magnetic strips on each stolen credit card.

When a credit card is used at a retail establishment, it is usually swiped through a transponder, which reads the CVC number at the head of the magnetic stripe and immediately sends it over a telephone line to the credit card company's central data-processing facility. The computers there check whether the card in question is expired, overextended, or stolen. If it is not, the computers send back an approval code within a second or two. (American Express uses two-digit approval codes, while Visa and MasterCard use four- or five-digit ones.)

Baumann had little doubt that most if not all of these credit cards had already been reported as stolen. If they hadn't yet, it was simply a matter of time.

But he had circumvented that process. Each credit card now had an approval code of the appropriate number of digits encoded in its magnetic stripe. Whenever a merchant swiped one of these cards through the transponder, the approval code would instantly appear on the transponder's readout. The machine would read the code—not send it out.

It was highly unlikely the merchant would wonder why the telephone hadn't dialed, why several seconds hadn't elapsed before the approval code came in. And if that happened, why, Baumann would remark that the magnetic stripe on the back of the card must have worn out. Too bad. And that would be the end of that. An excellent chance of success, with virtually no risk.

In his remaining time, Baumann ordered several sets of letterhead stationery for several notional, amorphous firms—an import-export company, a law firm, a storage facility.

And he reserved a seat on a Sabena flight from Brussels to London under a false name for which he had no documentation, knowing that, so long as he traveled within the European Commonwealth, he would not be required to show a passport. Then he booked a coach seat from London to New York under the name of one of his newly acquired American passports, that of a businessman and entrepreneur named Thomas Allen Moffatt.

Etienne Charreyron had arranged to use a deserted horse barn on the outskirts of Huy that belonged to a business associate who was in Brussels for the entire month. The associate had recently liquidated all of his family's livestock at auction.

The barn still smelled strongly of horse manure and damp hay and machine oil. The lighting was barely adequate. In the dim, dank interior, Charreyron opened a battered leather suitcase and gingerly removed three black plastic utility boxes the size of shoeboxes. The lid of each was a plate of brushed aluminum, and on this plate were three tiny bulbs, light-emitting diodes.

"This light tells you that the pocket pager is on and functioning," Charreyron explained to Baumann. "This one tells you that the battery is emitting power. And this one indicates that the timer is functioning."

Charreyron slid the aluminum plate off one of the fusing mechanisms. "I've set up two separate systems on opposite sides, for redundancy. Two nine-volt batteries, two sets of two screw posts each to connect to the blasting caps. Two timers, two pager-receivers set to the same frequency, two relays. Even two ferrite bars for antennae." He looked up. "It will beat the bomb-disposal people. Doubles the chances of the thing working, hmm?"

"And one microwave sensor."

"That's all there's room for, and certainly all you'll need."

"Shall we test one of them?"

"Yes, of course." Charreyron lifted one of the black boxes.

"Actually," Baumann said, grabbing another, "let's try this one."

Charreyron smiled slyly, seeming to enjoy the sport. "Whatever you like."

He brought the box over to an empty fifty-five-gallon steel drum at the far end of the barn and put it on a narrow wooden plank that had been placed across the open top of the barrel. He attached two blasting caps to it, then walked to the other side of the barn.

"First test," the Belgian said, "is for radio control."

He took a small cellular phone from his breast pocket, opened it, and dialed a number. As soon as he had done so, he looked at his watch. Baumann did the same.

The two men waited in silence.

Forty-five seconds later the barn echoed with the sound of a gunshot. The blasting caps that dangled from the fusing mechanism had detonated, giving off fragments that were contained by the steel barrel.

"A long delay," Baumann observed.

"It varies."

"Yes." The detonator that set off the blasting caps had been armed by a circuit that closed when the built-in pager received a signal sent by satellite. Depending on how much satellite traffic there was at any given moment, the page signal could be received in a few seconds or a few minutes. "What about the microwave sensor?"

"Certainly." Charreyron walked across the barn to the steel barrel and attached a fresh set of blasting caps to the fusing mechanism. He rearmed it and pushed a button to activate a time-delay switch.

"As soon as the timer runs down, the microwave sensor is armed. You can set the time delay for as short as ten seconds."

"And as long as—?"

"Seventy-two hours. But if you need a longer delay, I can easily replace it."

"No, that'll do."

"Good. I've set this for ten seconds. And now, the microwave—yes." From across the dim expanse, Baumann could see a red light wink on. "It's armed now. Would you like to . . . ?"

"Distance?"

"Twenty-five feet, but that too can be adjusted."

Baumann walked slowly toward the steel drum, then stopped approximately thirty feet from it. Then he approached step by step, until he was startled by the loud explosion of the blasting caps.

"Very precise," he said.

"It's top-quality," Charreyron said, permitting himself a proud smile.

"You do good work. But what about the signature, as we discussed?"

"That took me quite some time to research. But I came up with a rather convincing Libyan signature."

Most explosive devices leave "signatures" that permit an investigator to determine who originated them. They might be how the knots are tied, how connections are soldered, how wires are cut.

The Provisional Irish Republican Army, for instance, makes its bomb fuses in lots of a hundred or so. A number of PIRA technicians get together in a warehouse or barn and work without stop for a few days, making identical fuses, which are then parceled out. This has been confirmed both by intelligence and by inspecting the fusing mechanisms of unexploded PIRA bombs: one can tell from the identical, if minuscule, markings that every wire has been cut with the same pair of wirecutters. Some terrorist groups leave a signature unintentionally, out of sloppiness, because they have always constructed a bomb in a certain way. Some, however, do so deliberately, as a subtle way to claim credit.

"Now, as for shipping," the Belgian said. "You're certainly welcome to take them with you, but I assume you don't want to take that risk."

Baumann gave a small snort of derision.

"I didn't think so. The entire assembly can be broken down into its components, which all clip rather neatly into place. I'll go over it with you. That makes it easy to ship."

"But you won't ship them from Liège."

"That would not be discreet," Charreyron said, "given what Liège is known for. No, I will send them from Brussels. Concealed, let's say, in some harmless electronic thing like a radio. Overnight express, if you like. You simply give me an address."

"Fine."

"And—uh—there's the matter of payment. The pagers cost a bit more than I calculated."

Baumann removed an envelope of bills and counted out the amount Charreyron asked for. It was a reasonable sum—about 30 percent more than his original estimate. The Belgian was not trying to pull a fast one.

"Excellent," Charreyron said, as he pocketed the money.

"Well, then," Baumann said heartily, "please give my best to your lovely wife, Marie. Isn't she a curator at the Curtius Museum?"

Charreyron stared dully.

"And little Berthe—six years old and a student at the *école normale*, is that right? You must be proud."

"What the hell are you hinting at?"

"Just this, my friend. I know the address of your apartment on Rue Saint-Gilles. I know where your daughter is at this very moment, where your wife is. Remember what I said: if the slightest detail of our dealings is made known to *anyone*, the consequences for you and your family will be unimaginable. I will stop at nothing."

"Oh, please, not another word," said the Belgian, ashen-faced. "That is understood."

As they strolled out of the barn and into the blindingly bright afternoon daylight, Baumann considered whether to kill the man. There was a mild, cool breeze and the pleasant smell of newly mown grass.

Life is a series of gambles, Baumann reflected. Charreyron would not benefit in any way from turning in a South African mercenary whose name he didn't even know, and would certainly not wish to let the authorities know of his own past involvement in Luanda. And the threat to his family's well-being would be persuasive.

No, Charreyron would live. Baumann shook his hand cordially, got into his rented car, and drove off. Doing business with someone he knew from another life was an enormous risk—but so too had been his escape from Pollsmoor. He could not proceed with this undertaking until he knew for certain whether his whereabouts remained unknown.

There were ways to find out. He had been driving through the Meuse Valley, along the Sambre River, which meets the Meuse River at Namur. This stretch of the road was breathtakingly beautiful, with high cliffs and canals, farmhouses and the ruins of ancient brick buildings. After he'd passed through Andenne, and before he'd reached Namur, he pulled off the road and drove around until he located a long stretch of woods, a line of trees beside a clearing. There he switched off the engine.

CHAPTER THIRTY-FOUR

Of the fifty-six FBI field offices and four hundred resident agencies throughout the United States and Puerto Rico, the New York office is generally considered both the best assignment and the worst. From the ABSCAM convictions against members of Congress for taking bribes, to the siege against the five major Mafia families, to the bombing of the World Trade Center, New York has always had the sexiest cases.

New York is the largest of the field offices, with some twelve hundred agents. It occupies eight floors of the Jacob J. Javits Federal Building, at 26 Federal Plaza in lower Manhattan. Unlike all the other field offices, New York is headed not by a special agent in charge but by an assistant FBI director, because it is both bigger and more important than the others.

Sarah had always found the Javits building gloomy. Tall and plain, with a facing of black stone alternating with sandstone, it is set in the middle of a forlorn cement "park" studded with concrete planters holding marigolds, ferns, and petunias—some landscape designer's valiant attempt to make the setting cheery. Pigeons skitter across the broad granite ledges around a reflecting pool.

On her first morning, she arrived before eight, already perspiring from the heat. The one-bedroom furnished apartment she was subletting was on West Seventy-first Street near Columbus Avenue, very close to the subway stop, a Gray's Papaya, several decent pizza places, and a Greek coffee shop. For the first couple of days, she had lived on nothing but Greek salads and slices of pizza. What else could you ask for?

Daylight, perhaps? Somehow, by some ingenious stroke of architecture, all of the apartment windows gave onto shadowed air shafts. It was always midnight in her small bedroom, in the cheaply furnished living/dining room, dark enough to grow mushrooms.

For the first time in years, Sarah was living alone. It was disorienting, at times lonely, but not entirely unpleasant. She'd stayed up late the night before, reading in the tub and drinking wine. She played a recording of the Beethoven late quartets she'd picked up at Tower Records and listened to it until it began to sound like Philip Glass.

Jared was away at camp in upstate New York. For months he'd demanded to go to summer sleep-over camp, and she had kept refusing. The money was too tight these days, she'd explained; he could go to day camp near Boston.

But with the sudden transfer to New York, and the wrench that threw into her son's life, she had to scrape together the money. The new assignment brought with it an increase in salary, which made paying for camp feasible. Anyway, it was certainly better for him to spend a couple of weeks in camp (though he'd wanted a month) than to live in New York City, not a place for eight-year-old boys, she thought.

The lobby of 26 Federal Plaza was cavernous, with high marble walls, several long elevator banks, cash machines. She felt small. She presented her credentials at the reception desk, and was directed to Counterter-rorism, in a corner of the twenty-third floor.

A very tall, thin, good-looking man of forty intro-duced himself as Harry Whitman, the chief of the Joint Terrorist Task Force. He wore a khaki summer-weight suit with a standard-issue white shirt and, the one grace note, a bright turquoise tie.

"So, you're Sarah Cahill," he said. "Welcome."

"Thanks."

His office was sparsely decorated with a small, auto-graphed photo of Hoover—not a good sign, Sarah mused—and, for some reason, a large official photo of George Bush in a fake-gilt frame, propped on its side against the side of his desk. Bush had been out of office for years. Definitely not a good sign.

"You and the rest of the special task force will be lo-cated off-site," he said. "I'll introduce you to the others in a couple of minutes, and explain how the joint task force operates. You're in charge of a code-name opera-tion. But first things first. I guess Perry Taylor in D.C. liked you, but he likes you even more now."

"Why?"

"Thanks to your suggestion, Perry shook the bushes in South Africa for a lead on your terrorist."

"And?"

"We've got a name. By tomorrow morning we should have a face."

She felt her heart start to thud. "A name . . . ?"

"His name is Henrik Baumann."

CHAPTER THIRTY-FIVE

Baumann hiked around the perimeter of the clearing, satisfied no one was around, that no one could come upon him unexpectedly. From the truck he pulled out the MLink-5000, the satellite telephone that resembled a metal briefcase. He placed it on the roof of the car and unfolded it. The top, which flipped open like a book, was the flat-plate antenna. It was much less conspicuous than the older models whose antennas were large dishes.

Since the transmitter's beam width was much broader than that of the older models, aiming accuracy was much less crucial. As he adjusted the angle of elevation, he studied the little boxes on the LCD readout that indicated signal strength. When he had maximum signal strength, he turned the thumbscrews on the back panel and removed the handset.

Then he placed a telephone call.

From his years in South African intelligence, he knew the workings of the government of South Africa. He knew that any search for his whereabouts would move in one of two directions. It would either be instigated by South Africa and reach outward, or it would be instigated by another country and be directed *toward* South Africa.

The first direction—a request coming from South Africa and going to security and law-enforcement services around the world—was by far the more likely. A former member of BOSS had broken out of prison, had likely left the country: the South Africans would request help.

Less likely, but far more worrisome, was the second possibility—that some law-enforcement or intelligence agency had learned something about him and had turned to South Africa for help. This would most certainly indicate a leak in Dyson's coterie.

When governments deal with other governments, they almost always go through established channels. An official request to the South African government for information on one Henrik Baumann might come through diplomatic or intelligence channels; it might be sent to the attorney general, or directly to the South African police. But no matter where it was pointed, it would be funneled to one place. All prisoner records, including court statements, photographs, and the standard fingerprint record, S.A.P. 69, are stored in the centralized records of the South African Criminal Bureau in Pretoria. The Criminal Bureau, however, was a large bureaucracy. A request for records might be handled by any of a dozen or more people.

But a far smaller staff was employed at the Department of Customs and Excise, Baumann knew, processing and handling passport applications. Any thorough search for information on him would include a request for his original passport application. Years ago, there was just one person, a stout Afrikaner whose name Baumann had long since forgotten, who handled requests for copies of these applications.

The clerk in charge was no doubt a different person

by now. But there probably was still just one clerk in charge.

By his second call, he had reached the customs clerk in charge of passport application requests, a pleasant-voiced woman.

"This is Gordon Day from Interpol in Lyons. I'm following up on a request . . ."

"Sorry," the clerk said politely when Baumann had stated his business. "We're not supposed to deal directly with outside agencies—"

"Right," he said, the jolly British civil servant, "but you see, the thing of it is, the request has already been made, and I need to know whether the documents have been *sent*, is all, because there seems to be some foul-up on our end here, at headquarters."

"I haven't gotten any request from Interpol concerning a passport of that number," she said.

"Are you quite sure?" Baumann insisted.

"Yes, Mr. Day, I'm quite sure, but if you send me a fax with—"

"Is there another agency the request might have ended up at?"

"Not that I know of, sir."

"Oh, dear. Well, is it possible that our request was filed with another country's, like the French, maybe, or—"

"No, sir. The only request for that application I've received came from the American FBI."

"Ah," Baumann said triumphantly. "That makes sense. They put in the request to us, as well. Was the requesting officer a Mr. . . . Mr. . . . I must have it here somewhere . . ."

"Taylor, sir, from Counterterrorism?"

"Taylor! Right. Well, that certainly clears *that* up. Thanks so much for your help."

"Yes, sir, my pleasure."

Counterterrorism. The FBI. The Americans were on to him. A change in plan was most definitely necessary.

He would not fly to New York. No, that would not do at all. That would be a mistake.

He would fly to Washington.

CHAPTER THIRTY-SIX

Twenty years ago or so, Harry Whitman explained, an agent in the Criminal Division had attended the FBI Academy with a South African policeman. The FBI National Academy runs an intensive fifteen-week program at Quantico, Virginia, to train midlevel police officials in the latest investigative techniques. Out of the one hundred law-enforcement officials in each class, fifteen or twenty are foreign.

"This South African guy, name of Sachs, had gone to three FBI-run retraining sessions in Europe, so our people'd had a little bit of contact with him," Whitman said. He and Sarah stood at the entrance to his office. "We checked him out with State and the Agency, to see if maybe the guy went bad. Negative. Luckily for us, this Sachs fellow's now in the security services, so we got a line right into the heart of darkness. Had someone on the CIA team in Johannesburg make contact, real unofficial."

"The CIA guy asked the South African cop for information on the alias Heinrich Fürst?"

Whitman nodded. "And anything else he could get. Taylor's thinking was that if there was something rotten going on and our contact was party to it, this contact would trigger a flurry of communications. Right after our man met with this guy, we laid on the surveillance. Had the satellite cowboys monitor all signals traffic into and out of South Africa, checking the frequency of cable traffic to their embassy here."

"And?"

"And nothing unusual went out. No frantic calls or telexes. You can't prove a negative, but it's a good sign the contact's clean."

"Maybe."

"Next morning he came back to us with a name. Nothing on any Heinrich Fürst, but 'Prince of Darkness,' yes, oh my yes. 'Everyone in the intelligence service knows who *that* is—fellow named Henrik Baumann.' Code name, or cryptonym, is—or was—Zero, designating their most skilled agent. So we had our legat make an official request to several branches of the South African government, the attorney general, the police, blah blah blah, for all records on one Henrik Baumann. Passport applications, birth certificate, files, the works. Now we sit and wait. See if we really do have our man."

"Are they being cooperative?" Sarah asked.

"Are you kidding? They're frantic! They're all alarmed that a former South African agent may be involved in terrorism. Especially a white guy left over from the old regime. They love to dump shit on the old government. Actually, I should call the Communications Center, see if anything came in."

He picked up his desk phone and pressed a button. Sarah examined the discarded photograph of George Bush and wondered how long it had been resting on its side. Since Clinton's inauguration?

"*I* see," Whitman was saying to the telephone handset. "*I* see." His eyebrows were arched.

Sarah looked up at him curiously, trying to interpret his tone.

Whitman hung up the phone and looked directly at her with a peculiar smile. "We've got a full set of prints—"

"Great."

"—and a kink in the fishing line. Just over three weeks ago, our Mr. Baumann escaped from maximum-security lockup at Pollsmoor Prison. Pollsmoor police detectives discovered he was missing, found a couple of bodies, and opened an Escaping Docket to investigate an escape from lawful custody. They followed standard procedure— Form SAP-69, with the fugitive's fingerprints, and a dossier containing court statements and other records were sent over from central records at the South African Criminal Bureau in Pretoria. But nothing turned up, not a trace of our friend. The South Africans normally don't reach out to the international authorities in the case of an escaped prisoner, even a former member of their own security services. They'd all but given up looking for him, even put out a burn notice on the guy. Anyway, I'd say we've got the right man. Now let me take you to your lovely suite of offices and introduce you to the happy campers you'll be working with."

The "lovely suite of offices," as Harry Whitman had put it, was the penthouse of a decrepit building in midtown Manhattan, on West Thirty-seventh Street near Seventh Avenue. The neighborhood was lousy, the ancient clattering elevator even less promising.

Once Sarah got off the elevator at the penthouse, however, the scenery changed dramatically.

The site, which the FBI was renting from a company that sold display fixtures to retail stores and had recently relocated to Stamford, Connecticut, had last been used by the FBI for a Chinatown drug sting operation, and so the security was already in place. Sarah entered a reception area that was walled off from the rest of the floor. A phony name was on the wall.

A receptionist sat at a desk, Whitman explained, monitoring video cameras mounted in the hallways and fire stairs and buzzing in authorized visitors through the electronically controlled inner door. A volumetric alarm system was set up in the reception area; the rest of the space was alarmed with volumetric, passive infrared, and active point-to-point infrared systems. To allow people to work through the night in various parts of the offices, the alarm system was zoned. The safes were in one room, separately alarmed.

"Secure communications links," Whitman said as they entered what was once a showroom, now clearly the main command center. "This place cost us serious big bucks to set up, I might add, so I'm glad we're reusing it." He gave her a sidelong glance as if she were to blame. "Secure fax, secure computer terminal links, a line to the Watch Center at Langley, even a couple of Stus thrown in just for fun." "Stu" is intelligence-community lingo for STU, a secure telephone unit. In a separate room, also alarmed, were two STU-III secure telephones—black lines, as they are called, for calls up to the classification of top secret.

Several people Sarah didn't know were there, drinking coffee and reading the *Daily News* and the *New York Post*. The rest she recognized. Alex Pappas was engaged in animated, friendly conversation with Christine Vigiani from Counterterrorism in Washington. Both of them were smoking furiously. Russell Ullman from Washington was doing a crossword puzzle. Ken Alton was off by himself reading a book entitled *Schrödinger's Cat*, which she assumed was science fiction.

"All right," Whitman announced loudly, his hands thrust high in the air, waving for attention. "I assume everyone here has been detailed to the special working group of the Joint Terrorist Task Force. If you're not, you know too much already and I'm going to have to have you killed."

Polite chuckles all around. Whitman introduced himself and then everyone else to one another. Everyone in the room, Bureau or not, was wearing the FBI-regulation ID card, either clipped to a shirt or breast pocket or hanging from a metal chain around the neck. The FBI men were all wearing laminated dog tags and, so it seemed, Rockports.

Every FBI agent in the Joint Terrorist Task Force is paired with a New York City policeman. Sarah's partner was a paunchy, moon-faced police detective lieutenant named George Roth, who had a receding hairline, deep acne pits on identical spots on each cheek, broken capillaries spread across a bulbous nose, and a strong Brooklyn accent. He barely acknowledged her. He gave her an imperceptible nod and didn't shake her hand. He took a Breath Saver from a roll in his shirt pocket, popped it into his mouth, and lodged it against his left cheek.

Great to meet you too, Sarah thought.

Whitman sat on the edge of a desk and shoved aside an ancient-looking cup of coffee with a cigarette butt floating in it. "Okay, now, all of you were handpicked for this special group, but I've gotta lay down the law about secrecy right here and now. I can't stress enough how important secrecy is. A couple of you are from out of town, so you might not know what kind of shit will go down in this city if the word gets out that a major Wall Street bank *might* get hit with a major act of terrorism in two weeks. Panic like you've never seen. Those of you on the job know what that means.

"If you have to reach out to other departments in the city, don't tell 'em you're doing work on terrorism. You're looking for a fugitive, okay? And not a fucking word to the press, understood?"

There were nods, clearing of throats.

"When we were working on TRADEBOM, someone on the task force had a drinking buddy, a reporter for *Newsday*. Couldn't help blabbing. So what happens? *Newsday* runs an article about one of the terrorists we were going to arrest when we were good and ready, but no, now we had to swoop in on the guy way too early. Which screwed things up really bad. Now, that leak came from the full task force, which is big. There's only ten of you, so if there's a leak, you better believe I'm going to track it down. If any of you have drinking buddies in the press, I'd go on the wagon till this inquiry is completed."

The task force, he said, was code-named Operation MINOTAUR. He explained that the Minotaur was a mythological monster, ferociously strong, with the head of a bull and the body of a human. The Minotaur—he didn't bother to explain whether this was supposed to represent the terrorist they were after—fed exclusively on human flesh. It was perhaps an overly optimistic code name, for according to Greek mythology, the Minotaur was trapped in a place (the Labyrinth, constructed by Daedalus) from which it could not escape.

"Uh, how long is this 'special working group' supposed to go on for?" asked Lieutenant Roth. He gave "special working group" a heavy ironic emphasis. Sarah's heart sank at the thought of working with him.

"The director has approved a preliminary inquiry," Whitman said. "That means it's good for a hundred and twenty days. Theoretically, if there's good reason, it can be renewed for another ninety days. But I'd like to get this thing wrapped up way before that."

"Who wouldn't?" one of the agents mumbled.

"What do you mean, 'theoretically'?" Pappas asked.

"I mean, in our case Washington's giving us all of two weeks."

He was interrupted by a chorus of protests, whistles, catcalls. "You gotta be kidding," Christine Vigiani said.

"No, I'm not kidding. Two weeks, and then the search is shut down. And we don't even get a full-field. Now, for those of you new to the game, the main difference between a preliminary inquiry and a full-field inquiry is what you *can't* do. No wiretap. No surveillance. No trash cover."

"Can we ask people questions?" Roth said. "If we ask nice?"

Whitman ignored him. "Look, I know a task force of ten people is nothing. Some of you guys remember back in 1982 when they found cyanide in Tylenol, and this guy was extorting a million bucks from Johnson & Johnson. The New York office put three *hundred* agents on the search, from Criminal and Counterintelligence. I think a ten-man force is bullshit, but I guess Washington's trying out a small, flexible task force that's not as hamstrung by red tape and all that." He shrugged. "I don't make policy."

"Correct me if I'm wrong," Lieutenant Roth said mordantly, "but would it be accurate to say that we don't have jack shit on this guy? I mean, we don't even have this guy's *name*."

"Not quite," Sarah said. The others turned around to face her. She explained what they'd just received from Johannesburg.

Instead of the outburst of excitement or appreciation that she expected, there was a beat of silence, and then Agent Vigiani spoke.

"This guy escaped from prison in South Africa more than two *weeks* ago and we never heard about it?" she asked bitterly. "They didn't send out a heads-up, didn't alert Interpol, *nothing*? I don't get it."

"I doubt it was deliberate," Sarah said. "South Africa's been an outcast for so long that they're not used to sharing their internal problems with the international authorities. They haven't exactly gotten their act together."

"Oh, well, this is quite a relief," said Lieutenant George Roth. "Now we have a *name*. All we have to do is ask around—if we're permitted to do that—to see if anyone happens to know a terrorist named Henrik Baumann. Makes our job *so* much easier."

"A lead's a lead," Sarah said irritably.

"Your job is just about impossible," Whitman agreed. "Yes, we have a name, and we'll soon have prints, maybe even a photo. But we're still searching for a needle in a haystack."

"A needle in a haystack?" Lieutenant Roth replied. "More like trying to find a short shaft of wheat in a field that might be anywhere in Nebraska."

"We'll never find the guy with that attitude," Harry Whitman said. "You've got to believe the guy's out there. Each of you has to think of yourself as the fugitive. What he's doing, what he's planning, what he might have to buy, where he might be living. And everyone makes mistakes."

"From what you're telling me," Lieutenant Roth said, "this guy doesn't."

Sarah spoke without looking up. "No. He'll make a mistake. We just have to catch him at it."

CHAPTER THIRTY-SEVEN

During the lunch hour on February 26, 1993, at 12:18 p.m., a bomb concealed in a rented yellow Ryder truck exploded in level B-2 of the parking garage of the World Trade Center in lower Manhattan. An estimated fifty thousand people were inside the 110-story skyscraper, one of the World Trade Center's seven buildings, at the time. Tens of thousands were stranded in offices, stairwells, and elevators as a result of the explosion, including seventeen kindergartners from P.S. 95 in Brooklyn, who were trapped in an elevator. A thousand people were injured, mostly from smoke inhalation, and six were killed. One of the great symbols of New York City sustained almost a billion dollars' worth of damage.

After a painstaking investigation, eight men were subsequently arrested, of whom four were convicted of the bombing after an extraordinary five-month trial during which 207 witnesses were called, ten thousand pages of evidence amassed. The four men, all Arab immigrants, were followers of a blind Muslim cleric in a New Jersey mosque.

This was the worst act of terrorism ever to hit the United States up till that point. The bomb, which was built by amateurs, consisted of twelve hundred pounds of explosive material and three cylinders of hydrogen gas. It cost less than four hundred dollars to make.

Terrorism experts (an enormous number of them seemed to spring up all at once) all announced that America had lost its innocence, that America's cities had become fortresses. The security in major buildings, particularly landmarks, was enhanced. Parking garages were no longer quite so easy for just anyone to enter. Concrete stanchions were placed around public spaces so cars could not drive into them. Incoming packages were X-rayed. Visitor passes and employee identification cards were checked more rigorously.

Unfortunately, that heightened vigilance lasted for only a few months. Although the new security cameras and the concrete stanchions remained in place, the shock of the World Trade Center bombing gradually faded, and people returned to life as usual.

The terrorism experts declared that America had finally joined the ranks of Europe, Latin America, and the Middle East, where terrorism is a regular occurrence. Actually, the United States had seen terrorism before.

There had been a few isolated incidents: in Chicago in 1886, a bomb exploded in a crowd of policemen; in 1920, a bomb went off on Wall Street. In the late 1960s and early 1970s, there was a wave of leftist-radical bombings, but they were sparse, mostly done by the Weather Underground faction of the Students for a Democratic Society and other members of the "white left," who'd launched a campaign of urban terrorism hoping to spark a revolution. In a famous 1970 incident, leftist radicals had blown up the University of Wisconsin Army Research Center with a crude bomb made of diesel fuel and fertilizer. But the Weathermen dissolved in 1976 as a result of internal squabbling and by 1980 had more or less ceased to exist.

During the 1970s, the world was swept by terrorism,

but the continental United States was mostly left alone, with the exception of a series of attacks, from the mid-seventies to the early eighties, by the Puerto Rican independence group FALN. Most of the Puerto Rican attacks, however, were limited to Puerto Rico. In 1980, in fact, more Americans were killed by lightning than by terrorism—and that was, worldwide, a big year for terrorism.

From time to time in recent years, America has gone through terrorism scares—in 1983, when a U.S. warship accidentally shot down an Iranian passenger plane, and in 1991 during the Persian Gulf War. But very little ever materialized. Of the five terrorist incidents on U.S. soil in 1991, none was associated with the Middle East. Four took place in Puerto Rico; the only one that happened in the continental United States was an attack on the Internal Revenue Service Center in Fresno, California, on April Fools' Day by a group calling itself Up the IRS, Inc.

In fact, in the thirty-four terrorist incidents recorded in the United States and Puerto Rico between 1987 and 1991, not a single person was killed or even injured.

So while the bombing of the World Trade Center certainly jarred America into the realization that terrorism could actually happen here, that realization faded all too quickly. By the end of 1994, America returned to its normal state of blissful unconcern.

And then, on April 19, 1995, came the bombing of the Alfred P. Murrah Federal Building in Oklahoma City, the worst domestic terrorist incident in U.S. history. Like TRADEBOM, the bomb was loaded onto a yellow Ryder rental truck. This one consisted of a ton of ammonium-nitrate fertilizer. It killed 167 people.

Fortunately, by the early 1980s the Federal Bureau of Investigation had begun to take terrorism seriously and had set up six Joint Terrorist Task Forces around the country. The largest was in New York City. It operated out of 26 Federal Plaza and was commanded jointly by the FBI and the New York City Police Department. And for more than a decade—until the Trade Center bomb—it went without an international incident, a "major special," as such significant attacks are called.

The composition of the Joint Terrorist Task Force is always precisely 50 percent FBI agents and 50 percent New York City police detectives. Under the Memorandum of Understanding that established the task force, the FBI is the lead agency. The police members are sworn in as federal marshals to enable them to handle federal violations. A lieutenant oversees the policemen; an FBI supervisor oversees the agents.

It is a choice assignment for cops, and the task force members selected are always the cream of the detective corps. They tend to be senior detectives; the FBI members tend to be younger. They always work in teams of two and are further divided into squads—one that deals with Muslim fundamentalists, for instance, one for domestic terrorism, one for other international groups like the Sikhs or the Provisional Irish Republican Army.

The Joint Terrorism Task Force numbered no more than six cops and six agents in 1985. During the Gulf War the commitment increased to about a hundred agents and a hundred detectives. By 1994—after the Trade Center bomb—it had shrunk to thirty agents and thirty detectives. There was even talk at One Police Plaza and 26 Federal Plaza about disbanding the force entirely.

After all, TRADEBOM was an isolated event, was it not? And what were the odds, when you came right down to it, of such a thing ever happening again?

But then came Oklahoma City, and then it seemed

that America would never be safe from terrorism again.

At three-thirty in the afternoon, Baumann arrived at Dulles International Airport, outside of Washington. An hour and a half later, he carried his baggage through the terminal's Eero Saarinen–designed interior and got a cab to Washington. In his leather carry-on satchel, in several neat bundles, were Thomas Cook traveler's checks in various denominations totaling several hundred thousand dollars, payable to a fictitious corporation. Baumann knew that the Central Intelligence Agency uses unsigned Thomas Cook traveler's checks to pay its contract agents (often diverted from funds earmarked for the U.S. Mission to the United Nations). That way, there's no paper trail. Had the customs inspector opened his satchel and discovered the checks—which did not happen—there would have been no problem: such checks are nonnegotiable currency and cannot be taxed by U.S. Customs.

Baumann stayed at the Jefferson, because he had heard it was a comfortable and elegant hotel, and because it happened to have a room available for a harried businessman who'd just missed his plane.

It was too late in the day, by the time he arrived at the hotel, to make any calls, so he ordered a cheeseburger from room service, took a steaming-hot bath, and slept off his exhaustion. In the morning, refreshed and prosperous-looking in one of his businessman's suits, he devoured a large room-service breakfast, read *The Washington Post*, and set off for a walk.

When you call the FBI's general number, you do not hear the periodic beeping that signifies you are being recorded. But Baumann assumed the FBI did record all incoming calls, legally or not. The real problem, though, was not whether his voice might be taped. Had he called the FBI from his hotel room, a record would be made at the Bureau of the number from which he called. That would not do at all.

So he found a pay phone in the atrium of an office building from which he could call without too much background noise.

"I'd like to speak to Agent Taylor in Counterterrorism, please," he said. Someone named Taylor, from Bureau headquarters, was the authorizing official on the request to the South African Department of Customs for a copy of his passport application. That didn't mean Taylor was the investigator, just that he was the responsible authority. And it was a very good start.

"Mr. Taylor's office," came a friendly woman's voice.

"Yes, I'm looking for Agent Frank Taylor, please," he said.

"I'm sorry, this is Perry Taylor's office—"

"But this is Counterterrorism, right?"

"Yes, it is, sir, but there's no Frank Taylor—"

"Oh, gosh, I'm sorry, this must be the right Agent Taylor. I'm Paul Tannen from the *Baltimore Sun*, and I'm copyediting and fact-checking a piece on the battle against terrorism. The reporter mentions—well, it's got to be Agent *Perry* Taylor, and quite favorably, I should say, but you know how lazy journalists are these days, what with computers and everything."

The woman's voice brightened. "Yes, sir, that's sure the truth."

"I mean, you got spell-checks and word-processing programs and all that stuff. Good golly, a newspaperman doesn't even have to *write* anymore."

She laughed pleasantly, a high, musical, laugh. "Did you want to talk to Agent Taylor?"

"Golly, I can't be bothering him with proofreading queries, no ma'am, but thanks anyway. Well, thanks a lot, and—oh, right, one more thing. Our reporter talked to Agent Taylor at home. I *assume* he did, anyway. He lives in Washington, right?"

"Alexandria, actually."

Baumann gave a big, exasperated sigh. "You see what I mean?"

CHAPTER THIRTY-EIGHT

"As the case agent on the original investigation that led to all of us being here," Whitman said, "Ms. Cahill will be lead investigator, in charge of day-to-day operations."

Sarah cleared her throat and launched into a summary of the information they had so far and read aloud from a paraphrased summary of the NSA intel intercepts. Annoyingly enough, she explained, she couldn't give copies of the actual intercepts to them, since none of them had been cleared, though she was working on getting at least one of them cleared to act as liaison with NSA from now on. She didn't explain—no reason for them to know—that CIA and FBI were now at each other's throats over the leak of the NSA intercept to the FBI. But the two agencies were always skirmishing, and it would blow over. She explained about the CD-ROM that had been stolen from Warren Elkind and copied, and then returned to him.

"Has anyone talked to this Elkind guy?" asked Lieutenant George Roth, who then popped a breath mint into his mouth.

"Not yet," Sarah said. "The New York office sent a couple of agents to talk to him. They briefed him about the threat, but he seemed fairly unconcerned, said he gets threats all the time. Which is true—his security people are always handling one threat or another. But he won't talk, won't submit to questioning. His attorney was with him, wouldn't let him answer anything."

"Prick," said Roth. "We should just let the fuckers bomb the bank, or zap Elkind, or whatever they want to do. Serve him right."

"It's his right not to talk to us," Sarah said.

Pappas said, "We should try again. Maybe you should try talking to him."

"I'm working on it," Sarah said. "In my own way. He'll talk, I promise you. One of the main things we want to find out is what was on the CD-ROM in question. Ken, why would a terrorist want a CD-ROM?"

"The possibilities are endless," Ken said. "My guess is that the CD contains something that would allow the bad guys to penetrate the bank's security. Passwords, keys, that sort of thing."

"How easy is it to copy a CD-ROM? Is it tough?"

"Oh, God, no way. Shit, it's practically like photocopying the thing. For a couple thousand bucks you can get a CD-ROM player that has a writable CD-ROM drive in it. Pinnacle Microsystems makes one; so does Sony."

"All right. Russell, have you reached the Israelis, and are they being helpful?"

"Yes to the first, no to the second," Ullman replied. "The Mossad is one tight-lipped bunch. They wouldn't confirm that Elkind is one of their, what you call, *sayan*s. Wouldn't even say if anyone in Mossad had ever been in touch with the guy. Off the record they confirm they know about Elkind's kinky side, mostly because he's a big contributor to Israel and all that, and they like to be informed. They say they don't know anything about terrorism and any connection to Elkind, but they might just be playing it close to the vest."

"Anything from flight records?" Sarah asked.

"Nothing from any of the major carriers, or even the minor ones," Christine Vigiani said. "But I wouldn't expect to find anything unless he's traveling under his real name or a known alias, and he wouldn't do that if he's got any smarts."

"Sarah," Pappas put in, "we might want to contact every intelligence service we have ties to—the British SIS, both MI6 and MI5, the French SDECE, the Spanish, the Germans. The Russians may well have something in their archives from Soviet times."

"Good idea," Sarah said. "You want to coordinate that? Request any records of Henrik Baumann under his true name, any known aliases, the names of any friends or relatives or associates. Any name we can trawl up. This guy has a record of doing tricks in the terrorist business for years, so he has to have left some trail."

Pappas nodded and jotted down a note. "I should warn you, we may have to apply some serious pressure. Counterterrorism is like motherhood and apple pie—everyone says they're for it, everyone says they'll help, until it comes to the crunch. But I'll put out the word worldwide."

There was a hoarse bark of laughter, and Lieutenant Roth said: "I like this. This investigation is so top-secret we can't tell a soul, except for a few thousand people around the world, from Madrid to Newfoundland. That's really keeping the lid on."

"Look—" Pappas began with exasperation.

Sarah turned to the cop slowly with a vacant expression. "Lieutenant Roth, either you're with us or you're out of here. It's as simple as that. If you want to leave, please do so now."

She folded her arms and stared.

A crooked half-smile slowly appeared on one side of

Roth's mouth. He nodded, almost a bow. "My apologies," he said.

"Accepted. Now, Ken, we've already done a complete database search of Bureau records, but since this is your specialty, maybe you could go over it again and do it right."

"I'll try," Ken said, "but I really don't know squat about the terrorism indices."

"You'll figure it out in no time. Most of the good stuff is at CIA, which maintains the principal government terrorism database. It's divided into two parts—the interagency one, and another one that's parochial to CIA, containing operational information, sources and methods, and so on. Also I need someone—Christine?—to check out any connections between our terrorist and the right-wing maniacs who did OKBOMB."

"I doubt there's anything," Vigiani said. "This is clearly international—"

"I agree with you. But just run a check, okay? Rule it out."

"Sarah, what about Elkind?" Pappas said. "He's still the best lead we've got. If he can be persuaded his bank is being targeted, he's got to be a little more receptive."

"Yeah," Sarah said with a heavy sigh. "He should be, shouldn't he?" Unless he's holding something back, she thought.

Perry Taylor's telephone number and address were listed in the Washington metropolitan telephone book, in Alexandria.

Baumann rented a car, a black Ford Mustang, from Hertz, using one of the false U.S. driver's licenses, this one belonging to a Connecticut driver named Carl Fournier. Then he made the short drive to Alexandria and located 3425 Potomac Drive, a contemporary brick ranch fronted in weathered shingles.

Passing by at moderate speed, he saw that the front lawn was an immaculate bottle-green carpet, a veritable putting green. The only car in the recently blacktopped driveway was a hunter-green Jeep Grand Cherokee, Limited Edition, of recent vintage. The family car.

He returned to Washington and spent the day making various purchases at an electronics shop, a pet shop, and a sporting-goods store. He rose early the next morning and was in Alexandria by about five o'clock.

It was still dark, the sky streaked faintly with pink traces of the rising sun. A second car was now in the driveway, next to the Jeep: a metallic-blue late-model Oldsmobile. No lights were on in the house yet.

Baumann did not slow the car as he passed. The neighborhood was upper-middle-class, and a car that slowed or stopped would be noticed. Neighbors here, like neighbors everywhere, could be counted on not to mind their own business. They eavesdropped on domestic quarrels, noticed new cars, watched yard work (approvingly or not). The houses were set far apart; property lines were neatly marked by tall picket fences or short split-log ones, but there was little privacy. There would always be an early riser next door or across the broad suburban street, peering out as he or she arose.

He parked the car a few blocks away in the mostly deserted lot of a Mobil station and walked back to Perry Taylor's house. He was wearing a sporty cardigan sweater, a pair of Dockers khaki pants, new white Nikes. He belonged.

In one hand was a bright-red dog's leash, which jingled as he walked; in the other was an aluminum device the pet shop called a "Pooper-Scooper," used to clean up after your dog. He whistled low as he approached the house, softly calling: "Tiger! Come on, boy! Come on back, Tiger!"

As he walked up Taylor's driveway, he saw with relief

that the house was still dark. He continued to call out quietly, looking back and forth across the immaculate lawn for his errant pet. Finally he came up behind the Oldsmobile and quickly knelt down.

If Taylor or a neighbor chanced to catch him there, in this position, he had a ready excuse. Still, his heart thudded rapidly. Taylor was an FBI man involved in counterterrorism and had to be cautious.

In a few seconds, he slipped a tiny, rectangular object, a flat metal box no bigger than an inch a side, under the rear bumper of the Olds. The powerful magnet locked on instantly.

"Where are you, Tiger, old boy?" he called out in a stage whisper as he got to his feet.

There was some information he wanted to get from this car, but it would require him to switch on his Maglite. The pencil flashlight's beam was small but powerful, not worth the risk.

A light went on in a second-story window next door. Baumann casually strolled down the driveway, shrugging his shoulders and shaking his head in resignation, for the sake of the neighbor who, he assumed, was watching him.

CHAPTER THIRTY-NINE

The finest houses in all of Amsterdam are located on the Herengracht canal, in a long row of facades built in varying stunning styles and known as the Golden Bend.

One of the grandest of the houses, built in Louis XIV style, with a double staircase running through its magnificent entrance and frescoed ceilings, belonged to an American man in his early forties who had married an extremely wealthy Dutch woman and ran her family's banking concern.

Early in the morning, the telephone rang in the man's enormous, light-filled master bedroom, waking both the American and his beautiful blond wife. The man picked up the handset, listened, said a few words, and then hung up.

He began weeping.

"What is it?" his wife asked.

"It's Jason," he replied. "He's dying."

The man had been estranged from his younger brother, who lived in Chula Vista, California, for some five years. Five years earlier, the younger brother had announced that he was gay, news that had torn this conservative Republican family apart.

In the ensuing battle, the two brothers had fought,

and years of simmering resentments and rivalries had boiled over. They had not spoken since.

Now came the news that Jason, Thomas's only sibling, had an advanced, full-blown case of AIDS. According to his physicians, he might live for another week, no more.

Although Thomas was an American citizen, he had not left the country in more than two years, for a brief, unavoidable meeting in London. He despised traveling, and until this morning had intended never to leave Amsterdam again.

He got up and went downstairs, drank a cup of *koffie verkeerd* (coffee with hot milk) prepared by their housekeeper, and booked the earliest possible flight to San Diego for him and his wife. Then he went to the marble-topped bureau in his study, where he kept all of his important papers, to get his passport.

It was not there.

This was odd, because he had seen it there just two or three days ago, when he had to make a photocopy of his birth certificate. He searched the drawer again, then pulled the drawer out and looked in the space behind it to see whether it might have somehow slid out of the drawer.

But it was not there.

The cleaning lady who came in every other day had just neatened up his study a few days ago, but she would certainly never move it. Thomas doubted she'd ever opened this drawer.

By late morning, Thomas and his wife and the housekeeper had searched the house high and low, but to no avail. The passport was missing.

"Just call the embassy and tell them it's lost," his wife said impatiently. "You can get a replacement right away. We can't look anymore if we're going to catch the afternoon flight, Thomas."

He called the American consulate, on Museumplein, and reported his passport missing. After the typical runaround, he was told to come in and fill out some papers.

"Let me have your name again, sir," the woman on the other end of the line said.

He responded with great annoyance, because he had given this dull-witted woman his name no fewer than three times. He had even spelled it out, as if to an idiot.

"Moffatt," he said. "Thomas Allen Moffatt."

CHAPTER FORTY

The Mobil lot was too exposed, so Baumann found a nearby Dunkin' Donuts, which was open, casting a sulfurous fluorescent light on the cars parked in the small lot in front. He parked and went inside for a cup of coffee. The server was a small young woman with frosted blond hair. She handed him a large cup, black, and a plain doughnut, and cheerily wished him a good morning. From the vending machine at the entrance he bought an early edition of the *Post*.

In the car, he draped the newspaper over the steering wheel and perused it as he sipped his coffee. From under the front passenger's seat he slid the receiver, plugged it into the cigar lighter, and adjusted the antenna. Any passerby would think he was studying the paper, though he was actually examining the LCD readout. A flashing red dot told him that the "bumper beeper," or Hound Dog, he had placed on the Oldsmobile's bumper was transmitting a signal, and that the car hadn't moved.

The device emitted an RF signal. Some Hound Dogs trailed a black wire antenna almost a foot long, but not this. Not on the car of an FBI man. This particular solid-state model had a stubby antenna that wouldn't easily be detected.

The scope, beside him on the front seat, told him where the transmitter was and where he was relative to it. This would enable him to tail the FBI man without being detected. Even deputy assistant directors had once gone through training and knew to look for certain signs of surveillance.

There was a risk that the FBI did regular RF sweeps on Taylor's car, in which case the Hound Dog would be discovered; but they would not do them daily. In any case, he would have to move quickly.

By his second cup of coffee, at 7:50 A.M., the flashing red dot began to move.

He followed the FBI man from as much as half a mile behind. Only once did he come close enough to see Taylor. This was at a large intersection just outside the District. Taylor was in the right lane, near the entrance to a shopping center. Baumann entered the shopping center's lot and drove within line of sight.

With his Nikon 7×50 binoculars he was able to scrutinize Perry Taylor; because Baumann's rental car had tinted windows, Taylor could not see Baumann, even if he happened to look. Taylor looked to be in his late forties, perhaps fifty, of medium build. His gray hair was neatly cut, and he wore wire-rimmed glasses. He wore an olive poplin suit with a white shirt and a gold-striped tie: the consummate government bureaucrat.

An ID badge was attached to the breast pocket of Taylor's suit jacket by means of an alligator clip, which told Baumann that Perry usually kept his jacket on during the day. Whenever an FBI employee was in FBI space he was required to wear his ID badge.

Baumann let the metallic-blue Oldsmobile get a good distance ahead, and he followed carefully. Since he didn't know the streets of Washington, he made a few wrong turns and was stymied by a one-way street, but that was inevitable.

When the flashing red dot came to a stop once again, Baumann pulled up several car lengths away, and could see that Taylor had pulled into a small parking lot off a commercial stretch of Pennsylvania Avenue. Baumann double-parked half a block up the street and watched through the binoculars.

Perry Taylor got out of the car, placed a coin in the parking meter, and entered a delicatessen that advertised breakfast specials and takeout meals. Was he having breakfast? If so, this was a golden opportunity.

With some trepidation, Baumann left his car double-parked, strolled past the metallic-blue Oldsmobile, and quickly made a few mental notes.

One, there was an FBI parking garage pass on the dashboard. No surprise here; all employees who worked at FBI headquarters had the right to park in its garage. Unfortunately, the garage was well guarded and difficult to enter.

Two, if Taylor had set the car alarm, there was no visible sign of it. Likely he had not.

And three, there was a briefcase on the front seat, a gray Samsonite. This was most interesting, but how to get to it? It was possible, though not likely, that Taylor had left the car unlocked. Baumann passed by the car again, pretending to be looking for a street number, and with his glove-clad hands tried the driver's-side door. It was locked.

Then he noticed a small plate screwed onto the dash where it met the windscreen. Yes, of course. Engraved on the plate was the VIN, the vehicle identification number. Baumann drew close and copied down the long series of numbers and letters, and just then he saw Taylor emerge from the delicatessen, carrying a white paper bag—his breakfast? his lunch? Baumann kept walking toward the rented Mustang and got back into the car. He took note of the name of the auto dealership where

Taylor had probably purchased the car: it was emblazoned on the bracket that held the license plate. Then Baumann pulled into traffic and proceeded down the street and out of sight.

CHAPTER FORTY-ONE

Sarah and Pappas were not the first to arrive at Operation MINOTAUR's headquarters. By seven-fifteen, everyone had arrived except Ken Alton, who'd been at work into the early morning, rigging up in record time a local-area network, or LAN. Since each member of the task force had a computer terminal, this would allow everyone to gain access to files and records in the most efficient way possible. Ken had explained to Sarah that he wasn't particularly concerned about what he called interior defense, because every task force member had been thoroughly screened and vetted. Had there been more time, he would set up an adequate perimeter defense, with a "firewall" security system. But Ken was a perfectionist in everything except his grooming, and Sarah told him to leave things as they were. No time for anything elaborate.

The group broke up into teams and dispersed for the day, all of them equipped with a beeper in case Sarah needed to reach them suddenly. She and Lieutenant Roth moved to the office she had claimed as her own. Probably it had once belonged to the display company's president. For all the high-tech security that had been set up on the floor, many of the offices had been left untouched.

A ratty abandoned desk-and-chair set dwarfed the room, with its breathtaking view of the city. From up here it looked clean and galvanized and full of promise. The desk's surface was wood-grain Formica, patched at one corner with mismatched wood-grain contact paper. The high-backed chair was upholstered in mustard-yellow vinyl, with white cotton tufts sprouting through gaping holes in the seat. No wonder the furnishings had been left behind. The only official-looking thing in the room was the FBI-approved safe, a four-drawer Mosler combination safe, concrete-and-steel, good for material up to top secret.

"So, Lieutenant Roth, my sources tell me you're one of the best cops on the force, you were considered a genius when you were on the Fugitive Squad, you tracked down twelve fugitives in a year and half, you're great at passports and credit cards, and you've got some sort of unbelievable gift at finding people, some kind of sixth sense. I hope my sources are right."

Roth popped a Breath Saver. "They exaggerate," he said. "I'll do my best, all I can say."

"That's good enough for me."

"Okay," he said, as Sarah prepared to take notes. "There's an organization that might help called APPLE, for the Area Police Private Security Liaison program. I guess the S is silent. The members are the security directors of nine hundred buildings and companies in the city. Mostly they're involved with break-ins and domestic crime. They spend their time thinking about public toilets and loading docks and service entrances, but since the World Trade Center they've gotten pretty concerned about terrorism. The program coordinator is a buddy of mine. I'll give him a call."

"But if the Manhattan Bank is the target," Sarah said, "why bother with nine hundred other companies?"

"On the assumption that the Manhattan Bank might be one of a *series* of targets. Probably I'm wrong, but I figure it's safer to rule things out instead of being surprised down the line."

"What are you going to ask them?"

"If they've received any threats or noticed any suspicious behavior. This is New York City. Threats and suspicious behavior are a way of life, so the answer will be yes, and we'll have to screen. I mean, we got the resources, right, so why not squander them?"

"That's one way to look at it," Sarah said.

"Plus, I was thinking we should just go down the list of major landmark buildings and locations and keep them on our radar screens."

"Like the Empire State Building and the Trade Center towers?"

"And Rockefeller Center, Lincoln Center, the United Nations, the Chrysler Building, the Empire State Building, the Statue of Liberty, the New York Stock Exchange."

"The Statue of Liberty?"

"Hey, a bunch of Croatian nationalists planted a bomb there fifteen, twenty years ago. The thing went off. Fair amount of damage, luckily no injuries. The big lady's managed by the National Park Service, and they use electronic scanning equipment on visitor's packages."

She nodded, leaned back in the mustard-yellow chair. It gave a squeak of protest. There was a deferential knock at the door, and Russell Ullman entered, bearing a large manila envelope. "It's in," he said.

"What's in?" Sarah asked.

"The prints."

"The prints of your Prince," Roth said. "I told you someday your prints would come."

"We're on the home stretch," Ullman said. He could barely contain his excitement. "We got him now."

Lieutenant Roth rubbed a large, fleshy hand over his face. "Oh, is that right?" he asked, affecting the deepest boredom. "Kid, the race hasn't even started."

Sarah snatched the envelope from Ullman and tore it open. Roth was right. They hadn't even started.

It was a complete set of fingerprints, carefully done.

"Where's the photo?" she asked.

"They couldn't turn one up," Ullman said.

"*What?* What do you mean, they couldn't 'turn one up'? They couldn't find a photograph of the guy?"

"The South Africans say they're unable to turn up any photo of Baumann. In cases like his—deep-cover agents—the old secret service used to keep only one photograph, in its locked central personnel files. Reasons of security. But that one photograph appears to be missing—stolen, pilfered, something."

"Try the prison, Russell," Sarah snapped. "You didn't think of that?"

"No, I did," Ullman replied. "Pollsmoor photographs all incoming prisoners, like every other prison, and stores them in two different places, but both photos of Baumann have disappeared sometime in the last few weeks."

"Bullshit!" Sarah exploded.

"No, really," Ullman protested. "They did a thorough search, but the file photos have been stolen."

"How can that be?"

"Look," Ullman said, "for years the South African government did everything it could to keep this guy's face a secret. The way CIA does with its deep-cover agents. Maybe there were three extant photographs of him in all the government files. So if our guy had enough pull, or some powerful friends in the right places, it was no big deal to make those photos disappear. The

South Africans protected his anonymity so well and for so long that now—when they *want* a picture—they can't get their hands on one."

"Looks like your terrorist," Roth interjected, "has some powerful friends."

CHAPTER FORTY-TWO

Perry Taylor arrived at the FBI headquarters at 8:20 A.M. and pulled into the main employee entrance in the middle of the Tenth Street side of the building. This meant he would be in his office by 8:30 A.M. He was a punctual man, which was good for Baumann, because it meant he was also a man of regular habits, a most useful vulnerability.

Unfortunately, Taylor's car did not leave the FBI building the entire day. The red dot remained fixed and flashing: the Hound Dog hadn't been discovered, it was still transmitting, and the car hadn't been moved.

Baumann spent a few hours walking the streets around FBI headquarters. He bought a pair of cheap sunglasses and a Washington, D.C., T-shirt, and played the tourist. For lunch he got a hot dog from a stand at Tenth Street and Pennsylvania Avenue.

He noticed that the Pennsylvania Avenue entrance to the FBI garage was shut, the gates drawn, presumably for security reasons. The World Trade Center and Oklahoma City bombings had made the FBI understandably nervous. He saw that groups of tourists could gain access to the building by taking a guided tour. For no particular reason, except that he had time to kill, he took a tour at midmorning, which began in front of a display of America's Ten Most Wanted criminals and ended with a film about handguns.

The rest of the day he kept watch on the various employee entrances and exits to see whether Taylor emerged. He did not. Many FBI employees went out for lunch to the food malls nearby, and there was said to be a large and adequate cafeteria within the complex, but Taylor probably ate his lunch at his desk, from the white bag he had taken out of the delicatessen.

By four o'clock in the afternoon, Baumann had returned to his parked car and prepared for Taylor to leave the building. The red dot did not begin to move until 6:45 P.M. Baumann waited until Taylor was a good distance away before he began to follow. Taylor appeared to be taking the same route home he'd taken to work.

Baumann drove with a sense of discouragement. This could go on for days, and he would learn nothing unless he got into Taylor's office or home. Taylor was indeed going home, Baumann saw, but to be sure, he followed the Olds as far as he could prudently do so.

Getting into Taylor's home would not be a problem, although there was no reason to believe he would find anything there. Careful FBI men like Taylor did not keep a set of files at their homes. Getting into Taylor's office was possible, though perilous to the point of being foolhardy. Obviously he or someone who worked with or for him had been delving into Baumann's past. That meant he might recognize Baumann in person.

But even assuming Baumann entered the office wearing a persuasive disguise, what could he expect to find there, really, without being left alone—a highly unlikely possibility?

Baumann suspected that the gray Samsonite briefcase would contain Taylor's FBI building pass, a personnel list, or any of a hundred things. If Taylor were to stop somewhere on the way to or from work, Baumann would have an opportunity.

There was no keyless entry system on the driver's door, which was too bad, because that would have made it easy to get into the car. All Baumann would have had to do was to watch through the binoculars as Taylor keyed in the code.

If Taylor were to leave his briefcase on the front seat again, Baumann could just slip in a slim jim and have the car open in a matter of seconds, without anyone noticing.

If Taylor locked the briefcase in the trunk, that was a different situation. There were simple, brute-force methods. You could use a dent-puller to pop the trunk lock out, then open the trunk with a screwdriver. But no matter how carefully you did it, the damage would be immediately visible. Taylor would know someone had gotten into his trunk, and he would be immediately suspicious. Such a move would blow everything.

The smash-and-grab had to be ruled out.

Baumann returned to the Jefferson, made some notes, went out for a brief walk. From a pay phone he hadn't used before he called Perry Taylor's number. If Mrs. Taylor answered, he would ask for him, say he was an old friend, make it clear he was not a salesman of any kind. . . . But Taylor answered the phone himself.

"Hello," he said.

"Perry Taylor?" Baumann asked pleasantly.

"Speaking. Who's this?

"Mr. Taylor, according to our records, you don't subscribe to *Time* magazine, and we'd like to offer—"

"Sorry," Taylor said brusquely, "but we're not interested. Good night."

Baumann read for a while, an architectural history of New York City, and went to sleep early.

In the morning, Baumann followed the same routine, picking up Perry Taylor's signal from a half-mile away and following him at a distance. Once again, Taylor stopped at the delicatessen on Pennsylvania Avenue to buy what Baumann assumed was his lunch. He drove into the FBI garage by the same entrance on Tenth Street, and again did not leave the building until his workday was done.

In the meantime, Baumann had plenty of time to do what he needed to do. He returned to the Jefferson and placed a call to the auto dealership whose name— Brautigan Motors—was on Perry Taylor's license-plate bracket.

"Yes," he said when the service department came on the line. "I feel like such an idiot." He laughed. "This is Perry Taylor, and I bought a car from you guys, a '94 Olds, and I just went and locked my keys in the car."

From his brief conversation with Perry Taylor the night before, Baumann had learned the eccentricities of the FBI man's voice—a resonant baritone, a slight Southern accent, a careful enunciation. The imitation would fool anyone except a good friend; fortunately, the young man in the service department did not seem to know Taylor.

"Sorry to hear that, sir. I assume you don't have a spare set—?"

"I'm embarrassed to say it, but my wife has the spare, and she's in Miami Beach visiting the in-laws. Pretty swift of me, huh?"

"Mr. Taylor, I'm going to have to ask you for your VIN number, which is located on the car or in your paperwork. Do you think you can find that for me?"

"No problem, I got that."

"Great," the young man said. "Otherwise we *would* have a problem." Baumann gave him the VIN number. "Okay, now hold on a moment while I pull your file."

When he returned to the phone a few minutes later, the serviceman said, "I'm going to give you a number now, Mr. Taylor." He spoke as if Mr. Taylor were a simpleton, which was probably a fair assumption given the circumstances. He gave Baumann the number. "You bring that number—it's your key code, okay?—to any locksmith, and they can make you a new one. All right?"

"All right, great," Baumann said. "Thanks so much."

CHAPTER FORTY-THREE

The next afternoon, unfortunately, Perry Taylor drove home from work without stopping. Baumann placed a call to the auto dealership, asked for Kevin, the young man who had helped him, and thanked him for his help. It would not do at all to have Kevin call Taylor to make sure everything turned out all right.

The next morning, Taylor made his regular delicatessen stop, but that was too short a time to do anything.

That evening after work, Taylor made a stop at a Giant Foods supermarket a few miles from his home, part of a strip mall containing a People's Drug, a Crown Books, and a variety of smaller shops.

Baumann pulled into the lot just in time to see Taylor get out of the car.

The opportunity had come.

Taylor locked his briefcase in the trunk of the car. Baumann waited for him to enter the store before he went up to the Oldsmobile.

He had left the car alarm off again. Baumann nonchalantly inserted the trunk key in the lock and popped it open. Taylor kept his trunk immaculate—no debris, no old newspapers or rags or dog-eared magazines. There was only an unopened can of tennis balls and the gray Samsonite briefcase. He lifted it out, shut the trunk, and returned to his own, rented car.

Although the briefcase had a locking mechanism beneath its handle, three numbered dials, Taylor had not locked it, and why would he? It was safe in his trunk.

In one of the pockets there was a Smith & Wesson semiautomatic, Model 1006, which took 10mm rounds. There was also a datebook and a thick sheaf of file folders. As he went through the datebook and the files, wearing latex gloves, Baumann began to sweat. He turned the car on to get the air-conditioning going, but it did a feeble job. The car had to be in drive for the air-conditioning to really kick in.

Taylor was not holding a shopping list, so it was possible that he was only making a quick stop, in which case Baumann had to get through these files in a matter of minutes and return the briefcase to the trunk. Taylor must not know anyone had been in his car. Fortunately, Taylor had parked his Olds in a remote corner of the lot, where there was little foot traffic.

There were a lot of documents, many of them marked "Confidential" or "Secret," but that was meaningless. No one paid any attention to any document that wasn't marked at least "Top Secret." Baumann knew that in the U.S. government there are three levels of secrecy: confidential, secret, and top secret. Top secret is the highest level of secrecy; despite what is commonly believed, there is none higher.

But there do exist more than thirty *subsets* of classification, known as compartments. A person in the government may be granted access to one or more compartments, yet not for others.

Then Baumann found a document that was of interest, one he hadn't expected to find. Hadn't *hoped* to find, in fact.

It was a sheet of green paper marked AIRTEL.

Baumann knew enough about the workings of the FBI to realize that there were three categories of communications sent between headquarters and field offices. A routine communication was called a Letter and was printed on white paper. One level of urgency up from Letter was an Airtel, printed on green paper. At least, at headquarters it was green; the field offices got blue copies. In the old days, an Airtel was sent by airmail, although that distinction had long since become meaningless. Now Airtels (also known as "greenies") were either faxed or sent by courier. The highest level of urgency was a Teletype, on manila paper, which was once sent by Teletype and now faxed or couriered. The only operative difference between the two was the heading.

This particular Airtel was addressed to ADIC NY, the assistant director of the FBI in charge of the New York office. It was from Perry Taylor, and it listed members of a special working group of the Joint Terrorist Task Force, code-named Operation MINOTAUR, along with their affiliations. Five of them were FBI: two from headquarters, two from the Boston office, and one recently retired from the Boston office.

Baumann understood at once that these were the names of the FBI agents who had been assigned to investigate an "alleged," "impending" act of terrorism in New York City. It was Baumann they were after.

He had the names of his hunters.

He did not want to take the time to bring the papers to a photocopy shop, so he copied down the names and identifying information and replaced the papers neatly in the briefcase. Then he got out of his car, opened the trunk of Taylor's Olds, replaced the briefcase, and shut the trunk. He quickly leaned over to retrieve the transmitter from the rear bumper—it was too risky to leave it there any longer. He felt along the underside of the bumper until his fingers slid up against the magnetized transmitter and closed around it, and then he heard someone speak very close to him.

"Freeze," the voice said. "FBI."

Baumann whirled around and saw Perry Taylor standing just a few feet away, and he could not suppress a smile. He had been sloppy, or perhaps he had underestimated Taylor. Taylor must have seen someone standing next to his car, must have left the supermarket by some unseen exit. He had no shopping bags.

This was a very bad situation indeed, and Baumann's head spun. He did not want to kill Perry Taylor; that had not been his intention at all. Baumann gave an abashed smile, laughed awkwardly. He spoke in a Southern accent, which by now felt natural. "Of all the places to drop a contact lens," he said.

He could see Taylor hesitate. "Where'd you drop it?" Taylor asked skeptically. Had he seen Baumann open the trunk?

No one was walking by, no one even close. No one could see them. "Right . . . right here, somewhere, it's got to be," Baumann said, shaking his head. "Man, it's one of those days."

"I know what you mean," Taylor said. "Here, let me help you."

Of course: Taylor didn't have a gun with him. His gun was locked in his trunk. Taylor moved closer, pretending to help Baumann look for the lost contact lens, but really—Baumann was sure of it—to grab Baumann, catch him off base, perhaps attempt to disarm him.

"Thanks," Baumann said, and waited for Taylor to come closer, and when Taylor did, Baumann's right hand shot toward Taylor's throat, as quick as the dart of a snake's tongue, and got hold of the FBI man's trachea and squeezed, and Perry Taylor sank to the ground dead, looking very much like a middle-aged man overcome by the sweltering heat of a Washington summer evening.

Part 4

FINGERPRINTS

*Under fragrant bait there is certain
to be a hooked fish.*

—Sun-tzu, *The Art of War*

CHAPTER FORTY-FOUR

Police around the world still use the old Henry system of fingerprint classification, which groups fingerprints by their various features, their loops, arches, whorls, and ridges.

It is a fairly baroque system. A loop may be ulnar or radial; a central pocket loop may be plain or tented. Whorls come in four types: plain, center-loop, double-loop, or accidental. Additionally, a whorl can be an inside tracing, an outside tracing, or a "meet" tracing. Then there are ridges. Every fingerprint has a unique pattern of ridges, enclosures, ending ridges, and bifurcations, places where the ridge lines end or split in two. To make a positive identification, one must have eight or more points of identification, also called Galton's details, after the nineteenth-century English scientist Sir Francis Galton. Under the Henry classification system, unfortunately, comparisons have to be done manually, in a print-by-print search, which can take weeks or even months.

But since 1986 a different, computerized method of sorting and storing prints has been in use in the United States. It is called the Automated Fingerprint Identification System, or AFIS, and it uses high-speed optical scanners to analyze prints, digitalize them, and store them in computerized form. The position of minutiae are counted on a 512-pixel-per-inch scale and converted into a series of numbers, which can easily be compared with others. Loops and whorls are effectively turned into bytes and bits. Using AFIS, the FBI and major police forces around the nation have the remarkable ability to compare fingerprints at the rate of nine thousand a minute.

The FBI's Identification Division has the fingerprints of some twenty-four million convicted criminals on line, in addition to the print file cards of forty million other Americans, including federal employees and military veterans. And very recently, the FBI's AFIS has been electronically connected to AFIS machines at state capitals and major cities around the country. This network, the Integrated Automated Fingerprint Identification System (IAFIS), which is housed in a new site in Clarksburg, West Virginia, ties the local police booking station to the FBI in a paperless transmission system that will soon eliminate the old-fashioned fingerprint cards entirely.

The task force had been hastily assembled by beeper. Even Ken Alton, awakened from slumber, straggled in clutching a take-out cup of coffee. Sarah passed out copies of Henrik Baumann's "ten-print," his ten fingerprints compiled on a file card by the South Africans. On this form, each print was carefully rolled onto its own block. On the lower portion of the card were the "slap prints," the four fingers of each hand slapped down at once.

"You may not have any use for the prints," she announced, "but it's there in case you do. Those numbers there beneath each print are the Henry numbers, which the South Africans still use. Stone-age technology, but we're not in a position to complain. The Identification

Division is already working on these, blowing them up, tracing the ridges, and converting them to the AFIS system."

"What, no lip prints?" asked Lieutenant Roth dryly.

There were a few chuckles, some louder than others, as if this were an inside joke.

"Sorry?" Sarah said, mystified.

"It's a running joke," explained Wayne Kim from NYPD Forensics, shaking his head. "There've been a couple of papers in the *Journal of Forensic Science* on using lip prints for personal identification. They look at labial wrinkles and grooves, bifurcated, trifurcated, reticulate, stuff like that."

"I see," she said. "Now, a couple of things about these prints you may or may not know, since I know you're not all fingerprint jocks. Until we get the AFIS classifications, you can fax these ten-prints or receive latents by fax, but make sure to use not just the high-resolution fax, but the *secure* high-resolution fax, okay? And be careful, because even the high-res fax can introduce false minutiae. If you get a set of latents you think might be from our guy, I'd rather courier them down to Washington than mess around with the fax."

"Sarah," Ken said groggily, "what's the deal on reliability of AFIS matches?"

"Okay, the machine classifies the quality of the prints A or B. C is a reject. It doesn't give you a definite yes-or-no, this-is-it kind of thing. It'll give you a list of the top contenders in descending order by PCN number. A so-called perfect score is nineteen thousand, nine hundred ninety-eight. But remember, we're in the law-enforcement business, not the intelligence business, so everything we do has to stand up in court. And legally, even after the computer spits out the winner, ID's still going to have to chart it by hand, or rather by eye."

Ken nodded.

"We going to put this out on the NCIC?" asked Mark McLaughlin of the NYPD, who had sandy blond hair and a face dense with freckles.

Sarah shook her head. "NCIC uses a different system, a simple numerical classification the Bureau came up with in order to be able to store prints on computer. It's based on a line count of ridges between the delta and the core—you know, 'center loop, outside tracing,' or 'radial loop with a four count,' like that. It's actually a pretty crude system, useful for pointing the way and that's all. AFIS and IAFIS are really a hell of a lot more useful."

"And Albany, too, since we're assuming the guy's right here," Lieutenant Roth said. "The Division of Criminal Justice, Fingerprints Section. So if he's arrested and printed anywhere in the state, we've got him. I say it's worth the time to send prints on to every state to search for a match, and retain them if they're willing to. New York will, but a lot of states won't."

"So what do you want us to do with prints if we get any?" asked one of the street agents, Dennis Stewart, whose specialty was organized crime.

"We've got some basic equipment set up here," she replied. "A RAMCAM, the little fingerprint reader that makes a thermal picture of the print, and the CRIM-CON, which is hooked up to a video monitor. Lieutenant Roth is the man to see if you have a print—he'll be in charge of all that."

Later, as the group dispersed, Pappas approached her and spoke quietly. "Listen, Sarah, with all this sophisticated technology, it's easy to lose sight of the fact that all the fancy computers in the world aren't going to make up for some good solid shoeleather."

"So what are you saying?"

"I'm just afraid that the clock's ticking and we're being sidetracked by all these toys."

"Alex, we ignore the new technology at our own peril."

"You remember when the Reagan administration spent seventeen million bucks on a computer system they called TRAP/TARGIT that was supposed to predict terrorist incidents based on early signals? It was a complete bust. Never worked. A huge joke. I'm just wondering whether we shouldn't be doing some more basic, old-fashioned brainstorming. What are you doing tonight?"

"I'm picking up Jared from camp. Between six and seven at Penn Station."

"You two doing something, going out for dinner?"

"I didn't have any plans. I thought I'd see what Jared's up for."

"Maybe I could come by later, when Jared's asleep. No, I've got a better idea. Why don't you ask Jared when he gets in if he feels like having dinner with you and me at a nice Greek place I discovered on First Avenue. You and I can talk, and Jared can put in his two cents. But I don't want to horn in on your little reunion—"

"Oh, he always loves seeing you, Alex. But I don't know about Greek. You know how discriminating he is about food."

"McDonald's it is. The one at the intersection of Seventy-first, Broadway, and Amsterdam."

Alex Pappas devoured his Big Mac and fries with as much gusto as he did moussaka or spanakopita. A good portion of his fries, of course, went directly to Jared, who ate ravenously, as if he'd just come not from summer camp but a Soviet hard-labor camp.

In the two weeks since she'd last seen him, Jared seemed to have grown taller and more slender, more a young man than a pudgy little boy. Sarah could at times see him as an adult, a breathtakingly, head-turningly handsome man. And in the next instant he was again the kid in tie-dyed shorts with scuffed knees letting out a fake belch, telling them about all the games he'd learned at camp. "I can't wait to play in Central Park," he said.

Sarah shook her head. "Not without supervision, you're not."

"Oh, God, I don't need *supervision*."

"You're not playing in Central Park unless I'm there, Jared. 'Stranger danger,' remember?"

Jared pouted. "I'm not a baby, Mom."

"Central Park can be a dangerous place for kids. That's the rule. Only with supervision. Now, I'm going to be really, really busy during the days, and I don't want you staying in the apartment all day and watching TV, so I got you into the summer program at the YMCA near Lincoln Center. It's on West Sixty-third Street, not too far from here. Sort of a neat building. That's where you'll spend your days."

"YMCA?" Jared said. "I don't want to swim."

"It's not just swimming, it's arts and crafts and basketball and other games. You'll have a great time."

"Oh, God," Jared wailed.

"Believe me," Pappas said to him, "when you get to be as old as me, you'd give anything to be able to spend your days at a day camp. *Anything!*"

CHAPTER FORTY-FIVE

"If Baumann is indeed in New York City," Pappas said after Jared had gone to sleep, "he has to have entered within the last month, since his escape from Pollsmoor."

Sarah nodded. "That narrows the time frame, but we don't know if he entered legally or illegally. He's a pro, so he might have sneaked in without a trace. Which makes finding him just about impossible."

"You can't think that way. You have to think in terms of probabilities. Yes, people can and do enter the U.S. illegally by walking across the border from Canada—so you have the Canadians search their entry records."

"And if he came in by way of Mexico? We're screwed if we have to depend on the Mexicans to help us out."

"Think probabilities. Mexico's used far less often for illegal entries in cases like this."

"But what do we ask the Canadians to search for? They're only going to be able to help if he flew in on his own passport, under his true name. Which isn't likely."

"Granted, but it's still worth a try."

"And if he flew into the U.S. directly—whatever passport he used—there are lots of international airports. The guy has his choice. Wouldn't he choose some little, Podunk place like—oh, I don't know, isn't there an international airport in Great Falls, Montana, with just one INS inspector?"

"Not at all," Pappas said. "One inspector means much closer scrutiny, which he wants to avoid. Much better to enter the country at a large, crowded airport that's got six hundred people waiting to get through Customs and Immigration. All those people, and just one poor, overworked customs inspector for the teeming hordes. That's what I'd do—JFK or Dulles or Miami, something big like that."

"Great," she said bitterly. "So we're looking for a guy who entered the U.S. sometime in the last month. Under any name whatsoever. Just . . . a guy. That really narrows it, doesn't it?"

Pappas shrugged.

"And as if that weren't bad enough, I'm supposed to have people search entry records in every port of entry in the U.S. Why the hell aren't they all together in one place, in some kind of centralized data bank?"

"Because they aren't. Someday they will be, but for now all the searching has got to be done by hand. Could I trouble you for another cup of instant?"

"Sure." Sarah got up, went to the kitchen, put the kettle on to boil. As she waited, she mentally listed the airports in the United States and Canada. Montreal, Toronto, Vancouver, Washington (both National and Dulles), LAX . . . The list went on and on, and she began to lose track. And what if Baumann hadn't entered the country by air? It was maddening, hopeless.

She returned to the living room and put down a mug of instant coffee and one of Earl Grey tea. "Let's say he hasn't arrived in New York yet, hasn't even arrived in the country. In that case, we should contact Interpol and have them put out an International Red Notice." A Red Notice is an international lookout for a fugitive based on an outstanding arrest warrant for the purpose of extradition, sort of an all-points bulletin issued by Interpol's General Secretariat to the border lookout systems of all member countries. "Result, we'll get nothing and just end up alerting Baumann."

"Nothing necessarily wrong with that. Maybe that'll scare him, make him call it off."

"Not likely."

"No," Pappas conceded. "Not likely."

"I suppose we could blanket the city with a description. Damn, I wish we could find a photo! But even if we could, the word would be out about our existence, and the city'll go crazy."

"Not if we do it through the New York office and say we're on the trail of some guy who's wanted for some brutal crime in Europe or something."

She nodded. "All right, let's focus on the passport issue. Say for the sake of argument he entered the U.S. directly, but not on his own passport. What are the search options there?"

"Quite a few," Pappas said. "Can I smoke?"

"I'd rather you didn't, not with Jared so close by."

"You're no fun." He sighed, stretched his legs, took another sip of coffee. "We went through this drill in TRADEBOM," he said. "When we searched the apartments of some of the suspects, we found Nicaraguan passports—real, legitimate Nicaraguan passports."

"How'd they get them?"

"Who knows? Some corrupt Nicaraguan official sold blanks to the Sandinistas, who sold them, or gave them, to ideological soulmates. This stuff happens all the time, all over the world."

She thought for a moment. "So, what, we have our foreign legats talk to all their counterparts and local liaison?"

Pappas nodded.

She went on, "Ask every country we have dealings

with to check whether a passport was issued to this guy. Maybe even ask them to do a complete records check, if they're so inclined."

"But without a photo, we'll get squat. And not every country will comply. They'd be more likely to help out if they believe our guy *forged* one of their passports. But a lot of countries won't give us the time of day."

"Seems pointless."

"That's right. The thing we have going for us is, it's not likely—probabilities, again—that he'd use a foreign passport."

"Why not, if it's so easy to get one?"

"Because that entails going through both customs *and* immigration in most U.S. airports and having officials take a nice, hard look, and who needs all that? Certainly not our Prince of Darkness."

In her peripheral vision she saw that Jared was standing before them in his Lion King pajamas, squinting, hair mussed from sleep. "Could you guys keep it down?" he said grumpily.

"I'm sorry, honey," Sarah said.

"Sorry," Pappas said. "We'll be quieter. Hey, buddy, do you mind if I smoke in here?"

"No, Alex, it's okay. You can."

Sarah got up, gave Pappas a black look, and kissed Jared on the forehead. She took him back to bed. When she returned, they resumed in much lower tones.

"Okay, so he's got to get his hands on a U.S. passport," she said. "How does he do that?"

Pappas exhaled delicately out of one side of his mouth, ostentatiously keeping the smoke away from Jared's direction. "A number of ways. There's the classic method of going to a cemetery, copying down the name of someone who died in infancy who's also around your age, getting his birth certificate, then applying for a passport. Easier said than done; it's awfully labor-intensive, and more and more often birth and death records are collated, so you can't pull a fast one. No, he'd have to steal one or acquire a forged one."

"It's not so easy to forge a U.S. passport anymore."

"No, it isn't. Though admittedly not impossible if you hire someone really skilled. But that's a limited pool of talent."

"And if he *does* hire someone good?"

"If it's a top-flight forgery, we're not going to catch it anyway."

"Oh, come on, Alex, isn't there a computer network linking all border entry points? Called something like IBIS, for Inter—Interagency Border Inspection System? Correct?"

"Correct, but—"

"As I recall from New Agents training, we used to post watch lists and photographs of fugitives at border entry points, and the customs agent would consult his lookout lists either alphabetically or by passport number."

Pappas nodded and fished out another cigarette from the pack.

"But now we've got automatic document readers at most major ports, right? They optically scan the coded information at the bottom of the passport, and they're programmed to look for variances and patterns to make sure a passport is valid. So if our guy flashes a forged passport, isn't he going to be caught instantly?"

"If it's a lousy forgery, sure. But not if it's any good. You're dreaming if you think the system is set up to catch fakes. It's not."

"But if the number of a fake passport doesn't match existing passport numbers, won't it be flagged?"

"Wrong. More techno-lust. Little-known fact: the system doesn't notice passport numbers that don't exist."

"Jesus Christ. But surely lost or stolen passports are

logged onto the system. Otherwise, what the hell is it good for?"

"Yes, lost or stolen passports *are* entered into the computer, so if someone tries to use one, a 'red flag' goes up—an alert message or whatever it is. That's how we caught those terrorists who stole all those U.S. passports a couple of years back."

He was referring to a recent incident, which the FBI has never made public, in which a terrorist group seized fifteen hundred valid U.S. passports. But the FBI had each of the passports flagged on the INS computer system and thereby caught any terrorist who tried to use one.

"Which means," Sarah said, "Baumann's not going to use a *stolen* passport."

"Well, no, not necessarily. There's always a delay between the moment he, or someone else, steals a passport and the moment it goes onto the on-line lookout list. Maybe the guy he lifted it from doesn't notice for a couple of days. Or maybe the lady whose job it is to enter passport data into IBIS took the week off to visit Disney World with her kids."

"So he *can* use a stolen passport."

"Correct."

"Shit. All right, I've got it. We do a cross-check."

"Hmm?"

"Okay, so we know the automated, optically scanning document readers at all ports of entry store all information on who's entered the country, at what time, on what day and on what flight and where, right?"

"Right."

"That's all on an immense database at State. And we cross-check *that* list against a list of all passports reported lost or stolen within the last month. So in effect, what we're coming up with is a list of all lost or stolen passports that've been used since they were reported lost or stolen."

Pappas chuckled. "More of your beloved technology."

"Of course, it won't work if the passport Baumann used to get into the country was never reported. But say it was. Then we've got a list of all illegal entries, and we filter out that list, and we've got him."

"Can't be done," Pappas said flatly. "These are two separate, discrete databases. Sad, but true. We're not set up to do something like that. Sounds good in theory, but you'd have to check a list of thousands of stolen or lost passports against *millions* of people who've come into the U.S. recently—and do it *by hand*. It would take forever. Tedious, mind-numbing, and frankly impossible."

"That's why God invented computers."

"Listen, Sarah. For as long as I've been in the Bureau, that's never been done. Never. There's a reason for that."

"Yeah. They didn't have Ken Alton, computer wizard. I'll give him a call. He's probably just booted up his computer for the night."

"Don't get your hopes up, kid. And don't forget, even if you somehow find out what passport he used, he's already *in the country*."

"Shame on you, Alex. Then we've got us a trail."

"Hardly a trail."

"Oh, come on," Sarah upbraided him. "Then we've got us a damn good start."

"If we're lucky."

"Yeah, well, sometimes you've got to count on a little luck. Think positive."

CHAPTER FORTY-SIX

In a great city like New York, Henrik Baumann was in his element. He disappeared easily into crowds, his appearance always changing; he made his arrangements, established his contacts, bought what he needed in absolute anonymity.

In the beginning he took a one-bedroom suite on the forty-first floor of the New York Hilton, in what they called the Executive Tower. There were less expensive rooms, and nicer hotels, but it was height he was after most of all.

He set up the MLink-5000 satellite telephone on the sill of an east-facing window and opened its lid to aim the flat-plate array antenna, checked the signal-strength meter, and readjusted the angle of elevation. Rather than use the handset, he plugged into the phone's modular port a small fax machine he had purchased on Forty-seventh Street. On a table nearby he placed the cheap electronic typewriter he had bought at the same place, and several preprinted invoice forms.

For the first time he felt anxiety. The situation had changed.

He'd never intended to kill the FBI executive in charge of finding him, but the fellow had made it unavoidable. Baumann had done what he could to make the death look like a random act of violence. He had stolen Taylor's wallet and with a silencer-equipped pistol had fired two bullets into Taylor's head and throat. He had also removed from the briefcase the Airtel that listed members of the top-secret task force, but he took nothing else. Those investigating Taylor's death would, he hoped, think that Taylor's killer had not even gone into the trunk of the car. Even if they did suspect Baumann, they wouldn't know that he had found the list of task force members.

In any case, the FBI had learned enough of his undertaking to form an investigative body to look into it. This was serious. There was now a possibility that the mission would be blown, that he would be caught. And for the first time he wondered whether he should go through with it.

He had already received a good chunk of Dyson's money, and he knew he could disappear now if he had to and never be found. But he had never aborted a mission before, except on orders from above; men behind desks tended to be cautious, even fearful, by nature. He felt as if his work had barely begun. And he prided himself on his dexterity and cunning, his talent at remaining elusive.

The truth was, despite all the danger he felt sure he could forge ahead and not be caught. He had been hired to do a job—the largest, most ambitious undertaking of his lifetime—and he was going to do it. He knew he was the best at what he did; pride would not let him give up now.

So he turned his attention to where the leak might have come from. There were loose ends—there were always loose ends, you could not work in a vacuum—but he thought it unlikely the leak had come from his end. True, the bomb-disposal expert in Liège was aware of a small part of his operation, the nature and operation of the bomb. But he knew very little—and certainly not enough to have been the FBI's source.

No, the leak had to have come from Malcolm Dyson's team. The question was whether someone of Dyson's associates had been bent, or their security had been compromised.

Assuming the first possibility—that one of Dyson's people had talked—then the operation was as good as over. Godammit to hell, that was exactly why Baumann didn't trust groups! If this was correct, then Baumann would know soon enough. He would proceed as planned, but with even greater caution, and prepare to abort the mission if need be.

But what if the leak had not been human but mechanical, technical? A tapped fax or phone call, a bug in Dyson's offices? The Russians, the British, and the Americans all had the facilities to listen in on telephone conversations by means of satellites. But Dyson and his people would never talk on open lines; Baumann had specifically instructed them on this point. Yet what if Dyson's people had spoken openly over amateur equipment, encrypting telephones bought on the commercial market?

This was possible.

It was utterly inconceivable that his one, brief satellite communication with Dyson had been the source of the leak, since he had said only a few words and had not been at all explicit. Yes, the CIA and the NSA and GCHQ had the ability to use a spectrum analyzer to pick up this SATCOM's characteristic signal. But why would anyone be so motivated?

Baumann had learned through bitter experience how dangerous it was to communicate by even "secure" communications, and he tried to keep doing it to a minimum. When the Libyans had hired him to bomb the La

Belle disco in West Berlin in 1986, they had been foolish enough to send a "secure" message from Tripoli to East Berlin predicting a "joyous event" to take place at a club in Berlin. The Americans had intercepted the message and had frantically tried to close down clubs in Berlin, but didn't know which one was to be hit. The operation was almost blown, and Baumann was furious. Since then, the Libyans communicate only through couriers, human-to-human contact, the only safe way.

To use the SATCOM again was a risk, but a small one. Still, he would have to take extra precautions now. This would be his last telephone call to Dyson, unless there was a great emergency.

Hence the secure fax machine.

Baumann placed a secure call to the bank in Panama City, which confirmed that the second 3.3 million had been wired to his Liechtenstein account. Excellent; exactly one week remained until the strike date. Dyson had not been tardy with the money. Then again, 3.3 million dollars here and there was pocket change to Malcolm Dyson.

He then called the Liechtenstein bank and purchased slightly less than 6.6 million U.S. dollars' worth of gold bullion. He lost a few thousand dollars in the transaction, but it would be worth it in the long run.

Then he wrote out a message, which began: LEAK YOUR END. AMERICAN INTELLIGENCE PARTIALLY KNOWLEDGEABLE. THOROUGHLY SWEEP HOME, OFFICES, COMMUNICATIONS EQUIPMENT, CHECK PERSONNEL. DON'T USE TELEPHONE. I WILL BE OUT OF CONTACT. He ended it: HEREBY ACKNOWLEDGE RECEIPT SECOND PAYMENT.

Using the red-plastic-bound Webster's pocket dictionary he'd bought in Paris, a twin of which Dyson had, he encrypted the message by means of a simple substitution cipher and typed it out on one of the preprinted forms.

The text appeared to be an authentic-looking invoice requesting prices on a list of things—item #101.15, item #13.03, and on and on. Dyson alone knew this referred to page 101 in the dictionary, fifteen major words down on the page, etc. This simple cipher was almost unbreakable.

Baumann had set a five-minute window for Dyson to fax a similarly encoded reply. He ordered a room-service lunch, took a brief nap, and once again set up the MLink-5000.

Precisely as the five-minute window began, his SATCOM blinked to indicate an incoming signal, then the fax machine warbled and out came Dyson's reply.

He read it, and then, in the glass ashtray, burned it and all the other pieces of paper he had used. He flushed the ashes down the toilet, then went out for a stroll.

Christine Vigiani had been tasked to be liaison with the National Security Agency. In reality, this meant one thing only: find out whatever she could about the intercepted telephone conversation, and urge them to get more. Sarah had arranged to have her cleared at a high enough level to read the NSA telephone intercept.

Not only is the NSA notoriously secretive, but it is disinclined to share with rival agencies more than it absolutely must about its sources and methods. Vigiani was having a hell of a time finding anyone at NSA who knew what he was talking about and had the authority, or the willingness, to talk.

Finally, an NSA analyst named Lindsay called Vigiani on the STU-III secure phone. He was cordial and seemed familiar with the satellite intercept in question.

"The first thing we need to know," Vigiani said, "is whether you captured the telephone numbers of the caller or the recipient along with the conversation."

"No."

"You didn't? You're sure of that."

"Right. The answer is no, we did not."

"Neither one. Neither sender nor receiver."

"Correct."

"Why not?"

Lindsay paused. "How to answer that," he sighed. "What we got was a snatch of conversation in mid-stream, so to speak. A few minutes from somewhere in the middle of the phone call."

"But the satellite intercept—" Vigiani said, not sure of what she was saying.

Lindsay sensed her ignorance and responded in simple language: "It's actually rare to get the phone number that's being called," he said. "Pure happenstance. We'd have to have locked on to the call from the very first second, so we could hear the dialing or the touch tones being punched."

"It's really that crude?"

"It's what the technology allows."

"Well, what we'd like is for you to have your satellites search for this same encryption scheme again. We figure that whoever made this call will continue to use this encrypted phone, and so now that we know the key, we can just pick up anything in the ether with that configuration, or whatever."

"Doesn't work that way," Lindsay said. "Our satellites can't tell any particular encryption scheme is being used until the signal is down-linked and examined."

"You've got to be kidding me. Am I talking to the National Security Agency?"

Lindsay's response was cold silence.

"All right," Vigiani said, "what *do* you know about this intercept?"

"We know a number of things. We know it was a

digital signal, to start with, which is helpful, because there aren't that many digital phone signals out there in the ether yet. Soon, that's all there will be. But not yet."

"What else?"

"And we know which microwave relay station the signal was captured from, its exact location. It's the Geneva North microwave relay, numbered Alpha 3021, located on a mountain north of Geneva. If our caller uses this phone again, the signal will likely be transmitted using the same relay. We can target that station."

"Okay . . ."

"Also, each microwave relay station uses a known, fixed set of frequencies. We can tell our receiving station to listen in on these frequencies, scan them. Of course, we'll ask the British, GCHQ, to monitor the same frequencies and process them. If we're really lucky, we'll record another signal that won't decrypt."

"Fine," Vigiani said, "but this time get the phone number, okay?"

"Okay, right," the NSA man said dryly. "You got it. Whatever you want."

Vigiani got up from her desk and walked toward Sarah's office. There, gathered around Sarah in a knot, were most of the task force members watching Sarah speak on the phone. Everyone, including Sarah, looked stricken.

"What?" she said to Ullman. "What is it?"

"It's Duke," he said without even turning to her.

CHAPTER FORTY-SEVEN

Straining to keep a semblance of order and calm, Sarah stood before the MINOTAUR task force. "Whatever our private suspicions," she said, "we can't rule out the possibility that Perry Taylor died in a—well, I hesitate to use the word 'routine,' but there it is—a routine holdup. At least that's the way it looks to both the Bureau's Crime Labs and Washington Police Homicide."

"In a parking lot in broad daylight?" asked George Roth.

"It was early evening," she said.

"But the sun was out," Roth persisted.

"Okay, right, but his car was parked in a fairly remote area of the lot."

Pappas shook his head, but Sarah couldn't tell what he was thinking.

"Look," Roth said, "Baumann wants us to think Taylor was held up. Does anyone here seriously think that's what happened? I don't know Taylor. You feebees, tell me: was he a drug user?"

"Of course not," Vigiani said. "Obviously Baumann did this. Which means he's in the U.S."

Russell Ullman, to whom Perry Taylor had been something of a father figure, had been silent for most of the meeting. His eyes were rimmed in red. Now he spoke, his voice weak. "Has Crime Labs looked into the MO of the murders at Pollsmoor Prison to establish a correlation?"

"Yes," Sarah said. "But there's nothing."

"How so?" Pappas asked.

"Taylor appears to have died from bullet wounds in the throat and forehead at fairly close range."

"What do you think?" Vigiani exploded. "Baumann's going to leave a signature—a billboard saying, 'Here I am'? Come *on*!"

"All right," Sarah said calmly. "You all may be right."

Roth asked: "Any similarity between Taylor's death and the death of your call-girl friend back in Boston?"

Sarah shook her head. "Ballistics tells me no."

"If Duke was killed by Henrik Baumann," said Pappas, "that tells us he's not unwilling to kill a major FBI official, with all the heat that brings down. The question then is, what would his motive be? Nothing appears to have been stolen from Taylor or his car, except a wallet."

"Baumann might have wanted the ID cards," Ullman said. "Or he might have wanted to make it look like a mugging."

"The motive," Vigiani said, "was to try to paralyze the hunt for him. And if he'd kill Duke Taylor, he'd certainly kill any of us in an instant."

On Jared's third day in New York, on a Sunday afternoon, he insisted on going to the park to play. Sarah had worked all day Saturday, and had planned to work all day Sunday too, but at the last moment she relented. It was important for her to spend some family time with Jared. And she could do some work while he played. So they went to Strawberry Fields at West Seventy-second Street, and she read files while he batted a softball around by himself. It would have been a sad sight, this solitary kid in a brand-new leather jacket (a gift from Peter), tossing a ball up into the air and batting it, then running after it and starting all over again, were it not for the fact that he was so clearly enjoying himself.

In short order he had befriended another boy of roughly the same age who took turns pitching to him and then being pitched to. Relieved that he had met someone, Sarah returned to reading Bureau intelligence files on terrorist attempts within the United States.

The truth was, she was discovering, the Bureau's record on catching terrorists was spotty. In 1986, she read, a domestic group called the El Rukin organization tried to buy an antitank weapon from an FBI undercover agent, intending to pull off some terrorist act in the United States in exchange for money from the Libyan government. A couple of years later, the FBI arrested four members of the Provisional Irish Republican Army who were trying to buy a heat-seeking antiaircraft missile in Florida.

Fine, but what about all the black-market weapons sales that the Bureau *didn't* catch? Barely months after the TRADEBOM investigation, which Alex Pappas was justly so proud of, a ring of Sudanese terrorists was arrested in New York, and members of the Abu Nidal organization were apprehended in Ohio, Wisconsin, and Missouri.

Pappas talked of probabilities, but what were the odds, really, that the special working group would catch this terrorist—and without a photograph?

People liked to joke about the World Trade Center terrorists, with their rinky-dink operation, returning to Ryder Truck Rental to get their five-hundred-dollar security deposit back, but Sarah didn't find it amusing. Sure, the World Trade Center bombers were jokers, clowns, amateurs, but look what they had accomplished.

And imagine what a top-notch, professional terrorist like Henrik Baumann could do.

The Bureau had come close to cracking the Oklahoma City case, but so much of it was luck. One of the investigators had found a twisted scrap of truck axle with a legible vehicle identification number on it, and he fed that number into Rapid Start, one of the Bureau's many databases, and then we were off. That was good, basic scut work—but the Bureau had also lucked out when it was discovered that a nearby ATM video camera had captured an image of the rental truck that contained the bomb. And then a cop happened to stop a guy for speeding, a guy who happened to be driving without a license. How many lucky breaks could MINOTAUR really count on?

Perry Taylor's death had changed everything. None of them really believed he'd been killed in a routine mugging. It was as if Baumann were in the next room now. They could hear his footsteps, his breathing, his approach. He was no longer an abstraction, a code name. He was *here*.

Lost in her thoughts, Sarah didn't notice at first that Jared had disappeared.

She looked around, then rose slowly to get a better vantage point. She slipped the files into her shoulder bag. Jared was gone.

She was not yet nervous. Jared was impulsive, prone to run off without thinking, and now he had an accomplice.

She called his name. Several people turned around to look at her.

She called his name again, louder.

"Dammit, Jared," she said. "Where the hell are you?"

She tightened her fists in anger and frustration, walked aimlessly around the landscaped field, yelled for him.

No answer.

She told herself not to overreact, not to be overprotective. Any moment he'd pop up behind her, laughing at the prank he'd pulled off, and she'd deliver a stern lecture about not fooling around that way in a strange city.

And after she'd circled the field and realized he really wasn't there, that he probably wasn't playing a trick, her heart began thudding.

She followed the path near where he and his new friend had been playing, toward the northeast part of the field, which dropped off suddenly into a densely wooded area, and when she heard his cries she began to run.

Three rough-looking late-adolescent boys had circled Jared and were jabbing at him. One of them was grabbing his new leather jacket. Another was wielding a baseball bat. Jared's face was flushed, his eyes wide with fear.

"Hey!" she called out. "Back off! Leave him alone!"

They turned to look at her, and then two of them approached her.

"Mommy!" Jared cried out.

"Mommy!" mimicked one of them, with dreadlocks and a wispy adolescent goatee.

"Fuck you, bitch," the other said, waving the bat.

Sarah knew the basics of hand combat, but the truth was she had never had to defend herself physically, not once in her career outside of the FBI Academy, not once when she didn't have a gun, and right now her gun was in the office suite on West Thirty-seventh Street.

And then she felt a numbing blow to her abdomen, at precisely the same time that Jared let out a terrified scream, and she felt her purse being yanked from her shoulder. One of the young men had swung at her with the bat. With a great fury she lunged at the two attackers, while her son was slammed to the ground by the other, who yanked off his leather jacket. Jared let out a terrible scream.

She hit one of them in the jaw. He barely flinched, grabbed her waist, kneed her in the solar plexus, while the other approached, brandishing a bat. She screamed for help, but barely a sound escaped her throat. "Just leave him alone," she finally shouted, trying to regain her balance, but they kept coming at her, grabbing her neck, kicking at her abdomen. She screamed again.

"Back off!" said a male voice to her right. "You let her go!" She caught a glimpse of a slender bespectacled man in jeans and a dark-blue T-shirt, walking stiffly toward them. He lunged at the assailants. One of the kids, who had been menacing Jared, turned to fend off this newcomer; the one with the bat swung at him and cracked into his hip, hard.

The man doubled up in pain. His glasses skittered to the ground a few feet away, one lens popped out of the bent frame.

And then, as quickly as they had appeared, the three young men disappeared, tearing off at top speed. Jared was in a heap on the ground, sobbing. Blood was pouring down his forehead, sheeting down. She rushed to him, threw her arms around him.

"Oh, my God," she said. "My God. Are you all right? Are you all right?"

"Hurt," came his small, muffled voice.

"Oh, Jesus," she said, feeling his blood-sticky scalp for the source of the gushing blood. He'd been wounded in the head. She squeezed him tight, feeling his body rise and fall rhythmically with his sobs. He winced when she touched a spot, a large gash. She looked up, saw the man in the blue T-shirt getting awkwardly to his feet.

"Is he okay?" the man asked. He had soft brown

eyes, a tousled head of salt-and-pepper hair. He clutched his hip, bent down to retrieve his glasses, which looked damaged beyond repair. "Looks like he got hit bad."

"I—I don't know," Sarah said.

The man came closer, knelt down, touched Jared's head. Jared let out a yowl of pain. "It looks bad," the man said. "We've got to get him to a hospital. Is there one nearby?"

"I have no idea," Sarah said, now terrified as the realization struck her that Jared might in fact have been seriously hurt. "Oh, God. There's got to be one."

"Can you pick him up? If you can't, I can. He shouldn't walk."

"No," Sarah said quickly. She didn't want the stranger to touch Jared, though he was a nice-seeming man, maybe around forty, quite good-looking, and seemed gentle. "I'll carry him," she said.

"I'll get a cab."

The man ran ahead of them and flagged down a cab, which came screeching to a halt. He opened the back door, then came running back toward Sarah, who was struggling to carry Jared, and helped them into the cab.

"Get us to the nearest emergency room," the man ordered the driver.

In the cab, the man introduced himself. His name was Brian Lamoreaux, and he was an architect, a writer, and a professor of architecture and town planning at the University of Alberta in Edmonton. Things were moving so quickly that she forgot even to thank the stranger for coming along to help them.

When the cab stopped, Sarah allowed him to pick up Jared and escort them into the St. Luke's–Roosevelt Hospital ER. Jared's bleeding was still profuse, but it seemed to be slowing. Although he had stopped crying, he seemed dazed.

"I think he's probably okay," Brian assured her. "The

scalp always bleeds a lot. He probably got cut when he was shoved to the ground."

Brian dealt with the triage nurses while Sarah comforted Jared, and Jared was seen quickly. The examining physician asked if his tetanus shots were up to date. It took Sarah a moment to remember that Jared had had a DPT shot at the age of four or five.

The doctor wanted to take Jared away to suture his scalp, but Brian insisted that Sarah be allowed to accompany her son, and they reluctantly agreed.

As they wheeled Jared, Sarah noticed for the first time that Brian was limping slightly. She wondered whether the limp was from the blow with the bat. Jared, who was looking over at Brian, wasn't burdened with tact, and for the first time he spoke.

"Did you get hurt trying to help us?" Jared asked.

"Hardly at all," Brian Lamoreaux said. "Hip's bruised a bit, but I'll be fine."

"But you're limping," Jared persisted.

"I've had this limp for a long time," he replied. "Let's worry about you."

"How'd you get it?" Jared asked.

"Jared!" Sarah exclaimed.

"No, it's okay," Brian said. "I was in an accident once. Years ago."

"Wow," Jared said, satisfied.

The surgeon clipped the hair around the scalp wound and numbed the area with a syringe of something, chatting with Jared the whole time to distract him. Then, a few minutes later when the numbness had set in, he began suturing the scalp. Sarah held his hand; Brian sat in a chair nearby.

"Okay," the surgeon said to Sarah when the procedure was done, "he's going to be fine. He must have fallen against something on the ground, a piece of metal or broken glass or something, and got a fairly nasty laceration. What we call a 'scalp lac.' The scalp is richly vascular and bleeds like hell. Fortunately, scalp lacs are easy to suture."

"Shouldn't you check for concussion?" Sarah asked.

"No reason to," the doctor said. "He didn't lose consciousness at all, did he?"

She shook her head.

"Then no."

"What about infection?"

"I cleaned the wound with Betadine, then used lidocaine with epinephrine, then dabbed on some bacitracin. He's had his tetanus shots, so he should be okay there. I wouldn't worry about it. Just don't wash the hair for three days. Don't get the wound wet. Watch for signs of infection, like redness or pus. In a week the sutures can come out. If you have a pediatrician in town he can take them out, or come on back here. He'll be fine."

They sat for a while, the three of them, near a vending machine in the ER waiting area. Brian told Sarah he was working on a biography of a Canadian architect Sarah had never heard of. He was here because some of the architect's papers were in New York. Sarah said she was with the FBI, but was vague about what exactly she did, and he, apparently sensing her discomfort, didn't pursue it.

Abruptly, Jared asked, with his eight-year-old's straightforwardness: "Are you married?"

Sarah felt acutely uncomfortable. Was her son turning into a pander for his mother?

"I was," Brian said.

"Jared knows all about divorce," Sarah said quickly, mussing Jared's hair. "Doesn't he?"

"My wife died three years ago," he said.

"I'm sorry," Sarah said. She watched Brian as he talked to Jared. On closer inspection, she saw that he was prematurely gray; his face was youthful, although there were deep furrows around his mouth that looked like smile lines.

"How?" Jared asked.

"Jared!" Sarah said, shocked.

"No, it's a natural thing to ask. She was sick for a long time, Jared."

"What'd she have, cancer?"

"Come on, now, Jared!" Sarah said.

"Yes," Brian said. "In fact, she had breast cancer."

"Oh," Jared said, somewhere between sad and bored.

"She was young," Sarah said.

"It happens. It's a horrible thing." He paused. "You're divorced?"

"Yeah," she said, and quickly said, "You're great with kids—do you have a son?"

"Clare wanted to have a kid before she got sick. We both did. Before I got my Ph.D. and went into academia, I worked for the Canadian Government Children's Bureau as a counselor. I worked with a lot of kids Jared's age. He's a terrific little guy."

"I think so, but I'm biased."

"So, you're alone here? I mean, you and your son?"

Sarah hesitated. "Yeah, I guess you could say that."

"Me, too. It's a tough city to be lonely in."

"I said alone, not lonely. Anyway, it's a better place to be alone in than, say, Jackson, Mississippi."

"Listen, I hope this isn't too . . . forward, but I've got a couple of tickets to a performance of Beethoven's late quartets at Carnegie Hall, day after tomorrow." He reddened as he talked. "I got them for me and a colleague of mine, but—"

"But she can't make it," Sarah interrupted, "and you hate to waste a ticket, right?"

"*He*, actually. He decided to leave the city early and return to Canada. I don't know if this is your kind of thing, or whatever—"

"I'm sorry," Sarah said. "I love chamber music, and the late quartets are among my favorites, but I'm just not a reliable companion these days. I'm in New York on some very pressing business, and my pager's always going off, and I often have to go in to work at odd times of day or night."

"That's all right," Brian said.

"I don't think so," she said. She was drawn to Brian, but instinctively distrustful of any stranger in the city. "Thanks anyway. And—listen, thank you so much for your help."

"Can I take your number anyway?"

She hesitated, thought it over. "All right," she said, and gave it to him.

"So can I call you sometime?"

She shrugged, smiled. "Sure."

"I will. Jared, you're going to be fine. Just don't wash your hair for a couple of days. You heard the doctor."

"Yeah, I can deal with that," Jared said.

"I thought so. Take care." He shook Sarah's hand. "Maybe I'll see you again."

"Yeah," she said. "Maybe."

CHAPTER FORTY-EIGHT

The encrypted message Baumann had faxed by SATCOM emerged with a beep from one of Malcolm Dyson's personal fax machines in his inner office. From the rest room, where, wheelchair-bound, he found the simple act of relieving himself a veritable Bataan death march, he heard the fax and wheeled out to get it.

Faxes that came through these lines were for his eyes only; mostly they contained political intelligence of a highly confidential nature that could affect a major deal, or they spelled out details of blatantly illegal transactions he preferred his staff not to know too much about.

Recently the Dyson corporate jet had been flying to Moscow quite a bit, and to the Ukrainian capital, Kiev, where Dyson's minions were hacking through some Byzantine dealings in grain and sugar, Siberian oil, and copper refined in Kazakhstan. Most of these undertakings were extremely sensitive, involving massive bribes to politicians. Had one of them soured?

But this one, sender unspecified, was a meaningless jumble of words. He stared at it mystified for a few seconds until he realized that it was the substitution cipher he had worked out with Baumann.

He buzzed for Lomax and had him do the crypto-graphic heavy lifting. Lomax took the fax and the pocket dictionary to his office and returned half an hour later with the message in clear.

Dyson donned his reading glasses and studied the translation. "The hell's this supposed to mean?" he asked his aide. " 'Leak your end' and 'American intel-ligence partially knowledgeable'?"

Lomax answered with another question. "If there's a leak, how does he know it's from our end?"

" 'Leak,' " Dyson said with a scowl. "How serious a leak? He doesn't say he's abandoning the operation; it can't be that serious."

"I don't know."

"The fuck is 'partially knowledgeable,' anyway?"

"Don't know."

"I've told exactly two people," Dyson said. "You and Kinzel." Johann Kinzel ran the Zug, Switzerland, of-fice of Dyson & Company, and was one of Dyson's few confidants.

"You've hardly told Kinzel a thing," Martin Lomax reminded him. "The roughest outline, really."

"You two've talked about this, though, I'm sure."

"Of course," Lomax said. "He's made all the banking arrangements. But all of our conversations have been on the secure phone."

Dyson gave his underling a scorching stare. "On the Russian's phones, I assume."

"Of course."

Dyson shook his head. "Those phones are secure—the only ones I want you or Kinzel to use. What the hell does he mean? This office is swept every other day. Arcadia gets a good going-over every Monday. And we can't even raise the guy, can we? This is exactly how I didn't want it."

"At least we know he's in New York."

"Cold comfort. One week remaining, and we don't even know what he's done."

"The main thing is that you not be connected in any way."

"What about the hired gun who took care of the whore in Boston?"

"Died in an unfortunate car accident near his native Coventry, England."

Dyson gave one of his enigmatic smiles and reached for a Macanudo, whose end he snipped as meticulously as a surgeon. He lighted it with a gold lighter and turned toward the window. Martin Lomax stood in silence, knowing better than to interrupt one of his boss's reveries, which were more and more frequent of late.

Dyson found himself recalling the incident once again, for what seemed the millionth time. It had not made any of the newspapers, which indicated to Dyson that the U.S. government and its allies had pulled in a lot of chits. It had been a botch, all round, and the less known publicly the better.

Dyson had always feared the bounty hunters, but he had not counted on a bounty hunter working on contract for the U.S. government, a higher level of bounty hunter with the best intelligence.

Washington had obviously given up. All legal channels had been exhausted. The Justice Department's Office of International Affairs had passed on to State its request to extradite. State had sent it to the Swiss embassy. No dice. The Alien Fugitive Division of Interpol's U.S. National Central Bureau had been enlisted, to no effect.

Then someone at Justice, clearly frustrated beyond rational thinking, had come up with the idea: Screw the federal marshals. Send a contract employee to Monaco, where Dyson and his wife went twice a month. Grab the fucker. Just go in there and grab him and bring him back to the States, back to justice and Justice. Sort out the niceties later.

The attempted grab happened on a dark pathway near the casino. Two armed bounty hunters, actually. Taking on two of Dyson's personal bodyguards.

A full moon, a bright crystalline night sky. The twenty-sixth of June. Malcolm and Alexandra Dyson had just come from a night of baccarat, accompanied by their thirty-one-year-old daughter, Pandora, a delicately beautiful woman, their only child, visiting from Paris.

The ringing of Pandora's delighted laughter, the clove notes of Alexandra's perfume.

A scuff on the pavement, a rustling.

Dimly glimpsed out of the corner of an eye: a silhouette, a darting figure.

Dyson, always watching, always suspicious, felt his stomach constrict before his mind knew anything.

The sudden intrusion of a raspy male voice: "*Freeze.*"

Bertrand, Dyson's senior bodyguard, drew his pistol first, and the bounty hunters swiftly returned fire.

A sudden explosion, a series of rapid pops, the flashes of orange fire, the acrid smell of cordite. A woman's scream, which was really the terrified scream of two women. The flash of moonlight reflected in Pandora's earrings, a cough.

Bertrand saved Dyson's life, though not his legs, and died in the process. Both Dyson's wife and daughter were killed instantly. Dyson, paralyzed from the waist down, squirmed over to his dying wife and child and threw his arms around them both, half protecting, half embracing.

Malcolm and Alexandra Dyson's marriage had long cooled, but she had given birth to Pandora, and Pandora was Malcolm Dyson's whole world, the center of his life. He loved his daughter as much as any father had ever loved a daughter. He was obsessed with his Pandora; he could not talk about her without lighting up, without a smile or a glow.

Malcolm Dyson was a paraplegic now who carried his anger around in his motorized chair. Once he had lived for fortune; now he lived for revenge. *I'll never walk again*, he had once thundered at Lomax, *but with Pandora gone, why in the world would I ever want to?*

CHAPTER FORTY-NINE

Early Monday morning, Sarah arrived at headquarters, walking stiffly from the previous day's attack. She had placed Band-Aids over the cuts on her neck and the side of her face. There was a large bruise on her right cheek that had turned blue, another one on her forearm, and a particularly nasty one under her rib cage.

"What the hell happened to you?" Pappas asked.

She recounted the incident, assured Pappas that Jared was fine.

"Eight-year-old boys," Pappas said, "are a unique species. They're easily frightened and just as easily soothed. Plus, their wounds somehow seem to heal almost overnight—it's one of their chief physical properties."

Christine Vigiani approached, waited for Pappas to finish talking. In one hand was a curling sheet of slick fax paper; in the other was a cigarette, pluming smoke.

She said: "We got a photo."

Sarah whirled around. "Thank God. How?"

"I've been putting out intelligence feelers to all friendly contacts, as you asked me to do. I was sort of dubious, I'll admit it. But then all of a sudden, Mossad finally came through." The Mossad is world-renowned for its extensive photographic archives, some of which are stored on CD-ROM.

Sarah took the fax. "What is this?" she asked.

"An enlargement of a video image taken from a moving car in Johannesburg—a group of BOSS officers exiting a restaurant."

"This came over the high-res fax?" Sarah asked, plainly crestfallen. "This is it?"

"It's all they had, and since it comes from a single video frame—"

"Is this supposed to be a face? It looks more like a smudged thumbprint!" It was totally useless.

Vigiani took a drag from her cigarette, narrowed her eyes in silence.

"I'm sorry, Chris," Sarah said. "Nice try anyway, but this isn't going to do us any good."

When the group had assembled for the morning meeting, Sarah announced: "A few hundred copies of a South African computer Identi-Kit drawing of our good Prince are available up front, along with a spec sheet. Flash them around, or leave a copy if you think there's a chance he might come into an establishment. We've got to check as many hotels as we can, which means we'll have to call in some reinforcements from the PD and the Bureau. Remember, we're looking for a fugitive implicated in a murder. That's the public line."

"That's what he is," mumbled one of the cops.

"Do you know how many hotels there are in the city?" asked another one of the cops, a tall, thin, sandy-haired fellow named Ranahan.

"No," said Roth, holding a commuter's mug of coffee. He turned around to stare directly at him. "Exactly how many hotels are there in the city? I'd be interested to learn the number."

Ranahan coughed nervously. "How the hell do I know? A shitload."

Roth nodded meaningfully. "'A shitload.' *I* see. Is that privileged information, or can I leak that to the press?"

"Baumann is known to travel first-class," Sarah interrupted, "and to prefer first-class accommodations, so we should make sure to check all the top hotels, but also the bottom rung, the flophouses and boardinghouses. Those are the best places to ensure anonymity, better than the middle-level ones."

"I'll do the Plaza and the Carlyle," Ranahan volunteered. "George, there's a bunch of crack hotels in Harlem got your name on them."

"Keep the search to Manhattan proper," Sarah instructed. "White male, forties. Blue eyes, black hair, medium build, no known identifying marks. Bearded, but may be clean-shaven or have a mustache. Probably has a South African accent."

"What the hell does that sound like?" asked Special Agent Walter Latimer from the New York office.

"No one knows what a South African accent sounds like," said Ullman. "They might think it's an English accent, or Australian or Dutch or even German."

"Right," Sarah said. "Now, let's bear in mind that he can't exist in a vacuum, in isolation. What does he have to do in order to live in the city and make his preparations?"

"Does he have any known accomplices?" asked Vigiani. "Any major act requires some assistants or contacts. He's not going to just fly in, plant a bomb, and fly out. It doesn't work that way."

"He may want to open a bank account," Vigiani's police partner said. "Or rent a car or a truck or a van."

"Like maybe from Ryder Truck Rental in Jersey City," suggested Lieutenant Roth, a reference to the place where the Trade Center conspirators rented their van.

"He's a stranger in a strange land," Sarah said. "That's why he may call upon old contacts, friends or accomplices or contacts from the South African service or from past jobs. Chris, I'd like you to stay here and work the phones and the fax, see what you can turn up from friendly intelligence services in the way of known contacts. You didn't turn up anything on the domestic right-wing extremist groups, did you?"

Vigiani shook her head slowly.

"Didn't think so. Ken, what about the video frame Christine got from Mossad—any luck there?"

"I've been trying a bunch of times to enhance the photo using some not-bad photo-enhancement software. Some our own, some commercial 'paintbrush' stuff, but it's hopeless. There's no face there. I don't think the Mossad guys even had a lens on their camera."

"Thanks for trying," Sarah said. "Have you turned up any of our man's known relatives, associates, contacts, whatever?"

"Zero," Ken replied.

"Great," said one of the cops mordantly. "The guy has no friends."

"Yeah, well, if your name was the Prince of Darkness," said Roth, "you wouldn't exactly be popular either. 'Hey, hon, I've invited the Prince of Darkness over for dinner tonight. There enough lasagna to go around?' "

Sarah smiled politely, and a few cops chuckled appreciatively.

"One of the wizards at ID," Ken went on, "translated his ten-prints into a couple of different formats, NCIC and AFIS, in addition to the Henry system, and secure-faxed them to the French, the Italians, the Spanish, the Germans, the Israelis, and the Brits, for starters. A couple of the antiterrorist strike forces were really helpful. The Spanish GEO, the Grupo Especial de Operaciones—Special Operations Group, their antiterrorist group. The French GIGN, the Groupement d'Intervention de la Gendarmerie Nationale, France's crack antiterrorist unit. And the German GSG-9. They're all operational, but they all have direct lines to intelligence."

"And?" Sarah prompted.

"And we scored a couple interesting hits."

Several heads turned in his direction.

"In 1985 and '86 there was a string of fifteen bombings in Paris. Thirteen people were killed, more than two hundred wounded."

"Iranian, wasn't it?" Pappas said.

"I don't know—terrorism isn't my forte. But I do know that a Tunisian-born Frenchman was arrested and put on trial as the mastermind behind the campaign. He wanted to keep France from sending arms to Iraq during its war with Iran. Well, a big juicy latent thumbprint was found, clear as day, on a piece of duct tape used on one of the packages. The print was never ID'd—it didn't come from the Tunisian guy."

"Baumann," one of the cops said.

"The way it looks," Ken said. "Our guy gets around, or at least he's not discriminating about who he works for. And the Spaniards, the GEO, had a fairly good partial from his index finger, taken from the fuel line of a car back in 1973. Apparently our man was wearing latex surgical gloves, but when the latex in the glove is stretched tightly enough, the print comes through."

"What was the incident?" Pappas asked sharply.

"The assassination of Luis Carrero Blanco, the prime minister of Spain."

"Jesus, that was the Basques," Pappas said. "The Basque separatist movement ETA. You know, there was a rumor that they brought in an outsider. Baumann . . . is that *possible*?"

"Well, they scored a hit on the prints," Ken said, "so I guess so."

"The guy's not a ghost," Ullman said. "He does exist."

"Ken," Sarah said, "call up whatever you can on those events. I want names, contacts, *anything*. Have you been in touch with TRAC?" TRAC was the Terrorist Research and Analytical Center at Bureau headquarters in Washington.

"Oh, sure," Ken said. "I also reached out to INS, to see if they had any matches for the prints. My thinking was, maybe he applied for a U.S. visa under a false name. The answer was no, of course. He's way too careful a dude."

"Well, nice try, anyway," Sarah said. "And what about our cross-check?"

"A primo idea, oh esteemed leader." He explained to the others Sarah's idea. "But State is hamstrung by the Privacy Act, which protects passport information so ferociously that you can't just lump it all together in one nice, handy package."

Pappas gave Sarah a significant look. Sarah felt uncomfortable. "I like that," she said. "With all our personal rights to privacy, what about the right not to be blown up in a subway or a skyscraper or something?"

Ken went on: "Ask State a simple question like 'Can you tell if someone got into the country using a stolen passport?' and you get a load of bullshit. Like, 'Oh, we don't depend on the passport number for enforcement,' and 'Oh, there's lots of security features to prevent fraud, it could never happen.' Junk like that. But here's what they *don't* want to tell you: they do have a lookout system for lost or stolen passports, so it pops up on the screen at all major ports of entry. It's called the Consular Lookout and Support System. But it's not real-time or anywhere close. It's weeks and weeks behind the time.

So you steal a passport from a guy in London—I mean, right out from under his nose, so he sees you doing it—and you can use that passport to get into the U.S., assuming you look enough like the photo on the stolen passport. Because it's *weeks* by the time the London embassy sends—I mean, sends by *snail-mail*—the report of a lost or stolen passport to the U.S. and it's entered into the system."

"Can't you get a list of all passports reported stolen or lost in the last several months?" Sarah asked.

"That's the other thing. They don't have a way to do that, to collect the names and passport numbers in one file."

"You're kidding me," Sarah said.

"Unfortunately not. The U.S. State Department issues four million passports a year. And if you look at the figures for passports reported lost or stolen in 1992, for example, there were thirteen thousand, one hundred and one passports reported lost, and fourteen thousand, six hundred and ninety-two reported stolen. Of course, a lot of people who've actually lost their passport report it as stolen to save face, seem less clumsy. Yet State can't do a cross-check for you on stolen passports that were used after they were reported stolen!"

Lieutenant Roth remarked, "Let's hear it for the feds."

"So now what?" Sarah asked.

"So just because they can't do it doesn't mean *I* can't."

Sarah smiled wanly.

"Through the Bureau's link, I tapped into the Consular Lookout and Support System to see what passport numbers have been flagged as lost or stolen. Then simultaneously I went into the INS database that lists everyone who's entered the country by any port of entry."

"And if there's a match," Vigiani said excitedly, "you've got yourself a list of everyone who used a stolen

or lost passport to get into the country in the last couple
of months."

"Right," Ken concluded.

"And?" Sarah said.

"Well, I'm running the cross-check now, and I'll fill
you in as soon as you let me go back to my toys."

"You did all this over the weekend?" asked one of
the cops, a black man named Leon Hoskin, with more
contempt than awe.

"Computers never sleep," Ken explained offhandedly. "Some of these passport numbers will be automatic rule-outs, I suspect. Plus, I can eliminate females,
older folks, nonwhites."

"Don't," Sarah said. "Be careful about what you eliminate. A pro like Baumann can look older or younger
than he is, can dress like a nun or a wheelchair-bound
middle-aged man, for all I know. Don't be too hasty to
rule any of them out."

For some reason she flashed on an image of Jared
curled fetus-like on the ground in Central Park, then
saw the wispy goatee of her mugger.

She felt a surge of anger and of protectiveness, and
thought of how little progress they'd made, really, since
she'd arrived here, how much further there was to go
before there was even the remotest chance of stopping
the Prince of Darkness.

CHAPTER FIFTY

Warren Elkind, chairman and chief executive officer of the Manhattan Bank, had been under intensive FBI surveillance since Operation MINOTAUR had begun its work. Elkind had been unreceptive to repeated FBI inquiries, and therefore Sarah had ordered the surveillance, knowing in time they would find his weak spot.

There were several leading private bondage-and-discipline sex clubs in New York City, and considering his relationship with Valerie Santoro, the odds were great that Elkind frequented at least one of them. He did not, however, turn up at the two best-known ones, Pandora's Box and the Nutcracker.

At around four o'clock the next afternoon, Elkind left his office in the Manhattan Bancorp Building and began walking north up Lexington. His tails followed him to an office building on East Fifty-sixth Street between First and Second avenues, which was just a few blocks away.

Repeated calls to his office at the same time elicited the information that he was "out of the office," and then that he had "left for the day." As soon as surveillance had determined that Elkind's destination, on the thirteenth floor of the building, was the private and very exclusive Brimstone Club, Sarah's beeper went off.

She was there within twenty minutes, which, given the traffic, was impressive time.

The elevator took her straight to the thirteenth floor and opened on a small, dark, eucalyptus-scented waiting area with comfortable-looking couches around a black shag rug. On the wall were vast blowups of artistically grainy photographs of women posing provocatively in black leather. Behind a glass window, sitting at a counter, was a fierce-looking middle-aged woman with obviously dyed blond hair, an enormous bosom, and heavy purple eyeshadow. She glanced warily at Sarah and said, "Can I help you?"

Sarah had dressed casually in jeans and a buttondown polo shirt rolled up at the sleeves. She looked like an attractive young woman who was perhaps a graduate student, perhaps a professional on a day off. Hard to read, yes, but certainly not someone to beware of.

She had thought long and hard about her approach here, too. Flashing her credentials wouldn't get her beyond the waiting area, if they wanted to play hardball. If she bluffed her way in, she risked alerting him. Yet she had to get in somehow.

"A friend of mine suggested I check out working here, learn the trade," she said offhandedly.

"Uh huh," the blond receptionist said. "And who's that?"

"I'd rather not say, okay? A friend. I'm sort of into the idea of dominance."

She looked at Sarah neutrally yet appraisingly. "You have experience?"

"Some. I've played a little, with a lover. Done the clubs, the Nutcracker, you know. Now I'm sort of looking to do it professionally."

"You married?"

"No. My ex-husband's idea of dominance and submission was more mental than physical, if you know what I'm saying."

The receptionist gave a short laugh. "What toys are you familiar with?"

"Well . . . single-tail whips. Floggers. Some knifeplay, electrical play. CBT." CBT was the argot for cockand-ball torture.

"We don't allow the knife," the receptionist said. "No blood sports."

"I want a tour," Sarah said.

"I think one of the rooms is booked," said the receptionist.

"That's okay. Everything else, though."

The receptionist shrugged.

Another woman, this one with jet-black hair, gave the tour. She was stout and even more buxom than the receptionist, dressed entirely in black stretch fabric, and had a hooked nose. She introduced herself as Eva and gave an introductory spiel.

The Brimstone Club was one of New York's most exclusive houses of D&S, or dominance and submission. Its clientele, she explained, included some of the city's wealthiest and most powerful men and women. They ranged from corporate lawyers to music executives, from Wall Street tycoons to world-famous academics. No one from the lower or even middle echelons of society. A number of prominent public figures, a few extremely well known, came here regularly.

"Most of our members are men," Eva explained, "mostly submissives, though not all. Largely heterosexual, but not entirely. We have a staff of fourteen, including two men and twelve exalted mistresses."

Eva led Sarah down a low-ceilinged, acoustically tiled corridor. "We charge two hundred fifty dollars an hour, two-hour minimum. No sex or drugs allowed, and we're strict about that."

"So to speak."

She smiled. "So to speak. No intercourse or oral sex. No blood sports. Absolutely no hand releases. That's the law."

"How much of that five hundred do I get?"

"Forty percent of the hourly fee," Eva said.

"How many clients a day can I reasonably expect?"

"Look," Eva said, "there's always a surplus of mistresses."

"So how much time am I going to sit, waiting for someone who doesn't have a favorite?"

"If you're good, you can do maybe a thousand a day for the house, which means four hundred for yourself."

"You guys have an arrangement with any of the kinky clothing stores in the city? Any employee discounts or whatever? That stuff's expensive."

"Oh, sure. No nice clothes, no clients, simple as that. Yeah, we've got arrangements." She opened a door marked REST ROOM. A man in a maid's uniform was on his knees, furtively cleaning the tiled floor with a toothbrush and a pail of Lysol. Sarah noticed he was wearing a wedding band.

"That's not clean enough, Matilda," she barked. "Do it again!" She closed the door. "Anyway, that's the rest room. Unisex. His real name is Matthew. Matilda, when he's in the role. He's a sissy slave."

"Good help is hard to find, isn't it?" Sarah said.

"Not here. All right, now, there are five dungeons, all fully equipped." She pulled open a heavy steel door labeled DUNGEON TWO. Except that its walls were painted black, it could have been a doctor's examination room. Its equipment, however, would not have been found in most hospitals. There was a rotating wooden bondage table, a stretch rack, a cross outfitted with leather manacles. Against one wall was a long rack of whips and crops and other equipment Sarah didn't recognize. Against another wall was a black leather gym horse.

"That's Two. They're all pretty similar, with minor variations—suspension equipment, a pin chair, that sort of thing."

"Can I see the others?"

"Dungeon Three is in use, but I can show you the others if you want. Believe me, it's all pretty much the same thing."

"Forget it, that's all right."

"Our dominas typically wear leather, patent leather, latex, PVC, or English riding attire. We perform bondage, spanking, flagellation, and humiliation, all mild to severe. Puppy training, infantilism, genital chastisement, nipple torment, foot worship. All the usual."

When they had returned to the waiting room and Sarah had been handed a three-page form to fill out, she asked to use the rest room.

"Sure," Eva said, "go ahead. You remember where it is?"

"Yeah."

"If you want Matilda out of there, just order him out. He'd love it."

Unescorted, she followed the corridor to the rest room, passed by it, and found the steel door marked Dungeon Three, the one that was occupied. This had to be where she'd find him. She swung it open.

A beautiful redheaded woman in black PVC stretch pants, bra, gloves, and thigh-high black patent-leather boots with long spike heels was wielding a crop on a naked middle-aged man wearing only a black leather hood.

She turned toward the open door and said huffily, "*Excuse* me."

"Excuse *me*," Sarah said. "Mr. Elkind?"

A muffled, confused voice emerged from the hood: "Yes, mistress?"

"Mr. Elkind, it's Special Agent Sarah Cahill. I'm awfully sorry to disturb you, but I thought we might have a little talk."

The corporate headquarters of the Manhattan Bank were housed in a spectacular modernistic building designed by Cesar Pelli and located on Fifty-second Street near Lexington, very close to the headquarters of its leading competitor, Citicorp.

The executive offices were on the twenty-seventh floor, where Warren Elkind's suite of offices occupied a large corner of the floor, the area of a small law firm. The floors were covered with Persian carpets; antiques of burled walnut and fruitwood lined the corridors.

In his thousand-dollar navy-blue double-breasted suit with a gold tie, hair combed back, and seated behind his mammoth, bare desk, Warren Elkind once again exuded gravity. Sarah found it hard to reconcile this mandarin with the sweaty, paunchy figure she'd seen wearing nothing but a leather hood just half an hour ago.

Warren Elkind was the chairman of the second-largest commercial bank in the country. An Amherst graduate, he had been married to a wealthy New York socialite for twenty-some years and had four children. He was a director of PepsiCo, Occidental Petroleum, and Fidelity Investments, and a member of a number of exclusive clubs, from the Cosmos in Washington to the Bohemian Grove in San Francisco. A well-connected guy.

But rarely did he appear in the public eye. Here and there he gave a speech about bank regulation. Once in a while he and his wife appeared in the society pages of the *Times* at some benefit or other.

"Now," he said, "my lawyer will have a field day."

"So will the press," Sarah said. "And your share-holders. And the thousands upon thousands of employ-ees of the Manhattan Bank."

"Are you aware this is blackmail?"

"Yes," Sarah admitted blithely.

"And that I could get you fired for it?"

"Only if you could prove it," she responded. "But if I go down, I'll take you with me."

"What the hell do you want?"

"I thought you'd never ask. Mr. Elkind, we have some very good information that either you or your bank, or both, are being targeted by terrorists. And we've been trying to tell you this for over two weeks."

"Who?"

"We don't know."

He nodded slowly. "Probably the loons who did Oklahoma City. Those right-wing militia groups are convinced that the major banks are in some giant conspiracy with the Israelis and the Russians and the Trilateral Commission and the Council on Foreign Relations."

"I think whoever's behind it is considerably more sophisticated than any militia group. In any case, we need your cooperation. A few weeks ago you saw a call girl in Boston named Valerie Santoro, who was mur-dered later that same night."

Elkind stared levelly at her for several moments. His nostril hairs were white. His hands were perfectly manicured. "I don't know who or what you're talking about."

"Mr. Elkind, I understand your situation. You're a married man with four children, you're the chairman of a major bank, you have a reputation to protect. I under-stand why you'd rather not admit you know Valerie San-toro. But the potential consequences here are serious.

You should know I can make sure your name is kept confidential, that any connection to Ms. Santoro—"

"You understand English, don't you? I don't know who you're talking about."

"You should also know that a call was placed from a limousine rented in your name to a telephone number in the name of Valerie Santoro. We have records. That's point one. Point two, your name was discovered in Valerie Santoro's Rolodex. Now, perhaps we can talk for a few minutes."

Elkind looked at her for a long while as if deciding which way to play it. At last he spoke. "Listen to me, Special Agent Cahill," he said with quiet sarcasm. "I don't know any Valerie Santorini or whatever the hell her name is. You say a call to some woman was placed from my limo? What the *hell* makes you think I know anything about that? What the hell makes you so sure *I* made this call? How the hell do I know who had access to the limousine?"

"Mr. Elkind—"

"And you say my name is in some girl's Rolodex. So what?" He leaned over his desk, rustled through a pile of mail, and triumphantly waved a large junk-mail envelope. "I'm delighted and honored that some call girl in Boston put me in her Rolodex. And apparently I've also won *ten million dollars* from the Publishers Clearing House, Special Agent Cahill."

"Please, Mr. Elkind—"

"Ms. Cahill, in my position, you're a target for all sorts of schemers and loonies. These type of people prey on rich men like me all the time. They go through the *Forbes* Four Hundred, they buy addresses from these computer data services. I don't even know this woman, and I resent your wasting my time with this bullshit. If you're going to accuse me of the murder of some girl I don't even know, go right ahead. But you'd better have an ironclad case. And you'll be laughed out of a job. I'll see to it."

Sarah felt her face flush with anger. She studied the repeating floral pattern on the rust-colored carpet. "Is that a threat?"

"That's a prediction. I'm not without friends and allies. Don't fuck with me." He stood up.

"Sit down, please," she said. She took out a cassette tape recorder and hit the play button.

After she played the phone conversation between Elkind and Valerie, she said: "This, as well as your documented membership in the Brimstone Club, can become public knowledge through artfully placed leaks. Which means the end of your reign at Manhattan Bank. The humiliation will be too profound. Your board of directors will demand your immediate resignation."

"My private life is my own affair."

"Not for someone in your position of prominence."

"There's no difference between what you people are doing now and the way you went after Charlie Chaplin. You don't find it repulsive?"

"Oh, sometimes I do," Sarah admitted. "But this kind of gamesmanship is something I'll bet you're quite familiar with."

"That's Machiavellian—"

"Right—since the end justifies it. Everyone's always in favor of privacy unless we're invading the 'privacy' of terrorists or assassins—then they're all in favor of our 'intelligence.' I'd have thought that the threat of a terrorist attack on your own bank would have persuaded you to cooperate long ago, but I guess not. Now the choice is yours: tell me everything, or lose your career, maybe even your family."

Sarah called to mind the society-page photographs

she had seen of Warren Elkind's socialite wife, Evangeline Danner Elkind, at one benefit or another, duly recorded in *Town & Country* and the *Times*. She was an anorexic blonde, once beautiful but now the taut-skinned victim of one too many face-lifts. She was what Tom Wolfe called a "social X ray." She and her husband had four children, one at Choate, one at Exeter, one at Vassar, one doing drugs and living off Dad's money in Miami.

Obviously Evangeline Elkind knew nothing of her husband's proclivities, and the threat of public exposure was potent. Sarah was disgusted with herself, though outwardly she seemed calculating and cool.

Of course, it was far from a sure thing that to own up to his regular liaisons with Valerie would destroy his marriage and family. Marriages and families sometimes had unexpected artesian sources of resiliency. But his career as America's most powerful banker, or even second- or third-most-powerful banker, would assuredly be ruined.

She went on, "Valerie Santoro was hired to steal a CD-ROM from your briefcase—"

"Nothing was stolen from my briefcase!"

"No. She 'borrowed' it for a while, then returned it to the front desk at the Four Seasons."

He stared at Sarah again, and this time she was sure she could see the blood drain from his face. "What are you—"

"A CD-ROM. Did you 'misplace' it while you were at the hotel?"

"Oh, Jesus God. Oh, Jesus God." Elkind's face seemed to cave in.

"What happened to it?"

"The disk—I thought it fell out of my suitcase. I mean, it was meaningless to anyone else—no one would know what was on it. Then when it turned up, I knew it had just fallen out somewhere. The front desk said it had been found in a trash container—"

"What was on it?"

"Every year we get one of those CD-ROMs that's got an entire year's worth of authentication codes on it, a different computer 'key' for each day. They're used to send money around the world by computer, encoded digitally. That's why I was in Boston, for one of those bank security meetings. Once a year the heads of the bank, or their designated proxies, meet and exchange computer keys."

"Someone who had that cryptographic key—"

"—could get into our computers and falsify transactions and steal billions of dollars. Can't even think about it."

"But if the bank is suddenly missing an enormous sum of money, wouldn't the Federal Reserve just bail you out?"

"Christ, no. All these banking reforms. The Fed talks about 'moral hazard'—that we're not strict enough with depositors. The truth is, only eight percent of Manhattan Bank's assets are secure—in government bonds, triple-A-rated securities—basically liquid."

"Meaning?"

"Meaning it would only take a loss of about a hundred million dollars to make us insolvent. Now, will you just tell me what you want me to do, please?"

"I want to see your director of security," Sarah said. "Right now."

The Manhattan Bank's director of security was a formidable, very tall woman in her late forties named Rosabeth Chapman. She was ex-Bureau, which gave Sarah the notion that they'd have common ground on which to schmooze.

Rosabeth Chapman, however, was not a schmoozer.

She had the charm of a meter maid. She had a firm, intimidating way of speaking, a perfect pale-blond bouffant hairdo, precise pink lipstick. She spoke in a contralto, and her three male associates listened in respectful silence. Warren Elkind seemed to have a fondness for dominant women.

"You're asking us to activate a crisis-management approach. You want us to come up with a 'game plan,' as you call it. Yet you have absolutely no evidence of an impending attack on Manhattan Bank, whether the headquarters building or any of our branches."

"That's not quite accurate," Sarah said. "We have an intercepted telephone conversation—"

"Which is meaningless. It's talk; it's a hollow threat."

"Threats are more than we usually get in this business—" Sarah began.

"Are you aware how many threats are made against this bank?"

"What the hell else do you want?" Sarah finally burst out. "You want a ticking bomb? You want the whole building brought down? You want a signed statement from the terrorists notarized by a *notary public*— 'Oh, and make sure that little seal-punch thing hasn't *expired*'?"

Rosabeth Chapman shouted back: "You want to send a bomb squad around to search our headquarters and all the branches, is that it? You want to announce publicly that *someday soon*, we don't know when, Manhattan Bank is going to be struck by a terrorist? Do you have any idea what that will do to the bank's business?"

"All right," Sarah said. "Let's agree on this much. You'll send plainclothes teams around to inspect for bombs on a regular basis. The public won't have a clue. You beef up your security here and at all branches. Make sure Elkind's personal security is doubled or tripled. And for Christ's sake, change the bank's access codes *immediately*. Will you at least do that much?"

Rosabeth Chapman glowered. After a long pause, she said primly, "Yes. That much we can do."

CHAPTER FIFTY-ONE

Ken Alton emptied his Diet Pepsi and slammed it down on his desk with a hollow aluminum *thock*. "Hot damn," he said. "So Elkind talked. Let's hear it for compromising situations."

"Let's not dwell on that," Sarah said queasily, pulling up a chair next to his desk. She looked around at the wall of blue computer screens and keyboards and CPUs and cables that surrounded him. "I'd rather not think about it. He says the disk had an entire year's worth of computer passwords on it, a different one for each day. He said someone who had access to it could conceivably steal billions of dollars from the bank. This sound right to you?"

"Shit, yeah."

"How?"

Ken sighed the sigh of the expert who dreads the ordeal of having to explain in layman's language. "All right. Cash—good old-fashioned cash, the stuff we use to buy a cup of coffee or tip the waiter, that funny paper—that's disappearing, okay? Fast becoming history. Today, five out of every six dollars in the economy isn't cash but—*vapor*. Streams of zeroes and ones zipping around through cyberspace. A *trillion* dollars a day now ricochet around the world by computer. A *trillion*—can you get your mind around that?"

Sarah shook her head slowly, lost in thought.

"I mean, okay, you can argue that cash is an abstract concept, right? It's just a colored piece of paper printed up in some government printing press somewhere. Checks, too—what are they but fancy IOU notes? Okay, but the really big sums of money—the really cosmically huge amounts—they always move by computer. In the old days, when a bank wanted to send a million bucks, they sent a messenger out with a piece of paper, a cashier's check. Now it's almost always done by wire transfer—electronic funds transfer, to use the proper name. Man, I remember when the Bank of New York had some sort of software glitch, back in '85, and the Federal Reserve had to lend them twenty-three *billion* dollars overnight to bail them out."

"But what about theft?"

"Right, I was getting to that. This whole system makes it so goddam easy. Only shmucks go into banks with guns and ski masks on and try to steal the, what, maybe ten thousand bucks the average bank has on hand. That's pathetic. In 1988, some people in Chicago almost got away with stealing seventy million dollars from a bank, using electronic funds transfer."

"But they didn't get away with it."

"Yeah, but they were morons. Thing is, you rarely hear about the *successful* heists, because the banks don't want people to know how vulnerable they are. But around 1982 or 1983, this guy went into a bank in the U.S., I forget where, and did a little 'social engineering'—"

"Meaning?"

"Oh, that's computer hacker talk for using people to help you pull off some computer caper. The guy pretended to be from the Federal Reserve Bank doing something security-related, and he managed to transfer ten point two million dollars to an account in Switzerland, where he converted it to diamonds—and got away with it."

"Really?"

"Oh, yeah. And then there was this case in 1989, when a con man from Malaysia co-opted two employees of the Swiss Bank Corporation in Zurich in a huge scam, where they wired twenty million dollars to the New York branch of an Australian bank. The order was forged, but no one knew that. So the twenty million was zapped over to Australia, where it was drawn down quickly to a bunch of different accounts, and it just disappeared into the ether, leaving no trace. By the time Swiss Bank Corporation discovered what had happened, the money was pretty much all gone."

"So if someone had the computer passwords—?"

"Are you kidding, Sarah? Christ, someone clever could steal all of a bank's money, make it go belly up inside of a day. I think I should take a look at the Manhattan Bank's computers, don't you?"

CHAPTER FIFTY-TWO

If you were a drug smuggler seeking to get, say, a few thousand kilos of cocaine into the United States, you would probably resort to one of the time-honored methods devised by the drug cartels. You might conceal the goods in hollowed-out bars of aluminum stacked high in the cargo of a Venezuelan ship entering the Port of Newark. Or you might move the cocaine by truck across the Mexican border, buried in a shipment of roofing material.

If you were careful, and your shipping documents were in order, the odds would be in your favor.

But if instead you were smuggling in relatively small quantities of contraband, whether drugs or explosives or weapons-grade plutonium, there is another, far safer way.

You would simply use an international express package delivery service such as DHL or Federal Express or Airborne. Millions of packages enter the United States every day, roughly a hundred thousand sent by overnight express, and they are hardly ever subject to inspection.

"Express consignment operators," as the U.S. government formally designates international express courier services, are strictly controlled by the lengthy list of rules set out in Volume 19 of the U.S. Code of Federal Regulations, Part 128. They must demonstrate to the satisfaction of the U.S. Customs Service that their shipping facilities are secure, and that everyone who works for them has been subjected to a thorough background security check.

John F. Kennedy International Airport in Idlewild, New York, is the single customs entry point, the funnel through which all express packages from Europe must pass. In order to speed up the customs procedures, most of the express consignment shippers transmit a manifest in advance, by computer, to enable U.S. Customs to clear the planeload of packages in advance. After all, the U.S. Customs Service cannot possibly inspect even one of every thousand packages that pass through JFK.

Etienne Charreyron, the bomb-disposal expert in Lièges, Belgium, whom Baumann had hired to construct the fusing systems, sent two parcels on two separate days through DHL in Brussels. Each package contained a custom-designed fusing system, concealed in the hollow body of a Sony CFD-30 CD/radio/cassette player.

Charreyron knew the basic route of packages sent by DHL. He knew that Brussels was DHL's European hub. He knew that a package sent from the DHL office in Brussels was sent via one of DHL's private 727 jets, in which it was stuffed into one of six or seven large containers, or "cans," as they're called in shipping terminology. Each can might contain one to two thousand packages.

He knew that the packages containing the fusing mechanisms would arrive at one or two o'clock in the morning at JFK Airport, go through customs, and be loaded on a DHL jet to Cincinnati, DHL's U.S. hub, by nine in the morning. By the next day they would be in the hands of the man who had ordered them. In all, the transit time would be two business days.

Charreyron had done his homework, and he had chosen a good, low-risk way to send the detonators. But he had not figured on Senior Inspector Edna Mae Johnson.

Johnson had worked for the U. S. Customs Service for thirty-six years. A stout black woman of ferocious intelligence and unwavering attention, she was known by friends and admirers as Eagle Eye, and by many who got in her way by less admiring nicknames, most of them unprintable. Her husband of forty-odd years had learned the hard way not to bother trying to pull one over on Edna Mae.

So had the licensed customs brokers who dealt with her each night when the express consignments came in. They all knew that when Inspector Johnson was on duty, nothing would ever be allowed to slide by. Everything would go strictly according to Hoyle. With a fine-tooth comb—no, with a goddam microscope!—she went through the manifests, the airbills, and the commercial invoices (the official U.S. Customs form, actually called a Customs Entry, which listed a package's contents, value, and use), looking for any discrepancies.

A few of the customs brokers swore that finding a discrepancy gave Edna Mae an orgasm. If she found one, you could bank on the fact that she would make things right, even if it meant holding an entire planeload.

Two words everyone in the courier business most feared were "break bulk": this meant to make the shipping company open a container and spend three hours or so sorting through the two thousand packages for that one miserable little letter envelope whose paperwork was fouled up. Inspector Johnson certainly did not hesitate to break bulk. There were those who suspected she rather enjoyed it. When a customs broker groaned, she'd snap, "Well, *I* sure as hell didn't make the mistake. And you call yourself a business!"

So if you were in the express consignment business and Edna Mae Johnson was on for the night, you made extra sure to do things right. You made sure that the things they always wanted to inspect by hand—animal products, drugs, vitamins, foodstuffs—were put in a separate container, so you didn't delay thousands of other packages.

And you made sure that the declared value on the air-bill matched the declared value on the Customs Entry. And you made sure that no single shipment exceeded 550 pounds, that no single piece exceeded 124 pounds, that the total of the length, width, and height of a piece didn't exceed 118 inches.

If you didn't, Edna Mae Johnson most certainly would.

Actually all the paperwork on the DHL express consignment that night was perfectly in order. Inspector Johnson reviewed the manifest—she always worked from hard copy, because she was convinced that mistakes were made when the computer screen was used—and found nothing to object to.

As she continued processing the paperwork, she returned to her computer terminal and called up the consolidated Customs Entry. She saw a message flash on her computer screen: INTENSIVE.

The automated system was programmed to assign, completely at random, the designation "Intensive" every once in a while to an express consignment. "Intensive" meant that a hold was placed on the plane's cargo while a physical inspection was done.

She looked up at the customs broker and said, "Well, Charles, this is not your night. This shipment's going to hold."

"Oh, God," the customs broker moaned.

"Come on now, you'd better get to work and notify DHL. They've got some offloading to do."

Six large cans were removed from the DHL jet and transferred to a customs holding area. There, DHL employees were instructed to break bulk. A team of dogs was brought in to sniff the parcels. No explosives were found, but one DHL package sent from Florence, Italy, was discovered to contain seven large white truffles, packed in perfumed soap chips in a desperate attempt to conceal the truffles' pungent fungal aroma.

Inspector Johnson picked out a few dozen parcels and had them put through the mobile X-ray van. Several of them she instructed DHL employees to slit open. She did a visual inspection, satisfied herself that the contents were as described on the airbill, and had DHL employees reseal them with bright-yellow tape that informed the recipients that the parcels had been opened by U.S. Customs.

One of the parcels she put through the X-ray machine was, according to its airbill and its Customs Entry, a CD/radio/cassette player. Although the X ray showed that the piece of equipment inside likely *was*, in fact, a CD/radio/cassette player, Edna Mae Johnson didn't like its weight.

It was heavier than it should be. She was always looking for drugs, and Lord knows these drug dealers were always thinking of new ways to smuggle drugs. She had DHL cut the package open, and she took the matte-black Sony CFD-30 apart. As she did, she admired its sleek shape and thought how much her grandson Scott would like something like this. She wondered what it cost.

She took a screwdriver and carefully pulled off the bottom plate. Inside, instead of the normal guts, she found a black box with little lights on top of it. It was something electronic, and definitely something that didn't belong there.

"The hell—?" she said aloud.

The entire parcel was immediately sent over to the Bureau of Alcohol, Tobacco, and Firearms for inspection.

There, the dummy CD-and-cassette player was found to house a black plastic shoebox-sized utility box with a metal lid. The shoebox contained a microwave sensor as well as some peculiar fittings and brackets and wires and screw posts.

In one place, a battery was clearly meant to fit. And then there were those damned screw posts, which were meant to be attached to something. One of the ATF agents realized that if a blasting cap was attached to the screw posts . . .

No, it couldn't be, could it?

Inside the dummy shell of the Sony CD player was an ingeniously constructed fusing mechanism for an extremely sophisticated bomb.

CHAPTER FIFTY-THREE

At six in the morning, as Sarah was lying in bed trying to rouse herself, the phone rang.

Forty-five minutes later, she entered the conference room belonging to the assistant director of the FBI in charge of the New York office, a burly, six-foot-seven-inch, white-haired Irishman named Joseph Walsh. Seated next to him, and the only face she recognized, was Harry Whitman, the chief of the Joint Terrorist Task Force. She felt her stomach flip over when she was introduced to the two she didn't know, both in shirtsleeves: an overweight black man named Alfonse Mitchell, who was the first deputy commissioner of the NYPD; and the chief of detectives of the NYPD, a small, wiry man named Thomas McSweeney. This was a high-powered gathering, and it had to be serious.

In the middle of the table was a telephone speaker and a small, furiously percolating Bunn-O-Matic coffee-maker. She poured herself a cup of coffee, smiled at Whitman, and sat down.

"First things first," said Assistant Director Walsh, addressing Sarah directly. "I don't know if you'll take this as good news or bad news, but your investigation has been upgraded to a full-field."

Sarah nodded, betraying no emotion, certainly not the fear she felt. A full-field? A full-field investigation had to be authorized at the top, by the attorney general, through the FBI director. In order to authorize a full-field, there had to be a prima facie case. Why all of a sudden? What had changed?

He went on: "A component to a serious bomb has been found by United States Customs in a DHL shipment. Herb, can you take over?"

"Sure," came a voice over the squawk box. It belonged to Herbert Massie, chief of the Technical Section of the FBI's vaunted Laboratory Division. "Thanks to some thorough work by U.S. Customs at JFK, and some good luck thrown in, an ordinary-looking portable CD player was intercepted on its way from Brussels to Manhattan—actually, to a Mail Boxes Etc. location near Columbia University." The rustling of paper could be heard. "Inside it was what turned out to be a pretty fancy fusing mechanism."

"That's part of a bomb, Sarah," explained Alfonse Mitchell, the first deputy police commissioner.

Sarah mentally ran through several sharp responses, but merely nodded politely.

Over the speaker, Herb Massie's voice resumed: "I believe Agent Cahill worked Lockerbie, so she probably knows her bombs. Customs handed it over to ATF, who gave it to us. Well, actually, I had to do some shouting, but our techs got it pretty damned fast." In nonterrorism cases, the Bureau of Alcohol, Tobacco, and Firearms would normally be the investigating agency. In this case, however, the fusing mechanism was analyzed by Massie's section of the Crime Labs.

"When did the package come into JFK?" Sarah asked.

"Night before last."

"So it's supposed to have arrived at its destination by now."

"That's right," Massie replied. "Inside the shell of the CD player was a box measuring, let's see, nine point five inches long, five inches wide, and four point five inches high. It's got some interesting stuff inside. There's a pocket pager-receiver rigged to the relay."

"Radio-controlled," Sarah said. "Go ahead."

"There's also an electronic timer, which presumably goes off no matter what, unless it's deliberately stopped. "And here's the fiendish thing—it's got a microwave sensor rigged up in such a way that if anyone comes within twenty-five feet of the bomb, it'll go off. Talk about belt and suspenders."

"Agent Massie," interrupted the chief of detectives, "what have you people concluded about the sort of bomb that this . . . this fusing mechanism thing gets hooked up to?"

"A number of things. We know it's probably not meant to go off in an airplane."

"How do you know that?" asked FBI Assistant Director Walsh.

"It has no barometric capability or impact sensitivity. That means it can't be set off by a plane's reaching a certain air pressure, or landing. Also, since that pager inside is meant to receive a radio signal to set off the bomb, we know it's command-detonated."

Assistant FBI Director Walsh put in: "If the bomb's supposed to be detonated by means of a pager, doesn't that limit where the bomb could go? I mean, the radio signal can't travel everywhere, can it?"

Sarah nodded; that was a good point.

"Yes," Massie said. "We can be fairly certain that the bomb is not—*was* not—meant to go in a tunnel or a subway."

"Or an underground parking garage," Harry Whitman said, ever mindful of the World Trade Center bomb.

"Right," came Massie's voice. "All of those places are too shielded to allow the signal to reach the pager, at least reliably. You know how it is if you try to use your cellular phone in a parking garage, right?"

Thomas McSweeney, the chief of detectives, leaned forward and interrupted: "Can I go back to this microwave sensor thing? I guess what I'm saying is, why twenty-five feet? Doesn't that tell us something about where the bomb's supposed to be placed? If the bomb's on a street or any place where there's a crowd, the microwave would go off, right? So it's got to be placed somewhere where there ain't a lot of people."

"Yes," Sarah said. "Or else at night, in a deserted building."

"Could be," Massie said.

"There's another thing," Sarah said, looking around at the men, and pouring herself a second cup of coffee. "Probably the most important thing. The bomb's meant to go off no matter what, right? A timer, a microwave sensor, a radio-activated pager—one way or another, the bomb was designed to explode."

"So?" said Alfonse Mitchell.

"So now we know a lot about the *intentions* of the terrorist or terrorists," Sarah said. "Since there's really no way to shut it off, we know this isn't meant to be an extortion or blackmail attempt. That explains why we haven't received any demands, either by phone or by letter. *They don't want anything from us!* Unlike the normal terrorist—if there is such a thing—these guys don't want the United States to release prisoners or pull out of a war or some such thing. *They want to cause destruction no matter what.*"

"That's right," came Massie's voice after a moment's hesitation. The tension in the room was electric.

"Uh, Ms. Cahill," said Alfonse Mitchell of the NYPD, "you're overlooking the most important thing of all. There isn't going to be any destruction. *We have the goddam fusing mechanism!* Without it, our terrorists don't have a bomb, now do they?"

"Oh, that's good," Sarah snapped. "Would you like my group to start packing now, or can we have a couple of days to sort of wind down?"

"Sarah," Harry Whitman warned.

"I'm sorry," Sarah apologized. "That's just a ridiculous, even dangerous, comment to make. How do we know there aren't a dozen fusing mechanisms just like this one, that have already been sent into the country and have already been picked up? Or, if this really is the one and only, how do we know that my terrorist can't just pick up the phone and order another one? Have it sent in another way?"

"Right," said Assistant FBI Director Walsh. "We can't rule out that possibility."

Alfonse Mitchell sat back in his chair and sipped his coffee in smoldering silence.

"Agent Massie," Sarah said, "from what I know about how pagers work, you can't just buy a pager, you have to lease the telephone service at the same time, isn't that right?"

"Well, yes and no," Massie said. "You can buy a pager anywhere. But if you want it to *work*, you need to lease the service."

"Well, that's our lead," Sarah said, looking around the table with a smile. "We trace the pager to the paging service, and find out who signed on for the service. Even assuming they gave a false name, they have to give so much information when they sign up for a pager that we'll be able to trace—"

"No," Massie said. "Not that simple."

Alfonse Mitchell smiled behind his coffee cup.

"Why not?" asked Sarah.

"First of all, the serial number plate has been removed

from the pager. The designer of this thing seems to be fairly slick."

"But aren't there other ways—" Sarah began.

"You buy a pager from a paging company," Harry Whitman said, "and you lease the service, right? Then you buy another pager—just the pager, no service—from a second source. Now, each pager is programmed to respond to a digital code sequence. So all you do is you study the first pager, and alter the second one, so that it responds to the same digital code sequence as the first one—"

"You're losing us, here," interrupted Assistant Director Walsh.

"I get it," Sarah said. "The pager in the fusing mechanism works like the one that came with the leased service, but if we were to try to trace it, we couldn't. Very clever."

"You got it," said Herbert Massie. "But I've been trying to get to the main attraction, here. Listen up. Our techs have a theory as to who's behind all this."

"Who?" Sarah asked.

"Libya."

"Jesus!" exploded Harry Whitman.

"How do you know?" asked Assistant Director Walsh.

"All right," Massie said. "Someone in the lab is getting the day off. The timer is one of the ones Ed Wilson sold Libya back in 1976."

Sarah and some of the other FBI people present knew what Herbert Massie was talking about, but none of the police could possibly have been expected to know. Indeed, the story of Libya and its business dealings with the rogue CIA agent Edwin Wilson has been written about—but not entirely.

It is a matter of public record that Edwin Wilson—a CIA officer who went "off the reservation," as they say in the intelligence business—and an associate sold Muammar Qaddafi twenty tons of Semtex plastic explosive, which later turned up in numerous terrorist attacks around the world. It is also a matter of public record that Wilson sold the Libyan government three thousand electronic explosives timers.

What is not publicly known is where and how Wilson got them. He got them from the very source that custom-makes them for the CIA. Wilson placed the order for these three thousand timers with a man who lives outside of Washington, D.C., a renowned inventor with over six hundred patents to his name, who has for years constructed high-tech gadgets for the U.S. intelligence community. This man, who once built satellites for the Air Force at Edwards Air Force Base, is widely considered a genius.

This inventor knew that Edwin Wilson was an employee of the CIA—but not that Wilson was acting on his own behalf, not for the Agency. He should have been alerted by the fact that Wilson paid for the timers in cash, and not by purchase order. Wilson had cleverly duped him.

The gadgeteer designed and built three thousand timers, encased in black plastic, measuring three inches square by approximately half an inch high. On the outside of the timer was an LED and an on/off switch. The timer went from zero to 150 hours, in one-hour increments. As recently as 1988, these timers have repeatedly turned up in bombs set by Arab terrorists.

"So you think Henrik Baumann has been hired by the Libyans?" asked Sarah.

"It's possible. Looks that way," Herbert Massie said.

"Bravo," said Harry Whitman.

"Well done," Sarah said. "All right, now, I want that fusing mechanism put back together, boxed up, and delivered to that Mail Boxes Etc. site *today*."

"What the hell—?" said Chief of Detectives Mc-Sweeney.

"Sarah," said Whitman, "you're out of your mind."

"No," she said. "I want a surveillance team put on the site. At some point someone has to show up to claim the package. Let me remind you, we don't know it's Baumann, by the way. We *assume* it is."

"Agent Cahill," Massie's voice came, high and strained, "we're far from finished examining it."

"If we hold off any longer, Baumann's bound to get suspicious, and he won't show up. It's got to arrive today—one day late is okay, but no more. Also, I want a trap-and-trace on the Mail Boxes phone line, in case Baumann—or whoever it is—calls about the package. If I were in his place, I would."

"You didn't hear me, did you?" Massie said. "I said, we're not done. We're not packing this up yet."

Deputy Commissioner Alfonse Mitchell glowered at Sarah and shook his head slowly.

"Okay," Sarah said, backing down. "Get a duplicate of the tape player if you can, box that up in the exact same packaging, and get it over to Mail Boxes today, using a regular DHL truck, with their other stuff. Oh, and one more thing. Customs usually uses yellow tape to seal packages it's opened, saying 'Opened by U.S. Customs' or something like that. Make sure there's no yellow tape on it. I want it to look like everything went fine with it." She looked around the table once again. "We're going to catch the bastard," she said.

CHAPTER FIFTY-FOUR

In the next days, Baumann worked almost nonstop, renting not one but two furnished apartments in different parts of the city, under different aliases assumed by entirely different personas. He paid cash; let the real estate agents think what they wanted. Greed would always prevail; the Realtors would keep their silence. On a bleak, foul-smelling street not far from the Fulton Fish Market he took a short-term rental on a tiny street-level warehouse space barely big enough to park a compact car in.

He contacted the computer whiz (the "cracker," as he'd been taught to say), but the cracker, to his credit, insisted on meeting in person. Baumann knew only that the man was in his late twenties, was pompous to the point of megalomania, and worked only sporadically, but for fantastic sums of money. Most important, he came highly recommended by the intermediary in Amsterdam, who called him a man of rare skill, "ultra-slick, a serious wizard."

The cracker's name was Leo Krasner. He did work for businessmen who didn't like their credit ratings and wanted them repaired; for private investigators; for news reporters. He would work for any organization that interested him, except the government.

Krasner's fame had spread in the underworld of computer crackers early in 1991. It is a matter of record that during the Persian Gulf War of that year, the Cable News Network hired a number of computer hackers, crackers, and phreakers to circumvent the U.S. government's onerous press restrictions. These computer wizards were paid to intercept transmissions to and from military satellites and decrypt them. Krasner was heavily relied upon by CNN and other television networks, as well as by investors who wanted to know what was going on.

Baumann arranged to meet Krasner in a brightly lit but shabby little restaurant on the far West Side whose smeared plate-glass windows looked out onto the verminous street.

Leo Krasner was short, not much over five feet, and enormously obese. His doughy face was framed by immense porkchop sideburns. His unwashed hair spilled over his collar. He wore tinted aviator-frame glasses.

Baumann introduced himself, using an American alias and legend. Krasner offered a damp, pudgy hand to shake. After a minute or so of chitchat that was clearly going nowhere, Baumann came right to the point and told him what he wanted.

Krasner, who had been cupping his mouth in his small, round fist, looked up at Baumann slowly and gave a cryptic half-smile. A man sat down at a nearby table, set down a gym bag, and began to read a crummy paperback of Saul Bellow's *Mr. Sammler's Planet.* "This is some very high-profile shit," Krasner said. "It's going to bring down an enormous amount of heat. I may not be able to work for a very, very long time."

"Perhaps yes, perhaps no."

"I assume you're talking some very, very big bucks."

"A six-figure payment for a few days' work," Baumann said.

"*Six-figure*?" Krasner snorted. "Go find a high school kid. You gotta be kidding."

"Do you want to suggest a fee? You're the subcontractor, after all. Give me a bid."

"My bid is a million dollars, take it or leave it."

"I don't have anywhere near that kind of money," Baumann said.

"Then what kind of serious offer will you make?"

"If I really scrape and borrow and beg, I can come up with half that. But it will take enormous effort to scrape together."

"In gold. Currency's going to take a serious beating after this goes down."

"Done. Are you at all familiar with the systems used by the Manhattan Bank?"

"Sure, I know the Manhattan Bank. A little background work, a little calling around, and I'm all set." He extended his moist hand to shake. "No problem."

CHAPTER FIFTY-FIVE

Over coffee half an hour later, Pappas said: "They were right, Sarah. Had you given up that fusing device, you'd not only have lost an incredibly valuable mass of information, but you'd have risked losing a crucial piece of evidence."

"The idea wasn't to throw the thing away," Sarah said, exasperated because she knew Pappas was right. "It was to keep everything intact so as not to alert Baumann, and . . ." Her voice faded. "All right, I was wrong. I'll admit it."

Pappas nodded once. "Ah, well. To err is human, to forgive is not Bureau policy. Water under the bridge. Mail Boxes opens in, what, fifteen minutes or so? Hours are nine to seven, weekdays. You got a team in place?"

"Uniforms, but supposed to be some of New York's finest, whatever that means. They're already there, watching. What do you think about this Libyan timer?"

"Ed Wilson sold a bunch of timers to the Libyans, but who knows where they all ended up. By now, those timers have gone through a bunch of hands."

She nodded. "Arab hands."

"Odds are, yes."

"But I don't believe the Libyans are behind this thing."

"Why not?"

"The Libyans and the Iranians have a whole catalog of suicide bombers who can't wait to die for the greater glory of Allah. They don't need to hire him."

"He's the best."

"They don't *need* the best."

"You don't know that. You don't know what Baumann is up to."

"That's not my point. You hire the best to make sure you don't get caught, that the incident isn't traced back to you. The Libyans usually don't care if it is or not. If it *is* traced back to them, it makes them more formidable. They like that."

Pappas was silent, waiting for her to continue, and when she didn't, he said: "You might have a point."

At the same time, a DHL delivery truck was pulling up to Mail Boxes Etc. at 2840 Broadway, between 110th and 111th streets, next door to Columbia Bagels and not far from Columbia University. It was a legitimate DHL truck, making the first overnight deliveries of the day. Double-parked in front of the Mail Boxes store, the driver took out three express packages.

Two new employees were working the counter that morning at Mail Boxes Etc. One was a dark-haired man in his twenties, busy shelving boxes. The other, a pretty young blond woman, appeared to be a trainee working with a more experienced, though younger, woman. The blonde's hair was long and full, and it nicely concealed the tiny earphone she was wearing.

On Broadway, in front of the storefront, idled a yellow taxi, its roof light indicating it was out of service. The driver, a pudgy and balding man in a cheap-looking leather jacket and a frayed denim shirt, was examining the *Daily Racing Form*. Since he was far from the precinct in which he had once worked, he doubted any passerby would recognize him as Lieutenant George Roth of the New York Police Department.

The yellow cab—a real New York City cab that had been seized by the FBI in a drug raid—was the mobile command post. From there, Roth could communicate by radio with the two policemen inside who had been detailed to the working group on temporary assignment.

The eight members of the surveillance team had been fully briefed and outfitted with appropriate disguises and communications equipment. Wireless microphones were worn inside shirts or sweaters; earphones were concealed under wigs, baseball caps, or hats.

On the bustling stretch of Broadway in front of the storefront, an FBI agent in a spandex jogging suit was trying to change the right rear tire on his silver Corvette, another seized vehicle. A young Hispanic-looking man sat behind the wheel of a parked pizza delivery van. A hobbled old homeless woman pushed a grocery cart full of aluminum cans.

Another agent kept a lookout from the third-floor window of the office building across the street. Another, in a Con Ed uniform and hard hat, seemed to be inspecting a faulty electrical meter in an alley about thirty feet from the Mail Boxes storefront.

In the movies and on television, a telephone call can be traced in a matter of seconds. The reality, unfortunately, is far less impressive. A trap-and-trace, as it's called, can take five, ten, even fifteen minutes or longer, and quite often several separate attempts.

It is true that a service known as Caller ID is available in many areas of the United States, which allows you to learn the number of an incoming call even before the phone rings. But this service works only in telephone exchanges that use the fully computerized technology called SS7, for System Signaling Group 7.

And many telephone exchanges remain antiquated,

particularly in larger cities. NYNEX, the company that services Manhattan as well as much of New York State and New England, has been one of the slowest Baby Bells to update its technology.

Another problem with Caller ID is that it doesn't work on trunking systems, PBX systems, which are used in office buildings. Also, any subscriber can have the Automatic Number Identification (ANI) signal blocked, rendering Caller ID useless.

So the only reliable way to trace a number remains the old-fashioned trap-and-trace method, which can only be done by the telephone company, in its offices. The manager of Mail Boxes Etc., and his district manager, happily complied with the FBI's request to ask NYNEX to order a trap-and-trace for this particular store.

All that remained now was for Henrik Baumann—if indeed he was the recipient—to place a call and ask whether an express package had been received for a Mr. James Oakley. Even if Baumann called from a public pay phone, they might be fortunate enough to discover his location in time.

At 11:14 A.M., the call came.

The pretty young blond policewoman answered the phone and said perkily, "Your name, please?"

She signaled with her index finger. "Let me check, Mr. Oakley." She punched the hold button.

Her partner was already on another line to NYNEX telephone security, activating the trap-and-trace. As he held the handset to his ear, he said to the woman, "Keep him holding as long as you think you can."

"Right," she said. "But he said he was in a hurry, so I don't know how long he'll hold."

"Sure, he's in a hurry," the man said. "He's no idiot." Into the phone he said, "All right, good. Yeah, we will."

Ten seconds went by, then twenty.

"I'm going to have to pick up again and say something," the blond woman said, "or he'll get suspicious and we'll lose him."

"We got Manhattan," her partner announced. "Midtown. Let's go, man, let's go. Speed this thing up."

"Matt—"

"Yeah, yeah. Pick it up, tell him—think of *something*, for God's sake. Give us more time!"

She punched the hold button again to release it. "Mr. Oakley, we do have something here for you, and I'm trying to locate it. Was that an envelope or a box? It makes a difference, because we store them in different . . . Oh, shit. He hung up." She put down the handset. "We lost him."

Baumann, standing at a midtown pay phone, hung up the phone and quickly walked away. For reasons of safety, he did not like to stay on the phone for longer than twenty seconds. He did not know whether telephone-tracing technology had changed at all since he'd been in prison, but he did not want to find out. He knew that his package had arrived, which was the main thing. Even if they traced the call, by the time they got to this pay phone, he'd be long gone.

Perhaps he was being overly cautious. After all, it was highly unlikely that any law-enforcement authorities would have found out about this mail drop. But such instincts had kept him alive throughout a hazardous career.

It was out of this same overcautiousness that he donned a disguise—a long, shaggy brown wig, a natural-looking beard, a prosthetic paunch, a loose baggy white sweatshirt—and took a cab uptown to the Mail Boxes Etc. site, outside of which he did some preliminary surveillance. He found no reason to be suspicious, though if they were good, they would hardly be obvious.

He entered the small facility. The only other person

there was a young man standing at the counter, listening to music on Walkman headphones and filling out some kind of long form, which looked like an application for employment.

"Can I help you?" the young woman behind the counter asked.

"Not yet, thanks," Baumann answered, absorbed in a display of folding mailing cartons of various sizes. Then he turned back casually to the clerk and asked: "So where's Donna?"

"Donna?" the woman echoed dubiously.

"The woman who normally works the day shift here," Baumann said. He had come here twice before, each time in very different disguises, and had learned that a woman named Donna always worked days. "You know. Blond. Long hair."

"Oh, her. Sorry, I'm new. She's off for the day—went to the beach, I think. Why, you a friend?"

Baumann's instincts told him to leave at once. Both people behind the counter, he now realized, were new. He didn't like this at all. He also did not like the fact that the job applicant was wearing a Walkman. It made him suspicious. Headphones could be used to communicate with a command post. Then again, they could be entirely innocent. But his instincts told him not to take any chances.

"Yeah," he said. "Tell Donna that Billy said hi." He glanced at his watch as if late for an appointment, and walked out the door.

Halfway down the block he noticed that the young man wearing the Walkman had left a few seconds after he had and was heading in his direction.

He didn't like this either.

A few paces behind, Russell Ullman, who had been standing at the counter pretending to fill out a form for over an hour, spoke into his transmitter: "I don't know if this is our guy or not, but I'm going to follow him awhile, make sure."

"Got it," the voice in his headphones said. "Come on back soon as you're sure it's not our man."

"Okay," Ullman said.

Baumann suddenly darted across the street in the middle of the block, weaving between the moving cars, and walked along the other side of the block. As he rounded the next corner, he saw in the reflection in a plate-glass window that the young man was still behind him.

He was being followed.

Why? The only explanation was that somehow the fusing mechanism had been intercepted on its way from Belgium. True, there were many points at which it could have been intercepted, but . . .

Had Charreyron, the Belgian explosives expert, talked?

Unlikely, Baumann decided. If he had, he probably would have given up each of the addresses to which Baumann had requested the fusing mechanisms be sent. And since Baumann had already received one of them without incident, that seemed to rule out Charreyron as a leak.

No; the DHL package simply must have been intercepted. Such things happened, which was why he had had duplicate fusing mechanisms sent. In the real world, things went wrong; one made fall-back plans.

As he plunged into a crowd of tourists emerging from a bus, hoping thereby to lose the tail, he caught another glimpse of the follower in a mirrored storefront. The man appeared to be alone. Why, Baumann wondered, were there no others?

* * *

In his headphones, Ullman heard: "It's probably just some hinky guy. Lot of weirdos use private mail-box services to get sicko videos and child pornography, or whatever. You get his face? We didn't."

"No," Ullman said, "but I will." A woman passing by saw him talking to himself and veered away with alarm.

Baumann attempted several classic maneuvers to lose the tail, but the follower was too good. Obviously he was professionally trained, and talented as well. He didn't recognize the young man's face, but that meant nothing. Although he'd conducted some surveillance of the Operation MINOTAUR headquarters building, he'd not been able to identify any of the task force members. Also, Sarah never emerged from the building talking with anyone.

Baumann passed a small, dingy Chinese restaurant, stopped short, and entered its dimly lit interior. It took a few seconds before his eyes became accustomed to the dark. He sat down at one of the Formica tables. He was the only one in the restaurant. In effect, he was daring the tail to follow him in and reveal himself.

Ullman saw the fat man in the white sweatshirt turn abruptly into the Chinese restaurant. In front of the restaurant, he hesitated. It was obvious the man was trying to lose him.

Well, there was no choice.

He opened the restaurant door and stepped into the dark air-conditioned interior. He looked around. It was empty. In the rear of the restaurant, a Chinese man sat behind a counter punching numbers into a calculator. Ullman spoke into his transmitter, giving his location. Then he approached the Chinese man and said, "You see someone come in here?"

The man gazed warily at Ullman, then pointed toward the rear of the restaurant. Ullman saw a rest room, raced to it, flung open the door, and stepped in.

A sink, a toilet; no stall, no window, no place to hide. And no one here.

He quickly turned back to the corridor, looked left and right, saw the kitchen. This was the only place the sweatshirted man could have gone.

He pushed open the swinging double doors to the small kitchen, surprising a couple of elderly Chinese men doing prep work, cutting up vegetables. Without explanation, he walked in, looked around, saw no one else. Then he saw the delivery door and ran toward it, ignoring shouts of protest from the kitchen workers.

The door gave onto a narrow alley, where he was assaulted by the stench of rotten food garbage. He looked around and saw nothing. The man in the sweatshirt must have escaped through this door and run down the alley.

Shit.

He'd gotten away. Ullman stepped carefully down a slimy set of three iron stairs into the alley, past bulging black plastic trash bags.

"I think I lost him," Ullman said into his Walkman.

"All right," the voice replied. "We'll send a couple of guys down where you are to see if we can nab him."

Ullman glanced around, then moved quietly over toward the blue metal Dumpster, which overflowed with more disgusting food garbage, and as he glanced behind it, he felt something grab his throat. He lost his footing as he was yanked behind the Dumpster. He felt something squeeze his trachea with an excruciatingly painful force. He reached for his pistol, but before he could do so, something slammed into his right eye.

Everything went red. He doubled over in pain and gasped. For a moment he could not speak. He wondered whether his eye had burst. Somehow he realized that the object that had just smashed into his eyeball was the barrel of a handgun. With his one good eye he found himself looking into a man's ice-blue eyes.

"Who are you?" the man whispered.

"FBI," Ullman croaked. "Baumann—"

"Man, you got the wrong guy," Baumann said as he crushed the young blond man's trachea with one hand, killing him instantly.

The FBI man had been agile and strong, but also clearly inexperienced. And he had seen Baumann's face—disguised, yes, but that was still too great a risk. Baumann removed the dead man's wallet and found the FBI ID card, which identified him as Special Agent Russell Ullman. He pocketed the card and murmured to himself, "You got the wrong guy."

CHAPTER FIFTY-SIX

The plastic explosive Composition C-4, so beloved by terrorists, usually comes in rectangular blocks an inch high, two inches wide, and eleven inches long. Each block, wrapped in clear or green plastic, weighs one and a quarter pounds. Its color is pure white.

C-4's compactness makes it appealing to the U.S. military, and of course to terrorists. For terrorists, one of its most useful attributes is that it doesn't have an odor: it is therefore quite difficult to detect. It is not, however, *impossible* to detect.

What is unknown outside exclusive intelligence and law-enforcement circles is that certain types of C-4 are much more readily detectable than others. For obvious reasons, counterterrorists prefer that terrorists and potential terrorists know as little as possible about these various types of C-4.

Having served in South African intelligence, however, Baumann knew quite a lot about explosives. He knew that the active ingredient in C-4 is the compound cyclotrimethylene trinitramine, which is entirely odorless. In fact, it is the *impurities* in most plastic explosives that are sniffed out by trained dogs or mechanical sensors.

He knew, too, the well-concealed fact that all C-4 in America is made in one of seven manufacturing plants. Six of the manufacturers use either nitroglycerine or the compound EGDN in the manufacture of dynamite, which contaminates the C-4 made at the same time. This contaminant makes most C-4 detectable.

Only one company in America makes a pure, "un-contaminated" C-4. Baumann knew which one it was. He also had a reasonably good plan to get some.

CHAPTER FIFTY-SEVEN

As a technology procurement specialist in the Network Administration Department of the Manhattan Bank, Rick DeVore handled a lot of telephone solicitations. That was his job; he did it without complaining and was always friendly but firm. The truth was, in the computer business, a lot of selling took place over the phone, so you couldn't refuse to take calls. But if you stayed on the phone too long, you'd never get anything done. So Rick DeVore was quick to screen out the jokers, those selling junk, stuff he had no interest in.

The vendor on the phone this morning, however, seemed to know what he was talking about.

"Hi, I'm Bob Purcell from Metrodyne Systems in Honolulu," the voice on the phone said.

"How're you doing?" Rick said neutrally, not encouraging, but not discouraging either. Metrodyne was one of the hottest software companies these days, located in the hottest new city for software companies, Honolulu. They wrote add-ons for Novell networks.

"Good, thanks. Listen, I don't want to take up too much of your time, but I was calling to let you know about the availability of a new security NLM that allows for run-time encryption of files regardless of format or network."

"Uh huh," DeVore said, doodling on his pink "While You Were Out" telephone message pad. He flashed on a mental image of himself and Deb last night and wondered if it was true that men think about sex every five minutes.

The Metrodyne vendor went on, with increasing enthusiasm: "Every time you save a file it's automatically encrypted on your Novell network, and every time you open the file it's decrypted. It's really great. Just like the way a file is compressed and decompressed automatically, without the user even being aware of it. I think every Novell user should have it. I was wondering if you'd have some time for me to come by and talk to you about—"

"Gee, that sounds cool," DeVore said sincerely, "but you know, we don't use Novell anymore. We just switched to NT Advanced Server." This was Microsoft's networking software. "Sorry."

"Oh, no, that's great," said the salesman. "We've got a version that runs on NT too—we really want to address the variety of the marketplace. Do you mind if I ask, what are you currently using for security?"

"Well, I—"

"I mean, are you relying on what comes out of the box for security? Because we've engineered our product to make up for the weaknesses in NT's security. As you know, NT doesn't even do encryption, you've got to encrypt everything separately. But ours does across-the-board encryption—"

"Listen," Rick DeVore said, shifting into terminate-call mode, "I've pretty much said all I can responsibly tell you. Sorry. I'm really not at liberty to talk about this stuff. But if you'd like to send me a demo of your product I'd be happy to take a look at it. Okay?"

When he'd taken a mailing address and a contact name, Leo Krasner hung up the phone and turned to his SPARC-20 workstation.

He'd learned all he had to about what software the bank used.

CHAPTER FIFTY-EIGHT

The Technical Services analyst, on the secure direct line to the Hoover Building, sounded as young as an adolescent. His high-pitched voice actually cracked several times as he spoke.

"Agent Cahill, I'm Ted Grabowski," he said tentatively. "I've been assigned to work on the piece of equipment, the fusing mechanism."

"Mmm-hmm?" she said distractedly.

"Remember you asked me to check out whether there was any kind of signature on this here—"

"I certainly do remember." Identifying tool marks is one of the FBI's forensic strengths, and though it often requires painstaking effort, it is the most reliable "fingerprint" a bomb can provide. It is also admissible in court.

"All right, well, it's sort of confusing," Grabowski said. "Not really a coherent signature."

"The soldering?"

"The soldering joints are neat, maybe too neat. But it's the knots that got me."

"How so?"

"They're Western Union splices. Really nice work."

"Refresh my memory."

"They first used the Western Union splice with telegraph wire, in the old days, because those wires were subject to a lot of pulling, and you had to have a knot that could withstand a good yank. You sort of take the bare ends of two lengths of wire, set them down in opposition to each other, twist them, then raise the ends and twist them again, at a ninety-degree angle. Sort of forms a triangle, and you wrap some tape around it—"

"So what does this tell you?"

He paused. "It tells me—this is only speculation, ma'am—but it tells me the guy who made this was trained at Indian Head."

Indian Head was the Naval Explosive Ordnance Disposal School at Indian Head, Maryland, where all U.S. military bomb experts—"explosive ordnance disposal specialists," as they're called in military and intelligence circles—are trained. Although the CIA does have the facilities to train its own bomb experts, most of its people are trained at Indian Head as well.

"You're telling me this was made by an *American*?"

"No, ma'am, I'm not. You may not know this, but the Naval EOD trains some foreigners, too. One section at Indian Head is the course on improvised explosive devices—I know, because I took it. I'm just saying that whoever made this neat little fusing mechanism, it sure as hell wasn't a Libyan."

Christine Vigiani, smoking furiously, stood at the threshold to Sarah's office until Sarah looked up.

"Yes, Chris?"

Vigiani coughed, cleared her throat. "Came up with something you might want to take a look at."

"Oh?"

"I mean, it was really just a matter of putting two and two together. Our guy did Carrero Blanco, right? Hired by the Basques?"

"Okay . . . ?"

"So I got onto CACTIS and cross-referenced the Carrero Blanco murder, trying to find any other connections." She took a drag on her cigarette. "So come to find out, CIA has some excellent sources that say whoever it was who was hired by the Basques was hired soon afterward by the IRA."

Sarah sat up, her attention riveted.

"So I got in touch with Scotland Yard Special Operations. And there's solid evidence that our man also did the assassination of the British ambassador to Northern Ireland in the mid-seventies—you remember that?"

Sarah, of course, remembered it well. On July 21, 1976, Christopher Ewart-Biggs, the British ambassador to Ireland, was killed when a land mine detonated in a culvert under the road on which he was driving, in the countryside near Dublin. Ewart-Biggs had been ambassador for a mere three weeks.

The assassination was the work of the IRA's Provisional Wing. But it has long remained a matter of much speculation who actually carried out the bombing. British Intelligence later learned that it was a paid professional hit—that it was *not* done by the IRA.

But by now it is a matter of certainty within intelligence circles, based on forensic and intelligence data, that Ewart-Biggs was killed by the same mysterious person who killed Carrero Blanco in Madrid. The name has never been made public.

"This Baumann," said Vigiani fuzzily through a lungful of smoke, "is one mean motherfucker, if you'll pardon my French."

"Agent Cahill?" the Technical Services analyst said over the secure link a little more than an hour later. "Your question about the timer?"

"Yes?"

"Well, I think you may be on to something, ma'am. I looked at it real close, and a couple other guys here looked at it, and we all pretty much agreed it's almost identical to the timers that Edwin Wilson sold Libya in 1976."

" 'Almost identical'?"

"It's built just like those timers, ma'am, but it's not one of them. You know the black plastic box that houses the timer? Well, I ran the plastic through a melting-point test, and I found it melts at three hundred and forty degrees Fahrenheit, so now I can say for certain it's not the same timer."

"You're sure."

"Positive. We've got several of the Wilson timers, as you call them, and they're all made from a nylon resin, which melts at five hundred and two degrees Fahrenheit. But the one we got here, that's an acetel resin. This one's different."

"So it's a fake? You think someone made a fake timer that looked just like the Libyan one to make the bomb look like it was done by the Libyans?"

"That's what I'm saying, ma'am. There's no other reason why someone would construct a duplicate timer except to fool the counterterrorist folks like you. Someone's trying to snow us."

CHAPTER FIFTY-NINE

AAAA Construction and Excavation was an eyesore on the outskirts of the otherwise lovely Westchester County town of Mount Kisco, New York. It was nothing more than a small brick structure surrounded by trailers, set in a field of rubble, surrounded by alarmed barbed-wire fencing.

Four A, as its seven employees called it, advertised construction and specialty blasting in the Manhattan Yellow Pages, in a small red-outlined box that featured a line drawing of a crane with dirt cascading from its shovel. It was the first listing under "excavation" in the Yellow Pages, thanks to all those A's.

Its demoralized and underpaid employees thought a better emblem would have been a dollar bill with wings on it, to symbolize the fact that Four A had been losing money steadily for the last four years, ever since David Nickelsen, Jr., had taken over the family business after his father, the company's founder, suffered a stroke.

But AAAA Construction and Excavation suited Henrik Baumann's purposes just fine. He'd gone through the Yellow Pages listings of construction companies and rejected any that didn't have the licenses—from ATF and the local municipality—to use or store explosives.

That still left quite a few candidates. But of those, only a few fit the desired profile: small, privately held, and in sufficiently bad financial shape not to immediately turn away an English guy who was calling to discuss some private business regarding C-4.

Fortunately, David Nickelsen, Jr., was not overburdened with scruples. Baumann knew it would not be difficult to find someone in this line of work who'd do business with him. Nickelsen listened to the proposition of the well-dressed man who identified himself as John McGuinness from Bristol, England, and agreed to do business. Whether it was Mr. McGuinness's polite manners or his offer of fifty thousand dollars in cash that persuaded him, David Nickelsen, Jr., gladly accepted.

The Englishman explained that he represented a foreign buyer—he would not say more—who was having difficulty obtaining an export license for a major construction job in Kuwait. This buyer needed a five-hundred-foot roll of DetCord, several M6 Special Engineer Electrical Blasting Caps, and one thousand pounds of C-4, U.S. military designation Charge Demolition Block M-112.

But not just any Charge Demolition Block M-112. For technical reasons too complicated to go into, it had to have a specific manufacturer's code.

What Baumann did not bother explaining was that the numbers he gave the corrupt construction-company owner referred to a certain manufacturer and lot. He had found these codes in a list of government contracts published in a journal called the *Commerce Business Daily*.

David Nickelsen, Jr., had looked at him as if he were out of his mind. Your guys want plastic explosives or not? Yes or no? What's the deal here?

Baumann informed Nickelsen that the exact lot he wanted was being offered for sale, dirt cheap and right now, at a national auction conducted by a government agency called the Defense Reutilization and Marketing Service (DRMS), in Battle Creek, Michigan. DRMS is an arm of the Defense Logistics Agency, which is in turn part of the Department of Defense. Each month, DRMS offers surplus explosives, from government warehouses, for sale at drastically reduced prices. Anyone who has the proper explosives license can bid.

"All right," Nickelsen said, "I can buy this stuff today if you want."

"I do," Baumann said.

"Then what? How the hell'm I supposed to cover the fact that I made an illegal sale?"

"You don't. You have the C-4 shipped to you, and you store it in your certified magazine. You turn off the power in the electrified security fence—a lapse you will blame on one of your expendable employees. You let me know when it's there, and you receive the money. The following morning, you find the lock on your magazine cut. You are horrified, and you report the theft. And that is the end of it. You'll never see or hear from me again. And one last thing—the guys I work for are really intent on their privacy. One goddam word of this gets out—one bloody word—and your two little boys will be without a father. Simple as that. All clear?"

CHAPTER SIXTY

At the same time, Ken Alton was sitting at his work station, deep in concentration, surrounded by large blue-screened monitors, several keyboards, an impossible-looking tangle of wires, and heaps of empty Diet Pepsi cans.

"I've been in touch with the computer people over at Manhattan Bank," he said, "sort of familiarizing myself with the system. It's pretty secure, for a bank. But I'm thinking of going over there and getting my hands dirty, doing some hands-on work, checking things out."

Sarah nodded. "Great. Any luck on the passport search?"

"We're getting there."

"How close?"

"I'm winnowing. I'm down to forty-some names—we could hand-check them, but it would be a hell of a lot faster for me to narrow down to a name or two."

"What are the forty?"

"The intersection of two databases: every U.S. citizen who's entered the country since the beginning of the year, and all U.S. passports reported lost or stolen."

"Can I see the list?"

"It won't do you any good, but sure, if you want. Hard copy?"

"Please."

He tapped a few keys, and his laser printer hummed to life. "Done. But it's just a list of names, with Social Security and passport numbers, ranked in order of probability."

"Probability of each candidate being our guy?"

"You got it."

"Based on what?"

"Several different fields, or factors. Stuff like height, age, sex. To start, we know Baumann's five foot eleven."

"The passport people don't check height, Ken."

"Right, but if someone's very short—four foot eight, in one case—it's not likely to be Baumann, unless he had his legs sawed off. On the other hand, I'm not eliminating anyone taller, because it's easy for someone to look taller with lifts or special shoes, okay?"

"What about age? We've already agreed that he could look a lot older if he wanted to, with the right makeup."

"Granted, but he's not going to look eight years old, right? So there are some passport ages that probably couldn't be him. Anyone younger than twenty-five gets demoted in the probability ranking automatically. And there's itinerary."

"Hmm?"

"I'm proceeding on the assumption that Baumann didn't first depart the U.S. before he entered. In other words, he most likely acquired the passport abroad and used it to enter the country. Anyone who, let's say, entered the U.S. last week but *left* the country a week or two earlier isn't likely to be our terrorist. So he gets pushed down the list."

"Okay, good."

"Plus, I've gotten data from most, though not all, of the airlines these forty-three flew in on. Manifests, airline travel logs, flight logs. Those databases tell us a lot. For instance, did the passenger buy a ticket with cash? Odds are very high our guy did. If he didn't—down to the bottom of the pile he goes. Not out, but down."

"Makes sense."

"Oh, and we can eliminate anyone who entered the country *before* the date of Baumann's escape from prison." He retrieved a sheet from the printer, handed it to her. "So, what you're looking at is a work in progress. Not all the databases have been worked in. Another day or two, I should have it narrowed down to one name."

Lieutenant George Roth had just about given up searching the alley behind the Chinese restaurant, and he radioed in to report his lack of success. Then, as he turned back toward Broadway, something in a trash heap in a large blue Dumpster behind the restaurant attracted his attention. He moved closer to the refuse, holding his breath, and saw that his first impression had been right—it was a black leather shoe. He pulled at it, and realized that it was attached to a leg.

A few minutes later, the special working group assembled for an end-of-the-day full staff meeting, minus the two involved with the Mail Boxes Etc. operation, George Roth and Russell Ullman.

Sarah opened by briefing them in on the Mail Boxes watch. "Apparently someone called to ask about the package," she said, "but hung up before we could get a fix on his location."

"You think he got suspicious?" Pappas asked.

"Possibly. Could be he was just being careful."

"He might not ever come in to get the package," Pappas went on. "If it really is Baumann, he might not need it—he might have other fusing mechanisms. Baumann's probably quite thorough."

"True," Sarah said. "In any case, they'll page me if anyone shows up to claim the package." She went on to detail the other operations that were in gear.

A full-field investigation, which Operation MINO-TAUR had become, is extremely resource-intensive; it allowed them to use every weapon they had. These included clandestine microphones and video, direction finders on cars, trash covers, wiretap surveillance. Technically, a full-field was good for one year, but it was renewable—some full-fields, like the FBI's war against the Communist Party of the United States, had gone on for forty years. The problem was, of course, that they didn't have a year, even a month.

She related what Technical Services had discovered about the fusing mechanism. But the latest information, which she'd received a few minutes ago from the youthful-voiced Ted Grabowski, was the real story. "Once it was clear that the Libyan timer was a fake, a counterfeit, the techies began to look more closely," she said. "They did a microscopic examination, looking for tool marks. Remember the attempt to assassinate President Bush in Kuwait a couple of years ago?"

"Sure," Pappas said. "We found explosives, Det-Cord, and fusing mechanisms, and determined that the folks behind it were—who else?—the Iraqis. So what's the connection?"

"Well, the exact same pair of wirecutters that were used to make the Kuwait bomb were used to cut the wires in this fusing mechanism."

"Sweet Jesus," Pappas said.

"Hold on," Vigiani said. "You're saying the Iraqis made this thing?"

"No," Sarah replied. "The Iraqis didn't *make* the Kuwait bomb either—they farmed it out. It was a pretty fancy piece of handiwork, probably beyond the capabilities of the Iraqis."

"Sarah," Vigiani said, "I think I'm above my pay grade here. Can you explain it in simple terms?"

"Okay," Sarah said. "Baumann hired someone to construct a detonator and ship it in. Whoever he hired also did the Kuwait bomb. *And* was trained at the Naval Explosive Ordnance Disposal School—by us. So if we can find out who built the Kuwaiti fusing mechanism . . ."

"I'm intrigued by this counterfeit Libyan timer," Pappas said. "This attempt to lay a false trail. Why would someone do that?"

"To conceal their own involvement, lead us astray?" suggested Vigiani.

"Or else," Pappas said, "to pin it on the Libyans for some strategic reason. Either way, this is not normal terrorist behavior. This is the work of someone who wants no credit, no blame, no extortion. In short, Baumann has been hired by someone who simply wants to destroy some part of New York City, presumably the Manhattan Bank, without making a statement."

"Well," said Vigiani, "he sure as hell isn't going to do it without his fuse thing. And he still hasn't shown up to claim it, or has he?"

"Not yet, as far as I know," Sarah replied. "He may still. Not likely, I admit."

"Sarah," Pappas said, "what else does this fellow need to build a bomb?"

"An explosive, obviously. . . . Why, what are you getting at?"

"Well, terrorists love plastic explosives, Semtex and C-4 and the like, right? Which is very difficult to get on the open market. So he's either shipping it in somehow—"

"Yes," Sarah interrupted. "Or getting it here." She saw where he was going. "Yes, that could be a way."

"What, steal it?" Vigiani asked.

"Possibly, yes," Sarah said.

"So we put out a threat advisory?"

"Too public," Sarah said.

"Real sanitized," Vigiani said.

"Still throws up too many questions. We'll ask ATF to inform us of any thefts of C-4, dynamite, or other explosives, please report immediately, blah blah blah. And give our twenty-four-hour number. Without revealing why we're so interested. Concentrate especially on military bases."

Vigiani shrugged. "Worth a try, I suppose." She looked up as Ranahan and Roth entered the room. "Hey, any luck?"

The expression on the two men's faces told the assembled that it wasn't good news.

"What happened?" Sarah asked.

"It's Ullman," Roth said, ashen-faced.

"What do you—what about Ullman?" Sarah said, although she now knew.

"Dead," Ranahan said thickly.

"Oh, my *God*," exploded Vigiani.

Ranahan continued: "He followed a guy for a couple of blocks, then vanished without a trace in an alley behind a restaurant. When we stopped hearing his voice, we sent out some guys to track him down."

"I found him," Roth said. "Dumpster behind the restaurant. Under a pile of, I don't know, food shit." He sank into a chair. There was a stunned silence.

"Baumann?" asked Pappas.

"His MO, anyway," Roth said. "Same as the Pollsmoor killings. Done with bare hands, except for a blunt object used to smash in the eyeball."

"Russell must have been on to him," Vigiani said in a hoarse whisper.

"Maybe," Sarah said. "But Baumann's obviously on to *us*."

CHAPTER SIXTY-ONE

The doorbell chimed, and Sarah buzzed Brian Lamoreaux in. He was wearing a nubby brown jacket over a striped band-collar shirt and looked terrific. He smelled very faintly of bay rum cologne. He was wearing an Armani-type pair of glasses with a tortoiseshell inlay that made him look almost sexy.

"New glasses," she said by way of greeting.

"They're old, actually," Brian said. "I'm glad you could come with me tonight."

"I can't work all the time," she said, although in truth she wished she were back at MINOTAUR headquarters. Still, if she continued working the way she had been, she feared she'd go out of her mind.

From behind his back he drew a small bouquet of lilies, some of which were already wilted. "How nice," she said. "Thank you. But let me warn you again, if my beeper goes off while the music's playing, I'll have to leave you in the lurch."

"Understood. I'm a big boy. I can take care of myself."

Softly playing in the background was the E-flat adagio movement of the Haydn G minor piano trio, which was not helping much to calm Sarah down. This was their second time going out, and for some reason she was still nervous. She'd turned him down at the hospital, but accepted when he called later in the day to check on Jared. The next night they'd met for a drink at a Cuban café on Columbus Avenue, and she'd decided maybe there was something there.

Jared approached shyly. Behind him hovered his babysitter, a Marymount Manhattan College student named Brea, who said hi and didn't seem to know what to do with her hands.

"So, Brian," Jared said, "do you build buildings?"

"No, I just write about them," Brian admitted.

"Oh," he said, disappointed. "You like baseball?"

"The truth is, I don't follow baseball. I don't know anything about it. But funny you should mention baseball." He produced a small plastic-wrapped card and handed it to Jared. "Look what I found in the rubbish."

Jared looked at the object, and his eyes widened. "No way!" he exulted. "You didn't find this in the trash! Oh, my God, it's a Satchel Paige!"

"Isn't that nice of Brian!" Sarah said.

"It's *awesome*," Jared said. "It's a 1953 Topps!" He turned to Sarah and explained: "There's hardly any Satchel Paiges around—they didn't make Negro League cards."

Sarah said, "I hope it didn't cost too much."

"You know, Satchel Paige didn't even know how old he was," Jared said. "There aren't any official stats on him. He'd, like, pitch three games a day, day after day, and then he'd go down to South America and pitch down there. . . . This is so *excellent*."

The phone rang. Sarah felt an adrenaline jolt and turned to answer it, but Jared got to it first.

"Oh, hi," he said without enthusiasm, and Sarah instantly knew who was calling. "Yeah, I'm okay," he went on in a sullen monotone. "Everything's fine. Mom, it's Dad."

"Can you tell him I'll call him tomorrow from work?"

"Mommy's going out on a date," Jared said into the phone. As Jared hung up the phone, Sarah caught his eye and gave him a look. He stared back at her brazenly, as if to say, *I know what I'm doing.*

"Now *this* is an apartment building," Sarah said as they strolled past the Dakota, at Central Park West and Seventy-second Street. She was distraught and frightened by Ullman's death, barely able to think about anything other than her work now, and yet trying to mask it with a blithe air. "You know anything about this one?"

"The Dakota? Sure do," Brian said. "Well, it was really the first great luxury apartment house. Built in the 1880s by a guy named Edward Clark, the president of the Singer sewing machine company. People called it Clark's Folly, because it was ridiculously far from the center of town."

"Hmm."

"In fact, I believe it was named the Dakota for the Dakota Territory, because it was so far away."

"Who was the architect?" she asked without interest. What am I doing? she asked herself. Trying to keep the conversation going so I don't have to think about the nightmares?

"Henry J. Hardenbergh," he said. "One of the great architects of the time. And . . . I seem to recall something about how Clark bought the adjoining land and had a couple dozen row houses built on it. Then he put this immense power plant in the basement of the Dakota to supply electricity not just for the Dakota, but for all the neighboring row houses. *That's* some serious urban planning."

"Isn't this where John Lennon was killed?"

"That's right. . . . Sarah, no offense, but I have a feeling you're not terribly interested in an architectural tour right now. Something wrong?"

"No, I'm fine."

"Is it Jared?"

"Oh, no, Jared's doing fine."

"That was your ex who called, wasn't it?"

"Yeah. I don't know how the hell he tracked me down, but he's a resourceful guy. And it's not like I'm in the Federal Witness Protection Program or anything. I just . . . mostly, I guess I wish he'd leave us alone."

"He isn't the jealous type, is he?"

"Oh, he is. He's also the violent type."

Brian stepped to the curb to hail a cab. "Great," he said. "I could barely handle prepubescent thugs. I doubt I could stand up to a jealous cop."

There was a break after the A Minor Quartet. Brian whispered, "Boy, that slow movement isn't easy to listen to."

"What do you mean?"

"I think it's the most difficult passage in all Beethoven. Someone once compared this piece to a man who's trying to see how slowly he can ride a bicycle without falling."

Sarah laughed gently. The longer she watched him, particularly when he was animated by enthusiasm for whatever he was talking about, the more appealing she found him. The difference between him and Peter was so enormous it wasn't even funny. How could the same woman be attracted to such entirely different men? In the park the other day, she had pitied him, felt a sort of contempt for him, bumbling and ineffectual as he was. Yet he had been wonderful, attentive, caring, when he took them to the emergency room.

After the *Grosse Fuge*, the concert ended with the C-sharp minor Quartet, which Sarah considered one of the greatest pieces of music ever written. "Amazing, isn't it?" Brian said, taking her hand. "The adagio is one of the saddest things I've ever heard."

Sarah squeezed his hand and nodded.

They took a cab to his apartment, just off Sutton Place. She had promised herself she wouldn't end up at his place or in a hotel room, but she felt comfortable with him, and Brea, the babysitter from Marymount Manhattan College, had said she didn't mind if it was a late night.

His apartment was small but elegantly furnished, with a lot of books, mostly on architecture, and beautiful, comfortable furniture. She went into his kitchen and made a phone call to check on the babysitter, then returned and sank into a wonderfully overstuffed couch while he got some brandy.

"I like it," she said, indicating the whole apartment.

"Oh, it's not mine," he said. "I think I mentioned this colleague of mine from Edmonton—he and his wife are here on sabbatical, but they're spending the summer in residence at Taliesen, the Frank Lloyd Wright house in Wisconsin. They're only too happy to have me take over the rent for a few weeks."

"Well, you've seen the way I furnished my apartment," Sarah said. "Milk crates and moving boxes, right? It must be nice to be living in a place so finished."

He poured out two snifters of brandy and handed one to her. "Look, Sarah, we hardly know each other, so this may be way too aggressive, but let me just say this." He sat down on the couch beside her, at what seemed the perfect remove, neither menacingly close nor exaggeratedly far away. "I pick up vibes that you don't want to talk about whatever it is you do, whether you really work for the FBI or not. If that's the way you want it, that's fine. But I don't want you to think I'm not interested, okay?"

Sarah couldn't help smiling appreciatively. "Okay."

"So let's talk about the weather or something."

"Well," she said, "do you mind if I ask you something personal?"

"Me? I'm an open book."

"Your limp. You've had it for a while, right? Did you get hit by a car or something?"

"A couple of weeks after my wife's death, I got really high and drove into a telephone pole. Next thing I knew, I was in the hospital, and a couple of policemen came to visit me, and they told me that they hadn't found any skidmarks at the accident scene."

"Meaning what?"

"I didn't try to stop. I just drove into the telephone pole at sixty miles an hour."

"Trying to kill yourself."

"I don't remember it, but yeah, that's what they were saying."

"You loved her."

"Yes, I did. She was a wonderful, wonderful person." He hesitated a moment, a catch in his throat. "But that was a different part of my life, and this is no time to talk about all that, all right?"

"All right."

He got up to put some music on. For a few minutes he rummaged through a large collection of CDs.

She watched him as he stood. He had a wonderful, lithe body, broad shoulders, a narrow waist. It was not the body of a man who sat around, an academic or an architect; he obviously worked out.

"This is a wonderful Armagnac," Sarah said.

"Thanks. I thought you'd like it."

"I love Armagnac."

"Good. So do I. Do you like jazz vocals?"

"Of course. What have you got?"

"Let me surprise you."

He returned to the sofa and sat closer, watching her as the music came on, simple but highly syncopated jazz piano.

"Oscar Peterson and Ella Fitzgerald!" Sarah said. "One of the all-time great albums."

"You've got good taste in music," Brian said, and leaned over and kissed her lips. He held her face in both hands as if admiring an objet d'art. Sarah closed her eyes and parted her lips and tasted his tongue.

Oh, God, Sarah thought, let me just be right here, in the moment.

She put her hands on his back, against his shoulder blades, then ran them down to the firm, shirt-covered flesh of his lower back. She slipped her fingertips underneath his belt and rested them there, enjoying the warmth, the velvety feel of the swell of his buttocks.

His tongue moved slowly into her mouth, exploring the inside of her mouth, and he held her face even tighter.

"Sarah," he groaned.

Be in the moment, she chanted to herself. In the moment.

She felt her thoughts at last beginning to lift momentarily away from the inordinate tensions of her daily work, the deaths, the fear and uncertainty. She felt almost light-headed, and she was grateful.

His hands slid smoothly down her neck, over her shoulders, then came around to cup her breasts from the sides, gently. She felt enveloped by the warmth, felt aroused.

I can't believe this is happening, she thought. Can't believe this is happening. I don't know the man, don't know anything about him, don't—

He unbuttoned the top buttons of her blouse, nuzzled

warmly against her bare skin, then licked and kissed his way to her nipples.

"Mmmph," she groaned.

A new song began: "How Long Has This Been Going On?" Ella's voice, though past its peak, was husky yet agile. She belted out the lyrics, stumbled over one line, sang, *One more once and that makes tw—thrice!*

She slipped her fingers underneath the band of his jockey shorts, felt the silky smoothness of his skin. At the same time, he reached around to finish unbuttoning her blouse, then unfasten her bra, and she felt her nipples grow hard. He undid her skirt and let it fall to the floor, then unbuckled his belt and let his pants drop. She saw his erection tenting the white cotton of his undershorts, and she slowly slid them down.

Slowly, agonizingly slowly, his head moved downward, planting a trail of scorchingly hot kisses on her belly, the wisps of hair beneath her navel, and—

"Brian—" she said, a vain attempt to gain control.

Down there, his tongue fluttering like a butterfly, or a hummingbird, his head moving back and forth, then up and down, his tongue alternately rigid and probing, then soft and wet and oscillating. He kissed, sucked gently at her labia, *hummed* a few notes along with the song, sucked a little harder, hummed again, and then enveloped her clitoris and the hood around it with a luscious, feather-soft kiss. She rocked back and forth, undulating her hips as the teasing little tickle of pleasure built into a sharp-edged wave and grew stronger and larger and she heard something so far away, something—

—a mechanical noise, of the ordinary world, not of the world of pleasure into which she was floating—

—her pager. She groaned. Her pager had gone off.

Brian grunted his annoyance. "Not now," he said.

"I'm—I'm sorry—I have to . . ." She rolled over, took her cellular phone out of her purse. Naked, she took it into the bathroom, shut the door, clicked on the ventilation fan to muffle her voice.

"Yes, Ken," she said. "I really hope this is important."

"Sorry to bother you," Ken Alton said. "But yeah, I think it is. I got it."

"Got . . . what?"

"The passport. The passport Baumann used to enter the U.S. The name is Thomas Allen Moffatt."

Sarah disconnected, folded up the phone, and returned to the bedroom. Brian was lying on his back, a crooked half-smile on his face. "Everything all right?" he murmured.

"Everything's fine," she said. "Good news."

"Good," Henrik Baumann said. "We can all use good news. Now, where were we?"

Part 5

TRAPS

*When the strike of a hawk
breaks the body of its prey,
it is because of the timing.*

—Sun-tzu, *The Art of War*

CHAPTER SIXTY-TWO

At four-thirty in the morning, the narrow alley off the side street in the Wall Street area of lower Manhattan was dark and deserted. Opaque steam rose from a manhole cover. A discarded yellow wrapper from a McDonald's Quarter Pounder drifted along the wet asphalt like tumbleweed.

Two figures appeared at one end of the alley, one tall and lean, the other small and portly. Both were clad in heavy pants and boots, long-sleeved overshirts, and welder's gloves.

On their backs were mountaineering backpacks and air tanks connected to mouthpieces that dangled at their sides. They approached the steaming manhole. The taller one, who was carrying a four-foot crowbar, inserted the sharp end of the crowbar between the manhole cover and casing, then pushed downward with all his body weight.

"You see why I couldn't do this myself," Leo Krasner said.

Baumann did not answer. He kept pushing at the fulcrum until a low, rusty moan began to sound, then a higher-pitched squeak, and then the manhole cover began slowly to lift.

"Go," he said.

Krasner trundled over to the opening, turned his portly body around, and began clambering down the rungs of the steel ladder built into the side of the manhole. Baumann followed, sliding the manhole cover back with great exertion. Finally the ornamented iron cover was back in place. They were underground within one minute and thirty seconds.

First Krasner, then Baumann dropped from the end of the ladder into the still water below. Two splashes disturbed the silence. The smell was rank, overpowering. Krasner heaved; Baumann bit his lower lip.

They reached around for the silicone mouthpieces, pulled them up, and bit into the nubs that held them in place. Baumann switched on Krasner's air tank, then Krasner did the same for him. With loud hisses, they began inhaling the tanked air. Krasner took several deep, grateful breaths.

Despite the stench, they were standing not in sewage but in a few inches of runoff water from storm drains, which ran through miles of tunnels beneath the streets of New York. The oval concrete tube was seven feet or so high and about five feet wide, and it seemed to go on forever. These drainage tunnels served a dual function: along the top and the upper sides of the tunnel ran many cables for power and telecommunication links.

"We can leave the crowbar here or take it with us," Leo said.

"Take it," said Baumann. "Let's move quickly."

There was a splash, and a rat the size of a small dog ran by.

"Shit!" exclaimed Leo with a shudder.

Baumann pulled a caver's headlamp from his backpack and put it on. He checked the reading on his compass and zeroed his pedometer, then waited patiently for Leo to do the same. He did, and consulted a map that had been compiled by a group of crackers he knew who liked to do nefarious deeds in the city.

For almost a quarter of a mile they slogged through the tunnels, guided through the maze by their compasses, pedometers, and the surprisingly detailed map of the underground tunnels. A more direct route would have meant entering via a manhole on a much more visible major street, which was out of the question.

They came to a juncture between two tunnels whose curved walls were covered with a profusion of large oblong boxes connected to thick wire casings. Each removed his mouthpiece, then switched off the other's air tank. The air here was much better.

This was, Leo explained, one of the many central switching areas in which repairmen from NYNEX could access telephone lines. To Baumann's untrained eye, it appeared to be a forest of wires in maddening disarray.

"Each one is labeled with a tag," Krasner said, panting. "Series of numbers and letters. By customer account number. Fear not, I know the one we want."

Two, then three rats scurried by underfoot. One of them stopped to sniff something in the cloudy gray water, then moved on.

After a few minutes of searching, Leo located the right cable.

"Coax," he announced. "Just like they told me."

"Hmm?"

"It's coaxial cable—copper wire. Hell of a lot easier to splice."

"What if it had been fiber-optic cable?"

Krasner shook his head in disbelief at Baumann's ignorance. "I brought every tool we'd need, whether it was copper or fiber." With a pair of wire cutters he snipped the copper line and proceeded to strip it. "Problem with fiber is, they could tell if there's a tap on the line. The coefficient of the material you use to connect the two cut ends of the fiber will always change the characteristics of the light pulse. So it's going to be obvious to a monitor that there's a new material conducting the light pulse. It would be detected instantly, soon as they're on line."

He fed both ends of the copper wire into a square "breakout box," which was, he explained, made by a company named Black Box. This was a tap, a sophisticated, undetectable, high-impedance parallel tap for computers, often used for diagnostic purposes.

Then Krasner carefully removed from his backpack an NEC UltraLite Versa notebook computer no bigger than a hardcover book. He connected the breakout box to the serial port in the notebook computer.

"This baby's modified so it's got a gigabyte of storage capacity," he said. He set the computer down on a small shelf that jutted out from the wall. "All right, it's ten after six o'clock. We can't do anything till nine A.M., and all we really need to capture is maybe an hour's worth of traffic. In the meantime, I'm going to take a nap. The Manhattan Bank doesn't open for business for another, oh, three hours."

While Leo Krasner slept, Baumann sat next to him, thinking. He thought about his time in prison, about his childhood, about a woman at university with whom he had had a long and ardent relationship. He thought, too, about Sarah Cahill and the game of deception he was playing with her. If she had been distrustful of "Brian," she was quickly becoming less so. Already he had successfully invaded her life, and soon, very soon, there would be many more opportunities to do so.

Then Leo Krasner's Casio alarm watch finally beeped, jolting him awake. "Whoa," Krasner said through a yawn. His breath was fermented, noxious.

"All right now, we should have some action in just about three minutes. Let's boot 'er up."

A little over an hour later, he had a sizable amount of captured traffic outgoing from Manhattan Bank, all stored on his computer. "We got a shitload of information here," he said. "Pattern of transaction, transaction length, destination code. Everything. Now it's a simple matter to mimic the transactions and get inside." He pulled the connector out of the computer's serial port. "I'm going to leave the breakout box here."

"Won't it be detected?"

"Nah. The fuck you want, you want me to yank this thing off right now and interrupt the line? Then we'd *really* be screwed."

"No," Baumann said patiently. "The breakout box can't be removed until after transmissions have stopped, which means after banking hours. And yes, I most certainly want it removed. I can't risk having a piece of evidence here for longer than a day."

"You want to repair the patch, you do it," Krasner said.

"I'd be glad to do it, if I could be certain of my ability to do it perfectly. But I can't. So we both must return here. Tonight?"

Krasner scowled. "Hey, man, I happen to have a life."

"I don't think you have much of a choice," Baumann explained. "Your payment depends upon satisfactory completion of all aspects of the job."

The cracker was silent, sullen, for a moment. "Tonight I'll be analyzing the traffic and writing code. I don't have time to slog around the sewers tonight. It can wait."

"All right," Baumann said. "It will wait."

"Hey, and speaking of analyzing the traffic, I can't do shit without the key. You got it with you? If you forgot to bring it—"

"No," Baumann said, "I didn't forget." He handed the cracker a shiny gold disk, the CD-ROM Dyson had given him. It had been stolen—Dyson did not say how he had arranged this—from a high-ranking officer of the bank. "Here's the key," he said.

"How new is this? Passwords still valid?"

"I'm sure the passwords have been changed by now, but that's insignificant. The cryptographic software is unchanged, and it's all here."

"Fine," Krasner said. "No problem."

CHAPTER SIXTY-THREE

Malcolm Dyson switched off CNN and pressed the button to close the sliding panel on the armoire. He had been watching a business report on the computer industry and could think about nothing except the plan.

The soft underbelly of capitalism, he knew, was the computer. And not just the computer in general, the computer as an abstract concept, but one specific collection of computers, in one specific building in lower Manhattan.

Its location is kept secret, yet when you know the right people, you can find out. Bankers and money men occasionally talk about the Network over drinks late at night, speculating about what might happen *if . . .* and, with a shudder, dismiss the thought.

Great catastrophes can happen at any moment, but we don't think about them. Most of us don't give much thought to the possibility of a gigantic meteor colliding with our planet and extinguishing all life. With the end of the Cold War we less and less often think about what might happen if an all-out nuclear war were to erupt.

The destruction of the Network is every banker's nightmare. It would plunge America into a second Great Depression that would make the 1930s seem like a time of prosperity. This possibility is, fortunately, kept hidden from the ordinary citizen.

It is, however, very real.

Dyson had come up with the idea, originally, and Martin Lomax had provided the spadework, which he had presented to his boss six months ago—almost six months after Dyson was paralyzed and his wife and daughter were killed.

The report Lomax had written now lay in a concealed drawer in the desk in Dyson's library. Dyson had read it countless times since then. It gave him strength, got him through the days, diverted his pain, both physical and psychic. It began:

FROM: R. MARTIN LOMAX
TO: MALCOLM DYSON

First, a brief history.

In the years immediately after the California Gold Rush of 1848, the American banking system became increasingly chaotic. Banks would send payments to other banks by dispatching porters with bags of gold coins. Errors and confusion were rampant. In 1853, the fifty-two major banks in New York established the New York Settlement Association in the basement of 14 Wall Street to provide some coordination in the exchange of payments. On its very first day, the Association cleared 22.6 million dollars.

By 1968, this antiquated system began to break down. It was virtually impossible to get anything done. The era of teletype technology in the 1950s gave way to that of the computer in the 1960s. By 1970 the advent of the computer allowed the Association to be replaced by the Network, shorthand for the National Electronic Transfer Facility.

The Network began with one computer connected to a telephone. The newfangled system was at first distrusted by the world's banks, but confidence began to grow. Banks began to accept wire payments. Gradually, every major bank in the world sought to join the Network.

Today, over a trillion dollars moves through the Network each day—90 percent of the dollars used anywhere on earth. Since virtually all Eurodollar and foreign exchange trading is conducted in dollars, and the world's flow of money is centered in New York, the Network, and its Unisys A-15J dual processor, has become the very nerve center of the world's financial system.

How fragile is the Network?

A brief case history will illustrate. At the close of business on June 26, 1974, German banking authorities closed the Bankhaus Herstatt in Cologne, a major player in foreign exchange trading. At the end of the German banking day it was still noon in New York, where banks suddenly found themselves out hundreds of millions of dollars. By the next day, the world banking system had gone into shock. Only quick action by Walter Wriston of Citicorp averted a global crash. As president of the Network at the time, he ordered the Network to stay open through the weekend until all payments were worked out. Any bank that refused to honor payment orders was thrown out of the Network.

A direct terrorist strike on the Network's Water Street facility would trigger worldwide havoc. It would so seriously disrupt the U.S. stock market, Eurodollar payments, and virtually all foreign exchange and foreign trade payments that the world payments system would collapse at once.

The destruction of the Network would topple the

business world and plunge America and the world into a massive depression. The U.S. economy would be obliterated, and with it that of the world. America's reign as a global power would be ended, as the country and much of the world returned to an economic Dark Ages.

It is only a matter of luck—or maybe ignorance of how the capitalist world works—that no terrorist has so far targeted the Network.

But if we could locate a masterful, experienced professional terrorist with a strong motivation—financial or otherwise—to accomplish the task, it is my strong belief that no more effective revenge could ever be wrought on the United States.

CHAPTER SIXTY-FOUR

Now there was a name, the alias Baumann had used to enter the United States. In some ways it was a major victory; in some ways it was dust.

"He may never use it again," Roth said.

Sarah nodded. "If so, the lead's useless."

"Why would he use the name again, anyway? If he checks into a hotel, he does it under some fake name."

"Credit cards?"

"Does he have this guy Moffatt's credit cards too?"

"I don't know."

"And if he does?"

"Bing, we get him," Sarah said. "Pops up right away, and he's nabbed."

"He's not stupid. He's not going to use stolen credit cards. Anyway, the scummiest little dirtbag knows you gotta test out the card first—you know, drive into a self-serve gas station and try the card on one of those credit card thingos there, and if it's rejected, you know it's no good. Real easy."

"He may have to rent a car or a van."

"Right," Roth said. "But he'll need a driver's license to do that."

"He's got Thomas Moffatt's driver's license."

"Well, there you go. So what are you suggesting?"

"This is a specific terrorist threat on U.S. soil. It's a full-field investigation. That means we can task a hell of a lot of manpower if we want. This monster has already killed two FBI agents."

"You're not talking about sending a hundred guys around to every car- and truck-rental place in New York City, are you?"

"And neighboring New Jersey and Connecticut."

"You gotta be kidding."

"Hey, don't forget, we caught the World Trade Center bombers through Mohammed Salameh's driver's license, which he used to rent the van."

"Well, you're the boss," Roth said dubiously.

"I don't mean to be a killjoy," Christine Vigiani said, the standard gambit of every killjoy, "but the only reason everyone seems so sure Baumann used Thomas Moffatt's passport is the timing. Pretty slender evidence."

"Whoever used the stolen Moffatt passport entered the country twelve days ago," Pappas argued, "which is eight days after he broke out of Pollsmoor prison. The fit is too good. Plus all the other factors—"

"Chris," Sarah said, "there's no point in talking any further. We have a team on it in D.C. already, so we'll have our answer soon."

In fact, at that very moment, there were several FBI teams in Washington searching for Baumann.

One of the flight attendants had been located, at her apartment near Dupont Circle, and had actually laughed when the FBI agent asked her if she remembered the passenger in seat 17-C. The customs agent who had processed Baumann/Moffatt's entry was similarly incredulous. "You gotta be kidding," he said. "You know how many *hundreds* of people I processed that day?" FBI street agents were unable to turn up any cab drivers at Dulles who remembered taking a fare that resembled the sketch of Baumann's face.

Another FBI team was poring over the flight manifest that United Airlines had just faxed over. They were fortunate to be dealing with an American carrier, because foreign ones tended to be recalcitrant. Some airlines would not turn over their flight manifests without a criminal subpoena—difficult to get, because Baumann was not being sought in a criminal matter. Or they'd request a "national security letter," a classified document that must adhere to the attorney general's stringent guidelines on foreign counterintelligence.

Thank God for American multinational conglomerates. In a few minutes, the FBI team knew Baumann had purchased his tickets in London, with cash, an open return. They were also able to study the I-94 form that all arriving passengers are required to fill out. The address Baumann had given was false, as they expected it to be—no such street existed in the town of Buffalo, New York.

More important, they now knew which seat Baumann had sat in, which meant they knew the name of the passenger who sat next to him. Baumann had sat on the aisle, but on his right had sat a woman named Hilda Guinzburg. An FBI team visited Mrs. Guinzburg, a feisty seventy-four-year-old, at her Reston, Virginia, home and showed her a copy of Thomas Allen Moffatt's passport photograph from the State Department archives.

Mrs. Guinzburg shook her head. This was definitely not the man she had sat next to on her flight from London, she insisted. This confirmed that Moffatt's passport photograph had been doctored and used by someone else.

And the I-94 form was then sent to the FBI's ID section to test for latent fingerprints.

* * *

After changing out of his filthy clothes and showering, Leo Krasner went for a walk.

When he reached the burnished silver Manhattan Bank building, he strolled into the atrium as casually as he could and took the elevator to the twenty-third floor. The employee cafeteria was on this floor, so there was no security.

He found a bulletin board and posted a notice, then posted the identical notice on a board in an employee lounge. He posted several other copies on other bulletin boards on the floor.

Then he returned to his apartment and went to work.

CHAPTER SIXTY-FIVE

This is New York, where no one knows his neighbors, Baumann reflected as he turned the last key in Sarah Cahill's triple-locked door.

He was out of breath and soaking wet. It was half past noon, but the sky was dark, and torrential rain was coming down with a Biblical vengeance. He wore a raincoat, the sort of tan belted topcoat just about every man in the city was wearing right now, although he had bought his in Paris from Charvet.

He had heard that when it rains in Manhattan the city comes to a halt and it becomes impossible to get a taxi, and it was true. It had taken him a long while to find a cab, which had then become stuck in the midday rush-hour traffic, exacerbated by the weather.

Sarah would not be home for hours, and Jared was still at the YMCA. True, there might have been problems if Sarah's neighbors were home during the day (which they were not) or if one of them chanced to see him entering her apartment and mentioned it to her.

But this is New York. Strangers exhibit certain predictable behavior. Like women and their handbags. When a woman does not know you, she clutches her handbag as if it contained her life's savings, though in fact rarely does it hold anything besides lipstick, compact, keys, grocery receipts, dry-cleaning slips, a scrawled note, and keys.

When a woman feels she knows you better, she will relax that grip. It is a mark of intimacy almost animalistic in nature. In your apartment, preparatory to lovemaking, she will go to the bathroom and, depending on what she needs, may leave her purse on the coffee table in front of you. Sarah had gone to use the phone on her second visit to his apartment. This told Baumann that despite her tough demeanor, she was a trusting person.

The phone was in the kitchen, out of sight of the living room: Baumann had made sure the only telephone was in the kitchen. She had talked to the babysitter for four or five minutes.

That had been enough time, really much more than enough time. There are tools for this sort of thing; the most simple-minded burglar can do it. There is a long flat plastic box, hinged lengthwise, perhaps five inches long and two inches wide and an inch thick. Inside the box is a wax softer than beeswax, a layer on the top and the bottom.

He placed Sarah's key into the box and squeezed it tight until he had an exact impression of her key—actually, three keys. He had anticipated that he might have trouble getting the keys off the ring, so he was prepared. He used a box that was notched at one end.

Later, he used a very soft, very-low-melting-point metal that in the profession is called Rose metal. It is an alloy of lead and zinc. Its melting point is lower than that of the wax mold. He poured the metal carefully into the mold. This gave him a very weak metal key, which is good only as a template.

From a hardware store he got the right key blank. In a vise he positioned the Rose metal template atop the blank. He used a Number Four Swiss-Cut file, the lock-picker's friend, and cut his own key.

Now he quickly turned the keys in the locks and entered the apartment.

This was his fifth time searching Sarah's apartment. She was scrupulous and left no files lying around, no personal notebooks with notes on the investigation, no computer disks. She was making this difficult . . . but not impossible. He now knew where she worked—the top-secret location of Operation MINOTAUR. He knew the phone number of the task force's headquarters. Soon he would know more. At any moment she might let down her guard, begin to talk about her work, pillow talk, worried confidences. It was possible. At the very least, his proximity to her afforded him possibilities of access he'd never have dreamed of.

Yes, there were hazards. There was an element of risk for the hunted to befriend the hunter, spend so much time with her, make love to her. But it was not a great risk, because he knew there were no photographs of him. Apart from a very generic and useless physical description—which could have described 20 percent of the males in New York City—the task force had no idea what he looked like. The South African secret service had no photographs of him on file, and the prison's photographs had been destroyed. It was a certainty that the FBI had put together an Identi-Kit, but it would do them no good. Whatever the South Africans had feebly attempted to put together would bear no resemblance to the way he looked now, not in a million years.

They might know his true eye color, but that was easily taken care of. Changing the color of one's eyes can be as simple as using standard, generally available colored contact lenses, but this is not a disguise for professionals. A careful observer can always tell you are wearing corneal contact lenses, which can raise nettlesome questions. Baumann had had special lenses custom-designed for him by an optometrist in Amsterdam. They were prosthetic scleral soft lenses, which cover the entire eye, not just the iris, and can be comfortably worn for twelve hours. The color tones were natural, the lenses large, with iris flecks (which standard contact lenses do not have). The most suspicious observer would not have known that his eyes were blue, not a gentle brown.

Naturally, if she became suspicious, she would have to be killed at once, just as he had killed Perry Taylor and Russell Ullman. But why in the world would she suspect she was sleeping with the enemy? She wouldn't.

It was all a game, an exhilarating game. A dance with the devil.

As he combed the apartment, in all the likely hiding places and the not-so-likely ones, among Jared's belongings, he could hear faint traffic noises from the street, a car alarm, a siren.

And then, at last, there was something.

A notepad. A blank notepad on her bedside table. The top sheet was blank, but it bore the imprint of a scrawl that had been made on the leaf above it. He rubbed lightly against the indentation with a soft lead pencil, and the scrawl appeared, white script against black.

Thomas Allen Moffatt.

They had one of his aliases. How in the world had they gotten it? So they likely knew he had used the stolen Thomas Moffatt passport to enter the country.

He exhaled very slowly. A near miss. He had reserved a van for tomorrow in Moffatt's name.

Well, that would have to change.

CHAPTER SIXTY-SIX

"A nuclear weapon," Pappas said, "is not what I'm worried about."

"Why not?" Sarah asked.

"Don't get me wrong, I don't mean a nuke wouldn't be terrifying. But the physics of an A-bomb are easy; it's the actualization that's tough. It's far too impractical, too difficult to construct."

"But if our terrorist has the resources and the ability—?"

"The plain fact is, a nuke would destroy much of the city, and that's not what the intel intercept seems to be hinting at. They're talking about a *targeted* attack on a *bank*, not on the entire city."

Sarah nodded. "Makes sense. We can't rule anything out, but in some ways a giant conventional bomb is scarier, because it's much harder to detect. *Much* harder."

"Right."

"So what are my options?" she asked.

"Obviously you can't order a bomb sweep of the entire city. But you can order sweeps of every Manhattan Bank branch office. That's certainly feasible. We have the personnel for that right here in the New York office."

"NYPD Bomb Squad?"

"They only get called in when you have a bomb ticking right in front of you. Otherwise they don't move. They're good, but you've got to have a bomb."

"And if we *do* have a bomb?"

"Then it's your call," Pappas said. "But you're not only going to have an emergency on your hands, you're also going to have an ugly turf battle. The NYPD Bomb Squad is one of the oldest and most experienced in the country, but they're experienced mostly with relatively low-tech stuff, homemade bombs and the like. Then you'll have ATF, which has the responsibility for all crimes involving explosives. They have the bomb capability, and they're going to want to play. And then there's the Army, which is responsible for bomb disposal over the entire continental landmass of the United States, other than in the sea or on the bases of other military services. They're going to want in, and they're going to argue—quite rightly—that they're substantially better equipped than the NYPD."

"And there's NEST," Sarah said.

"Right," Pappas said. "And ever since Harvey's Casino, they're going to want to play too."

NEST is an acronym for the Nuclear Emergency Search Team, the best bomb squad in the United States by far and, naturally, the most secretive. It is part of the U.S. Department of Energy, but is actually managed by a private contractor. Charged with searching for and rendering safe all suspected nuclear explosives, NEST is based in Las Vegas, Nevada (the Nevada nuclear weapons test site is ninety miles away). A portion of its equipment is also located at Andrews Air Force Base in Maryland, and its East Coast facilities are based in Germantown, Maryland.

The incident involving Harvey's Casino in State Line, Nevada, near Lake Tahoe, will not soon be forgotten by those in NEST. In 1981, a man who owed the casino a gambling debt of a quarter of a million dollars decided to liquidate his debt in the best way he could think of. He placed a complex, though not sophisticated, bomb in the casino, consisting of a thousand pounds of dynamite, and made an extortion demand: forgive the debt, or the place would blow up. Either way, he figured, he couldn't lose.

The bomb, which had six different fusing systems, sat there ticking for three days while everyone argued about whose responsibility it was. No one was avoiding responsibility; on the contrary, quite a few different parties wanted to take charge of defusing the bomb.

There was the city—which really meant two guys from the fire department who'd gone through a rudimentary three-week training program at hazardous devices school. They had the backing of the politicos. Then there was the Army, which announced that it had the legal responsibility for the bomb. NEST showed up, did a careful study, and declared, this is one complex bomb; why don't you let us handle it? But the city told both NEST and the Army to take off; its two firemen would take care of the bomb.

Both NEST and the Army were faced with a dilemma: if the city handled the bomb and anything went wrong, they'd both be held responsible, legally and morally. So they came to a decision. Throw us out of town, they declared—in writing. Otherwise, we'll move in and attempt to render it safe.

The city did as they asked and told the Army and NEST to leave town by sunset.

The explosion that resulted caused some twelve million dollars' worth of damage and left a huge gaping hole in Harvey's Casino. The firemen who had insisted on rendering the bomb safe unfortunately did not have much of a grasp of elementary physics. Never again would NEST give up control to the locals without a fight.

"Okay," Sarah said. "I'm going to hold out the possibility it's a nuke."

"*What*?" exploded Pappas. "There's no goddam *reason* to believe it's a nuke, and if you want to scare half—"

"I know, I know," Sarah said. "But it's the only way DOE will be willing to call in NEST, and we're going to need the resources of the best. And when we need them, we're going to need them fast."

CHAPTER SIXTY-SEVEN

Dressed in a European suit, Baumann fit right into the throngs of Wall Street businessmen swarming to work this morning. He might have been a cosmopolitan banker, an Anglophilic bond salesman.

He stood on Water Street and gazed casually across the street at the ordinary-looking office building. Hundreds of thousands of people passed by this building, people whose livelihoods depended upon Wall Street and who probably never gave the building even so much as a passing glance.

On the street level were administrative offices of a small bank called Greenwich Trust. On the upper floors were various other offices. The building's lobby was green Wall-Street-office-building marble. There was absolutely nothing distinctive about the building.

Except for what was on the mezzanine level, behind unmarked doors accessed by a card-key system.

There, well protected and hidden from the world by the anonymity of its setting, was the Network, the nerve center of the world financial community. By now, Baumann knew quite a bit about what was behind those walls and doors. He knew there were two Unisys A-15J mainframes and optical disk pads for read-write media storage. In case of fire, Halon suppressants would instantly be released into the room. In case of power outages or surges, the machines would run on current that emanated from storage batteries fed by the city's power grid. The batteries would sustain operations until diesel-powered generators could be switched on.

There was electrical backup and telecommunications backup, and the dual processors provided computer redundancy. There were twenty-two electronic authentication boxes made by the British firm Racal-Guardata to screen all incoming messages for code flaws before permitting them on the mainframes. By algorithmic means, checking for both number and spacing of characters, the authenticators would defeat interdiction.

The builders of the Network had done extensive risk analysis. Even in constructing the facility they had used union labor only up to a point, then brought in their own technicians to do the sensitive internal wiring. Regular maintenance was done by their own internal technicians too.

But when you came right down to it, it was early-1980s technology, really, with only the most rudimentary security precautions taken. It was nothing short of a scandal how the planet's entire financial system could be brought down by one act of destruction visited upon this ordinary-looking office building in lower Manhattan.

After the World Trade Center bomb, there was talk about how badly damaged America's financial structure had *almost* been. That was nonsense. The World Trade Center bomb had killed a handful of people and closed some businesses for a while. That was nothing compared to what was about to happen here, across the street.

A trillion dollars moved electronically through one floor of this office building each day—more than the

entire money supply of the United States. Immense for-
tunes moved through here and around the world at the
speed of lightning. What, after all, is a treasury bill
these days but an item on a computer tape? The fragile
structure of the planet's finance depended upon the
function of this room full of mainframes. It teetered on
the confidence that this system would function.

Interrupt the flow—or worse, destroy the machinery
and wipe out the backup records—and governments
would shake, vast corporations would be wiped out.
The global financial system would screech to a halt.
Corporations around the world would run out of money,
would be unable to pay for goods, would have to halt
production, would be unable to write paychecks to their
employees. How astonishing it was, Baumann mused,
that we allowed our technology to outpace our ability
to use it!

This was the genius of Malcolm Dyson's plan of vengeance. He had targeted his revenge both selectively
and broadly. A banker named Warren Elkind, the head
of the second-largest bank in the country, had turned
Dyson in for insider trading, and would now pay for his
perfidy. A computer virus would invade the Manhattan
Bank and cause all of the bank's assets to be transferred out around the world. Not only would the Manhattan Bank be shut down, but it would be plundered of
all its assets. It would be broke.

I don't want Warren Elkind killed, Dyson had said. I
want him to suffer a living death. I want his livelihood
to be destroyed, the bank into which he's poured his
life to come toppling down.

Dyson knew that the failure even of such an immense
bank would not seriously weaken the U.S. economy.
That blow would come a day later, when the Network
was brought down just before the end of the business
day. Then the entire economy of the United States, which

had sent agents to kill Dyson's wife and daughter, would be dealt a paralyzing blow, from which it would not recover for years.

It was, really, a clever plan, Baumann reflected. Why had no one thought of it before?

CHAPTER SIXTY-EIGHT

Saturday morning, and Sarah took Jared to the St. Luke's–Roosevelt emergency room to have his stitches removed. By late morning they were back at home. Sarah was about to call Brea, the babysitter, and return to the MINOTAUR headquarters, when Brian called.

"You're home," he said, surprised. "I was wondering if you and Jared might want to take a walk around the city."

"A walk?"

"I want to show you two my favorite place in New York."

"Let me make a few calls," Sarah said, "and see how much time I can spare this afternoon. But I should warn you—"

"I know, I know. The beeper."

He met them in front of their apartment building and took them downtown on the subway at West Seventy-second and Broadway.

"Where are you from?" Jared asked Baumann on the ride downtown.

"Canada."

"But where?"

"A town called Edmonton."

"Where's that?"

"It's in Alberta. It's the capital."

"Is that a state?"

"Well, we call it a province. It's five times the size of New York State."

"Edmonton," Jared mused. His eyes suddenly widened. "That's where the Edmonton Oilers are from!"

"Right."

"You ever meet Wayne Gretzky?"

"Never met him."

"Oh," Jared said, disappointed.

Sarah watched the two of them sitting next to one another, noticing that Jared had started to become relaxed around Brian, that there was a chemistry there.

Baumann said, "You know, basketball was invented by a Canadian, a hundred years ago. The first basket was a bushel basket used for peaches."

"Uh huh," Jared said, unimpressed by Canada and its legacy. "Can you throw a pass?"

"As in American football?" Baumann asked.

"Yep."

"No, I can't. Sorry, I can't play football with you. I'm a klutz. Do you like football?"

Jared hesitated. "Not really."

"What do you like?"

"Tennis. Softball."

"You play ball with your dad?"

"Yeah. You play ball?"

"Not so well, Jared. But I can show you buildings. Maybe *you* can show *me* how to throw a pass someday."

As they walked to the Woolworth Building, Baumann said, more to Jared than to Sarah, "This was once the tallest building in the world."

"Oh, yeah?" Jared objected. "What about the Empire State Building?"

"That wasn't built yet. This building was completed in 1913. Only the Eiffel Tower was taller, but that doesn't count."

"Do planes ever crash into the tall buildings?"

"Once in a while," Baumann said. "A plane once crashed into the Empire State Building. And I know that once a helicopter trying to land on the roof of the Pan Am building broke apart, killing a lot of people."

"A helicopter! Helicopters can land on the Pan Am building?"

"No more. They used to, but since that horrible accident, helicopters can only land in officially designated heliports."

He brought them up to the main entrance on Broadway, with its ornately carved depressed arch, and pointed out the apex of the arch, the figure of an owl.

"That's supposed to symbolize wisdom and industry and night," Baumann said. He had always been an architecture buff; his time in Pollsmoor had given him ample time to read architectural histories. As a cover it was natural.

"How come those are empty?" Jared asked, pointing at two long niches flanking the portal.

"Excellent question. A well-known American sculptor was supposed to carve a statue of Frank W. Woolworth for one of those spaces, but for some reason it never got done."

"Who was supposed to be in the other one?"

"They say Napoleon, but no one knows for sure."

In the lobby, Baumann pointed out a plaster bracket near the ceiling, which he called a corbel. Jared could see only that it was a figure of a man with a mustache holding his knees, coins in both hands.

"Who's that, do you think?" Baumann asked.

"Some old guy," Jared said. "I don't know. Weird-looking."

"It is sort of weird-looking, you're right. That's old Mr. Woolworth," Baumann said, "paying for his building with nickels and dimes. Because he paid all cash for the building. Mr. Woolworth's office was modeled on Napoleon's palace, with walls of green marble from Italy and gilded Corinthian capitals." Jared didn't know what Corinthian capitals were, but it sounded impressive.

"Where do you want to eat supper? McDonald's?"

"Definitely," Jared said.

"What do you know about the Manhattan Bank Building?" Sarah said suddenly.

Baumann was suddenly very alert. He turned to her casually, shrugged. "What do I *know*? I know it's second-rate. Why do you ask?"

"Isn't it designed by some famous architect?"

"Pelli, but not *good* Pelli. Now, you want to see good Pelli, take a look at the World Financial Center in Battery Park City. Look at the four towers—how, as the buildings rise, the proportion of windows to granite increases until the top is all reflecting glass. You can see the clouds float by in the tops of the towers. It's amazing. Why are you so interested in the Manhattan Bank Building?"

"Just curious."

"Hmm." Baumann nodded contemplatively. "Say, listen," he suddenly exclaimed, putting a hand on Jared's shoulder. "I've got an idea. Jared, do you think you could teach me how to throw a pass?"

"Me? Sure," Jared said. "When?"

"How about tomorrow afternoon?"

"I think Mom's working."

"Well, Sarah, maybe I could borrow Jared for the afternoon, while you're at work. We could go to the park, just Jared and me. What do you say?"

"I guess that would be all right," she said without conviction.

"Yeah!" Jared exclaimed. "Thanks, Mom!"

"Okay," she said. "But you promise me you'll be careful? I don't want anything to happen to your head."

"Come on, don't worry so much," Jared said.

"Okay," she said. "Just be careful."

Late at night, the phone rang. Startled out of a restless, anxious dream, Sarah picked it up,

"You fucking some guy?"

"Who is—"

"You fucking some guy? Right in front of my son?"

"Peter, you're drunk," Sarah groaned, and hung up.

The phone rang again a few seconds later.

"You think you can take him away for the summer?" Peter shouted. "That's not the arrangement. I get him on weekends. Yeah, you thought I wouldn't track you down, did you?"

"Look, Peter, you've had too much to drink. Let's talk in the morning, when you're sober—"

"You think you can get away with it? I got news for you. I'm coming to visit my son."

"Fine," Sarah said, depleted. "So come visit."

"He's my little boy. I'm not going to let you take him away from me."

And he hung up.

In a tiny apartment a block away, Baumann listened on the phone.

"*Fine. So come visit.*"

"*He's my little boy. I'm not going to let you take him away from me.*"

Sarah's ex-husband hung up, and then Sarah hung up, and then Baumann, intrigued, hung up too.

People say things over the phone they should never say, even the most suspicious people, even professionals who know what can be done with a telephone these days. The personal conversations Sarah had were

sometimes useful to Baumann, but it was the business
chats that had been most informative.

Baumann had heard everything Sarah Cahill had
said on the telephone ever since the day after they slept
together. Her ex-husband had called once. A few female
friends from Boston had called, but she seemed not to
have many friends. When she used the phone it was
usually for work. Jared had had long, rambling, trivial
conversations with a few of his buddies; Baumann never
wasted his time listening.

It is not easy to tap a phone or bug an apartment.
Placing the tap is easy—that isn't the problem. The
problem is the technology.

If you plant a bug in the walls of a room, or in a phone,
or even in the A-66 connection panel on the floor of the
apartment building, you must stay very close at hand,
because most bugs broadcast on VHF, which stands for
"very high frequency." You must have an apartment
nearby, or remain in a van within a few hundred yards,
and that was not possible in this case. Once there was a
vogue for something called the "infinity transmitter" or
"harmonica bug," but it ties up the phone line and is easy
to detect and doesn't work all that well, anyway. The
CIA met with its inventor and said sorry, but no thanks.

For a while, intelligence agencies were excited about
something called the laser microphone—the watchers
try to bug a room by shooting a beam of light on the
room's window from the outside. The sounds in the
room make the window glass vibrate, and the vibrations
of the glass in turn vibrate a small glass prism attached
to the outside of the window, which redirects the light
beam back toward the watchers. You look at that shimmering spot with a telescope equipped with a photo-
cell, which converts the light to an electrical signal,
which is then amplified and converted back into sound.

Nature and architecture and logistics, however, tend

to get in the way. Traffic sounds almost always interfere, as well as noise from TV and radio, even water moving in pipes. And you must find a vantage point directly opposite the room in question, which is not always easy to do in the city. The technology is very impressive, but except in the most ideal circumstances it works poorly.

So you spend a little money—ten thousand dollars, in fact—and you act the jealous boyfriend. You go to a private detective and say you're convinced your girlfriend is fucking around, you're sick of this shit. I want you to hang a wire on her, you say. I want it to come to me. Once it's in place, you tell the detective, you're out of the loop.

Private investigators are asked to do this kind of thing all the time. They have contacts at the telephone company's central station, cooperative guys, guys they know they can do business with.

When you're on the inside, it's easily done. The cooperative guy at the phone company, who doesn't want to know a goddam thing about it, puts in a parallel connection in the appropriate frame.

Baumann rented a tiny apartment in Sarah's neighborhood, because the telephone there was serviced by the same central office that serviced hers. There was nothing in this tiny apartment but a telephone and a call diverter. It recorded every single conversation made on Sarah's telephone line, and when the call terminated it dialed out to Baumann's apartment off Sutton Place. Now it was almost as if he had an extension in Sarah's apartment.

When she talked on the phone, he could hear everything she said.

CHAPTER SIXTY-NINE

By the time Leo Krasner arrived at his apartment, there were several messages on his answering machine responding to the notices he had posted not half an hour earlier. By midafternoon he had received eighteen calls from secretaries and other office workers (sixteen female, two male) at the Manhattan Bank.

One by one he returned the calls.

"The term paper's on a computer disk," he told the first secretary, "but my computer's busted. Thing is, I need some really good editing—you know, just go through it, correct the spelling errors, grammatical mistakes, punctuation, all that junk. Thirty pages."

But he needed it done tomorrow, by the end of the day. It was urgent. Who else but a desperate business-school student would pay three hundred bucks for an hour's work?

The one he finally settled on said she did not have a home computer, but would work on it tomorrow during her coffee breaks and her lunch hour. She promised to be done by the end of the business day.

They agreed to meet at the cappuccino bar in the Manhattan Bank Building atrium, first thing in the morning.

CHAPTER SEVENTY

On the way to Central Park, just before noon the next day, Jared sulked. Two new friends from the Y went to a video arcade after camp got out every day, unaccompanied by an adult, and they had invited Jared. "Look, I'm sorry, but the answer is no," Sarah said. "I'm glad you have some new friends, but I don't want you going out unless a grown-up is with you, or Brea, or me."

"It's like two blocks away from the Y," he protested. "And it's not like it's just me alone. There's three of us."

"No. Look what happened to you in the park when I let you go off by yourself—"

"Jesus Christ," Jared said, sounding like his father. "You're being ridiculous."

"Hey," she said. "You heard me. The answer is no."

"That's just stupid."

"That's just careful," she said as they crossed the street to the park. "I don't want anything happening to you."

He raised his voice. "How come you always treat me like I'm a baby?"

Brian approached, wearing a sweatshirt. He gave Sarah a peck on the cheek, patted Jared on the shoulder. "I'm ready, coach."

"Yeah," Jared said sullenly.

Sarah left them there and went to work, arranging to meet them at the same spot in exactly two hours.

Jared taught Brian the fundamentals of going out to catch a pass. "You start running first," Jared said. "*Then* I throw it."

"Okay," Brian said as he took off. The ball came soaring toward him. He dove for it and missed. The ball spiraled into the air, while he slipped in the mud and tumbled onto his back. Jared burst out laughing, then Brian started laughing.

Both of them grass-stained and covered in mud, laughing. They sat in the grass, as Brian caught his breath. He put his arm around Jared. "You know, my parents were divorced when I was a boy, too," he said.

"Really?"

"Yeah. I know how lousy it is. And—well, this is something I've never told anybody before. When I was nine—just a year older than you—my parents fought all the time. All the time. They got divorced when I was ten, but it took them years, years of fighting. And one day when I was nine years old, I got so tired of them constantly fighting that I ran away from home."

"Really?" Jared said, rapt.

"That's right. I just packed my favorite toys and some clothes and packed them in a bag, and then I got on a bus and rode for an hour, to the end of the line."

"Far away?"

Baumann nodded, imagining a Canadian boyhood, enjoying the lying, which he knew was convincing. "And I spent the night in a field, and the next morning I got back on the bus and went home. By then my parents were terrified. Seemed as if the whole town was looking for me. The police sent cars around to find me."

"What did your parents do? Were they mad?"

"Oh, very. Very angry. But for a day they were united,

a team. For that one day they stopped fighting. They were worried about me. So, you know, you should try to look at things from your mom's point of view. She worries about you, because she loves you. There's a lot on her mind, and she's doing some dangerous work, isn't she?"

"Yeah," Jared said. "I guess."

"I mean, she told me she's in charge of a group of people who are looking for someone. Did she ever tell you anything about her work?"

"A little bit, I guess."

"So you know she worries a lot, right?"

Jared shrugged.

"What did she tell you?"

CHAPTER SEVENTY-ONE

Leo Krasner worked most of the night, several times cursing the goddam Englishman who had hired him to do this job.

But by dawn he had finished. The end result was a computer diskette that appeared to contain only a thirty-one-page "term paper" on market economics and monetary policy, which Krasner had plagiarized from a college introductory economics textbook and then rendered semiliterate, strewn with typos and basic grammatical errors. Of course, the only part of the disk of any interest to him, the sequence of code he had so laboriously written, was cloaked in a hidden attribute and would remain invisible to the user.

At a few minutes to nine o'clock he walked into the cappuccino bar in the Manhattan Bank building, wearing his only blazer and tie. His blue oxford-cloth button-down shirt was too small at the neck; perspiration darkened large ovals under the arms and in the middle of his chest.

Mary Avakian, administrative assistant to the Manhattan Bank's senior vice president for personnel, popped the diskette into her disk drive as soon as she'd poured herself a mug of coffee (light with two sugars) and set to work on it right away.

She copied the contents of the disk to her C-drive, which meant copying it to the bank's LAN, or local area network. She glanced at the text. Boy, this guy wasn't kidding. What a mess! And this guy, who could barely write, was probably going to walk out of business school and start at six figures, while she slaved away for a lousy twenty-four thousand.

During her coffee breaks and lunch hour she slogged through the guy's term paper. The spelling was so bad she couldn't even rely on the spell-check. It took her an hour and a half, and it wasn't exactly easy sledding. But for three hundred bucks, tax-free, she really had no right to complain. For three hundred bucks, she'd edit this guy's work again anytime he asked.

CHAPTER SEVENTY-TWO

That evening, Sarah and Brian took Jared out to dinner at a steakhouse, where Jared was able to order a cheeseburger and fries. Brian ordered a large salad and a plate of pasta, explaining that he was a vegetarian. After dinner, the three of them were ambling toward Sarah's apartment when they heard a voice.

"Jared."

Sarah and Jared turned around simultaneously, recognizing the tall blond man running toward them on the street as Peter.

"Hey, little buddy, how're you doing?"

A look of concern passed over Brian's face, and Sarah was noticeably tense. He hung back as Peter approached Jared, arms wide. Jared looked stricken.

"Give me a hug, Jer," Peter said, leaning down toward Jared. He was in street clothes, slacks, and a hunter-green polo shirt.

Standing stiffly, Jared kept his arms at his side and glared at his father.

"Come on, now, buddy," Peter said, giving his son a bear hug anyway. Straightening up, he turned to Sarah and then to Brian. "So," he said. "I hope I'm not interrupting something."

"Not at all," Brian said. "Just returning from dinner." He extended his hand. "I'm Brian Lamoreaux."

Peter smiled at him as a snake smiles at a rabbit. "Peter Cronin. So you're Sarah's latest."

Brian half-smiled uncomfortably. "I should probably leave you three alone," he said.

"No, Brian," Sarah said. "Please."

"I've got a long day tomorrow. I should really be getting home."

"Brian," Sarah said. "Don't."

Peter slipped one arm around Jared's slender back. "How was camp, Jerry? Hey, I've missed you."

Baumann lingered awkwardly in the background, shifting from one foot to the other, eyes watchful.

"So you've been real busy looking for your mad bomber," Peter said to Sarah. "So busy you don't have time for Jared, right? You're parking him in some YMCA all day—you think I don't know that?"

"Will you please get out of here?" Sarah said.

"No, sorry, I will not," Peter said. "I've come to see Jared for a couple of days. Come on, buddy, let's get your things, and come on with me. I'm staying at the Marriott Marquis. We're going to see the sights of New York City that your mom is too busy with her boyfriend and her task force to show you."

"Come on, Peter," Sarah said.

"No, Dad, I don't want to go," Jared said, face flushed. "I'm having a great time here."

"Hey, little buddy—"

"You can't make me," Jared said. His eyes narrowed, in unconscious imitation of his father. "You can just go on back to Boston. Just lay off."

Peter stared at Jared, then at Sarah. A slight twist of a smile played on his lips. His face, too, began to redden. He spoke to Sarah in almost a whisper. "You're turning him against me, is that it? You think you can do that to my son?"

"No, Dad," Jared said. "She doesn't even talk about you. It's me. I'm sick and tired of you bullying me around."

Peter continued staring, alternating between son and ex-wife. He licked his lower lip, then smiled viciously.

He started to say something, then turned slowly and began walking away.

CHAPTER SEVENTY-THREE

Shortly after midnight Baumann left Sarah's apartment. The street was empty, chilly, lit by soft oblique early-morning sunlight. As he walked, he became aware of someone following him.

He turned around and saw Sarah's ex-husband, Peter Cronin.

"Oh, hello," he said.

Cronin held his face a few inches from Baumann's. He shoved Baumann into the mouth of a narrow alley a few feet away and began moving closer, his breath hot against Baumann's face. He placed a large hand on Baumann's shoulder and flattened him against the brick wall. Baumann looked around: there was no one in sight. They were alone. No one was passing by.

"Let me be really clear with you, Brian. I'm a cop. I got resources you wouldn't believe. I'm going to look into your past, find out all about you. You wouldn't *believe* the shit I can find out about you, you asshole. The shit I can do to you. I can get you *deported*, motherfucker."

"All right, enough," Baumann said quietly.

"*Enough*, motherfucker? *Enough?* I got news for you, fucker. I did a little checking on you, big guy. There's no record of any 'Brian Lamoreaux' entering the country. Either you're here illegally or you aren't who you say you are."

"Oh, is that right?" Baumann said phlegmatically.

"That's right, buddy. I'm going to turn your whole life inside out, you little shithead. I'm going to make your life a living nightmare, and then I'm going to—"

There was a loud snap, the unmistakable sound of bone cracking, and now Peter's head was turned around almost 180 degrees. He seemed to have turned to look at the opposite wall; but, his spinal column having been severed, his head was grotesquely out of position. His eyes glared angrily, his mouth gaping in midsentence, frozen in death.

Baumann eased the body to the ground, then took out an alcohol wipe from his pocket and cleaned the prints from Peter Cronin's neck and face, and in a matter of seconds he was out of the alley and on his way.

CHAPTER SEVENTY-FOUR

At two o'clock in the morning, Henrik Baumann and Leo Krasner were slogging through the tunnels beneath the Wall Street area of New York City. Though burdened as before with backpacks and air tanks, they moved more quickly this time, finding their destination without pedometer, compass, or map.

They arrived at the central switching area and removed their breathing apparatus. Krasner, angry at having to do this menial task, took out his tools in silence.

Then he turned around and, short of breath, fixed Baumann with a menacing glare. "Before I do jack shit, you listen to me."

Baumann's stomach tightened.

"I'm not as stupid as you seem to think," Leo said. "This whole ridiculous idea of making me go back down here in this fucking cesspool and fix the splice—let's just say I've got a bad feeling about this."

"What's that supposed to mean?"

"We both know you could have left the box here and no one would ever have detected it. Just coming back down here again is a bigger risk than leaving the breakout box on the line. So why would you want to take a chance like that?"

Baumann furrowed his brow. "I don't want—"

"No, I'm not done, dude. If you have some idea about wasting me down here, you can forget about it. I taped our first meeting. If I'm not home in a couple of hours, a phone call is going to be made."

"What is this?" Baumann said darkly. At their first meeting, Baumann had carried a small, concealed near-field detector that would have detected a running tape recorder. He was sure Krasner was bluffing.

"It's my life insurance policy," the cracker said. "I've dealt with assholes like you before. I know the sort of shit you guys sometimes try."

"This is a business deal," Baumann said quietly, almost sadly. "I certainly have no intention of killing you. Why should I? We are both professionals. You do the work I've asked you to do, you get paid—rather generously, yes?—and then we never see each other again. For me to do anything else would be insane."

Krasner stared at him for a few seconds longer, then turned back to the wires. "Just as long as we're totally clear on that," he said, as he removed the breakout box and respliced the copper cable on which Manhattan Bank's encrypted financial transactions traveled.

When he had finished his work, he turned around and smiled at Baumann. "And that, dude—"

Baumann reached out his hands with lightning speed and swiveled the computer wizard's head until the vertebrae cracked audibly. The mouth was open in a half-smile, half-grimace; the eyes stared dully. The large body sagged.

It required considerable effort, but Baumann was strong. He hoisted the dead body and carried it to a blind end of the tunnel, where he deposited it in a crumpled heap. With alcohol wipes, he removed any fingerprints from Krasner's face and neck.

In this section of the tunnel, there was a good chance that the body would remain undiscovered for weeks, if not longer, and by then it would make no difference anyway.

CHAPTER SEVENTY-FIVE

Early the next morning, Christine Vigiani was informed that there was a call for her on the STU-III secure phone. She went into the secure communications area, lighting a cigarette as she walked, and picked it up. "Vigiani," she said.

"This is Larry Lindsay at NSA."

Vigiani was silent for a beat too long, so he went on, "Your liaison, remember?"

"Oh, right. What's up?"

"Let's go secure," he said. "This is sensitive."

Vigiani called Sarah's apartment. Sarah answered on the first ring.

"Hope I'm not waking you," Vigiani said.

"Nope, I'm just having my coffee. What's up?"

"I think I have your deadline."

"What are you talking about?"

"The deadline. The day the attack's going to take place. I think I have the date."

"Oh?"

"GCHQ picked up another piece of an encrypted phone conversation from the same microwave relay station the last intercept came from."

Sarah sat up straight.

"They were targeting Geneva North microwave relay station, listening on a number of specified frequencies, when they came across a signal that wouldn't decrypt. They pulled it down and put it through the Cray. And lo and behold, it turns out to be the exact same encryption scheme as the first one."

"What's in the conversation? More about Baumann?"

"No, it was some guy—the same guy as in the last intercept—calling a banker in Panama, authorizing a payment. He was very detailed about it. He wanted to make sure one-third of 'the money' had been paid out at the beginning, and then another third last week, and then the *final payment* three days from now. June 26. He said a major 'incident' was going to take place in the United States on June 26, and only once that 'incident' took place was the money to be released. He wasn't more specific than that."

"Three days from now . . ." Sarah mused aloud. "You're right. That's the target date. That's when the bomb's going off."

She hung up and turned to Jared. "I want you to take my cellular phone. Put it in your backpack."

"Wow," Jared said.

"This is no game, Jared. You are not to use it. Don't show it around, don't play games with it, you hear me? It's only if I have to reach you."

"What are you going to use?"

"We have other cell phones at work I can use."

"Cool," Jared said.

In the very small, unfurnished apartment a block away, Baumann put down the phone, pursed his lips, shook his head slowly.

CHAPTER SEVENTY-SIX

When Leo Krasner bragged to Baumann that he'd "taped" their first meeting, he hadn't been bluffing. But he hadn't been so foolhardy as to conceal a tape recorder on his person, because he knew there were devices that could detect such things—portable, hand-held bias-oscillator detectors or metal detectors, that sort of thing.

No, he had done something far more effective.

After Baumann had first called, Krasner had insisted they meet at a brightly lit restaurant, not in some dingy pub. He had enlisted the help of a friend, a fellow hacker and cracker, who showed up at the restaurant with a gym bag.

The gym bag, set down on a table near where Baumann and Krasner were meeting, had black nylon mesh at either end to provide ventilation for sweaty gym clothes. But the mesh served another purpose as well. A video camera could clandestinely film through it quite well—and did.

While the video camera ran, Krasner's friend read a book. He sat for a good long while, and then left.

Thus Krasner had a clear videotape of his meeting with Baumann, whose name he of course didn't know, from which he had chosen several excellent still frames of the man who had hired him. Using his Xerox color scanner for maximum resolution, he had scanned the clearest black-and-white image into one of his computers.

The man could track him down, could find his apartment, could find the video and the stack of black-and-white glossies. But only someone a good deal more computer-adept than that guy would realize that his photo was hidden in a silicon chip.

Neither was Leo Krasner lying about a phone call being made if he did not return to his apartment by a certain time. Using the same simple technology employed in burglar alarms that automatically telephone the police when they're tripped, he connected an autodialer to a timer and an answering machine on which one outgoing message had been recorded.

At exactly nine o'clock in the morning following Krasner's last trip through the underground tunnels, the autodialer called 911 and played the message.

CHAPTER SEVENTY-SEVEN

At nine in the morning exactly, a call was answered by one of the sixty-three 911 operators at work in one large room at One Police Plaza. "New York Police 911," she said into her headset. "Your call is being recorded."

She was met by silence, and was about to disconnect when she heard the whine of a tape recorder, and then a male voice began to speak.

"My name is Leo Krasner," the voice said hesitantly, "and I want to report myself missing. This is not a joke. Um . . ." There was a rustling of paper in the background. "Please listen carefully. It is possible I have been abducted, but it's . . . um, even more likely I've been murdered. If I have been, there is a very good chance my body can be found in a tunnel whose precise location I will now describe. . . ."

As the tape-recorded voice of Leo Krasner continued speaking, the 911 operator grew less and less skeptical. It was too sober-sounding to be a prank. She typed the information—name, address, the possible location of the man's body—into her computer terminal, forwarding it to the appropriate police dispatcher, who sat in the adjacent room.

Calls that come into 911 are "stacked" on the computer screen in order of priority, from a full Priority One on down to a Ten, a complaint about a barking dog or loud music in the middle of the day—which could wait or simply be ignored.

Although this was not an emergency situation, the call was treated as Priority Three, as are all "found bodies," to which an ambulance was required to respond.

An ambulance, the fire department, the NYPD Emergency Service Unit, and a two-man car were all sent to investigate.

CHAPTER SEVENTY-EIGHT

"Can I help you?"

The receptionist for the Information Management Group at the Manhattan Bank greeted the large, unkempt man before her as if he'd wandered in off the street reeking of Night Train.

"Special Agent Ken Alton, FBI."

The receptionist stared at the leather-encased badge, then back at Ken, as if unable to reconcile the two. "What can I do for you, Agent . . . Alton?"

"I need to talk to your boss," Ken said.

"May I ask what this is in reference to?"

"Yeah. It's in reference to this visit. Can you please get him?"

"Do you have an appointment—?"

"Right *now*," Ken said.

With a grimace, the receptionist lifted her telephone handset and buzzed her boss.

Ken Alton had all but taken over the workstation belonging to the Information Management Group administrator, who stood by anxiously, watching. "I told you," the administrator said, "we've run an exhaustive series of diagnostic tests, and our systems seem to be secure. No break-ins."

"Do you have anything to drink?" Ken asked as he scrolled down a directory on the screen.

"Coffee?"

"I'd prefer Coke or Pepsi. Diet. Now, I need to know if you've seen any unusual transfers of funds in the last couple of days. Unusually large amounts, or anything unaccounted for, or . . . Hold on a sec. Just one second."

"Yes?"

"Take a look at this executable file. This is in, like, a million places."

The network administrator, a slight black man with graying hair so closely cropped it almost looked shaved, bent to look where Ken was pointing. "I'd have to get the manual," he said.

"All right," Ken said. "I want to take a copy of this file off the machine, put it on a nonconnected machine. Break it down into assembly language and see what it would be doing if it ran. Or maybe run it, and see what happens."

"What do you think it is?"

"Don't know. You tell me if this EXE should be here."

"Okay."

Twenty minutes later, Ken looked up at the network administrator with alarm and said, "Holy shit, man! This is a fucking virus! If this thing ever runs—"

"What? What is it?"

"—Your whole system would be fucked. You got a serious problem here. Shut down all users."

"*What* are you saying?" the administrator gasped.

"You heard me. Shut down the system."

"Are you out of your *mind*? I can't do that. This is

the busiest day of the week! It's a peak day for network traffic—"

"Go, man!"

"If I shut down the system, the entire bank grinds to a halt!" the man shouted at Ken, folding his arms. "Files can't be accessed, transactions can't be processed, every single branch office—"

"Will you just goddam *do* it?" Ken bellowed. "Send out a message to all users—"

"Look, you can't just shut down the whole goddam bank like that! You think—"

"Oh, God. Oh, Jesus God. Forget it."

"What are you—?"

Ken pointed at his monitor. He thrummed the keys, but the screen remained frozen. He ran a finger along the row of keys, then pressed his entire hand onto the keyboard, but nothing appeared on the screen. "It's too late." Ken said, his voice shaking. "*Shit!* I don't know if it was timed to go off now, or it got activated by my taking a look at it."

The network administrator turned to a monitor at the adjoining workstation and banged at the keys, but it too was frozen. Shouts began to rise from the adjoining desks, until the entire computer center was chaos. People were running down aisles; the place had gone mad.

"Frank!" someone shouted, running toward the administrator. "We got a freeze-up!"

"*What the hell is going on?*" the man thundered to the enormous room.

Ken replied, his voice now almost inaudible: "You got yourselves a virus that's taking over the whole system, the whole bank. A serious, fucking, monster virus."

Racing for a taxi, Ken Alton nearly stumbled twice on his way out of the Manhattan Bank Building's atrium. It was raining with such force the rain seemed to be coming up from the steaming pavement. It was morning, but the sky was dark with storm clouds.

He didn't have an umbrella, of course, and his clothes were totally soaked through. A cab slowed down for him. Then a middle-aged woman darted in front of him and flung herself into the cab's backseat. He called her a colorful name, but the slamming of the door kept her from hearing him.

Several stolen cabs later—damned New Yorkers get aggressive when it gets wet, he thought—he sat cocooned in the stifling warmth of a taxi hurtling toward Thirty-seventh Street. He leaned back and tried to gather his thoughts.

A virus. A goddam polymorphic computer virus. But what kind of virus was it? What was its intent? A practical joke—to gum up the works for a day or so? Or something more sinister—to wipe out all records of the second-largest bank in the country?

The idea of a computer virus—a piece of software that reproduces itself endlessly, spreading from computer to computer, copying itself ad infinitum—was relatively recent. There was the Internet Worm in 1988, the Columbus Day virus in 1989, the Michelangelo virus in 1992.

But how had it gotten in? A virus can be planted by any number of means. Someone inside the bank could have done it, or someone from the outside who had somehow gained access to the bank's computer facilities. Or an outside phone link. Or an infected diskette. There was a famous story, famous at least among computer types, about a guy who rented a plush office space in London, pretending to be a software company. He persuaded a major PC magazine in Europe to attach a free diskette to copies of the magazine. The diskette contained an AIDS questionnaire as a public service: you popped it into your computer, and the program asked you a series of dopey questions and then gave you an AIDS "risk assessment."

But it also did something else to your computer. It sent a virus burrowing its way into your machine that, after a certain number of reboots, hid all your files and flashed a bill. The bill directed the by now panicked users to send a sum of money to a post office box in Panama in exchange for a code that would unlock their files. The extortion scheme would have worked had some very smart hackers not broken the code and solved the virus.

Ken knew several people who were far more expert in the subject than he. As soon as he got to headquarters, he would have to figure out a way to send this virus on to his friends without infecting their systems, so they could examine it.

But this goddam cab was taking fucking forever. He took out his cellular phone, and he punched out Sarah's number.

CHAPTER SEVENTY-NINE

Most people fly on jets blissfully unaware of what keeps them aloft. So too do princes of capitalism wheel and deal in vast, inconceivable sums of money, ignorant of how their money travels magically from New York to Hong Kong in seconds. As long as the machinery works, that's all that counts.

But Malcolm Dyson had always been a get-under-the-hood-and-fix-it kind of guy. He knew how the fuel systems and the drive trains of all his cars worked.

He knew, too, the machinery of capitalism, knew how incredibly fragile it was, knew the precise location of its soft underbelly. He worked a long day in his library at Arcadia, and then pressed a button on his desk that pulsed an infrared beam at the Louis XIV armoire in a niche to his right. A panel slid open with a mechanical whir and the television came on: CNN, the top of the hour, the world news.

The announcer, a handsome young man with immaculately parted dark hair and sincere dark eyes, said good evening and read the lead story off his Tele-PrompTer.

"A computer virus has paralyzed the operations of America's second-largest bank," he said. "A spokesman at Manhattan Bank said that bank officials had no idea how the virus infected the bank's computer system, but they believe it was the result of a deliberate attack by computer 'hackers,' or 'phreakers.' "

A graphic appeared next to the announcer's head, a photograph of the sleek world-famous Manhattan Bank Building. He said, "Whatever the source, Manhattan Bank chairman Warren Elkind announced that the multinational bank was forced to close its doors at eleven o'clock Eastern Standard Time this morning, perhaps forever."

Dyson shifted slightly in his wheelchair.

"The bank's computers went haywire this morning, with all terminals freezing up. It was later discovered that a malfunction in the bank's electronic payments system caused the withdrawal of all of Manhattan Bank's assets, estimated at over two hundred billion dollars globally, and transferred as-yet-undetermined, enormous sums of money to banks around the world— estimated at over four hundred and thirty *billion* dollars, far more than the assets in the bank's possession.

"The consequences for the American economy are, according to the Federal Reserve chairman, incalculable. We have two reports now, from Washington, where the White House is said to be 'gravely concerned' as this disaster unfolds, but first from New York City, where an estimated three million small investors and bank depositors have had their entire life savings wiped out."

Then there was videotape footage of desperate crowds storming Manhattan Bank branch offices in Bedford-Stuyvesant and the Bronx. Dyson took a cigar from the humidor on his desk and snipped its end with intense concentration, muttering, "You ain't seen nothin' yet, folks."

CHAPTER EIGHTY

Warren Elkind's inner office was chaos. His desk phone rang nonstop; young men and women rushed in and out with messages. It was crisis mode. His bank was crashing and burning. Sarah stood at his office door, still.

"Where the hell have you been?" Elkind shouted to her across the room. "This fucking computer virus, or whatever the hell it is, has emptied the bank's coffers, down to the last penny, and now they're telling me they're never going to unwind this mess—"

"So now you want to talk."

"Christ! All right, I want everyone out of here. Everyone!"

When the office was cleared out, Sarah came closer. "When you called me, you mentioned Malcolm Dyson. You think he's behind this?"

"How the hell do I know? I'm saying it's a possibility."

"There's nothing in your FBI file about Malcolm Dyson."

"It's sealed, for God's sake!"

"What's sealed?"

"The scumbag probably blames me. He was indicted in the biggest insider-trading scandal ever to hit Wall

Street, which is why he went fugitive, but he probably blames me. Thinks he'd still be a U.S. citizen, free and clear and living in Westchester, if I hadn't turned him in."

Sarah said, coming still closer: "Did you turn him in?"

"It wasn't exactly that way," Elkind said.

"You were the witness that turned him in," Sarah said. "You were the only one who knew. You made the case."

"He needed the bank's help in financing an immense stock buyout, and he offered to cut me in. I refused. I'm a banker, not a kamikaze pilot."

"You turned him in to the SEC," Sarah prompted.

"Not quite so simple."

"Nothing ever is."

"After the SEC got on to him, he invited me to lunch at the Harvard Club. He wanted to make sure we 'got our stories straight'—i.e., that I'd lie for him. By then I'd agreed to cooperate with the SEC. The SEC investigator wired me. He wanted to tape a tiny microphone and battery pack to my undershirt, but I wasn't wearing any, and they didn't want to tape it to my skin. So the guy offered me his undershirt to wear! I told him, look, I don't wear polyester blends. But I wore the guy's undershirt anyway. They found an empty supply closet next to the dining room and sat there while I broadcast to the tape recorder. I was terrified Dyson would find out."

"I guess he eventually did. He didn't threaten you or anything?"

"No. The one time I was convinced he'd go ballistic, and go after me, was when he was almost killed by the feds, in a botched shootout. I didn't go out in public for weeks, let me tell you."

"When was that?"

"The date, you mean?"

"Right."

"I'll never forget it. It was the day of my wife's birthday—we were at '21' celebrating, and they brought a phone to the table. It was one of my clients in Europe. He told me Malcolm Dyson had been fired on by U.S. marshals in an ambush in Monaco, that his wife and daughter had been killed, and that he'd been wounded. That he'd probably be paralyzed for life. I remember thinking, shit, I wish they'd gotten him too. When you strike at a king, you must kill him, as the saying goes. This was going to be one guy out for revenge. That was June twenty-sixth."

"That's tomorrow."

June 26 was also the day when, according to the second telephone intercept, the final payment was scheduled to be made to a Panamanian bank.

"Excuse me," Sarah said. "I've got to get going."

CHAPTER EIGHTY-ONE

"I want you to contact the Justice Department," Sarah told Vigiani, "and get a list of all known employees, colleagues, associates, and friends of Malcolm Dyson, who might be located in Switzerland. Then get in touch with NSA and have them pull up voice samples of any of those people they have in their archives. And have them try to do a voice match with the two voices in the intercepted phone conversation."

There was a knock on the door to Sarah's office. Roth pushed it open, saw that Sarah was meeting with Vigiani, but barreled ahead anyway: "Listen, Sarah, I got a call—"

"Roth," Sarah said curtly, "I'm in a meeting."

"Yeah, well, you might want to listen to this. We just got a call on the twenty-four-hour line from the police in Mount Kisco, New York. Responding to that NCIC lookout we put out."

Sarah looked up. "Yes?"

"A couple of hours ago they got a theft report from an excavation company out there. One thousand pounds of C-4 plastic explosive was stolen from its warehouse last night."

Sarah stared. "How much?"

"A thousand pounds."

"Holy shit," she said.

"So what you're telling me," Assistant Director Joseph Walsh sputtered, "is that you don't know crap."

"No, sir," the FBI explosives analyst replied, coughing nervously into a loose fist. "I'm telling you we can only ascertain broad generalities."

Walsh was intimidating enough in manner. He did not need to plant his burly six-foot-seven-inch frame next to the diminutive explosives expert, towering over him, as he was doing now. Sarah and Harry Whitman, the chief of the Joint Terrorist Task Force, watched the interplay with grim fascination.

"Jesus Christ," Walsh thundered. "We have the fucking fusing mechanism. We know a thousand pounds of C-4 has been stolen. What else do you want? A blueprint and a wiring diagram? A guided fucking tour?"

But the explosives expert, a small and precise man named Cameron Crowley with a graying crew cut and a pinched pink face, was not put off quite so easily. He had done excellent work after the World Trade Center bomb and Oklahoma City, and everyone in Walsh's office knew it. On reputation alone he could coast. "Let me tell you exactly what we do know," he said, "and what we *don't* know. We know a thousand pounds of C-4 may—I repeat, *may*—be part of this bomb. We don't know if the theft of this plastic is a coincidence, or whether it was done by, uh, Baumann."

"Fair enough," Sarah put in to encourage the man.

"But assuming Baumann stole it, we don't know if he's planning one bomb or a series of bombs. We don't know if he's planning to use all of the thousand pounds in one bomb. That's a hell of a lot of explosive power."

"What's a 'hell of a lot'?" asked Walsh, as he pivoted to return to his desk.

The expert sighed with frustration. "Well, don't forget, it only took one pound of plastic to bring down Pan Am 103. Four hundred grams, actually. A thousand pounds can certainly do a lot more damage than was done in TRADEBOM. That wasn't even dynamite—it was a witches' brew of ammonium nitrate and all sorts of other stuff—but it blew out a six-story hole in the tower. It had an explosive force equivalent to over a thousand pounds of TNT."

He explained that on the table of relative destructiveness as an air-blast explosive, TNT is 1.0, ammonium nitrate is .42, dynamite can be anywhere from .6 to .9, and C-4, Semtex, and British PE-4 all have a value of 1.3 or 1.35. "So," he concluded, "weight for weight, C-4 is about a third more powerful than TNT."

"Can it bring down a building?" Walsh asked impatiently.

"Yes. Some buildings yes, some no. Not a huge building like the World Trade Center." He knew there had been four studies done on the engineering aspects of the World Trade Center complex, which determined based on vibration analysis that the World Trade Center buildings could not be knocked down by any bomb short of a nuke. "In any case, it depends on a whole lot of factors."

"Such as?" Whitman prompted.

"Location of the bomb, for one thing. Is it going to be placed outside or inside the building? Most bombs are placed outside buildings so that the damage will be visible, easily seen and photographed, for maximum psychological impact."

"If it's placed inside the building . . . ?" Sarah asked.

"The rule of thumb is that a bomb confined inside a building will do five times more damage than one placed outside. Then again, look what happened in Oklahoma City."

"You're still not telling us *anything*!" Walsh shouted.

Sarah could see Cameron Crowley compress his lips to contain his irritation. "Blast analysis is a complicated business," he said quietly. "The geometry of the charge has some effect on the peak pressure of the shock wave that emanates from the explosive. The shock waves always move at a ninety-degree angle to the surface of the explosives. We don't know if the charge is going to be shaped, or spherical, or what. Is there any way for the explosive to vent and thus be diffused? Also, we don't know what building it's going to be placed into. Different substances have different abilities to withstand the shock front. Glass generally yields between one and three p.s.i. when hit with a front-on load. A typical masonry wall—a good, well-made brick wall—will break at eight to twelve p.s.i. And if there's steel reinforcing, well, steel has a modulus of elasticity, called Young's modulus—"

"Goddammit," Walsh said. He was not a thick or ignorant man, far from it, but he was famously impatient with scientific bluster that served in his opinion to muffle practicalities. "What you're saying is that a thousand pounds of C-4, if placed intelligently inside a reasonably sized Manhattan office building, can do a fuck of a lot of damage."

"Yes, sir," Crowley said. "A fuck of a lot."

The intercom on the AD's desk buzzed. Walsh lumbered over to it, hit the switch, and said: "Dammit, Marlene, I said hold all calls."

"Sorry, sir, but it's urgent, for Agent Cahill."

"Oh, for Pete's sake. Cahill?"

Sarah strode to the phone. "Yes? Alex, I'm in a—Uh huh . . . I don't understand, what do you mean he called it in himself? . . . All right."

She hung up and turned to the three FBI men, who had been watching her throughout the conversation.

"That was Alex Pappas. Roth got a call from NYPD Homicide. They located a body in a drainage tunnel under the streets in the Wall Street area. The victim seems to be the guy who planted the computer virus in the Manhattan Bank."

"*Baumann*?" Whitman gasped.

"Some guy Baumann hired, a computer-hacker type."

Walsh sat bolt upright. "How do you know this?"

"Seems the victim had had a call put in to 911 after his death."

"The hell you talking about, Agent Cahill?" Walsh thundered.

"It's complicated. Seems this computer guy was afraid he'd be knocked off. Had some tape recorder call 911 with a report of his own homicide. I didn't quite follow. The point is—"

"Is this for real?" Whitman said.

"Apparently so. An emergency-medical team and some guys from the fire department went down in the tunnels and found a body. Homicide and some of our people are on their way over to the victim's apartment right now."

CHAPTER EIGHTY-TWO

Ken Alton examined the computer equipment at Leo Krasner's apartment with the admiration of a fellow hacker. He whistled. The guy had a nice Macintosh Duo with a docking station for a removable Powerbook, a couple of enormous Apple color screens, an IBM with a Pentium processor, and a SPARC-20 Unix-based workstation, all networked together. There was also a new 1,200-d.p.i. color PostScript printer and a Xerox color scanner.

Jesus, there was even an alpha-test prototype from the Hewlett-Packard/Intel/Sun consortium, the HPIS-35. This was a scientific workstation containing a network of five high-performance RISC processors in the SPARC/Pentium family, plus three gallium-arsenide multiprocessors from HP Labs.

Very cool.

He tried to access the HPIS-35 and the SPARC-20, but a password was necessary—of course. He said, "Shit," got to his feet, and lumbered around the apartment.

"What?" Roth asked.

Ken ignored him. He wandered around, thinking.

In the bedroom, on the nightstand, Ken found a

palm-top computer. And he knew he had the problem solved.

The palm-top could be connected to the workstation by means of a spread-spectrum link. In other words, the guy could use his palm-top in the bedroom to do stuff on the workstation in the living room. And of course there was a protocol built into it that accessed the workstation by giving the password. This was for easy access.

Even geniuses got lazy once in a while, Ken knew.

Quickly he listed the files on each machine. Some of the documents looked potentially interesting, but then, on the SPARC, he came across a couple of intriguing files, intriguing because they each had a JPEG extension. JPEG was a standardized image-compression mechanism, so named for the committee that wrote the standard, the Joint Photographic Experts Group. Each file with a JPEG extension was around 39K in size, just about the right size for a good-quality black-and-white photograph, but probably not big enough for color.

Ah, Ken thought. Hence the scanner. All you do is run a photo through the scanner, which stores the image in either color or in a gray-scale. A black-and-white photo is broken down into particles, or pixels, each of which is assigned a gray-scale value between 1 and 256. The JPEG program takes this big hunk of data and identifies the redundancies in it and then compresses it. So you end up with a computer file, a binary file, a bunch of ones and zeroes. The compression certainly isn't perfect—it's "lossy," as the techies call it—but it has the advantage of making extremely small files if you use the default quality setting.

Ken didn't know exactly how JPEG worked—you heard buzz phrases like discrete cosine transforms, chrominance subsampling, and coefficient quantization—but he knew how to use it. That was all that counted.

Well, he mused, if he's storing images, he's got to have a display program on here, something that will grab the image and convert it, an interactive image-manipulation and display program.

He typed "xv brit.jpeg &" and hit enter. This was the command for a common display program.

"Whaddaya got there?" Roth asked, standing over Ken's shoulder.

"We'll see . . ." Ken said.

In a few seconds the screen was filled with a high-resolution photographic image of a man, a dark-haired, dark-eyed, ruggedly handsome man of around forty. Though the picture seemed to have been taken with a long lens in some kind of public place, a restaurant or something, the man's face was perfectly clear.

"Is that the dead guy?" Roth asked.

"No," Ken said. "Leo Krasner's tape-recorded message to 911 said he had a picture of the man who had hired him. This has got to be one of the pictures in question."

"Who is—?"

"I think it's Baumann."

With a few more keystrokes, he converted the JPEG file to PostScript, a format for printing images, and sent it over to the printer.

"Hey!" Roth shouted to the others. "I think we have our guy."

CHAPTER EIGHTY-THREE

As supervisor of the Information Processing Division of the Greenwich Trust Bank, Walter Grimmer, fifty-two, was in charge of the bank's Moore Street facility, located just off Water Street in lower Manhattan—in the same anonymous building that housed the super-secret Network.

Grimmer had been with the bank for sixteen years, after twelve years at Chemical Bank. He didn't particularly like his job, didn't like his colleagues. In fact, when you came right down to it, though he was a CPA, he didn't even enjoy accounting. Never had. He loved his wife and his two daughters and enjoyed puttering around their house in Teaneck, New Jersey. But he had already begun counting down the months until retirement.

There were many more of them.

And it was days like today that made him think seriously about early retirement. The day had started with a call from a new assistant to the bank's chief financial officer, letting him know about an imminent visit from the FDIC. Great. How could you top that? Maybe at his next checkup the doctor would find a polyp.

Oh, the FDIC, the goddam FDIC. The Federal Deposit Insurance Corporation was the bane of Grimmer's existence.

The FDIC supervised all state-chartered banks, which meant banks that weren't members of the Federal Reserve, weren't national, didn't have the initials "N.A." in their legal title. They rated these banks for soundness, on a scale from one to five, one being the best. This was called a Uniform Bank Rating, the CAMEL rating. "CAMEL" was an acronym derived from a jumble of factors: capital, asset quality, management, earnings, and liquidity.

Depending on the bank's CAMEL rating, which was always kept secret from the bank, the FDIC inspected the bank either annually or every eighteen months. The eighteen-month cycle was for banks rated one or two. Banks rated three or less, or which had assets of over $250 million, were inspected annually.

Walter Grimmer didn't know for sure, but he suspected that Greenwich Trust rated a middling three. Which meant that every year, a team of eight to twelve FDIC examiners barged in and took over the place for as much as six weeks. They reviewed the bank's loan portfolio, the adequacy of its capital in relation to the risk of its portfolio, the stability of its earnings, its liquidity. Then they brought the whole happy adventure to a rousing finale with a wrap-up meeting with the bank's president and executive committee.

Loads of fun. And Walter Grimmer, lucky Walter Grimmer, had the honor and privilege of serving as the bank's liaison to the FDIC.

The guy who'd called this morning, the assistant to the chief financial officer, had phoned to let Grimmer know that for some damn reason the FDIC had to come back for an *additional* examination, as if once a year weren't enough. Computer runs had been ordered. Something like a dozen boxes of documentation for the

FDIC were going to be shipped in late this afternoon, and Grimmer was supposed to sign for them.

Did it have something to do with the collapse of the Manhattan Bank?

Was that why the FDIC was making a surprise visit?

"Where the heck am I going to put a dozen boxes?" Grimmer had wailed. "I don't have room here for a dozen boxes!"

"I know," the assistant said sympathetically. "The delivery service will bring them right down to the basement of the building and leave them there until FDIC shows up tomorrow. Just overnight. Then it's their problem."

"The basement? We can't leave them there!"

"Mr. Grimmer, we've already cleared it with the building manager. Just make sure you're there to sign for them, okay?"

The deliveryman from Metro-Quik Courier Service groaned as he pulled his delivery truck up to the modern-looking building on Moore Street, in the Wall Street area. The damned street was paved with cobblestones, which really did a number on the truck's suspension. It was a narrow, one-way street that ran from Pearl Street to Water Street. He'd had no problem picking up the boxes at the storage facility in Tribeca, but he'd gotten lost several times trying to find the downtown facility of the Greenwich Trust Bank.

At least the boxes were filled with paper, not floor tiles or something. He loaded the twelve sealed boxes, each sealed with bright-yellow tape marked FDIC EVIDENCE, onto a dolly and moved them into the basement of the building.

"Sign right here, please," he told Walter Grimmer as he handed him a clipboard.

CHAPTER EIGHTY-FOUR

Vigiani burst into Sarah's office without knocking. "We got a match."

"A match?"

"I mean, the NSA did. That phone intercept. We got the names to attach to the voices now."

"Let's hear."

"A guy named Martin Lomax, who's apparently a close associate of Malcolm Dyson's, and someone named Johann Kinzel, who's Dyson's money man."

"Great work. I think we just locked this up. We've got a prosecutable case now. Bravo."

Pappas knocked on the door and said, "Sarah, we need to talk."

She knew Pappas's face well, knew it was serious. "What is it?"

"There's been another murder," he said. "There was a body found in an alley in your neighborhood. The report just came in."

"Whose?"

"Sarah," Pappas said, putting his arm around her, "it's Peter."

* * *

Hunched over the toilet, vomiting.

Bitter tears burning her nostrils. She wanted to call Jared, wanted to go get him now, didn't know what to do. There was a right time, a right way, to tell an eight-year-old something so wrenching.

Then she remembered she had given him her cellular phone this morning to keep in his backpack, in case she needed to reach him. In case of emergency.

But no. She couldn't call him. It had to be done in person.

It would be harder because of Jared's anger toward his father. The wounds were already open; the pain would be unbearable.

She needed to go for a walk.

Roth called headquarters, asked for Sarah. Pappas answered. "She's not here," he said. "I don't know where she is. I just gave her the bad news about her ex-husband. She left about fifteen minutes ago."

"I'll try her at home," Roth said. "If you see her, tell her we got our guy."

"What do you—"

"I mean, we got a picture—a photo of Baumann."

"What are you talking about?"

But Roth hung up, and then dialed Sarah's apartment. He got the machine, calculated she might be on the way home, maybe to get her kid, so he left a message.

In a coffee shop across the street from headquarters, Sarah sat, red-eyed, dazed.

Peter was dead.

How could it possibly be a coincidence? What if Baumann had meant to get her, and had got to Peter instead—Peter, who was in town and might well have tried to go to her apartment . . .

Jared. *Was Jared next?*

She had to get back to work immediately, today of all days, but somebody had to get Jared out of YMCA day camp. Pappas couldn't do it. She needed him at head-quarters.

At a pay phone on the street, she called Brea, the babysitter, then hung up before the phone began to ring. Brea was at her parents' house in Albany, upstate. The fall-back sitter, Catherine, was in classes all day.

Then she dialed Brian's number.

In the small, unfurnished apartment, Baumann lis-tened to the message Lieutenant George Roth was leav-ing on Sarah's answering machine.

Leo Krasner hadn't been bluffing. A phone call would be made, he said. He had a photograph, he said.

Frozen, Baumann sat with his mind racing. Tomor-row was the 26th, the anniversary of the day on which U.S. federal marshals had killed Malcolm Dyson's wife and daughter, the day Dyson wanted it all to happen.

But now they had a photograph.

They had his face.

Sarah would recognize the face. He hadn't counted on that.

Well, the bomb was already in place. Waiting until tomorrow meant the entire mission might be sabotaged.

He could not take that chance. He would have to move things up. Dyson would certainly understand.

He would have to move now.

Then suddenly another phone rang. This call was being forwarded from his display apartment, the one where he took Sarah. Baumann could tell by the ring.

It was Sarah.

"Brian, *please*," she said, her voice verging on the hysterical. "I need to ask you a favor."

* * *

Roth slammed down the phone in Leo Krasner's apartment.

"Shit," he said. "Where the hell is Sarah?" Then he said loudly, to the apartment in general, "You think this guy maybe has a fax around here somewhere?"

CHAPTER EIGHTY-FIVE

Outside the YMCA on West Sixty-third Street, Henrik Baumann stood, dressed in a blue polo shirt and chinos and sunglasses.

Jared emerged, looking disoriented. He smiled when he saw Baumann, came up to him and gave him a high-five.

Baumann flagged a cab. They got in, and he directed the driver to head toward Wall Street.

"Where are we going?" Jared asked.

"Your mom wanted us to go for a little outing."

"But the camp director said you were going to take me home because my mom couldn't get off from work."

Baumann shook his head absently.

"The director said Mom wanted you to take me right home," Jared said, puzzled, "'cause something important was going on."

"We're going on a little outing," Baumann said quietly.

It was a few minutes after one o'clock in the afternoon, still the lunch hour, so the streets bustled despite the weather. Although he was moving the operation up by an entire day, the timing was still good, because it was the middle of the day, when the Network operated at maximum capacity.

When the cab reached Moore Street, it pulled up before the new twenty-story building that housed the Network's computer facilities. Baumann got out with Jared.

"What's this, Brian?" Jared asked. "Where are we?"

"It's a surprise," Baumann said.

He took Jared around to the rear of the building and found the yellow-painted emergency-exit door he'd identified earlier.

He pulled out the key he had made a few days before, unlocked the door, and entered, taking the service stairs to the basement.

"Sarah," Vigiani said as Sarah entered headquarters. "There's a fax coming in for you. Slow as shit."

"Who's it from?"

"Roth. Says he's got a photograph of Baumann."

Her heart suddenly hammering, Sarah went over to the fax machine. Now she saw why it was coming through so maddeningly slowly. It was a photograph. The bottom was coming out first, a thick white border, and then a dark area, millimeter by millimeter. *This could take forever.*

She stood over the fax. The suspense was unbearable. In two minutes, the photograph had come through almost completely.

She looked at the face, felt her insides twist.

She looked again. She felt vertiginous, about to lose consciousness. The face seemed to rush toward her like a speeding train, like some special effect in a movie. She gasped.

Brian.

Part 6

THE HOMING

In difficult ground, press on;
in encircled ground, devise
stratagems; in death ground, fight.

—Sun-tzu, *The Art of War*

CHAPTER EIGHTY-SIX

Baumann switched on the lights. The basement was low-ceilinged, bare, and quite large, the size of the entire floor above it. He had, of course, been down here several days earlier to survey it, and he knew where the furnace room was, where the supply rooms were, and which part of the basement lay directly beneath the computer facility.

"Why are we here?" asked Jared.

"I told you. I have to do an errand before I take you home."

Jared shook his head. "Mom's in trouble or something. She said it's something serious." He raised his voice. "I should go home now."

"Soon. When I'm done with my errands. And please keep your voice down."

Backpack on his back, hands on his hips, Jared looked at Baumann defiantly. "Hey. Take me home now."

"I told you, soon."

"*Now.*" Jared's voice echoed.

Baumann moved suddenly, quickly clapping his hand over Jared's mouth as Jared flailed his arms, kicked, his screams muffled.

* * *

Sarah could handle a great many things, from threats to the national security to kidnappings to murder; she had acquired an ability to steel herself against fear and great tension; but nothing could shield her against this. Not her years of training, not her professional experience, not the methodical flow charts she'd been taught, the A-then-B-then-C techniques that served so well in emergencies.

But they did not work when your son has been kidnapped by a professional terrorist, and Sarah knew that was in effect what had happened, except that she had voluntarily, unthinkingly, turned her son over to the kidnapper.

She felt sick to her stomach.

Her chest tightened. The blood roared in her ears.

My God oh my God oh my God.

Everything took on a jerky, unreal quality, as if she were in some old newsreel, jumpy and badly spliced.

Years ago, when Jared was eight months old and they were living in Frankfurt while she worked Lockerbie, she was trying to go over some case files while Jared crawled around the apartment floor. There was a spiral staircase in the middle of the living room that she knew was treacherous to a crawling baby. It was steep and made of steel. She shuddered to think of what would happen if the baby ever fell down the stairs. She'd blocked off the landing with an overturned chair.

She must have been too absorbed in a file, because she suddenly heard a crash and then all was quiet. She looked up and saw what had happened. Jared had managed to wriggle beneath the chair and had plummeted down the staircase.

She felt her stomach turn cold. Everything in the world stopped. She found herself standing over the staircase, staring in shock. Her mind was operating in slow motion, but so, thank God, was the rest of the universe.

Jared had fallen down half the stairs, his tiny head lodged between the railing and a riser. He was silent.

She was convinced he was dead. She had killed this beautiful little being by looking away for an instant. Her fragile little son, with the winning, gummy smile and his two brand-new teeth, that little kid who had his entire life ahead of him and depended upon her utterly to protect him, was dead.

She leaped down the staircase and grabbed the still body and could only see the back of Jared's head. Was he dead, was he unconscious? Would he be blind, paralyzed for life? Suddenly Jared let out a great, blood-curdling scream, and she yelled with relief. She tried to pull his head out, but it was stuck. Pulling and twisting as gently as she could, she extricated his head from the gap between stair and riser and looked at his bruised red face and saw he was all right. She cuddled him to her shoulder and chanted, "Oh God, oh God, oh God."

He was fine. Ten minutes later he stopped crying, and she gave him a bottle of formula.

Only then did she realize how much of a hostage a mother really was.

Now, her mind spun with thoughts as she sank into a chair, momentarily weak and dizzy.

That "Brian Lamoreaux" was the cover for a South African–trained terrorist named Henrik Baumann was grotesque, yet in some horrible way logical. What did she know about the man except that he had tried to save Jared and her in Central Park . . .

. . . in a setup, that was suddenly clear. He had arranged the mugging—probably had paid some eager teenagers to attack this little boy for the sheer fun of it and some cash besides, a good-faith payment up front and the rest afterward. Then he had "happened" to be there, and had rushed in to help them out—a clever way to meet a woman suspicious of this new city. He must have known they didn't have his photograph, or else he would certainly have never dared to insinuate himself into her life; the risk of exposure would otherwise have been far too great. He acted the bumbling, frail intellectual, the exact opposite of his true persona, but could not disguise his naked body—his muscular, powerful torso, his broad thighs, his well-defined biceps. Why had she given so little thought to his superbly conditioned, sinewy body? Yes, men worked out these days, so why wouldn't a Canadian architecture professor? But why hadn't she suspected that there was something not right about this man she knew hardly at all?

She thought of the few nights they had made love—what a misnomer, what a fraudulently inappropriate phrase; no, they had had sex—and felt a shiver of revulsion and a wave of nausea.

Revulsion, not betrayal. She cared now only about Jared.

Everything moved in slow motion, stop-action photography, unreal. She was trapped in a nightmare.

After a minute, the paralyzing fear gave way to steely resolve. She ordered all members of the task force to assemble at once, then she put in a request to the Department of Energy to mobilize the Nuclear Emergency Search Team.

She had to find Jared. To find Jared was to find Baumann; to find Baumann was now a matter of pressing concern to the entire FBI, to the City of New York.

Baumann surveyed the twelve banker boxes, stacked in four piles of three each, lined up against one wall. Each box was sealed with bright antitamper tape marked FDIC EVIDENCE.

He knew that no one in the building would have touched those boxes during the few hours he'd have to leave them there. After all, he had arranged with the Greenwich Trust Bank for these boxes of FDIC "evidence" to be held in the basement for an audit tomorrow. The officer at the Greenwich Trust Bank had in turn contacted the building manager and secured his approval to leave the boxes in the basement storage area overnight. The space was often used for deliveries, so the building manager had no objections.

The boxes contained the C-4, but since plastic explosive is roughly twice as heavy as the paper that was supposed to be inside, he had only half-filled the boxes with C-4 and then placed stacks of phony bank papers on top of the explosive. The weight of each box was therefore reasonable, and in any case, sealed as they were, no one would dare open them.

It made sense, certainly, for these boxes to be stacked here, but the precise location was no accident. They were against the elevator shaft, in the core of the building. Like most buildings, this one had an extremely strong core and was cantilevered out from that. To set off the bomb here was to maximize the chance of bringing the building down and ensuring that the Network was destroyed. It was a simple matter of structural engineering.

And just a floor above were the Unisys mainframes of the Network.

From his briefcase he drew out a roll of what appeared to be white clothesline. With a commercially available pre-inked rubber stamp, he had marked it ANTI-TAMPER/DO NOT REMOVE/TAMPER DETECTION SYSTEM IN OPERATION. He looped the cord securely over and around the twelve boxes several times.

This was the DetCord, the diameter of which was two-tenths of an inch. One end of it, tied in a triple-roll knot, he fed into one of the boxes and into the C-4 explosive.

Then he drew out from his briefcase a black box with lights on its brushed aluminum lid, labeled EVIDENTIARY SECURITY SYSTEM. Although it appeared to be the security-system control box, this was in fact the fusing mechanism. One had been confiscated by the FBI, but another had arrived by separate means, as he had arranged. He connected the mechanism to the DetCord, which was connected directly to the C-4. The pager, a fall-back option, would not be necessary now.

The fusing mechanism included an omnidirectional microwave detector.

This was quite a clever device. It had been constructed to defeat the bomb-disposal people, assuming they showed up in time, which was highly unlikely.

It was a volumetric device that worked on the principle of the Doppler shift. In effect, it was a booby trap. The area around the bomb, in a radius of twenty-five feet, was now filled with microwave energy. A steady-state pattern had been established. If a human being walked through the field at anything even close to a normal pace, the waves would be reflected, and the sensor would close a circuit, detonating the bomb.

He was about to depress a button on top of the fusing mechanism when he heard a voice.

"How're you doing?" asked a guard, a slender young black man with a shaved head and a brass stud earring in his left ear. He seemed to have appeared out of nowhere.

"Fine," Baumann said, smiling jovially. "How 'bout yourself?"

"All right," the guard said. "What you got there?"

"One shitload of documents," Baumann said.

"So, you're with the bank?"

"FDIC, actually," Baumann said, hoping the guard wouldn't ask how he'd gotten into the basement. "Something wrong?"

"You're going to have to move those on out of here," the guard said. "Can't stay down here. Fire department regulations."

Baumann looked at the guard curiously. "Gosh," he said. "I thought my boss cleared this with the building manager—a Mr. Talliaferro, right?"

"That's the guy, but he didn't tell me anything about leaving any boxes."

Baumann suddenly heard a clanging sound from not far away in the basement, and he wondered whether the guard heard it too. He shrugged and rolled his eyes. "Man, this whole day's been like this," he said. "You want me to get my boss to call this guy Talliaferro? I mean, these'll be gone first thing in the morning." He watched the guard keenly, wondering whether he could hear the clanging, calculating whether he could kill the man right here, in a busy office building in the middle of the day, whether it was worth the risk.

The guard hesitated, looked at his watch. It was clear he didn't want to wait around for someone to call someone else who'd then call him and say, yeah, it's okay.

"All right, forget it," the guard said. "'Long as they're gone first thing tomorrow morning, like you say."

The clanging grew louder, more insistent. It had to be the boy, whom he'd locked in a supply closet.

"Oh, they will be," Baumann said with a groan. "I can't do my job without 'em. They'll be gone. I promise."

"Hmm," the guard said, nodding, as he turned away. He paused. "You hear something?"

"I don't think so."

"There. Banging."

Baumann pretended to listen. "Sounds like the old water pipes knocking."

"Over there," the guard said, pointing.

The clanging was rhythmic, insistent. A regular tattoo. Clearly made by a human being.

Baumann drew closer to where the guard was standing, as if trying to listen at the same spot. "I still think . . ." he started to say as he reached over with both powerful hands and broke the man's neck, and then he finished the sentence ruminatively: ". . . it's the old pipes knocking."

CHAPTER EIGHTY-SEVEN

"Sarah—" Pappas said, holding a phone up in the air.

"What is it?"

"It's Jared."

"Oh, thank God," Sarah said, and pressed the flashing extension button. "Jared!"

His voice was small and distant-sounding. "Mom?"

"Honey, are you all right?"

"I'm scared, Mom." He was on the verge of tears. "Brian was supposed to take me home, but he took me somewhere else—"

"But you're okay, aren't you? He hasn't hurt you, has he?"

"No. Well, he put this thing in my mouth, but I got it out."

"Where are you?"

"I don't know. He locked me in a closet. In the basement of some building. Kind of like a big glass-and-cement building. Looked like a bank, sort of. I've been banging on the pipes to try to get someone's attention." His voice rose in pitch. "Mom, I'm scared of him."

"Of course you are. He's a scary person, but we'll come get you. Honey, now tell me as much as you can about where you are, what you saw when you—"

"I think I hear voices—"

And the call was disconnected.

After twenty minutes of concentrated work, checking and rechecking all fittings and connections, Baumann was finished. The bomb was now armed, which meant that the entire basement area was off-limits. Anyone passing within twenty-five feet—a guard, a janitor, anyone—would set off the bomb, which would destroy the building, with Baumann still in it. To protect himself until he got out, he had jammed shut the external locks of all doors to the basement. They could be opened from the inside, but not the outside. After he was gone, if a bomb squad somehow managed to force a door open— well, that would be unfortunate for them.

Baumann was excited and nervous, as he was when- ever he did a job, although he had never before done something of this magnitude.

He glanced at his watch. The helicopter was probably on its way to take him, and his hostage, from the roof of the building directly to Teterboro Airport, a few miles from the city. That way, there was no chance of an arrest at the Downtown Manhattan Heliport.

The helicopter pilot might not come through— Baumann trusted no one, and had considered that possibility—but it was unlikely. He had offered the pi- lot so much money it was impossible to imagine that he wouldn't be there. Moreover, there were probably a dozen appropriate pilots who would have gladly taken his assignment, but this one seemed the most likely to keep the bargain, the most motivated.

"Did he hang up?" Pappas asked.

"I don't *know*," Sarah said. "The line went dead. He said, 'I think I hear voices,' and the line went dead."

"Either he discovered Jared, or Jared hung up so he

wouldn't be overheard. We'd better hope it's the latter. And we'd better hope he calls again. It's our only hope."

"Alex, Jared doesn't know where he *is*. He just knows he's locked in a room in the basement of some kind of bank building, and that could be a thousand places."

"That's not what I mean," Pappas said. "Next time he calls, we'll run a trace."

"It's a cellular phone, Alex!"

"Boy, you're so upset you're not thinking clearly."

"I can barely think. We can trace it, can't we?"

When a couple of criminals kidnapped an Exxon executive a few years ago, she suddenly recalled, they'd used a cellular phone to call in their ransom demands, mistakenly thinking cellular phones can't be traced. That had been their undoing.

"But only if Jared calls again," Pappas said.

CHAPTER EIGHTY-EIGHT

There are only four places in Manhattan where a helicopter is permitted to land, four officially designated heliports. One is at West Thirtieth Street and Twelfth Avenue, by the West Side Highway; another is on East Thirty-fourth Street; still another on East Sixtieth Street.

The fourth is the Downtown Manhattan Heliport, located at Pier Six on the East River. Some people call it by its old name, the Wall Street Heliport; helicopter pilots just call it Downtown. It is run by the Port Authority of the City of New York and has twelve parking spaces for choppers.

Since space in the city is so prohibitively expensive, most of the helicopter charter companies that do business in Manhattan are located in New Jersey. One of the smaller charter companies, based at Allaire Airport in Farmingdale, New Jersey, fifty-five miles to the southwest of New York City, was Executive Class Aircraft Charters, certificated by the FAA as an air-taxi operator. Of Executive's six full-time pilots, Dan Hammond was, at fifty-one, the oldest. Flying was a young man's game, and there were hardly any helicopter pilots older than fifty-five. Most of them were in their late twenties or thirties. It wasn't a matter of burnout, but of the medical exam you had to take every year to qualify. The longer you lived, the more likely you were to fail the medical, for one reason or another. And once you flunked the medical, they wouldn't let you fly.

Dan Hammond's ugly little secret was that his hearing was going. They hadn't caught it on last year's exam, but his doctor had told him he'd never pass this time. His ears had done yeoman work for fifty-one years, and now, after a quarter-century of rock concerts (the Stones, the Dead) and flying in noisy old Hueys in Vietnam, the Bell 205, and then thousands of short hops in the Jet Rangers, they were signing over and out.

It didn't make much difference to Executive if Hammond was forced to resign. There were dozens of low-time, upstart, rookie pilots, with the bare minimum of a thousand flight hours in a turbine helicopter, waiting in the wings to take his place. So what if the low-time kids didn't know how to fly the ASTAR, the jewel of Executive's fleet? A hundred hours of flying time and they could do it too.

It was time to leave, anyway. The economy was lousy, which had really hit the helicopter charter companies hard. Executive Class Aircraft Charters was on the verge of bankruptcy.

It was awful good timing when some crazy rich guy called yesterday to charter the American Euro-Copter AS350B ASTAR, formerly known as the Aerospatiale ASTAR 350B. So what if his request had been peculiar, even illegal?

The rich guy wanted to be picked up in the Wall Street area, but not at the Downtown Manhattan Heliport. No, the guy was either too lazy or too self-important to get in his limo and drive a couple of blocks to Downtown.

He wanted to be picked up at a rooftop heliport—on the roof of his building. He was trying to impress some friends.

Hammond had told the guy that you just couldn't do that anymore, not since the city ordinances changed after that horrible accident on top of the Pan Am Building when a chopper broke up landing and pieces went everywhere and even people on the street were killed. Anything outside of the four Manhattan heliports was controlled airspace. You violated that and the FAA would serve your balls for canapés.

"But what would the penalty be, really?" the rich guy wanted to know.

"A fine and suspension or revocation of my airman's certificate," Hammond had replied.

"Tell the FAA you had to make an emergency landing," the rich man said.

"Emergency landing?"

"Say you were having difficulty with your controls. Say there was a flock of birds in front of you. Then they won't revoke your airman's certificate."

"They'll still fine me."

"I'll pay it."

"I might lose my job," Hammond said, though the prospect of that didn't exactly sicken him.

"I'll make it worth your while," the rich man said.

Hammond had accepted the offer. All you really needed to land safely was an area one hundred feet by one hundred feet that was clear of power lines.

The rich guy had made a down payment of five thousand bucks, with the rest payable upon arrival at Teterboro Airport.

A hundred thousand bucks would be enough for Hammond and his wife to make the down payment on the bed-and-breakfast in Lenox, Massachusetts, they'd been eyeing for years.

A hundred thou would spring Dan Hammond from a job that he was about to lose anyway.

It was not a tough decision to make.

CHAPTER EIGHTY-NINE

The man from FBI Technical Services arrived twenty minutes later with a steel case of equipment. He unpacked a notebook computer and hooked it to a high-frequency ICOM receiver, an IC-R7100 with a specially designed antenna that filtered out all signals except those in the 800-to-900-megahertz range. Most cellular telephones broadcast in the 870-megahertz range.

Whenever a cellular phone broadcasts its signal, there really are two transmissions being emitted. There is the one you hear—the voice—and there is the carrier signal, which broadcasts at 4.5 MHz above the primary signal. The carrier signal gives a listening receiver the phone's identification number, the frequency it is transmitting on, and the "cell," or area, in which the caller is located.

All the technician had to do now was to wait for Jared to call again. Once the call came in, he would monitor the signal 4.5 MHz above the frequency of the call, thereby zeroing in on the cellular identification number.

That number would next be programmed into the linked computer, which was equipped with special law-enforcement software and had been preprogrammed with all existing cellular frequencies, provided by the FCC.

Cellular telephone calls constantly jump frequencies as the caller moves between cells, so the cellular phone tells the receiving cell—by means of the carrier frequency signal—when to do the "hand-off," when to switch frequencies, and to which one, depending on which cell is strongest.

Knowing which cellular identification number to look for, the computer can tune the receiver, ever scanning, ever running its search program. That way it can quickly identify which cell the call is being made from.

With Jared inside a building—i.e., stationary—the task would probably be easier. That meant he was located within one "cell," presumably somewhere in Manhattan.

If, that is, he called again.

Seven minutes after the technician arrived at Operation MINOTAUR's headquarters, he did.

Sarah picked up the phone and heard Jared whisper: "Mom—"

"Jared, oh, thank God. You're all right?"

"Yeah." He said it with a trace of his usual petulance, which made Sarah smile with relief.

"Now, Jared, listen carefully. Don't hang up, whatever you do. What does the building look like?"

"It's—it's a *building*, Mom, a modern building, I don't know!"

"What's the name of the bank?"

"It's only on the first floor—"

"*Which bank?*"

"I think it's Greenwich something—"

"Greenwich Trust! Jared, can you get out of there?"

"The room's locked. It's like totally dark in here."

"Where is he? Jared, what's he doing right now?"

"He's—" Jared lowered his voice to a whisper that

was almost inaudible. "He's coming toward me. I can hear him right outside the door."

Sarah's heart drummed in her chest like a hummingbird's. "Oh, God, Jared. Be careful."

The technician, hunched at the receiver next to Sarah, said, "Getting there. Keep him on longer."

She heard a voice in the background, a man's voice, shouting something, and then she heard the phone clatter to the ground, and then there was Jared's voice, a faint cry. "Help me!"

"Five more seconds!" the technician shouted.

But the phone was dead.

Panicked, Sarah turned around, saw Pappas watching wide-eyed, saw the technician hunched over the receiver.

"You didn't—" she said, afraid to ask whether he had traced the call.

"Not yet," he admitted.

"Oh, Jesus!"

"No, wait," the technician said.

"But the line's disconnected!"

"That's all right," he said. "The phone's still on."

"What do you mean?"

"Whether the phone's in use or not," the tech said, his eyes not leaving the computer screen, "still transmits . . . eight seven two point oh six megahertz . . ."

"What?" Sarah said.

"Long as the phone's turned on—whether it's in use or not—as long as the phone is powered on, it keeps transmitting back and forth to the closest cell. That's how you can tell the strength of the signal before you use the phone. It's—Yes! I got it!"

The open door to the supply closet cast a bright light on Jared, who, Baumann now saw, was speaking on a cellular phone. Who would have thought it? Baumann grabbed the child and placed a gag in his mouth. Over it he pressed a short piece of duct tape.

"Let's go, little one," he said, more to himself than to the boy. "Time to get going."

CHAPTER NINETY

The cellular telephone company that served Sarah's Motorola was NYNEX Mobile, which has 560 cell sites in the northeastern United States. In Manhattan, NYNEX has between thirty and forty cell sites; it prefers not to make public the precise figure.

When a call is placed from a cellular phone, whether mounted in a car or hand-held, the signal is relayed to the closest cellular site, which is little more than an antenna connected to sensitive radio-frame equipment. There are two types of antennas: directional, which is a rectangular box measuring three feet by one foot; and omnidirectional, which is straight and cylindrical, about an inch thick.

In cities like New York, these antennas are usually mounted on the roofs of buildings, except where a building is particularly tall, in which case they are mounted on the side of a building. The brains and guts of the cellular site, however, occupy an area approximately the size of a twelve-by-six-foot room, usually in leased space within the building itself. There, large radio-frame equipment receives and processes the signals, then sends them via telephone lines to regular telephone-company switching centers.

A cell may be as large as several square miles or as small as one building. This is because of the peculiarities of how Manhattan is built. The problem is not population density but topography: the profusion of extremely tall buildings with relatively narrow streets below. This makes it difficult for radio waves to travel to street level—where most cellular phones are used.

Because of the topography, for instance, there is a cell site in Rockefeller Center that serves an area of no more than two square blocks. There is even a cell site in a large Wall Street–area building that covers only that building.

The Wall Street region presents a number of problems for NYNEX Mobile, for several reasons. There is a large density of people in the area who use cellular phones. Also, many of those people use their cellular phones inside buildings, most of which are old, solidly constructed, thick-walled—and therefore difficult for radio waves to permeate. And the area has the same topographical challenges as Midtown—very tall buildings built on very narrow streets.

NYNEX Mobile compensates for those difficulties in two ways: by mounting some of their directional antennas on the sides of buildings, pointed down at the street, to maximize reception; and by placing more antennas per square mile in the region—four in the New York stock market area alone.

There are more cellular sites in the Wall Street area than anywhere else in the city, which means that each cellular site is relatively small—an area of a few blocks, instead of a few miles. This simple fact of telecommunications life in Manhattan turned out to be the very break Sarah needed.

NYNEX Cellular Site Number 269 was an area of approximately three irregularly shaped city blocks almost at the southernmost tip of Manhattan Island, near

the South Street Seaport. The omnidirectional antenna received and transmitted signals to and from all
NYNEX-serviced car phones and cellular phones situated within a chunk of real estate bordered by Water
Street, Broad Street, Whitehall Street, and the one-
block-long Stone Street. Running parallel to Stone, and
dividing the almost-but-not-quite-rectangle into three
wedges, were two short streets, Bridge and Pearl. Jut-
ting into the rectangle from the Water Street side, and
ending at Pearl, was Moore Street, one block long and
paved in cobblestone.

Contained within this area are the blue-glass tower of
the New York Health and Racquet Club; a large, twenty-
story NYNEX building; and, across Water Street, a new
forty-story office-building tower adorned with art deco
ornamentation and built around a sizable plaza. This is
One New York Plaza; beneath it is a shopping arcade,
which can be entered at the corner of Water and Broad.
On Pearl Street is the immense forty-story blue-glass
tower called the Broad Financial Center, headquarters
of the NASDAQ Financial Exchange. Across Whitehall is a pair of black forty-story towers, One State
Street Plaza and Battery Park Plaza.

A team of twenty-two uniformed cops and FBI street
agents was dispatched immediately to search the area
for any building that contained a sign for the Greenwich
Trust Bank.

A cell site is not a precise designation: there are areas of overlap, sections of streets that may be serviced
by one of two or even three different cells. It was clear,
however, that the cell site that was transmitting back
and forth to Sarah's Motorola phone was Cell Site 269.
Jared was stationary, located within one building, so
there was no handing-off between cell sites to compli-
cate things.

Moreover, each NYNEX cell site is configured into

three "phases," which divide the area into three segments: alpha, beta, and gamma. If the cell site is a circular pattern, as it roughly is, each phase of each antenna serves one-third of the area of that circle.

From the carrier frequency signal, the FBI tech was soon able to determine that Jared was transmitting from the gamma phase of Cell Site 269, which narrowed the search down to no larger than a one-square-block area. This meant the area around Moore Street, between Pearl and Water.

One of the search team assigned to the Wall Street area, a rookie cop named Julio Seabra, turned right up Moore Street, which was narrow and paved in cobblestone. For some reason, there were security cameras on the second-floor level of the buildings here, trained on the street. And then he saw a gleaming new twenty-story structure of glass and steel. There, at street level, was a two-foot-square brass plaque indicating the presence of an office of the Greenwich Trust Bank.

Officer Seabra stared at the sign for a few seconds before he remembered to radio the command center.

"We got the address," Pappas shouted.

"Oh, thank God," Sarah said. "Where?"

"Not a skyscraper or anything. Some twenty-story building right off Water Street, on Moore."

"What's in it?"

"A Greenwich Trust office on the street level, which is how the street cop pegged it. Not a branch office or anything, but some administrative offices—"

His desk phone rang, and he picked it up before the first ring was finished. "Yep?" He listened for a few seconds, then his eyes became round. "Christ almighty."

He hung up the phone. "On the mezzanine level of that building, unmarked and basically invisible to the public, is a huge data-processing center called the Network, which is—"

"All right," Sarah interrupted. "Alex, I want you and two junior people to stay here. One is to man my phone in case Jared calls again. The other stays by the STU-III in case of direct contact from CIA or anyone else. You run the show here. Roth, you I want downtown with me, directing operations, being traffic cop. Everyone else reports immediately to NYO Command Center."

"Right."

"Okay, I need you to establish phone contact with whoever's in charge of the Network. If there's any way they can do it, I want them to shut down operations immediately. Notify all member banks to halt all funds transfers. And get us a cruiser immediately."

"You got it."

"I want the entire block evacuated, including all surrounding buildings."

Roth snapped, "Are you crazy? You know how many huge motherfucker office buildings are down there? There's New York Plaza, One State Street, Battery Park, a NYNEX building, the Broad Financial Center—"

"Do it," Sarah said. "Notify the police commissioner—we've got the authority—and block off the streets with pylons and sawhorses and cruisers and patrolmen, whatever they've got. Block off sidewalks. I want every patrolman they can get down there. No one is to enter the area. I want every building evacuated."

"Jesus," Roth said. "If Baumann's in the Network building and everyone rushes out of there at once, we'll never find the guy."

"Roth, my son is in there."

"Sarah." It was Pappas. "You're both right. We have to empty the building at once, but at the same time we have to look over everyone who leaves."

"Impossible, Alex!" Sarah said.

"No. It's not impossible. Remember Mecca?"

"Mecca? What are you—"

"1979. The Grand Mosque in Mecca. A textbook example of this."

"Alex, we don't have any time for anything complicated."

"Sarah! It's not complicated. We need to round up some riot-control buses, that's all."

He explained quickly.

"*Do it*," she said. "And somebody help me find my vest."

The police car sped down Seventh Avenue, siren wailing and turret lights flashing, turned left onto Houston, then right onto Broadway.

In the backseat, as Roth made arrangements on his cell phone, Sarah watched Broadway go by in a blur.

Oh God oh God oh God, she thought.

Jared. Oh God.

If Baumann had taken Jared hostage, how had Jared managed to make phone calls undetected?

Where was he?

She heard Roth say, "A thousand pounds of C-4. Assume, worst case, the whole load is in the bomb." He paused to listen, but only for a moment, and then he went on: "That's enough to bring down the entire building, depending on placement of the device. Possibly kill everyone inside. Definitely do severe damage to neighboring buildings and pedestrians."

Sarah's mind raced, her body racked with tension. To save Jared was to stop the incident. This she repeated like a mantra, because she could think only of her son. She knew, but would never admit, that suddenly she didn't care about the case, didn't care about her work, didn't even care about the incalculable damage the bomb was about to do.

The rain had stopped, but it was still overcast, the skies a metallic gray.

Would he kill Jared?

He had murdered—both wholesale and retail, as she thought of it. Retail murders were one-on-one, wholesale the acts of terrorism he'd engineered. In some ways, retail murders were the most chilling, and he was capable of snuffing out an individual life, face to face. Would he really hesitate to kill Jared if he deemed it necessary?

Well, perhaps. He hadn't killed Jared yet, or so she hoped. Perhaps he planned to use him as a hostage, as insurance, as a human shield. She prayed Jared was still alive.

How had she been fooled so easily? How could she, so suspicious by profession and by training, have been taken in? Why had she been so willing to see him as a warm and likable man? How could he have concealed so well the essence of who he was?

He was a master of disguise, yes, but perhaps it wasn't so hard to devise a disguise when your face was unknown. But it was his physical awkwardness that had deflected her suspicion. Had she not *wanted* to see the contradiction, really?

By the time the cruiser turned off Whitehall to Water and swung the wrong way up Moore Street, an immense crowd was already gathered in front of the building. Blue and red police lights were flashing; sirens were screaming from several different directions. Policemen were stopping and re-routing traffic on Water Street back down Whitehall or Broad. The area around Moore Street was blocked off with sawhorses marked POLICE LINE—DO NOT CROSS. Several fire trucks came barreling down Water Street, their sirens wailing. A couple of TV vans were already there, although how they'd been alerted so quickly, Sarah had no idea. So too was the NYPD's Emergency Services Unit.

As she jumped from the car, she wondered, How could everyone have gotten here so quickly?

Then she saw the answer. The NYPD Bomb Squad had arrived and taken over the scene, as they always did. Someone had called them in, probably one of the cops on the scene. At any moment the NEST teams would arrive and then there would be a turf battle from hell. Unless she stopped it.

She looked up at the building and whispered, "Jared."

CHAPTER NINETY-ONE

As the hour approached, Dan Hammond began to wonder whether the rich guy would really come through with the hundred grand he'd promised for flying into controlled airspace and landing on the roof of a Wall Street building.

True, the guy had showed up in person and put down five thousand bucks in cash. That was a good sign. The usual procedure was to give a credit-card guarantee on Amex or Visa, and then Executive billed you after the flight.

The company said they charged $825 per flight hour, but you never got into a helicopter for less than fourteen hundred dollars, to be honest. So five thousand bucks was a hell of a lot, but it wasn't such a crazy amount to put down.

This is probably my last job for Executive Class Aircraft Charter, Hammond reflected. Fitting that it should be in the best chopper they had, the ASTAR.

He loved flying the ASTAR, loved the look and feel of it. It was a French-made helicopter—actually, it was produced by a French-American firm—and so it didn't operate in quite the same way as American choppers. That made it a tough helicopter to fly.

For one thing, the ASTAR's rotor system turned the opposite way from the American rotor system. When you were trimming it in flight, you had to put in opposite control movements for antitorque, to keep the nose straight. Instead of applying left pedal when you added power, you applied right pedal.

Once you got used to that, it was a pleasure. It was powered by a French jet engine, the Turbo Mecca, a 640-shaft-horsepower engine. It cruised at 120 knots, the fastest single there was. It was also expensive, costing over a million dollars.

But it was a beauty. The fuselage was of a unique design, sleekly built and sweeping in appearance. It was jet-black, with titanium and plum striping and a silver lightning bolt down the expanse of fuselage. Its windows were deep-tinted. Its blades were blue, its interior tan. There were even oriental rugs to make the executive passengers feel at home. It seated four passengers, and one pilot, comfortably; it was air-conditioned and equipped with a telephone and a CD player.

The ASTAR was different, too, in that it had a panoramic passenger area, a 180-degree field of view. Your basic American helicopter had club seating, whereas this was like the interior of a luxury car. The pilot and passengers occupied the same cabin space. Also, its cabin was far quieter than those in American choppers, in which you really couldn't hold a conversation. In the ASTAR you could talk in normal tones.

Altogether, it was a spiffy helicopter, Dan Hammond thought, just the right one for his farewell flight.

CHAPTER NINETY-TWO

At McGuire Air Force Base in New Jersey, three Lockheed C-141 Starlifter aircraft were landing, bearing multiple cargoes of gear on pallets. There were radios and beepers and cellular phones and PBX telephone equipment; there was every tool and widget detector imaginable, from screwdrivers to Heckler & Koch MP5 submachine guns and Haley & Webber E182 Multi-Burst stun grenades employing high candela and decibel levels: a dazzling array of state-of-the-art weapons, surveillance devices, communications equipment, and radiation-detection equipment for locating clandestine bombs or stolen fissionable material.

Separately, over the course of several hours, more than thirty members of the NEST render-safe team had arrived on commercial flights from around the country.

"All right, I want everything from Broad to Whitehall, and from Water to Pearl, secured and blocked off," the man in the BOMB SQUAD wind-breaker announced to the squad members milling around him.

Sarah marched up to him and flashed her credentials. "Special Agent Cahill, FBI," she said. "I'm in charge of this operation."

"Oh, really?" the commanding officer of the Bomb Squad said, giving her a bored glance. "Not anymore, you're not."

The New York City Police Department's Bomb Squad is the largest and oldest full-time bomb unit in the country. Operating out of the Sixth Precinct, at 233 West Tenth Street, between Hudson and Bleecker, it handles some thirteen hundred calls a year to look for and disarm explosives. The squad is made up of six teams of two detectives, labeled A through F; the commanding officer is a lieutenant, and below him are four sergeants.

The Bomb Squad is part of the NYPD's Scientific Research Division, which is a unit of the Detective Bureau. But to be precise, though squad members wear gold badges, they are not detectives but "Detective-Specialists," which is something of a slap in the face to this all-volunteer, brave-to-the-point-of-foolhardiness group.

According to the *Patrol Guide* protocol, the Bomb Squad can appear on a scene only when called in by the Emergency Service Unit. They had been summoned on this occasion by ESU after one of the patrolmen searching the area realized there was a serious possibility there was a bomb in the building. The patrolman was simply doing his duty.

Until NEST's arrival, Sarah didn't have a card to play: the Bomb Squad was in charge. But once NEST showed up, the unit's Rules of Engagement—the most sweeping and comprehensive of any U.S. elite force—would place it unquestionably in charge.

There was a squealing of brakes. Sarah saw with enormous relief that NEST had arrived.

A CNN reporter was doing a stand-up in front of the tumultuous crowd surrounding the Network building on Moore Street.

Pappas and Ranahan stared at the television screen.

". . . a bomb in this building," the reporter was saying, "which houses a sensitive and highly secret Wall Street computer facility. In the basement of the building, according to police sources, there is believed to be as much as one thousand pounds of C-4 plastic explosive."

Then, footage of hordes of people evacuating neighboring buildings. Several people had been trampled in the ensuing panic. None had been killed, but several were injured.

"Police sources tell CNN that all entrances and exits to the Moore Street building have been blocked off except the main, front entrance. After a standoff between federal and local authorities, a team from the Department of Energy known as NEST, the Nuclear Emergency Search Team, has taken control of the scene."

There was a shot of the front of the Network building. Six buses had been lined up, three on a side, forming a narrow passageway, a chute, that led directly from the building's front doors to a courtyard across the street.

The buses looked like regular city buses except for one crucial difference. Steel plates attached to the sides of each bus had been lowered to the pavement so that no one could crawl out underneath them. In effect, the buses formed high metal walls that would keep anyone from escaping. Everyone evacuating the building had to pass between the specially modified buses to the courtyard, where everyone could be inspected or even questioned if need be.

This same method had been used in 1979, when armed Sunni fundamentalists had seized the holiest of Islamic shrines in Mecca, Saudi Arabia, with twenty thousand people trapped inside. Saudi troops had to figure out how to get the religious pilgrims out without letting the terrorists lose themselves in the escaping

ierd. They used riot-control buses to construct a corridor through which the pilgrims were funneled to a
nearby stadium, and there questioned.

Pappas smiled to himself.

Fire department volunteers stood both inside and
outside the front entrance, rushing the panicked workers through the revolving front door three at a time and
into the bus corridor. Once safely in the courtyard across
the street, each person was looked over by a small team
of observers from MINOTAUR, led by Vigiani and
Sarah.

The process did not go smoothly at all. The lobby
swarmed with people, many banging against the plate-
glass windows in terror.

"I'm going to die in here!" one woman kept shouting.

"Let us out!" a man yelled.

The building's windows, like those of many office
buildings in the city, could not be opened, but on the
street people could hear thudding. In one office on
the sixth floor a metal desk chair was hurled through
the plate-glass window, scattering shards of glass
over the sidewalk. A voice screamed out in terrible
agony, "I can't stand it!" and then a woman in her
early twenties jumped from the jagged hole.

The impact of the pavement hurt the woman badly,
broke several bones, but she survived the fall, which
the police and fire department crews feared would encourage others to do the same.

The commander of the Bomb Squad, though chafing
at being supplanted by NEST, picked up a bullhorn and
announced: "Stay in your offices! There is no reason to
panic! There is time!" But he didn't believe what he
himself was saying. Poor bastards, he thought.

For the most part, Sarah and Vigiani were able to scan
the emerging workers at great speed. Baumann was a

master of disguise, but from a distance of a foot or two, he would not pass by undetected.

A few men were detained—bearded men, including one with long hair who worked in computers in a law firm on the second floor—but after a few seconds of additional inspection they were cleared.

"I'm going to sue your fucking ass," the long-haired man said.

"Good luck," Sarah said tightly.

There was another crash, as a desk was hurled out of a twelfth-floor window. Fragments of glass hit several onlookers, drawing blood, though no one was seriously hurt.

"Anyone attempting to leave except through the front entrance will be detained," a metallic voice thundered.

"Who the fuck cares?" a middle-aged man shouted from the lobby. "We're all going to die!"

Sarah turned to Vigiani. "All right, now you take over. I'm going in."

"You're . . . *what*?" gasped Vigiani.

"Going in the building," Sarah said, striding off.

"You're out of your mind!" Vigiani shouted after her.

"Yeah," Sarah said softly to herself, "but I'm the boss."

CHAPTER NINETY-THREE

At the same time as the police and firemen were herding office workers out of the building, NEST had already begun to move equipment up a loading ramp and into the rear service entrance of the building.

They were escorted by a tight blue knot of uniformed patrolmen who made sure no one was able to escape the building as they entered. Several persons attempted to force their way past the NEST men but were grabbed by the policemen.

The first to enter was the NEST commander, Dr. Richard Payne, a tall, lanky man in his forties with a head of prematurely gray hair. Dr. Payne, who had a Ph.D. in nuclear physics, was in his regular life a special projects manager in the Advanced Technology Division of the Idaho National Engineering Laboratory. In the U.S. government's bureaucratic hierarchy he was a GS-15. He had wide experience in nuclear weapons and was considered brilliant by everyone who'd ever dealt with him.

Alongside him was his number two on this assignment, U.S. Army Lieutenant Colonel Freddie Suarez, from the 112th Explosives Ordnance Division Detachment in Fort Ritchie, Maryland. Behind them the other members of the team pushed carts bearing enormous and impressive-looking equipment.

In normal circumstances, theirs was a fiendishly difficult job. Like all bomb squads, they were trained to find the device and circumvent any booby traps that prevented them from gaining access to it. After that came diagnostics: examining the device, determining how it worked. Then the device was rendered safe. If need be, this was preceded by damage-mitigation efforts.

But unlike any other bomb squad, they often— though not always—dealt with nuclear devices, or at the very least with extremely sophisticated improvised explosive devices.

They'd had ample time in the last few days to examine the fusing mechanism that had been intercepted at the airport. Although there was no guarantee whatsoever that the bomber would use an identical fusing mechanism, or even anything close to it, they were prepared in case he did.

Yet these were far from ideal circumstances. The rule book said you did not attempt to defuse a bomb until the entire area had been secured and evacuated. In fact, the rules said you needed a thousand feet "under cover"—but everyone knew that was impossible in Manhattan, where you'd be lucky to back people up to the next corner.

As he pointed his team toward the stairs to the basement, Dr. Payne thought grimly, At least I'm paid to risk my life. All these other people went to work this morning fully expecting to go home to their families and their pets and their houses and apartments. Alive.

"All right," Dr. Payne told his assembled team in the crowded stairwell outside the basement of the Network building. "The locals have already sicced their dogs on the lobby of the building and found nothing."

He didn't have to explain to his men that when it came to sophisticated explosives, bomb-sniffing dogs are all but useless. They are fine for TNT or dynamite or other run-of-the-mill explosives. Even for C-4, if they got close enough, which meant within inches.

The NYPD Bomb Squad's dogs had sniffed nothing, but they had not gone into the building's basement. The doors to the basement were locked. Likely that was where the bomb was. From a structural-engineering point of view, that was the most logical place.

In fact, although the NEST men didn't yet know it, bomb-sniffing dogs would not have discovered anything even if they had found the banker boxes and peed on them, for the C-4 that Baumann had used in the bomb emitted no odor the dogs could detect.

It was a fair assumption, based on the intel they'd been given, that a C-4 bomb was beneath the lobby, but the team's first order of business was to make absolutely certain. If they could.

The mechanical version of a bomb-sniffing dog is a vapor detector, of which there are several types. Richard Payne had chosen an ion-mobility vapor detector, the size and shape of a medium-sized suitcase.

But they were working in the dark: if the bomb was in the basement, they had no idea where it was located in the basement, and it could be anywhere. They gathered in the stairwell beside the white-painted steel door that led to the basement. They did not try to force the door, because they assumed it was booby-trapped.

The shut door made it difficult for the vapor detector to operate well at all. Built into the machine was a vacuum pump, which would suck in air at a fair clip. But the bomb could be hundreds of feet away. Suarez held the intake nozzle to the floor, at the slight gap between door and floor. The machine was switched on.

Air was drawn into the vapor detector's lungs, trapping a sample that could be diagnosed.

After a few minutes, Lieutenant Colonel Suarez gestured for it to be switched off. If there was C-4 behind the door, it was not registering. Maybe it was too far away.

He shrugged.

Dr. Payne shrugged in reply.

There still might be C-4 there. They would have to do other tests.

It is a serious misconception that members of bomb squads like the Nuclear Emergency Search Team don't get frightened. In a situation in which a bomb might go off at any moment, causing maiming or death, it is only human to be scared.

But there is a difference between fear—which, reined in and redirected, can fuel intense concentration—and anxiety. Anxiety, in the form of uncontrollable apprehension and distress, is the most dangerous thing a member of a bomb squad can face, far more perilous than any bomb. A bomb is logical (whether or not we understand its logic), and a person with anxiety is not.

Dr. Payne and Lieutenant Colonel Suarez and the twenty-eight other NEST members who lined the stairwell were professionals and were experienced in rendering bombs safe. Still, each one was deeply frightened. There was far too much about this bomb that was unknown.

Simply put, they did not know whether the bomb was set to detonate if anyone came near it. The fusing mechanism had been intensively examined in a Department of Energy laboratory to determine how much energy it would take to set off the detector, whether there was a sensitivity switch or a variable resistor. Dr. Payne had himself plotted the RF (radio frequency) emanation relative to the position of gain control. He knew how much motion would set the thing off. He knew that it was designed not to respond to motion beyond twenty-five feet.

But he didn't know whether the sensor had been dialed up, extending the safe line to forty or fifty feet or more. And it was possible the sensor wasn't even on.

He had no idea.

This much he knew for sure: his men had not set off the bomb. Wherever the safe line was, they hadn't stepped over it.

But it might be located at the doorjamb, and they would have to assume that it was.

If there was indeed a proximity detector in force, Payne thought, most likely it affected the area on the other side of the door. Microwaves, for all practical purposes, do not go through steel.

But to be safe, they could not risk encroaching even an inch beyond where the closest man—Dr. Payne—was standing. All of their tests had to be conducted from their present positions, and no closer.

The first order of business for the team was to rule out the presence of a nuclear weapon. To do that, they had to test for radioactivity. Not knowing what was in the nuke, or even if it was a nuke at all, they had no way of knowing whether to test for alpha or beta particles, or gamma waves, or for neutron emission. Each is detected by means of a separate procedure. They could test either for whatever radioactive substance was in the bomb or for the "degradation material," the substance the bomb material would degrade into.

Dr. Payne knew they were not close enough to test for alpha or beta emissions. That left neutrons and gamma. If their detectors "smelled" a large quantity of gamma waves and a small quantity of neutrons, they were probably dealing with uranium; if they "smelled" the opposite, it was probably plutonium.

Their tests told them that the bomb inside the steel door was not nuclear.

That was a relief, though it lasted only a few seconds.

In a darkened room on the building's fifth floor, Baumann was working with a soldering iron and a pair of wire cutters. Jared, his arms and legs bound, wriggled on the floor a few feet away, thumping his duct-taped feet against the floor in an ineffectual attempt to summon someone, anyone. But the floor was tile over concrete, and the thumping made barely a sound, and in any case, the top floors of the building were by now evacuated. There was no one on the floor to hear him.

Baumann continued to work, his concentration undisturbed.

CHAPTER NINETY-FOUR

The next order of business for the NEST men was to determine whether the microwave detector had indeed been turned on. If not, they could force open the steel door and safely approach the bomb to render it safe.

If it was . . .

Well, the first thing was to determine whether it was on or not. To do that, they used a device known as a microwave sniffer, which looks for emanations in the microwave wavelength, above ten gigahertz. A version of this same device is used to test kitchen microwave ovens for leaks.

A junior member of the team, an Army sergeant named Grant who was trained in explosives detection, took the microwave sniffer's long, flexible antenna and pointed it at the steel door as Payne directed him to do.

"Dr. Payne," he said, "we're just not going to get anything. This door here is steel, and microwaves are pretty much blocked by steel, sir. It's going to mask the microwave emanations."

"That's right," Payne said. "But keep at it, please."

Sergeant Grant had served in the Army long enough

to know how to take orders with grace, so he continued, though with a trace of reluctance. The microwave sniffer was silent.

"You want me to sort of snake this antenna under the door?"

"*No*, Grant. That's a huge risk. Bad idea."

"Sir," Grant said, "Like I said, this here door—" But he was interrupted by a rapid, high-pitched beeping. The sniffer had gone into alarm mode.

The antenna, which Grant had pointed at the crack between the bottom of the steel door and the concrete floor, was being bombarded by microwaves exceeding its preset threshold.

"Oh, shit—" Grant cried out.

The microwave detector was not just in force on the other side of the door. Microwaves were leaking under the door. If anyone moved even a few inches closer to the door, there was a risk the bomb would be set off.

"Freeze!" Payne shouted. "*Everybody freeze!*"

The beeping continued.

"All right," Dr. Payne said in a quiet, steady voice. "The thing hasn't exploded. That tells us something. But any further motion might set it off."

"Jesus!" Grant whined. He was frozen in an awkward position, partially bent toward the floor, his extended right hand gripping the microwave sniffer's antenna. It was pointed at the gap between floor and door, which was no bigger than a quarter of an inch. The antenna was approximately six inches from the floor. He shifted slightly.

"Don't move a fucking *muscle*," Payne hissed. "We're picking up the microwaves that are coming through from under the door. The door is sealed tight against the doorframe everywhere except against the floor."

"I can't stay this way," Sergeant Grant moaned.

"Goddammit," Payne said, "don't move a muscle or you might just kill us all." He felt his body flood with panic.

Grant's eyes widened. Except for the rapid beeping, the entire stairwell was silent. Thirty men were standing almost completely still. From a distance there were faint shouts, distant sirens; but here the only sound was the papery whisk of their windbreakers as the men shifted stance ever so slightly, and the mechanical beeping.

"Now, listen," Payne said. "Everyone, look down at your feet."

Obediently, everyone on the team did.

"Memorize that position. Keep your feet in *exactly* that position. Even a reflection of a body might be picked up through that gap. I don't know why we haven't set it off yet—maybe the sensor just switched on. But if you move your feet, you may cause it to detonate."

"Oh, please, God," someone said.

"If you have to move, move parallel to the door. You're less likely to set it off that way. But if I were you, I wouldn't move a fucking muscle."

"I—can't—" Grant gasped. A tiny, liquid noise came from near the sergeant's feet, which Payne quickly realized was a trickle of urine. A long stain darkened his left pant leg. Payne, though as frightened as any man here, felt acutely embarrassed for Grant. No doubt Grant knew that this would be his last assignment with NEST.

Yet Payne could not help thinking, morbidly, that this might be his own last assignment as well.

One of the men—the one who had just said, "Oh, please, God"—was, in shrink jargon, decompensating. He was a scientist from DOE headquarters, a young man, in his early thirties, and he had begun to babble.

Payne ignored him, praying only that the young man

wouldn't move. If he did, at least he was one of the far-
thest from the door. Although he had broken out in a
cold sweat, he knew he could not afford to divert his attention to this man, or to Sergeant Grant, who, despite
his accident, at least had the self-control to remain frozen in position. Important decisions had to be made.

There is a concept you often hear among bomb-
squad technicians: the bomb's *wa*. A bomb's *wa* is its
overall state of being.

In order not to disturb a bomb's *wa*, you have to understand and appreciate its *wa*, and Payne had not yet
done that. He only knew that opening the steel door
would likely disturb the *wa*.

Payne could feel his anal sphincter squeeze tight as
his body grew increasingly tense. This was a phenom-
enon well known to bomb techs—"asshole-puckering,"
they called it. The detector was beeping furiously, telling them that the wrong move would detonate the bomb.
Yet you couldn't see anything, couldn't smell anything.
What did the beep signify? How sensitive was the microwave field?

"Grant," he said gently, "can you listen to me?"

"Sir," Grant croaked.

"Grant, I want you to move that antenna upward by a
few inches. Do you understand me? Slowly and steadily.
Upward."

"Yes, sir," Grant said. With a trembling hand he
inched the antenna up. As he did, it shook up and down.

"Steady, Grant."

"Doing my best, sir."

The beeping stopped.

Sergeant Grant had moved the antenna less than six
inches up from the floor, and apparently it was now out
of range of the microwave sensor. "That's the safe
line," Payne whispered, more to himself than to the

others. "The microwaves are not moving through the steel door."

He had received his Ph.D. in nuclear physics at CalTech and was well versed in the strengths and weaknesses of the microwave sniffer. For instance, they now knew how strong the emissions were—that was on the receiver's readout—but without opening the door to the basement they could not know how far they were from the bomb. That meant they couldn't map the microwave field, couldn't learn how close they could safely get to the bomb before it would detonate.

Was there a dead zone? They couldn't even tell that. Typically, a microwave sensor employs a Doppler shift, which means that the signal creates a constant pattern of microwave energy. The sensor looks for any change in the reflected pattern of that energy. A change occurs when an object within the sensor's field moves. If you are standing absolutely still in the field, nothing will happen.

Of course, *some* motion had to be tolerable: what if the air-conditioning caused a curtain near the bomb to ripple? So the detector calculated the amplitude of change over time. Any change that was strong—or long in duration—would set it off, the exact definition of "strong" or "long" having been preset in the detector.

Also, as Payne knew, you could beat a microwave sensor if you knew how. There were ways. If you approached the sensor *very* slowly, you might not set it off.

But if you allowed your arms to swing at your sides even slightly, you'd probably get nailed, because your arms would be moving toward and away from the sensor at a greater rate of speed, a greater rate of change, than the rest of your body.

That wasn't even a possibility now, however. Without

seeing the bomb and being able to estimate its distance from where they were standing, they certainly could not risk approaching it.

And here was the bitch of it. How could you kill a bomb when you didn't even know where it was?

CHAPTER NINETY-FIVE

Within fifteen minutes, the line of evacuees from the Network building dwindled and then stopped. Another announcement was made over the PA system, but ten minutes later no one had emerged.

None of the workers who had filed out of the building bore a remote resemblance to Baumann.

Inside the building, Sarah made her way up the stairwell. She had searched the first four floors, but no Baumann. And no Jared.

On the fifth floor, she walked silently down the empty corridor, checking office after office.

Dr. Payne made a swift calculation.

They were detecting microwave energy, but did that really mean they couldn't move? He knew that the range of detection is always greater than the range of function—that is, they could "see" the microwave emitter, but the emitter couldn't necessarily see them. There's always a threshold of acceptable leakage, just as a microwave oven might leak microwaves, but people don't necessarily get cooked standing in front of it.

Payne had examined the fusing system. He knew

now how much energy it needed to set off the bomb. The more he repeated his mental calculations, the more sure he was that the amount of microwave energy leaking under the steel door was not enough, if reflected backward, to trigger the detector.

They were safe where they were. They could move.

"All right," Dr. Payne said. "The safe line is on the other side of the door. There's some stray microwave leakage, but we're safe as long as we stay on this side. Everyone, back off from the door. You, Grant, and you, O'Hara"—he pointed at the DOE scientist who had lost it—"get out of here. I don't want to see you again."

On this side of the door, on this side of the safe line, they could move. The microwave sensor, he now realized, would detect motion on the other side of the door only.

This was good. This gave them considerably more room to maneuver.

This also meant they could remotely "look" at the bomb using a technology that remains to this day highly classified by the U.S. government. They used a device called a neutron backscatter, which emits a stream of neutrons at a very specific energy level. The stream is fired at the target, and then the backscatter measures the rate at which the neutrons come back at it—that is, the extent to which the neutrons are absorbed.

The neutron backscatter has the ability to penetrate metal liners and walls, so the steel door was not an obstacle. Using the same physical principle employed in an HED—a hydrogenous explosives detector—it looks for hydrogen. The neutron backscatter they were using was unusually powerful. Payne flipped the switch, checked the readout.

"Well, there's explosive material there," Dr. Payne

muttered to Suarez. "A shitload of it, from what I can tell."

"Now what do we do?" Suarez asked.

Dr. Payne did not reply; the truth was, he had no idea. He was winging it; in times like this you always had to wing it and trust your instincts.

"All right," he said at last. "I want the generator moved out here."

"You want to do *what*?" asked Suarez.

"Like I said," Dr. Payne said. "The generator."

"You want to do the EMP? Jesus—"

"I want to burn out its solid-state mind, and I don't even know if *that's* going to do it."

The electromagnetic-pulse generator was powered by a huge capacitor, really a bank of capacitors that required an immense power source. As the capacitor was wheeled into place beside the steel door to the basement, Lieutenant Colonel Suarez said, "Sir, with everyone out of the building, the situation is no longer life-threatening. Textbook says we're not supposed to risk *our* lives if the situation's not life-threatening. And the building's empty."

"Except for the terrorist."

"Except for the terrorist, yes, sir."

"The terrorist, and a child. And if this building goes up, those aren't going to be the only ones killed."

"Sir, the textbook—"

"Fuck the textbook," Dr. Payne said. "Get the door open."

"Sir, we can't," Suarez said.

"Well, we can't shoot *through* the goddam thing! We can't aim the EMP unless the door's open. *Get the goddam door open! Now!*"

"It's locked, sir." Suarez was doing his best to keep his cool. "We can't use explosive breaching techniques, sir. You don't breach the door of a magazine."

"Dammit," Dr. Payne said, "get out the halligan tool." This was a standard piece of equipment used to force open doors.

"Bad idea, sir. Respectfully. Looks like the door lock has been jammed with epoxy or Krazy Glue or something. It opens outward, toward us. It has to be opened from inside. Gently. But it looks as if it *can* be opened from the inside."

"If we force it . . ." Payne mused aloud.

"If we force it, we're introducing a violent motion, and you don't want to introduce energy into a bomb situation, right? If we use a halligan, we could set the thing off."

"Shit. You're right, Suarez. Good thinking. All right, do we have anyone already inside the building?"

"I don't know—"

Dr. Payne picked up his walkie-talkie and, calculating that it was safe to broadcast on this frequency, called Lieutenant George Roth. "Do we have anyone already in the building?" he repeated.

Sarah turned in the empty corridor.

Suddenly there was a static squawk.

It was her walkie-talkie, coming to life.

"Cahill, Cahill, ERCP," came a flat, mechanical voice. ERCP referred to "Emergency Response Command Post," the label NEST was using to avoid alerting any reporters who might be listening in.

"ERCP, Cahill, go ahead."

"There's a back way into the basement. We need you to enter the basement and open a door for us."

CHAPTER NINETY-SIX

Fueled by anger and determination and fear, Sarah ran down to the lobby and, in a dim corner, just as the floor plans had indicated, located the little-used basement door.

It was jammed shut from the outside, the lock plugged with the broken end of a key and some Krazy Glue. Baumann clearly didn't want anyone to enter the basement.

The door couldn't be forced. That might set off the bomb.

There had to be another way to get into the basement.

Desperate, she ran across the lobby. How could she get into the basement without using the doors?

She passed a maintenance closet that had been propped open by a galvanized steel bucket and wet mop. She stopped, opened the closet door all the way, and saw the pipes at the back, running vertically up and down through the building.

The answer.

They ran through a shaft, roughly two feet square, into the basement. There was space in front of the pipes, not a hell of a lot but perhaps enough.

She leaned over and peered down the shaft.

The drop to the basement floor was probably eight or nine feet. Several of the pipes made sharp right angles into a wide, dull gray, steel ventilation duct. The duct was some four feet wide. Wide enough to shield her movements from the microwave detector.

She pulled off her shoes and her jacket and squeezed into the narrow space, grabbing on to the pipes as she moved. It was a tight squeeze, but she realized quickly she could make it through.

It was like crawling through the narrow neck of a cave.

She shimmied down, holding on to the pipes, lowering herself as much as she could toward the floor of the basement. Then the pipes veered off at sharp angles in different directions. A drop of some six feet remained.

She eased herself down slowly, carefully. Shielded by the duct she dropped noiselessly to the ground.

She gasped when she almost stumbled over the body of a uniformed man, crumpled on the floor in front of her. It looked like a security guard, probably someone who had tried to stop Baumann.

She spotted a long stack of boxes roped together, on top of which sat a small black box, which flashed in the sputtering fluorescent light.

If you can see it, it can see you, Dr. Payne had said. But from how far?

Estimating distances didn't come naturally to her, but she had learned to do it, and she now calculated she was ninety to one hundred feet from the device.

She stopped, pressed the transmit button on her walkie-talkie. "ERCP, ERCP, Cahill," she said. "I'm here. I see it. How much time is remaining?"

"Cahill, ERCP. We don't know," Payne said. "We figure that as long as the terrorist is in the building, it's not going to blow."

"Good."

"Uh, Agent Cahill, I wouldn't be so relieved if I were you. The device has got a ground-plane antenna protecting a circular area, with a possible operating range of forty to sixty feet. If you're beyond sixty feet from it, you're safe. Now, I want you to move forward slowly."

"How slowly?"

"I can't answer that. If you're far away from it, any movement will be perceived by the sensor as much slower than if you were right up next to it."

"Give me a rate of speed!"

"As slowly as you possibly can. Recognizing that we're all under the gun—there's got to be a clock ticking, but we just don't know when zero hour is. Let's say slower than one step per second. We estimate the sensor can 'see' someone walking at the rate of one step per second, so keep it slower than that."

"Jesus, that's slow!"

"Keep your arms against your side. No, better—keep your arms folded against your chest. Whatever you do, you must not allow your arms to swing. The microwave's going to see a rapid fore-and-aft like a champ. You want to avoid creating a Doppler shift."

"Meaning what?" She knew bombs, but not to this degree.

"Just . . . just keep your body as still as possible. Keep flat against the wall. Inch along it. A few inches a second, no faster. Now, whenever possible, keep solid objects between you and the bomb—the furnace, machinery, whatever's down there. Anything RF-opaque. According to our examination of the device, it's a bit above ten thousand megahertz, so bricks and dense masonry like concrete and steel will be pretty effective at blocking it."

Sarah inched toward the main basement area, then stopped. She raised the walkie-talkie to her mouth, realizing that this was probably the last time she'd be able to use the walkie-talkie as long as she was down here: from now on, she'd have to keep her arms folded.

"There are some large objects," she said. "A water heater. A row of something. But there are gaps between them. *Huge* gaps. I'm not going to be able to always keep solid objects between the bomb and me."

"Do your best," Payne instructed. "In the gaps, be sure to move as slowly as possible. This is a volumetric device."

"Meaning—?"

"Forget it. You must not change the reflected patterns of the microwave. It sees rate of change. You've got to minimize your effect on the rate of change of the energy pattern by minimizing your body motion."

"*I don't know what the hell you're talking about!*"

"Move very slowly and steadily, Agent Cahill. And *go!*"

Oh, dear God, she thought. Sweet Jesus God.

Jared was in the building, had to be in the building, upstairs. She could not think that he was dead. He was alive, he had to be alive, but silenced somehow.

An FBI agent could, under some circumstances, be called upon to sacrifice his or her own life. But not the lives of their loved ones. That was not in the employment contract.

Now as she inched along the cold damp basement wall she felt a waft of ice-cold air and smelled the old familiar dirt smell of mold, a smell she associated with her childhood, and therefore found oddly reassuring.

One . . . two . . . one . . . two. A slow-motion side-shuffle. Her hands gripping her chest, flattening her breasts. One . . . two . . . one . . . two. Her legs trembled with the enormous exertion it required to keep them from jerking away from her. Brushing against the cold damp wall, one, two . . .

. . . Up to the water heater, a behemoth, floor-to-ceiling, wall of steel, blasting heat, pilot light twinkling. Easily eight or ten feet long. She reached it, recoiling from the overpowering heat, exhaled.

It bought her ten feet, she thought. Ten free feet. She slid against the wall, quickly now. She felt a prickly flush of heat, and the sweat began to run down her arms, down the inside of her arms, down her breasts, tickling her. Rivulets of sweat ran down her inner thighs. Fluorescent light flickered sickly greenish-white.

She came to the end of the heater, and there was a gap, a space of another five or six feet, before the next shelter, which she now saw was long and rectangular, a tall row of filing cabinets.

Immediately she slowed her pace, inched along. As she edged, she stared at the black box, her eyes glistening with fear, feeling as if the invisible microwaves could feel her, were invading her body, arrogant and intrusive and everywhere. Now, from this angle, she could see a tiny pinpoint of light, a ruby-red dot, on top of the black box. What was it, an indicator? Would it wink at her if it caught her moving? Would it wink in the split second before the building was incinerated, turning her and her little boy into ash? Or would there be no warning at all? Would she move a few inches per second too quickly, enraging the red-eyed monster, and never know anything?

She stared, and she thought about Jared, and she began to formulate a plan, anything to distract her, send her mind elsewhere, anywhere, while she edged along the dank wall to the file cabinets, light flickering fluorescent-green.

Another twenty-five feet to go, and then she would have to move along another wall before she reached the door.

Hugging her chest harder, her clothes soaked through. Thinking of Jared, cowering in a room somewhere.

She glided along the wall behind the filing cabinets, mindful of the gaps between the cabinets, through which the microwaves could pass. She had to move slowly here too, just as slowly, because of the gaps. Then she came to another open space. This one seemed miles long, seemed to stretch an eternity. Inched now. A muscle twitched, something connecting hip to leg, a slight jerking motion, and she froze. Her heart knocked against her rib cage. Stood still, holding her breath. Waiting for the ruby-red light to wink at her. It didn't. She exhaled slowly. Moved again to her left. One . . . two . . . one . . . two . . .

Could hear voices on the other side of the heavy steel door, which was coming closer inch by inch. The NEST men issuing and receiving instructions, setting up their machinery, waiting for her to ease open the door. Her walkie-talkie crackled; she ignored it.

"Cahill, Cahill, ERCP, are you there yet?"

Her arms glued to her breasts, she inched, inched, not answering. Sidled up to the next RF-opaque obstruction, which seemed to be ductwork, but this one was narrow, maybe five feet of relief, which was nothing.

She thought of Brian/Baumann. Flashed on the Identi-Kit sketch, which was a bad cartoon, looked nothing like the real thing. What did Baumann really look like? Did she know? Who was he? She inched along in the next open space, and now she felt the snugness of the corner, cold and damp and pleasantly rounded.

Negotiating this turn was not easy. She swiveled in slow motion, trying to understand the physics of the microwave sensor.

Stared at the unwinking tiny red dot.

Sidled, inch by inch by inch. Hugging herself tighter and tighter. Felt a tickle in her throat. Had to cough.

Now it was all she could think about—*don't cough, coughing will cause your head to jerk*. The tickle was unbearable.

She inched along; the tickle subsided.

Now the door was close enough to reach out and touch, and it took all of her willpower to keep from doing it. Must keep her arms folded. Must move slowly, inch by inch.

How far was she, how far was the door from the bomb?

Never good at estimating distance, and never was it so important. Fifty? No, more. Sixty? Maybe. Sixty was the cut-off. Within sixty feet, the sensor could read movement. A little more, perhaps. Sixty-five feet?

Hard to know.

Yes. Sixty-five feet.

Voices on the other side of the door grew louder.

Until she had reached the doorframe, sidled her body along until she stood directly in front of the door, and she slowly, slowly eased her hands down, as if caressing her breast, her abdomen, her hips, straightening them, moving them along the contours of her body agonizingly slowly, until both hands grasped the steel doorknob and she turned it, and it didn't move, and she turned harder, and still it didn't move, and then a *twist* of both hands and the knob turned. The door had been jammed so that it couldn't be opened from the outside, yes, but inside it could be opened, thank God, and, *yes*, it opened out, not into the room, thank God.

"I'm there," she said.

"Great," she heard a voice say. "Well done. Careful, now. No big movements."

She pushed against the door, gently but firmly.

And slowly.

Agonizingly slowly, she eased it open, inch by inch. Never had she opened a door so slowly.

—and she heard: "*Goddammit, it's going to blow!*"

She shouted: "It's okay! It's more than sixty feet from here, I'm sure of it!"

She heard shouts, a scream, and she felt the floor come up and smack against the back of her head, as someone forced her to the ground and out of the way of the machinery.

She looked around, saw that the stairwell was empty, realized that the NEST men had moved out of the building, as per procedure.

"All right, Agent Cahill, let's go! Move it!" came the voice of the man who had pushed her to the floor. He was wearing a bulky green suit, armored with Kevlar panels, and a helmet. "Out of the building!"

"No!" she shouted. "I'm not moving!"

"*Get the fuck out of here!*"

"Back off!" she shouted. "I'm staying here. My boy's in there."

"Move it! Out! You're not in charge now—we are. Only Suarez can stay here, and he's operating the machine."

"Sorry," Sarah said, steely. "If anything happens, I want to be here to assist. So prosecute me later. I don't give a shit."

She saw Lieutenant Colonel Suarez smile. "Yeah, she's right," he said. "I might need an assist. Let her stay."

Suarez aimed the antenna at the bomb and fired off a super-high-powered blast of electromagnetic energy.

There was a loud crackling sound. Sarah, crouching out of the way of the EMP, felt the hair on the back of her neck stand on end. It felt as if the shock were running through her body.

There was a burning smell.

There, some seventy feet away, was the pile of boxes,

DetCord looped around them. On top was the fusing mechanism. Its tiny ruby-red LED light was dark.

"Is that it?" Sarah asked.

"I—I think so," Suarez said. "Uh, the sensor isn't picking up any microwave emissions. Tom?"

The man in the green Kevlar protective suit said, "Spectrum analyzer finds no evidence of any electric flow. No current flowing through the thing."

"Approach the device," Suarez ordered.

The helmeted man in the protective gear lumbered through the doorway.

Sarah held her breath, found herself praying.

Suarez explained to her: "Everything about it seems to be dead, but EMP won't defeat a mechanical fuse, so he's got to look for himself."

Tom approached the device, walking up to it slowly, and did not feel his foot brush against a taut, almost invisible wire. He unfolded a flat, canary-yellow screen and placed it behind the black box, then pointed a small cylindrical object at it.

Suarez explained: "Those are CB2 screens. They fluoresce when hit by X rays. He's using a Min-X-Ray SS-100 portable fluoroscope to send X rays through the thing, so he can see an image on the screen. He knows what to look for—mostly, any deviation from the device you folks intercepted."

"Looks clear," Tom shouted.

"Clear," Suarez shouted to the rest of the team members, some three hundred yards off.

Tom opened the black box and looked inside. All the solid-state electronic guts of the fusing mechanism had been fried.

The bomb was dead.

But something caught his eye, just a glint at first, and he felt his stomach go cold.

It was a large mechanical stopwatch. A big, old, round-faced stopwatch that appeared to have been modified. A sweep second hand was moving at a normal pace, but to Tom, seized with panic, it seemed to be racing.

Two wires came out of the watch, snaked out of the box into the explosives.

He whirled around, saw the simple trip wire he had set off as he approached the bomb. A low-tech kind of thing commandos used in the jungle. The kind of thing that's not affected by electromagnetic pulses or anything fancy like that.

The second hand continued to sweep along the face of the stop watch, toward a steel pin, and when it made contact, the bomb would blow. A sixty-second stopwatch. Less than thirty seconds remained.

From behind him, Tom heard a shout: "What the hell . . . ?"

"Back off!" Tom shouted hoarsely. "It's not dead!"

A simple booby trap, Tom thought. It hadn't been in the mechanism they had inspected. Of course: Baumann trusted nobody, not even whoever had made his fusing mechanism. He'd put in a backup.

Two wires.

Two wires emanated from the watch. What did that mean?

Did he dare cut the wires?

What if it were a collapsing circuit, which meant that if you cut the wires, the circuit would automatically close, and the fucking bomb would go off?

Tom felt his fingers tremble.

Cut the wires or not?

Two wires.

Less than ten seconds remained.

No. A collapsing circuit always needed three wires.

Just over five seconds before the steel second hand touched the steel pin . . .

He snipped the wires.

Involuntarily, he winced, braced himself.

A second . . . two . . . three.

Nothing.

He exhaled slowly, felt tears spring to his eyes.

The thing was dead. He turned around slowly, numbly, and said, too quietly: "The render-safe is complete. The thing's dead."

Suarez sank to the ground in involuntary expression of relief. Sarah braced herself against the doorjamb and stared at the bomb in disbelief. Tears of relief welled up in her eyes.

"The render-safe is complete," Suarez called out. "The thing's dead."

And then Sarah's walkie-talkie crackled. "Cahill, Cahill, Roth."

"Roth, Cahill," she replied. "Go ahead."

"We've spotted your man."

CHAPTER NINETY-SEVEN

The area six miles in radius from the center of La Guardia Airport is officially La Guardia airspace. As Dan Hammond's ASTAR approached the uncontrolled airspace above the Downtown Manhattan Heliport, he was contacted by La Guardia Class B service operations. Flying into a high-density air-traffic area as he was, his craft was now under strict ATC control. ATC mandates your helicopter route, at a prescribed altitude. For each flight, you're issued a transponder code, which was in this case 3213. The transponder code tags up on the radar screen with your tail numbers, also known as registration numbers or N numbers. The tail numbers used to be painted only on the bottom of the aircraft, but now they are required to be visible from both sides. Also, because of drug-smuggling problems, the numbers are now required to be fully twelve inches high, which makes them visible from quite a distance.

Now, as he steered the chopper off into the controlled airspace just north of the helipad, he heard, "Helicopter three two one three, you're north of your prescribed route. State your intentions."

Hammond hit the talk switch. "I've—I've got

problems—" he started to say, which was the beginning of his prepared line.

But the ATC interrupted: "Uh, helicopter three two one three, we've got a NOTAM posted for the area you've just entered." A NOTAM is a Notice to Aviators and Mariners which declares a certain area off-limits.

A NOTAM? For what? Now, Hammond was momentarily confused. Who the hell would have expected this? What was the NOTAM all about?

He hit his talk switch again to ask.

CHAPTER NINETY-EIGHT

She raced up the stairwell to the twentieth floor of the building, up a narrow set of iron stairs that led up to the roof, and stepped out of the roof exit into the dank gray late-afternoon air. She gasped for breath. Behind her in the stairwell waited several police backups. Several much taller buildings loomed on two sides. Shouts and sirens and the honking of car horns rose from below.

Two shapes were silhouetted against the glare. She couldn't see their faces, but she recognized them at once.

Jared. He was gagged and handcuffed. One heavy steel handcuff tightly encircled both of his tiny wrists. The other end of the cuff was attached to the plastic handle of a rectangular object, a box of some kind, which Sarah at once realized was a child's plastic lunchbox. She looked again, not comprehending. Could she be seeing right?

His silken voice filled her with horror.

"Sarah," Baumann said with repellent gentleness, "I don't want to hurt Jared, but I will if I absolutely must. It's up to you to see that doesn't happen."

"Your bomb's dead," she said, short of breath, gasping. "It's pointless now for you to keep going." She moved closer so that her walkie-talkie, locked in transmit mode, could pick up their conversation for the benefit of the listeners down below.

"No closer, please. Now, I'd rather get out of here than stay. So now you and I will make a deal." It was strange: he was speaking in a South African accent and sounded like a different person.

"What do you want?" Sarah said, queasy with disgust at negotiating with this monster.

"In just a few minutes, I will be leaving the building. I'm taking Jared with me."

"What do you mean, taking him *with* you?" She was exhausted, bone-tired, and couldn't believe what she was hearing. Now she could see Jared's face. His eyes were wide with fright; he appeared frozen.

"Only for the first part of my journey. Just far enough to guarantee safe passage. Traveler's insurance. I promise you Jared will not be hurt as long as you cooperate."

"You *promise*—!"

"There's no reason for me to hurt your son. I'm quite fond of him."

Something was gradually coming over her now, an iciness, a fusion of hatred and determination and fierce protectiveness that made her less afraid. "Take me instead," she said, and took another step forward.

"Please, Sarah," Baumann said. "For Jared's sake, stay where you are. Listen carefully, please. I don't want you or your people to make any mistakes. First I must make a phone call." Baumann pulled from a pocket a cellular phone and punched a few numbers. He listened for a couple of seconds, then punched a few more. "There," he said. "Thank you, Jared, for the use of your phone. Now the bomb is armed." He put away the cell phone and held up a small object Sarah couldn't quite make out. "This is a dead-man switch, Sarah. You know how it works, I assume. This button is connected to a small radio transmitter, and to a signal generator that produces a continuous tone. It's transmitting that tone now. A one-milliwatt transmitter—very low-powered. Good only for line-of-sight. As long as I keep the button depressed, the signal is transmitted. But if I let go of the button, my transmitter stops sending the signal."

"What are you saying?" she said, although she knew. Her voice shook.

"In Jared's lunchbox is a small explosive device—half a block of C-4 connected to a blasting cap, which is connected in series with a paging device that has been modified. I've just called the pager, which caused the relay to close. Now there's only one thing that's keeping the bomb from detonating: the signal that my transmitter is generating. The normally closed relay is connected to a radio receiver—a scanner programmed for a specific frequency. As long as the receiver hears a signal—a continuously transmitted signal—it keeps the switch open, and he's safe. But if the signal stops, or is interrupted, the relay closes, closing the circuit between battery and blasting cap, initiating the C-4. The bomb detonates. And Jared is gone. Just half a pound of C-4, no more, but quite enough to turn him into mist." Jared's eyes closed.

"You're sick," Sarah murmured. "You're sick. He's a child."

"So, if anything happens to me—if, let's say, you or any of your people are so impulsive as to shoot me—I release pressure on the switch, and the bomb blows up. If you try to jam the signal, the receiver will no longer see a clear signal, and Jared will die. If you attempt to grab Jared, you will take him out of the line of sight of my transmitter, and he will die. And don't even think of trying the standard FBI negotiation tactic of waiting me out, because if the battery in either my transmitter or Jared's receiver runs down, the bomb will go off."

"And how do I know you're telling the truth?" she asked hollowly. She knew that NEST, as well as members of her own team, were listening to this exchange over her walkie-talkie, and she was terrified that some hothead might make the mistake of trying to rush Baumann somehow.

"I suppose you don't, do you? But do you want to take that chance?"

Sarah stared at Baumann, then at Jared, and said with a sudden passion: "How can you do this? Don't you care for Jared, even a little?"

Baumann smiled cynically. "Don't bother, Sarah."

"I understand who you are, what kind of thing you are. I just thought you had some feelings for Jared. Would you really do this to Jared? I don't believe you would."

Baumann's smile faded. She was right; he did feel almost tender toward the child, but such feelings were treacherous, and his escape was paramount. He knew Sarah would never allow her son to be harmed, and that was the point, after all.

"Don't test me, Sarah," he snapped. "Please don't test me. Now, Jared is going to accompany me to a nearby airport. When I'm safely aboard a plane, he'll be returned to you. Understand, Sarah, that if anyone makes an error, or is too aggressive, and Jared is killed, his blood will be on your hands."

Sarah heard a faint noise in the distance, and she looked up. Gradually the noise grew louder, a noise she recognized. She looked up at the sky, startled at first by the *whump-whump-whump* noise. It was a helicopter, black and sleek, with tinted windows.

In the NEST command post, Dr. Richard Payne turned away from the walkie-talkie. "Suarez," he barked, "get over here. I need some equipment."

*   *   *

The *whump-whump-whump* of the helicopter rotor
blades was now deafeningly loud and directly overhead.

Baumann shouted: "Are we clear? Are we in agreement?"

Sarah looked at Jared. Tears ran down his cheeks.
"Yes," she shouted back. The decision was not difficult.
But could she trust him to release Jared once the heli-
copter landed? What choice did she really have?

The chopper blades whumped and thundered.

Baumann walked to the helicopter, clutching Jared.
The fuselage of the helicopter hovered above the
roof of the building, then softly landed. From below,
through the racket, he could hear sirens, saw the reflection of red and blue lights against the surrounding
buildings.

He jumped through the open helicopter door and
shoved Jared onto the seat next to the pilot's. With a
quick, unseen motion, he clicked off the bomb inside
the Power Rangers lunchbox, then switched off his
transmitter.

The helicopter idled in place. Baumann barked to
Dan Hammond: "You, out of the chopper. We're not
going to Teterboro." Hammond, frightened but at the
same time clearly relieved, climbed out of his seat and
slipped past Baumann to the door of the helicopter,
then stepped onto the roof. Baumann slid over and took
the controls.

"You're damn right we're not," came a voice from
immediately behind him. Baumann felt the cool steel
of a gun against his temple.

The voice came from Lieutenant George Roth, who
emerged from a crouch from behind the high-backed
front seats where he had waited unseen, concealed behind a tall red first-aid chest.

"You're making quite a mistake," Baumann told

Roth, taking his hand off the collective. "The child is wearing a bomb."

"I know about the bomb," Roth said. "Otherwise I'd have nailed you already."

Baumann smiled, but his smile was ice. He reached down and swiftly retrieved a pistol from a concealed ankle holster, leaped from the seat, and spun around to face Roth, pointing his gun at the cop. Audacity, Baumann thought, was the hallmark of a commando, not a cop. "Would you like to get out of this helicopter, or would you like to die?"

The two men eyed each other tensely. "Looks like a standoff to me," Roth said. "I got a better idea. Better for both of us. You let the kid go. I'll take his place. Sarah gets her kid back, and you get a hostage."

"And if I don't agree to that?" Baumann asked.

"Then I guess we all blow up. I don't care. I've been feeling a little suicidal these days anyway."

"And if it becomes known that a member of the New York Police Department killed a child?"

Roth shrugged. "Who's going to know anything? You're the guy made the bomb. Let the kid go."

"Thanks, but no," Baumann said. "The child is a better hostage, to be quite honest. And in any case, I'd rather not find out what you have up your sleeve."

"Look," Roth said. "This isn't just some hostage we're talking about. This is a kid I thought you liked. You don't want this on your conscience."

"Believe me," Baumann said, "I don't want to hurt a hair on the child's head. If anything happens to him, it will be because of your carelessness."

Roth considered his next statement for a few seconds, though it seemed an eternity. "All right," he said. "Let me tell you what we've done in the last couple of minutes. You know that we've got a bunch of guys down there from the Nuclear Emergency Search Team, and if you know shit, you know these guys are the best in the business. While you and Sarah were talking, her walkie-talkie stayed open and broadcast to the NEST guys. So they heard everything you said. They heard your description of the bomb you set up. And so these guys have been using one of their toys called a spectrum analyzer to figure out what kind of tone you're broadcasting, and the frequency you're using, and all that shit. Simple thing to duplicate the tone, and then set a transmitter to broadcast that exact tone on the same frequency. Easy stuff. Amateur hour. Took those geniuses five minutes. Meanwhile, I haul ass over to the heliport, couple blocks away, and jump on the chopper. They're bombarding the air with that exact tone, transmitted on just the right frequency. So Jared's bomb isn't going off. You can toss the button out the window. Go ahead. It's not going to blow."

"That's very good," Baumann said. "I could almost believe that."

"Go ahead," Roth said. "Try me. Toss the button out the window."

"Do you really want to play a game like this with the life of a child?"

"Hey, wait a second," Roth said, as if suddenly realizing something. "You don't *believe* me, do you? You really *don't* believe me, do you? Then let me give you some numbers, buddy. You're broadcasting on a VHF frequency of one hundred forty-seven megahertz. The frequency of the tone is seventeen point five kilohertz, which I'm told is the same thing as seventeen thousand five hundred cycles per second."

Baumann did not smile now. He felt a droplet of perspiration run down the side of his face as he realized that Roth was telling the truth. They had duplicated the tone. Silently, he cursed his own arrogance.

"So I guess what I'm thinking," Roth said, "is that you just lost your leverage, know what I'm saying?"

"And if your calculations are off by the slightest bit, well . . ."

"You see," Roth said, as reasonably as if he were wrapping up the sale of a used car, "we really don't want to take that chance either, frankly. So here's what I propose. Let Jared go. And keep me here in his stead. You'll have your hostage, and Sarah gets her son. Everyone wins. What do you say, hmm?"

Baumann hesitated, considered his options. There was, he had to admit, little room to negotiate. The bomb had been rendered inert. Even if they didn't know he had disengaged it, the NEST people had defeated his system. He could move more quickly with his gun than the cop, certainly, maybe even kill him—but then there was a good chance the cop would fire and wound Baumann, and that was a chance not worth taking. Why hadn't the cop killed him already? he wondered. Was he bluffing, lying about the signal generator? Possibly— but the cop was acting far too boldly. He wouldn't act this way if a child's life was at stake, particularly Sarah's child. More likely, the cop didn't want to risk any gunfire that might somehow affect the transmitter. A smart calculation.

"All right," Baumann said.

"Take the bomb off the kid," Roth said.

"You can do it yourself," Baumann said.

Baumann handed Roth a small key. "Unlock the cuffs," he said.

Roth took the key and unlocked Jared's handcuffs. He noticed they were the type widely used by policemen, Smith & Wesson Model 100 swing-throughs.

"Put the device on the seat next to you," Baumann said. "Don't worry, I've already disarmed it."

Roth gingerly placed the lunchbox on the seat. He could see red marks on the outside of both of the boy's wrists.

Jared reached up and gently pulled at the duct tape over his mouth. His eyes teared up as the tape came off. He pulled out the gag. A large red area around his mouth showed where the tape had chafed his skin.

"You okay?" Roth asked.

"I don't know," Jared said miserably. "I guess I'm okay, yeah."

"Okay," Roth said to Jared, "now you get out of here."

On the roof of the building, Sarah, now joined by several NEST members, watched the idling helicopter.

"What the hell is Roth doing?" Sarah asked.

"We intercepted the helicopter and forced it to land," Vigiani explained. "It was in violation of a NOTAM. It was Roth's idea to get on board at the heliport and have it continue on to pick up Baumann."

"God, I hope he knows what he's doing," Sarah said.

"I think he does," Vigiani said.

And then Sarah saw Jared climb down the helicopter's three small steps and run across to the roof to her and virtually leap into her arms. She squeezed him tight. He was weeping, and then she was weeping.

"Oh, Jared, honey," she said.

The pilot limped over to the watchers. "Asshole better be careful with that chopper," Dan Hammond said. "Expensive piece of machinery."

"You're lucky to be alive yourself," Vigiani said. "And not in prison."

"Hey," Hammond said. "We got a deal. I cooperated. You guys better keep your half of the bargain."

Inside the helicopter, it was just the two men now, facing each other, guns trained on each other.

"Now," Baumann said, "since I'm getting into the pilot's seat, you're going to have to drop your gun first."

Roth stared. "You kill me," he said defiantly, "and there's nothing going to stop the sharpshooters on the roof from dropping you. You know that."

Baumann nodded. "Believe me, a live hostage is far more valuable to me than a dead cop. Drop the gun."

Roth considered taking the brave shot, but knew he was outclassed, that Baumann could kill him in a split second and then take his chances with the sharpshooters. He had to trust Baumann's survival instincts.

He lowered the gun, then dropped it to the floor of the helicopter.

"Now, empty your pockets," Baumann ordered.

Roth did so, dropping change and rings of keys to the floor.

Lightning-fast, Baumann smashed the butt end of his pistol against Roth's temple, just hard enough to knock him unconscious. Roth sagged to the floor of the helicopter. Baumann didn't want to kill him or even disable him. It was better for Roth to remain a living hostage.

Baumann handcuffed Roth to the steel frame of the seat and jumped into the pilot's seat. He inspected the controls, familiarizing himself with them. It worked differently from any helicopter he had piloted before.

He did not see Roth stir.

He did not see Roth's eyes flutter open.

Out of Baumann's sight, Roth opened his eyes. Slowly, he slid his left hand, the one that wasn't handcuffed to the seat, down toward his belt, slipped his index finger inside the belt, felt around until he had located the concealed pocket in which he always kept his spare handcuff key.

It is a little-known fact that virtually all handcuffs

use the same universal key. The cuffs that connected Roth's right wrist to the seat frame—a Smith & Wesson Model 100—could be unlocked by the key to Roth's Peerless handcuffs. Thank God Baumann hadn't used the much rarer Smith & Wesson Model 104, the high-security model, which had its own unique key.

From this angle Roth could not see Baumann, but he knew from the sound of the engine that the helicopter was still idling atop the building. Quietly, he slipped the key into the handcuff lock. With a slight twisting motion of his wrist, he got the handcuffs open.

Then, stealthily, praying Baumann was too preoccupied to see, he slid one hand up to the seat and toggled the bomb back on.

With one smooth motion he rolled over and out of the door of the helicopter, down five feet or so, landing on the roof of the building.

Baumann looked up just in time to see Roth roll out of the helicopter door, but he did not panic. He pulled the collective and lifted the helicopter up into the air, up above the building.

Baumann understood how things worked. He knew that the FBI and the police had nothing larger than small arms, which could not shoot down a helicopter. He also knew that, according to the century-old Posse Comitatus Act, the U.S. military was prohibited from acting in a domestic law-enforcement capacity. Which meant that the military could not shoot the helicopter down from the sky.

His hostage—first Jared, then Roth—had afforded him the opportunity to take off. That was really all he needed. The helicopter lifted high into the air above lower Manhattan and headed toward a remote area of New Jersey, and Baumann was filled with pride, with a knowledge that he had just surmounted the greatest challenge of his career, that although he had made mistakes, there was still none better.

"Roth!" Sarah shouted. "What—what happened? What about the bomb?"

"Bomb?" Roth asked innocently, and shrugged. He was still a bit unsteady from toppling onto the roof. He went up to Dr. Richard Payne of the Nuclear Emergency Search Team. "Your signal generator thingamabob," Roth said, reaching under the waistband of his blue police uniform, just below his paunch, and removing an oblong object the size of a cigarette pack. He handed it to Payne. "Thanks."

Sarah saw the exchange of knowing glances between Roth and Dr. Payne, and didn't understand what was going on.

But then her attention was diverted by an explosion half a mile away or so, directly over the Hudson River.

Actually, there was first a great flash of light, a bright yellow-white light that grew steadily in intensity, followed by an explosion, an orange ball of fire that gave off smoke both white and black. The helicopter, a flaming orb, pitched wildly in the air, and as it fell apart, a million pieces plummeted to the river below.

"Roth," Sarah said, embracing him. "Normally I don't like it when my people keep me in the dark—but I suppose I'll have to make an exception this time. Good job."

It had all come clear to her. NEST, listening in to the transmission over her walkie-talkie, must have provided Roth with a transmitter that would work with the bomb that Baumann had engineered. They'd handed it to Roth before he boarded the helicopter a few blocks away. Strictly speaking, she thought, Roth hadn't done anything illegal.

Actually, that wasn't quite true. He hadn't actually detonated the thing himself, but he'd switched the bomb on, while the transmitter concealed in his waistband stayed on—it had been on since before Baumann had gotten into the helicopter—and as long as Roth was within a few hundred yards of the bomb it wouldn't detonate.

Roth had been bluffing, at least in part—he hadn't told Baumann that he had a transmitter hidden in his pants, and that that was the only tone source. As soon as the helicopter moved out of the range of the transmitter—over water, just as the NEST team had calculated, though it was a risky calculation, to be sure—the bomb had gone off. But no one would ever know, and certainly no one on the roof of the building would ever say anything, not even to each other, about what had happened. No one would ever be able to prove anything, and after all, justice had been done.

All in all, the explosion had taken less than a second.

CHAPTER NINETY-NINE

Malcolm Dyson switched off CNN and wheeled around in a fury to the bank of telephones next to his desk.

"The goddam so-called Prince of Darkness fucked it up!" he shouted to the empty study, and was surprised when someone answered.

"That he did," said a man who was coming through the door, accompanied by two other men. Dyson looked around, bewildered. Three others were climbing in through the windows. He recognized their dark-blue windbreakers, the big yellow block letters. They were federal marshals of the United States government, he could see. He would never forget the first time he had seen these dark-blue windbreakers with the yellow lettering, on the night that his wife and daughter were killed.

"What—?" he began.

"That he did," the man said. "He gave us an extraditable offense, Mr. Dyson. But you and your people helped us too."

"The hell you talking about?" Dyson managed to choke out.

"See, now that we've got hard evidence of your role in international terrorism, the Swiss government will no longer protect you. It *can't*. It's given you up. You're being extradited to the U.S." The marshal cuffed Dyson and, with the others, led him away, out of the study and down the long main corridor of the mansion Malcolm Dyson called Arcadia. "A nice place you got here," the lead marshal said, gawking. "Very nice indeed."

CHAPTER ONE HUNDRED

The burial service was held at a bleak cemetery south of Boston, where the Cronin family had several plots. Jared didn't cry. Neither did he cry at the funeral. He was stoic, impassive, and talked hardly at all.

Teddy Williams cried, though, and they were genuine tears, and Sarah cried as well, and her tears were genuine too. The sky was gray, the clouds drifting by like cigar smoke.

After it was over, but before the small crowd dispersed, Pappas turned to Sarah and smiled sadly.

"How you doing, boss?" he said.

"The way you'd think," she replied.

"True you're being promoted to headquarters?"

She nodded again.

"The big time, huh? Onward and upward."

"I guess."

He lowered his voice so Jared couldn't hear. "Jared'll get through this okay. He's a strong kid."

"Yeah, he'll be okay. It's hard for him—all the more given how, you know, ambivalent he was about his father."

"Same for you, I expect."

"Yeah. But less so. I didn't like the guy, but we had a

son together. The most precious thing in my life. So you can't exactly call it a mistake that I married him. I mean, I shouldn't have, but I did, and something wonderful came out of all that hell."

"Your luck with men's bound to change."

"Maybe," she said, and turned and walked over to Jared, took his hand. Pappas took Jared's other hand, and together the three of them walked toward the car. "I guess anything's possible."

CODA

Sweet Bobby Higgins was tried and eventually found innocent of the murder of Valerie Santoro.

Malcolm Dyson was imprisoned in the United States and died of a heart attack in prison.

The Manhattan Bank was declared insolvent, its stock worthless. The Federal Reserve Bank negotiated a deal with Citicorp to buy what remained of the Manhattan Bank's assets. Warren Elkind committed suicide two days later.

AUTHOR'S NOTE

The Network does exist, though under a different name and at another location in New York City. Some of the details, particularly those having to do with security, have been fictionalized or deliberately obscured.

But the vulnerability remains real. In 1992 a *New York Times* correspondent wrote of the real-world equivalent of the Network: "Were the flow to stop unexpectedly, financial empires would teeter and governments tremble. . . . If something were to go seriously awry in the nearly perfect world of electronic money, the whole system could come to a wrenching halt in the twinkling of a gigabyte."

ACKNOWLEDGMENTS

I'm grateful to the extraordinary number of people who helped in the research of this novel.

In the Federal Bureau of Investigation—officially and unofficially, active and retired—quite a few counterterrorism experts gave generously of their time and expertise, particularly Robert J. Heibel, of Mercyhurst College, Special Agent (retired) Gray Morgan, Special Agent Deborah L. Stafford, retired Deputy Assistant Director Harry "Skip" Brandon, Peter Crooks, Hank Flynn, and James M. Fox, former head of the FBI's New York office. They aren't to blame, of course, for whatever factual liberties I've taken.

Just as accommodating was the Central Intelligence Agency, both officially and unofficially, but I can publicly mention only Vince Cannistraro, former head of CIA's counterterrorism operations and analysis, and a formidable terrorism expert. Other experts in terrorism who helped were: Neil C. Livingstone, David E. Long, and Mark D. W. Edington. (A few people on the dark side of the terrorism industry were very helpful, but probably wouldn't take kindly to being thanked by name.) I also thank my colleagues in the Association of

Former Intelligence Officers and Elizabeth Bancroft of the National Intelligence Book Center.

In law-enforcement and police work: Curt Wood, commander of the Fugitive Apprehension Unit of the Commonwealth of Massachusetts Department of Correction; Beverly Deignan of MCI Cedar Junction at Walpole; former New York City Police Commissioner Robert J. McGuire; James R. Sutton; Lieutenant Colonel Neal Moss of the South African National Police; Paul McSweeney of Professional Management Specialists, Inc.; and, in the Boston police, Frank Williams, Bobby Silva, and most of all, Sergeant-Detective Bruce A. Holloway.

I received some crucial cyberassistance from Eric Wiseman, Simson Garfinkel, Bob Frankston, Tom Knight of the MIT Artificial Intelligence Laboratory, Marc Donner, Dan Geer, David Churbuck, Donn B. Parker, Peter Wayner, and my good friend Bruce Donald. In surveillance and satellite technology, I was helped by H. Keith Melton and Glenn Whidden; in forgery, Frank W. Abagnale; in medicine and forensics, Dr. Stanton Kessler of the Boston Medical Examiner's Office, and my brother, Dr. Jonathan Finder.

For initiating me into the mysteries of the eight-year-old in the 1990s, I'm grateful to Tom McMillan and Christopher Beam. Thanks as well to Bobby Baror, Amram Ducovny, and two close friends: Rick Weissbourd; and Joe Teig, actor and cartographer.

I'm grateful as well for the early enthusiasm of my agent, Henry Morrison; Danny Baror of Baror International; Deborah Schindler; Caron K at Twentieth-Century Fox; and above all, Richard Green and Howie Sanders of the United Talent Agency, who lit the fuse.

The manuscript benefitted enormously from the astute editorial assistance of my brother, Henry Finder; from my chief technical expert, Jack McGeorge of the

Public Safety Group, who knows almost everything; and from the superb editing of Henry Ferris at William Morrow.

Thanks, finally, to my wife, Michele, who was there from the start with love and support, and to our daughter, Emma, for elucidating to us the Meaning of Life.